ASHES TO ASHES

LILLIAN STEWART CARL

D0756904

AN AUTHORS GUILD BACKINPRINT.COM EDITION

AN AUTHORS GUILD BACKINPRINT.COM EDITION

Published by iUniverse.com, Inc.

For information address:
iUniverse.com, Inc.
620 North 48th Street, Suite 201
Lincoln, NE 68504-3467
www.iuniverse.com

Originally published by Diamond Books

Grateful acknowledgment is made to Strathmore Music and Film Services for
permission to reprint lyrics from
"Ferry Me Over" by Andy M. Stewart, copyright © 1986.

ISBN: 0-595-09448-1

Printed in the United States of America

For Robert Walker and his family,
whose help and inspiration
have been priceless.

October

Chapter One

THE CASTLE'S TURRETS rose like a beckoning hand above a
crimson sea of maple leaves. Rebecca would have missed the
exit from the interstate if it hadn't been for that stone imperative,
a seventeenth-century Scottish castle springing from the soil of
central Ohio like a burp in time and space. The incongruity was
both engaging and unsettling.

Two miles of narrow asphalt corrugated by the wheels of farm
equipment brought Rebecca to a cast-iron gate in a stone wall.
A board creaking from a signpost proclaimed "Dun Iain." She
wrestled her Toyota into the driveway and stopped. The gate was
open. They'd told the man from the museum her date of arrival.
Good. It wasn't polite to arrive unannounced.

To arrive here at all was a victory of exasperation over comfort. Rebecca's stomach trembled with the same blend of anticipation and anxiety she'd feel when Ray teased her into jumping
off the high-diving board. But he hadn't teased her into coming
here. That had been her own idea, whether he liked it or not.
They were just engaged, not married. Rebecca tightened her
jaw, quelled her stomach, and accelerated up the driveway.

The castle was impressively picturesque at the end of its avenue of trees. Its builder, John Forbes, had studied his prototypes
well. The Scottish stately homes that had been on the history
tour Rebecca and Ray had taken last year—Scone, Glamis,
Blair—had all been entered through avenues of trees.

Only this avenue was of Canadian maples that flamed like
torches in the crisp October afternoon.

The trees parted. The castle loomed over her like a megalith at Stonehenge. Rebecca drove cautiously over the gravel of the parking area and stopped beside a red Nova with a rental agency sticker on the bumper. Her car exhaled a cloud of exhaust and subsided. It would have to be replaced soon, with money she didn't have and wouldn't be getting here.

"So," Ray had said. "You're spending part of the fall semester sorting junk at some two-bit San Simeon for nothing more than room, board, and a pittance from the executor? Just what are you trying to prove, Kitten?"

As if they both didn't know. When she'd left her engagement ring with him, for safekeeping, of course, Ray had looked at her with the hurt appeal of a puppy put out for the night.

Rebecca thrust the car keys into her purse, threw open the door, leaped out, and slammed it shut with a much harder push than was necessary. A butterscotch and white cat, sunning himself on a low wall beside the parking area, regarded her with sardonic detachment. Dun Iain's scattered windows peered down at her, multiple eyes sparkling in a sly and secretive humor.

She'd stewed over Ray all the way from Missouri, and gabbled endlessly about him to Jan during her quick visit in Putnam, just across the highway. "Something you'd like to recommend?" she asked the cat. He closed his eyes in the feline equivalent of a shrug. You're here. That's a start.

"Right," said Rebecca. The breeze fanned the heat from her cheeks.

She might have come a hundred miles from Putnam and the interstate; the only sound was of the crimson leaves shuffling in the wind, and the distant hum of an airplane. She squinted into the brilliance of the sky. There it was, a tiny insect toiling eastward. Something about the echo of those distant engines on a fall day was unbearably poignant; her heart swelled with longing for—for something. Decision, probably.

Her eye followed the plane until it vanished behind the castle. A fairy-tale castle, the State of Ohio guidebooks would say. But Dun Iain was a large house, only suggesting an L-shaped medieval keep.

The walls were beige harl, a kind of pebbly stucco, tinted pink by the maple leaves which surrounded them. They leaped in one sheer expanse from the ground to the fifth story, where they blossomed not into toothed parapets but into turrets and dormers. Atop them jostled chimneys and cupolas, which were in turn elbowed aside by a pla form with a balustrade. Its severe right angles failed to intimidate the subtle curves of the rest of the building.

The roofs were a dark greenish gray. Eriskay slate, Rebecca remembered, imported at horrendous expense. Authenticity at all costs, even to the shot holes concealed by grinning gargoyles in the stonework at the base of each turret. A magnificently quixotic, defiantly eccentric structure, Dun Iain, less Camelot than *Alice in Wonderland*.

A fairy tale, she told herself. The innocent gloss of some fairy tales couldn't hide the surreal twisting of the ordinary, the dark obsession, which lay beneath. Even the Disney version of *Alice in Wonderland* had once terrified her, the red queen shouting "Off with her head!" while Alice can't wake up from her dream turned nightmare.

The airplane was gone. A cold gust of wind sang through the trees. Rebecca shivered and turned briskly to tidying up the car. From the trunk she took her suitcases and the sacks of food. If the man from the museum was like all men, he'd been living on nitrate-laced bologna on white bread and chemical-doused sweet rolls. From the backseat she took the jug of apple cider purchased at a roadside stand; hopefully it wasn't contaminated with salmonella or whatever bug caused food poisoning. Biology wasn't her field.

She scooped the Burger King wrappers from the floor where Jan's children, despite their mother's admonitions, had let them fall. Not for the first time she tried to feel condescension toward her former roommate, who had dropped out of college to marry. Not for the first time she failed.

Locking the car, Rebecca hoisted her packages and crunched over the gravel toward Dun Iain. The only apparent door was set in a bulge at the internal angle of the building's "L." It was a massive affair of wooden slabs and iron braces that looked ready to repel invaders at any moment.

Someone was looking out a window above and to one side of the door. Rebecca couldn't produce a friendly wave with her arms full, so she tilted her head with a smile of greeting. But as soon as she focused on the window the shape was gone, plucked away into the shadowed interior, leaving her with a quick impression of a tall, thin figure and a pale face.

Well, if that was the way Dr. what's his name Campbell of the museum was going to be to his new colleague . . . An agonized shriek shattered the stillness. The cat dematerialized in a puff of fur. Rebecca's heart plummeted into her stomach. Her feet did a quick jig on the gravel—run away, no, run forward. She dropped the suitcases, laid down the sacks, and sprinted for the door, her purse on its shoulder strap flying behind her.

The door was heavy. She threw her entire weight against the wood and it yielded without the hideous screech she'd have expected. She took two bounds into the interior and stopped, blinking in the abrupt musty dimness. There, light spilled down a staircase.

Another high-pitched shriek thinned into hysteria. Rebecca stumbled past a massive shape that only resolved itself in her mind's eye into an open coffin, its occupant's hands folded in prayer, when she was already on the bottom of the staircase. What kind of place was this, anyway! She raced up the steps and into a wide doorway.

She burst past a carved screen into the Great Hall of the castle and collided with the end of a table. The room was small, as halls went, but large enough to contain her entire efficiency apartment. A vast hearth and mantel opened on her left. To her right were the smeared panes of a window glinting in the light of a wrought-iron chandelier.

Something was wheezing, half strangled. She spun around. Above her, on a wooden musician's gallery, a tall, slender man stood arguing with a decrepit set of bagpipes. Rebecca deflated with a wheeze of her own.

The pipes were winning the argument. The man blew mightily into the mouthpiece and squeezed the bag of faded tartan under his arm. The instrument emitted another squeal of indignation, like a woman goosed by a sailor.

"Thou unravished bride of quietness?" suggested Rebecca giddily.

The man jerked as though jolted by an electric shock. His face blanched and snapped toward her voice; his eyes bulged. The pipes in his suddenly flaccid arms whistled in a long exhalation like a gramophone record running down.

Now she'd scared him in turn. Nothing like starting off on the wrong foot. Rebecca tried a smile somewhat less broad than the Cheshire cat's. "Ah, excuse me—I'm Rebecca Reid. I guess you must be . . . ." She dredged frantically and his first name plopped onto her tongue. ". . . Michael Campbell from the British Museum."

Michael closed his eyes for a moment, allowing the natural

glow of the Scot to return to his face. He laid the bagpipes down, disappeared, and reemerged through the wooden screen. Wiping his hands on a T-shirt which read, "Disarm today, dat arm tomorrow," he seized her hand, shook it perfunctorily, and dropped it. His mouth emitted an unintelligible string of diphthongs and glottal stops.

This was more than embarrassing, it was positively mortifying. Rebecca's smile expired. Michael waited patiently, head cocked to the side, one side of his mouth tucked in a grimace that offered no assistance. Then, with a rush, some synapse in the back of Rebecca's brain wrenched the sounds into words: "From the National Museums o' Scotland. And there's nae need tae go creepin' aboot the hoose like that."

"I wasn't creeping," Rebecca protested. "You saw me from the window, you knew I was here."

"Oh, aye?" His blue eyes widened and then narrowed, as if surprise gave way to cunning. He turned away, his shoulders moving in something between a shiver and a shrug.

He had to have rushed downstairs from the window and snatched up the pipes as soon as he'd seen her. He must be very shy. Or ill mannered. Unless . . . "Is there someone else here? The housekeeper?"

"She'll no be in until the morn. There's no one else here." He stood, hands braced on the carved back of a chair, looking at a spiral notebook laid on the table amid a scattering of dishes and bric-a-brac. His fingers were interesting, long and lean, but his back was singularly uncommunicative. Rebecca peeked around him to see a page filled with neat columns of words and figures preceded by the script *L*'s of pound signs.

Rebecca plowed doggedly on into the silence. "I'm from Dover College in Missouri. I answered the advertisement in the *Journal of British Studies* placed by the State of Ohio."

"Who'll be takin' the house in January whether I've finished skimmin' the cream or no."

You've skimmed the cream? Rebecca's head tilted inquisitively. Each burred *r* in young Dr. Campbell's voice was a tiny buzz saw; obviously he resented the state thrusting an assistant on him. Maybe he was one of those paranoid types afraid some other scholar would steal his academic thunder. And yet he was simply taking inventory.

Maybe he thought she was there to check up on what he chose to take back to Scotland, as if he couldn't be trusted to be fair and honest. She said in her most professional voice, "I exchanged letters with Mr. Adler, James Forbes's executor. I've studied up on Dun Iain and both the Forbeses, father and son. I'll be getting my own doctorate in British history as soon as I finish my dissertation, so I'm qualified to help you skim the cream, as you say."

Michael released the chair, slapped shut the notebook, and turned back to her. A glance no doubt identical to the one he'd use to appraise a letter or a vase took in her stockings, sweater, and tartan skirt—an ersatz tartan, at that—the careful makeup and shoulder-length brown hair that was lovely but pathetically impractical.

So I like to look nice! Rebecca spoke more tartly than she'd intended. "Mr. Adler assured me I could do my own research while I—we—catalog the artifacts. There's no better collection of Scottish historical artifacts on this side of the Atlantic. I know how to work, don't worry. I supplemented my scholarships slinging hash at a Steak and Ale."

Michael's eyes glazed. That bit of slang was apparently beyond him, and he wasn't about to ask what it meant. "Of course there're no better collections. Forbes was a glorified thief, preyin' on the poverty of the old families and plunderin' the birthright of Scotland."

Typical man—when in doubt, attack. "The laws on the exportation of antiquities weren't as strict seventy or eighty years ago. If some of the old families had to sell the contents of their attics to feed, clothe, and educate their children, maybe they thought they got the better end of the deal."

"Thirty pieces of silver for the history of Scotland?"

"Which has been dirtied by a bunch of bloody Yanks?" Rebecca asked. "That history belongs to us, too, you know. My great-grandfather Reid left Ayrshire a hundred years ago because he couldn't support his family in Scotland the Brave." She cut herself off with a swallow and inspected the dusty toes of her shoes. Hard to believe that was her own voice being so rude to a foreigner, even a contentious one.

She glanced back up to see those brave Scottish eyes sparking not with anger but with a humor as sharp and dry as single-malt whiskey. "And today the old families can't even sell their birthright. They have to make Disneylands out of their homes. People who a hundred years ago would never have been allowed in the back gate now stand gawpin' over the Countess of Strathmore's knickers. You have to be independently wealthy to live in Scotland the now—all the jobs are in soddin' great factories in Birmingham and Manchester.''

Rebecca, having enjoyed the Countess of Strathmore's antique underpants, couldn't resist adding, "In England."

"Among the Sassenachs," he returned. "Chance would be a fine thing."

She assumed that remark was meant as sarcasm, something along the line of "that'll be the day," and offered him a grin of complicity. "Sassenach," huh? The word was more or less Gaelic for "Southerner" but had come to be a derogatory epithet for "English." No wonder Michael had flared at her when she'd inadvertently assigned him to an English museum; he was a patriot, working for a pittance for his country. Such idealism was refreshing.

The angle of his chin repelled her grin. He scooped impatiently at the strands of hair falling across his forehead. His hair was also brown, shorter on the top and sides than in the back, where it reached the neckband of his shirt. The style was part intellectual, part rock star, part uncivilized Highland chieftain. Rebecca wondered whether he'd had it cut that way on purpose or whether he'd been the victim of a schizophrenic barber.

"Well, then," Michael said, "I'll help you wi' your cases. It's time for tea." He strolled to the door and clicked off the chandelier.

Twilight surged into the room. The windows, although large, admitted only a thin brassy gleam. The chairs and tables, the fireplace and gallery, became only quick sketches of objects, without substance, like shapes in a dream. "Thank you," Rebecca said to her erstwhile colleague, but he was already out of the room. With a shrug, she followed.

From a solitary bulb in the ceiling of the landing a few watts of light trickled down the steps, causing the oblong shape in the shadowed pit of the entrance hall to phosphoresce. Michael started down two steps at a time. Rebecca walked more slowly, asking, "What is that?"

"What?" He turned at the foot of the stair.

"That . . ." She couldn't say coffin, it couldn't be that. "That box there," she ended lamely.

"This?" He found another switch. The shape coalesced into a white marble sarcophagus topped by the effigy of a woman, her cap, gown, and steepled hands finely detailed. Michael bowed, his hands sketching an elaborate flourish. "May I present Her Majesty, Mary, Queen of Scots? Poor, lovely, romantic, stupid Mary. I thought you said you'd studied Forbes and Dun Iain."

"I have," Rebecca returned. She knew that the elder Forbes had been besotted by the tragic story of Mary Stuart, and that he'd had a half-size replica of her tomb in Westminster Abbey carved of white marble. "I just didn't know he kept his toy sarcophagus in his front hall."

Another quick glint of humor, and Michael went striding across the parking area. Stupid Mary? A fine sentiment for a patriot. Rebecca spared a quick look at the marble face. Supposedly it had been modeled on Mary's death mask; its serene half-smile suggested the queen had welcomed death, however gruesome. Off with her head indeed!

Rebecca hurried out the door and almost collided with Michael coming back in. "Get your pokes," he said.

She rescued her sacks of groceries. The bronze evening sunlight, filtered through the maples, swam with russet dust motes. The farm road was out of sight beyond the trees. Next to the house was a clapboard and shingle shed, and across the dark green lawn, not far from the driveway, was a dovecote, a low rounded structure perforated by stone lattices.

"I need to be lockin' up the now," Michael called.

"All right, I'm coming." Rebecca checked to make sure her car was locked. She barely made it back inside before he swung the door shut with a crash and brandished a ridiculously large iron key. "I suppose," she said, swept against a set of flags furled at Mary's regal feet, "the really valuable things in Dun Iain don't look valuable. You know, all that glitters isn't gold."

He shot her a sharp and suspicious glance. She raised her brows indignantly; come on, that remark hardly expressed criminal intentions! "Kitchen's in there," he said, jerking his head toward a door to the left of the staircase, and he rammed the key into a massive lock.

Rebecca bit her tongue before she said, "Yes, your grace," and dropped him a curtsey. Who did he think he was, the Duke of Argyll? Probably whatever scion of the Campbell family was the duke was more polite than this, his poor relation. She couldn't imagine anyone looking—and being—less of a threat than she was.

She found the light switch inside the kitchen door. A wonderfully bright bank of fluorescents illuminated a kitchen much younger than the house. Range, refrigerator, telephone—more incongruities, but she wasn't about to complain. She laid the sacks on a vinyl-topped work island and put up the perishables: low-fat milk, skinned chicken breasts, and broccoli. She hadn't been far wrong about Michael's eating habits. The refrigerator contained only a package of processed cheese, two tomatoes, and an open can of frozen orange juice protruding a spoon like a sneering tongue. A couple of cans of Canadian beer sat on the counter. Efficiently she stowed them away, too, and turned to look for a bread box.

Michael's Reeboks were padding up the staircase from the entry. "Your room's on the second floor. The char aired it out yesterday."

Rebecca abandoned the rest of the groceries, hurried out of the kitchen and up the stairs behind him. She squinted into the room across the landing from the Hall. This was her room?

"This is the study," Michael announced. A shaft of sunlight picked out a Chippendale secretary piled with papers and trinkets. Beyond the boundary of the light, the shadows, even darker by contrast, swarmed with opaque shapes that might be cabinets and bookcases. A human form stood with preternatural stillness against the far wall. Rebecca's eyes narrowed. "Suit of armor," said Michael, and started up the next flight of stairs.

Rebecca rolled her eyes, as much at herself as at him, and followed. What he called the second floor Americans called the third; in British the first floor was the ground floor. Some people had the knack of making her feel dumb. And she'd thought Ray was exasperating.

This staircase was a circular one, so steep and narrow the only banister was a rope wound around the central pillar. The stone treads spiraled upward into shadow. The two sets of footsteps, magnified by the thick walls, wafted faintly up the stairwell and died away in the dark recesses of the upper stories. The shaft was a giant chimney flue, stirring with a chill draft like the breath of the house itself. Rebecca tasted acrid dust, musty leather, and furniture polish.

Michael led the way into a corridor. A solitary light bulb revealed three doors, one in each wall. Michael threw open the one across from the stairwell. "Bathroom and toilet." The porcelain fixtures were of 1920s vintage, forty years after the house was built. Fortunately the Forbeses' taste for authenticity hadn't extended to chamber pots under the bed.

"Bedroom." Michael dropped the suitcases inside the left-hand door. One last ray of sunshine illuminated a canopied bed, a huge carved armoire like something out of *The Lion, the Witch, and the Wardrobe*, a dressing table, and an inappropriate but welcome space heater installed in the fireplace. It looked clean and comfortable; Rebecca hadn't expected a luxury hotel.

Something oozed suddenly around her ankles. She jerked, imitating Michael's electric jolt of startlement. The butterscotch and white cat crouched at her feet, the fur on his neck bristling, yellow eyes focused on some infinite point beyond the confines of the landing or of the castle itself. How did he—that's right, she'd left the front door open when she'd rushed in.

"Well," said Michael, nudging the animal with his toe and getting a disdainful glance in response. "Greyfriars Bobby watchin' for old James?"

"I beg your pardon?"

"Didn't you know, then, the man was found dead by the caretaker at the foot of yon staircase?"

Rebecca's hair bristled like the cat's. "Here? I—I thought he died in the hospital, I guess." She cleared her throat. No, there was no chalk mark outlining a body on the broad planks of the floor, just the cat crouching and looking at—at something. "Not surprising a ninety-six-year-old would fall down a spiral staircase. The cat was James's? What's his name?" She bent to stroke him. He hollowed his back evasively and glided up the stairs.

Michael actually emitted a chuckle. "James had more of a sense of humor than his dad. He named the cat Darnley."

"For Henry Stewart, Lord Darnley, Mary's second husband?"

"Always thought old Harry was a bit of a tomcat, myself."

"He probably fathered more than James I, you're right."

"James VI of Scotland, James I of England," Michael corrected. "If you don't question that James was really Mary's bairn."

Rebecca stared. That was an uncanny shot, coming so close to the subject of her dissertation. If the Erksine letter was really here at Dun Iain, it might answer that exact question. His comment was a good omen, she told herself, and stepped into the bedroom.

The sunlight brightened a magnificent Sargent portrait, a

woman in 1890s Gibson Girl garb, hair piled lavishly on her head, bosom upthrust, jewels at her throat. But her face was thin and pale, her eyes too big, hinting of anguish. The jewels seemed to choke her. The artist had skillfully shown the discrepancy between luxury of dress and poverty of emotion. "Mrs. John Forbes?" Rebecca asked, looking up at the painted face. "The candidate for martyrdom? No wonder she died young; it must've been quite a burden putting up with the old crock."

"She could've flitted anytime."

"No, she couldn't. Back then a woman's place was with her husband and son. Especially a wealthy woman, with no skills beyond piano-playing and embroidery. Where could she have gone, what could she have done?"

"If you choose to suffer fools gladly, there's no excuse for you," Michael pronounced.

And that, Rebecca responded mutely, is certainly something you'll never be accused of. She pointed to the doorway opposite the bedroom. "What's in there? More skeletons in closets?"

If Michael heard her teeth grinding, he ignored them. "That's the piper's gallery. Naething there but a set of ill-tempered pipes. No bogles to leap out and scare you."

"And you?" she replied with a laugh. "You almost cartwheeled when I spoke to you." Through the door she glimpsed an elaborate plaster ceiling half erased by twilight, the vault of the two-story Hall.

"You crept up on me," he repeated indignantly.

Her laugh evaporated for lack of nourishment. Rebecca realized she was exhausted; she'd gotten up before dawn to drive here. She threw her purse onto the bed and flicked open the closest suitcase. "I'd better unpack now."

Michael thrust his hands into the pockets of his jeans and with disgruntled courtesy asked, "Would you like a cuppa?"

"Sure, thanks."

The soft pad of his footsteps faded away. Somewhere wood creaked and something, a hot water pipe, probably, sighed. Somewhere the cat glided through the shadows searching for its master, James Forbes, the bachelor, the miser. He'd mised enough to keep this place, with its compelling, disturbing discrepancies, going. And his heart was in the right place, to have willed the fruits of his father's rapacity back to Scotland.

Rebecca laid her makeup case on the dressing table. In the frame of the slightly tarnished mirror was a postcard picture of

Dun Iain. Or was it? She pulled the card out and turned it over. The legend declared the structure to be Craigievar, the Aberdeenshire castle which was Dun Iain's prototype.

If Rebecca had known last summer she'd be working at Craigievar's bastard child in America, she'd have rented a car in Perth and gone there. But then, Ray would have pointed out that the tour bus was already paid for, the countryside was the equivalent of the wilds of Africa, and the natives drove on the wrong side of the road. "That's just the way things are, Kitten," he'd have said patiently, and emitted another cloud of smoke from his pipe.

Prying Ray from his routine for that trip had been quite a feat, even though once there he'd followed her in bemused pleasure from site to site. But then, back home, it'd been back to the schedule. Tuesdays they'd eat pizza, half black olives for him, half green peppers for her. Sundays they'd attend the concert at Clemens Auditorium. Fridays he'd bring his overnight bag to her apartment and turn another page in *The Joy of Sex*.

Three years ago his calm, quiet, predictability had been endearing, evidence of his conscientious effort to do right by her. Rebecca wasn't sure when it'd become stultifying. She'd told him she'd eat olives if he'd eat peppers, that she'd buy tickets to a football game if he'd go with her, that some Friday she'd like to wing it without the book.

He'd responded with loving pats on the head. She'd been considering dynamite in his coffee when she heard about the position at Dun Iain.

Rebecca unpacked her tape player, found a plug, and snapped in a Mozart tape. The music was tinny and shallow, absorbed by rather than dispelling the silence. The walls seemed to lean disapprovingly inward. She turned off the player. On the mantelpiece she laid her dog-eared copy of *John Forbes: Man of Iron*; the thirty-year-old biography had cost her quite a trek through the secondhand bookstores in Kansas City.

She'd left her typewriter in the car. No great loss if it disappeared; it was a manual her parents had given her as a high school graduation present almost ten years ago. Oh, for a computer.

A programmer's job, Ray frequently pointed out, would pay much better than her teaching job. And grad school was such a financial drain. If she wrote off her quest for a Ph.D., she could get that new car, that computer, a larger apartment. She already knew word processing, after all. Like a human Cuisinart she processed the musings with which Ray fertilized assorted philosophy journals: "Aristotle's Poetics Revealed in *Saturday Night Live*," or "Sartre's *Being and Nothingness*: the Paradigm of the Eighties."

"Publish or perish," he'd say cheerfully. "You're such a big help, Kitten. I'm all thumbs when it comes to a keyboard."

The armoire reeked of lavender. Rebecca searched for a plastic air freshener but found nothing. She hung up her blouses and dresses and left the doors open, threw her satin stocking bag into a drawer, and checked the level of fluid in her contact lens case. A picture of Ray, looking professorial against a row of fake photographer's books, went on the bedside table beside the case holding her glasses. Last Friday she'd had a headache; Ray, the *Joy of Sex* page all picked out, had been miffed. This was a man so set in his ways he'd ordered bourbon in Edinburgh.

Rebecca leaned on the embrasure of the windowsill. Publish or perish. Even if she—when she—published the Erskine letter and joined Ray in the rarefied atmosphere of a doctorate, nothing would change. On that hypothetical future date she could marry him, and nothing would change.

Her jaw ached, a sure sign of words left unsaid and emotions unexpressed. Elspeth Forbes gazed down from the paneled wall, not completely unsympathetic. Jan, amid the riot at the Burger King, had opined that distance fanned a large flame and extinguished a small one. Only twenty-four hours distant, Rebecca told herself, and she already had a damn good idea just which one she'd singed her fingers on.

The sunlight ebbed from the world outside. The maple trees faded to gray. She was inside those multiple eyes looking out. In the twilight the lawns and trees lost all depth, as though they'd been painted on the panes of glass. If she raised the window, she might raise the landscape itself, seeing behind it nothing, the castle the only reality.

Rebecca shook herself, turning back into the room. It was almost dark, illuminated only by the feeble light from the corridor. She clicked the switch by the door but the bulb in the midst of the ornate plaster ceiling didn't respond. She tried the bedside lamp with the same result. All right, then, time to make Dr. Campbell disgorge a couple of light bulbs as well as that cup of tea. And a sandwich would be good. A little food and a stress vitamin would steady her nerves.

Rebecca closed the door into the piper's gallery and peered up into the darkness blotting the upper staircase. She would explore the rest of the house tomorrow, in the daylight. If it contained enough of what Ray called junk, working even with His Grace Michael the Grouch Campbell would be worthwhile. After all, she was here to do two jobs, her own and the state's.

Starting down the staircase, she visualized Michael, festooned in the great kilt of the seventeenth century, lifting a lamp on the landing. In his informal twentieth-century clothes, longish hair, and defensive posture he appeared barely twenty. He was probably closer to thirty, one of those aggravating men who look like boys until they're forty, at which time they become distinguished.

Something bumped on the staircase over her head—the cat, no doubt. The breath of the castle wafted coldly down the back of her sweater. Not sure if she was joking, Rebecca repeated under her breath the old Scots prayer: "From ghoulies and ghosties and long-leggety beasties and things that go bump in the night, Good Lord deliver us."

She skimmed by the black yawning apertures of Hall and study. The bright light from the kitchen made the model tomb look like a child's plaster-of-paris school project. Michael was singing something to the effect that it's good to be young and daring. His bravado scraped her mind like chalk skreeking across a blackboard. No one could really be daring, given the constraints of culture and sex and economics.

At least he sounded more cheerful now. She hadn't crept up on him. He'd seen her from the window . . . The cat, Darnley, wasn't upstairs but sat licking his paws on Mary's marble stomach much as his namesake must once have curled against Mary's skin.

Rebecca stopped dead in the entry. From the kitchen Michael's voice stuttered to a halt. One beat, two, and then he bellowed. "Blast you, woman, if I'd wanted my beer cold I'd have put it in the fridge myself!"

And then again, Rebecca thought with a frustrated stamp at the unforgiving stone of the floor, wasn't there also a prayer about deliverance from the wrath of the Campbells?

Chapter Two

REBECCA DREAMED SHE was in the upholstered seat of a tour bus, tied up like a Christmas package. Outside the window, green countryside lapped at the walls of a pink-beige castle. She had to have something inside that building. Urgently she banged her head on the glass. She wasn't tied, she realized; Ray's arms held her, his voice whispering soothing condescensions. The bus roared away in a cloud of exhaust. The castle—Dun Iain? Craigievar?—disappeared behind ribbons of asphalt and slipped forever from her grasp.

The roar of the bus grew louder. Rebecca swam suddenly from sleep, her mind clutching one thought: that prayer was not for deliverance from the wrath but from the greed of the Campbells.

The noise was a vacuum cleaner. The housekeeper was here. Rebecca fought off the smothering embrace of the blankets and sat up. So much for the romance of sleeping in a canopied bed. Claustrophobic, that's what it was. After all, the original purpose of a canopy was to protect the sleeper against zoological paratroopers from a thatched roof.

She should never have drunk that tea. Michael had brewed it strong enough to dissolve a spoon, assuming she would dilute it with milk. She hadn't, and had gulped cup after cup of the scalding stuff over sandwiches and banalities. When they'd adjourned next door, to the room which was fitted out with reclining chairs and a TV set, her eyelids had fallen to half-mast. She'd left Michael watching an old episode of *M*A*S*H*, replaced the two light bulbs, and gone to bed.

But then, perversely, her eyes had popped open. The house

had creaked and sighed, the wind had moaned around the turrets, and Michael had clomped endlessly up and down the staircase and across the ceiling above her head, his footsteps as ponderous as her own heartbeat.

Ray smiled from his photo beside her bed, his bland, Slavic face bisected by stylish glasses. He'd paid more than his half of that tour of Great Britain; if it hadn't been for him, she'd never have been able to go. Better to be shipped about like a package than to miss the trip entirely.

She threw back the covers and groped for her slippers and her glasses. The window overlooked a static vista of central Ohio, the sky smudged with cloud and the maples tossing in the wind. Under that pewter sky their leaves were less crimson than splotches of dried blood . . . Rebecca laughed at herself. What an image. Get away from Ray's dampening influence for a day and already her imagination had become overactive.

Nikes, jeans, and a Pringles of Scotland sweater made a suitably efficient outfit. She pulled her hair into a ponytail, embellished it with a scarf, and considered the effect. Without its framing waves her face seemed pinched; the cheeks that yesterday had been fashionably hollow looked this morning as though they'd been sucked dry by a vampire. Her brown eyes were as disproportionately large and dark as those of Elspeth Forbes gazing from her portrait just over Rebecca's shoulder.

The woman's necklace was gaudy but gorgeous, garnets and jet centering on a fiery gem that looked like the Hope diamond. The Hope was rumored to have brought bad luck to its wearer, and Elspeth's slightly dazed, slightly desperate expression looked as if she believed hers, too, to be cursed. The biography didn't say why she died so young. Of homesickness for her native Dundee, possibly, or from a broken heart. Rumor had it she'd been married off to the much older John Forbes after an unhappy love affair with a fellow Scot.

Rebecca inserted contacts into her eyes and gold studs into her earlobes. She applied light touches of blush, eye shadow, mascara, lipstick. There, she looked healthier. Cosmetics were expensive, but it was self-respect to look as nice as possible.

She headed for the staircase. A middle-aged woman was halfway up, lugging a vacuum cleaner and a basket of cleaning paraphernalia. "Let me help," called Rebecca.

The woman jumped and clutched at the breast of her flowered blouse. "Sweet Jesus, girl, don't sneak up on a body like that!"

With a distinct sense of déjà vu—this hadn't been funny the first time—Rebecca bared her teeth in an innocent smile and said, "I'm sorry. I was just on my way downstairs. I'm Rebecca Reid."

The woman peered up at her through blue horn-rimmed glasses. A red slash of lipstick emphasized the downturned corners of her mouth. Judging from the creases in her cheeks, that disapproving frown was her usual expression. She released her blouse and with an elaborate sigh said, "Dorothy Garst. You're the schoolteacher from Missouri?"

Rebecca stepped back as woman and machine arrived on the landing with a clash of metal against stone. "From Dover College."

"Aren't you the lucky one, getting to work with Dr. Campbell. Isn't he a case? I'd always heard Englishmen weren't very friendly. And that haircut!"

"I wouldn't let him hear you call him English," Rebecca replied. "Has he been here long?"

"A week. I keep hoping he'll start talking to where I can understand him, but he hasn't yet."

Michael would probably have to be tortured to make him give up one rolled *r*. "He's quite a change from Mr. Forbes, isn't he?"

Dorothy leaned forward, nodding curtly. Her gray perm, set like cement on her head, didn't budge. "Not much of a change, no. Neither one of them wants me to touch anything. How can I clean the place properly if I can't move things? But no, it was 'Leave that whatsit alone, Dottie,' when old James was alive, and now it's "Leave that whatsit alone, Mrs. Garst.' "

"Some things that don't look valuable are," said Rebecca placatingly.

"Old books that attract mice and pictures of people in funny clothes?" Dorothy's washed-out brown eyes narrowed into slits. "I bet you're here to look for the Forbes treasure."

"Treasure?"

"Mr. James kept going on about how his father had brought a treasure back from England . . ."

"Scotland," Rebecca murmured.

"And hid it somewhere in the house. But if you ask me . . ."

Rebecca didn't. She explained. "The obviously valuable pieces, like jewelry, are in the bank. There aren't any pieces of eight, I'm afraid."

"If you ask me," continued Dorothy without taking breath, "he was just touched in the head. Senile, you know. He didn't act like he was rich. He paid me, and Phil Pruitt, the caretaker, and Phil's son Steve who does some gardening, but he never went out and got himself anything nice from the new Wal-Mart. Kept living here with all this junk. If he'd had him a room over at Golden Age Village, he wouldn't have fallen down these ridiculous stairs. Right here's where Phil found him, end of August." She seemed disappointed when Rebecca wasn't startled.

"He was here alone at night?"

"Ah . . ." Dorothy straightened and stepped back, her eyes sliding away. "He—er—he didn't want anyone here with him."

"He must've been in good health, then, and could do for himself."

"Not really. He'd gotten pretty feeble and hadn't been out of his room by himself in two months. A nurse came in every day to check him over and keep him tidy. Though how anyone could stay clean in this dusty old place . . ." Dorothy adjusted her glasses and peered critically at a wonderful Landseer landscape hanging in the stairwell. "Well, I tried to help."

Rebecca frowned. "If Mr. Forbes was that decrepit, what was he doing on the staircase?"

"He'd gone soft in the head," insisted Dorothy. "No telling what he thought he was doing." Grasping her vacuum and her basket, she headed on up the stairs, presenting Rebecca with a vision of her rear end like a sausage encased in pink double-knit slacks. "I'd better get going—still got the rooms up above. I did yours yesterday. I have a system, a rotation pattern . . ."

That voice had enough vinegar in it to etch tracks in the stone steps. Fortunately the vacuum roared into life and blanked it out. Rebecca shook her head, half amused, half appalled. So the local gossip was that there was a treasure here. Romantic fancies, no doubt. Forbes's stocks and bonds weren't nearly as interesting as some mythical trove.

The old man had fallen down these very stairs and died there, alone, in the darkness . . . All right, Rebecca thought, she certainly wasn't going to be intimidated by that macabre image. She turned and climbed up to the fourth floor. And it was the fourth, despite Michael's calling it the third; when in Rome do as the Romans, or the Americans, do.

Through the door on her left she saw a bedroom littered with cast-off T-shirts, papers, and books. *The History of Scottish Sec-*

ond Sight lay open on the unmade bed, Michael's idea of light bedtime reading. There was no corresponding picture of a woman on his bedside table. The lawyer, Adler, had mentioned to her that the young Scot was single.

Scrubbing sounds emanated from an adjoining bathroom; Dorothy was removing toothpaste and whiskers from the sink just as Rebecca had once cleaned for her brothers. She was the only daughter, after all. One thing she'd always appreciated about Ray was how tidy he was. Not only did he wipe out the sink, he even hung his dirty shirts back in the closet.

A large bedroom was straight ahead and a small one to the right. The floor above had the same plan, except that here, on the level of the turrets, the rooms bulged into oblong protuberances filled with furniture. Every available space was distended with richly draped beds and cluttered tables, cabinets, and shelves, every wall was hung with tapestries and artwork. Impassive painted eyes followed her at every step.

On the next floor, the sixth, a long room stretched completely across the building. Couches and tables arranged on a hardwood floor proclaimed this to be a ballroom. A scrapbook lying on a chair held faded sepia photos of bustled ladies and boatered men picnicking in Dun Iain's fantastic shadow. Beyond the long room was a warren of smaller ones. Servant's quarters, probably. Nowhere did Rebecca see any signs of Dorothy's mice. No wonder Darnley the cat was so sleek and self-satisfied.

It was lighter up here, the walls thinner and the window embrasures not as deep. From one of the overhanging turrets the parking area seemed a long way down, Rebecca's and Michael's cars and Dorothy's Fairlane looking like miniatures on an architectural model. The only noise this high up was the murmur of the wind and Rebecca's own footsteps, each producing a faint but precise squeak from the old floorboards.

And it was cold, bone-chillingly cold. Rebecca fantasized about vats of hot coffee. Just a few more doors. Behind two were rooms crammed with piles of crates, boxes, and old books. A third opened onto a straight staircase. Light and an icy draft spilled down the steps. Ah, the roof. A sudden explosive burst of beating wings and swooping shapes made her leap back, slam the door, and stand against it, swallowing her heart back into her chest. Nesting blackbirds, she assured herself. Not an Alfred Hitchcock movie.

Rebecca rubbed her hands together as much in glee as to warm them. What a place! The corners were subtly curved, the walls met at eccentric angles, alcoves hiccuped at odd places. The ceilings were glorious confections of molded plaster like wedding cakes, and most of the walls were wood-paneled. The house itself was a treasure.

And had she really seen unique and wonderful artifacts tumbled indiscriminately with pure rubbish, or was she just wishfully thinking herself into hallucination? Even the famous Curle portrait of Mary, Queen of Scots, hung on the wall by a bed draped and canopied in crimson silk. Forbes Senior had been a magpie collector, buying on whim and leaving his acquisitions strewn about without any discernible order. Junk, Ray would've said, just as Dorothy had. What did he know? This wasn't his field, it was hers.

Dun Iain was a modern Pompeii, a labyrinth of walls and rooms and passages drifted with the remains of ancient fires—politics and religion, love and hate. Drifted with the ashes of time, waiting to be sifted by an academic arson team. Campbell and Reid, Rebecca thought wryly. Abbott and Costello.

Footsteps pattered across the floor of the ballroom. Rebecca looked around but saw no one. She must've heard Mrs. Garst's steps on the staircase. A strange echo, to make the steps appear to be on wood rather than stone, but that's what it had to be. The steps hadn't squeaked as hers had.

It was cold, and so silent she could hear her own pulse in her ears. Coffee, definitely. Rebecca started down the nearest flight of steps, another spiral staircase but not the same one she had come up.

She passed a back door into the large fifth-floor bedroom, another one into the corresponding room on the fourth, and then a long doorless stretch of curved wall. Tiny windows admitted watery light and an occasional glimpse of the surrounding trees, their dark carnelian contrasting oddly with the muted green of the lawns. There was Dorothy, leaning against the toolshed smoking a cigarette. That's why she'd abandoned the upper story—break time. She'd certainly made quick work of all those flights of stairs.

A third door was at the bottom of the cylindrical stairwell. Rebecca opened it, peeked out, and found herself in the far corner of the Hall from the piper's gallery. All right, then. She had it figured out. The building was a fat "L" shape. The Hall on the second floor and the ballroom on the sixth extended completely across their respective legs of the "L." The smaller rooms were set into the "L" like building blocks. No need to unroll a ball of string behind her as she'd first feared.

She strolled down the main staircase, pausing to look quizzically at Mary Stuart's inscrutable marble smile. Darnley had been sitting on the sarcophagus last night even as funny bumping noises came from upstairs. The hot water pipes, probably. Dun Iain would have made even phlegmatic Ray jump at his own shadow, let alone Michael, or Dorothy, or Rebecca herself.

She stepped into the brightly lit haven of the kitchen. An enamel kettle simmered on the range. Michael sat at the table, a mug of tea at his fingertips, a book propped against the marmalade jar. Darnley dozed on a chair, paws tucked in, looking like a furry butterscotch and white tea cozy.

"Good morning," Rebecca essayed. Her lips stopped before they could form the words "Dr. Campbell." He simply didn't have the august air of a Ph.D., even though he looked more domesticated than he had yesterday. His hair was smoothed tidily from his face as if awaiting the powder and ribbon of an eighteenth-century portrait. His sweatshirt was a conservative blue that reflected the blue of his eyes, its chest embossed with a white Saint Andrew's cross.

"Good mornin'," he replied. "I wasn't going to knock you up, but then the char came hooverin' in."

You weren't going to what? Rebecca was wavering between indignation and a whoop of laughter when she realized that she'd foundered on the shoal of dialect. He was being polite. She hazarded, "You weren't going to wake me, but the cleaning lady turned on the vacuum?"

"Thought you'd be needin' your sleep," he said equably. "Tea?"

"I'll fix some coffee, thank you." She lifted the kettle from the burner and asked, remembering the incessant beat of footsteps during the night, "What time did you get to bed?"

"Right after you. Slept like a bairn until seven, when I heard Mrs. Garst lettin' herself in."

She glanced curiously at him. How could he lie with such a straight face? Why bother to lie at all? But his eyes were fixed guilelessly on his book. She attacked a jar of instant coffee, promising herself to buy some real coffee in Putnam at the first opportunity.

Darnley opened one eye, decided there were no cat comestibles forthcoming, closed the eye. Michael marked his place, unfolded himself from the chair, and headed for the range shoving his sleeves up to his elbows. "The toast should be ready. There's no egg or sausage, but you could have a grilled tomato if you'd a mind to."

"No, thank you," returned Rebecca. He threw open the oven and filled a toast rack with slabs of dry toast. Good God, the man could cook. Rebecca's father and brothers had always demanded their toast and muffins, eggs and bacon, before her long-suffering mother had had a bite for herself.

Michael dealt out butter, plates, napkins, and cutlery. Rebecca watched, delighted to have someone wait on her for a change. She decided she'd give him an A for effort and an F for consistency. "The Forbeses had a toast rack. They really were Anglophiles. Or—there must be a better word—Britophile or something like that."

"Even the lingo is Sassenach," Michael snorted.

Rebecca laughed. "Let me guess. You're from one of the Campbell strongholds in Argyll with walls fifteen feet thick."

"No . . ." Michael sat on the cat. Darnley squalled and leaped for safety. Michael swore, reversed course, and collided with the counter. Rebecca winced, looking after the cat as he whisked into a small doorway in the corner of the room. But anything moving that fast couldn't be hurt.

Michael sat warily down with an embarrassed grimace she at first attributed to the cat incident. "No, I was born in Torquay."

"Torquay? The resort on the English Channel?"

"My parents ran a guesthouse called, so help me, Granny's Hieland Hame. My father wore the kilt and piped the boarders into dinner. Tryin' to make a livin', mind you, playin' music hall Scots like they do in the big hotels in Edinburgh."

No wonder he was embarrassed. But it would've been easier to lie about his birthplace than about his wandering around during the night. "Your family didn't have any antiques to sell for thirty pieces of silver?"

"Those jokes about thrifty Scots aren't all music hall blether. When you're poor, you have to be thrifty."

"Tell me about it," replied Rebecca sardonically.

Michael plopped marmalade onto his toast. "Accuse me of havin' the zeal of the convert, if you will, but we did flit to Inverness to live wi' my grandparents when I was eight. I wasn't born a Scot, really, but I was brought up one. No a teuchter,

though, I promise you that. As for my family bein' from Argyll
or Breadalbane or whether some ancestor found it expedient to
take the name of the local imperialists, I dinna ken. Don't
know,'' he translated.

He was trying so hard to be considerate Rebecca didn't tell
him not to bother, she understood the Scots dialect. Some of it.
"Teuchter?'' Her mouth couldn't squash the word like his could.

"Country yokel. Used to mean Highlander. Now it's a term
of ridicule. Like—oh—redneck, perhaps.''

"Like Sassenach?''

He grinned. His face was transformed, a Scotch mist dispelled
by sun.

Dazzled, she went on, "And you play the bagpipes, too?''

"I was first piper in the Mitsubishi Glendhu Distillery Pipe
and Drum Band. Kilt, bonnet, the lot. Won a prize in the Edinburgh Festival.''

"Mitsubishi what?''

Michael's grin skewed with that dry humor she'd glimpsed the
day before. "You get those pieces of silver where you can the day.''

"Of course.'' Rebecca responded with an answering grin. The
ceiling lights dusted his hair with auburn, and his eyes danced
like sunshine on a loch. When he was good, she thought, he
was very good. Quickly she scrunched her toast and dropped
her eyes to the book on the table. *MacKay's British Antiques.*
"Studying up?''

"I'm a historian and a museum curator, no an antique dealer.''

"You were qualified for this job.''

"I got it the same way you did, by volunteerin'. No other way
I could afford to see America. More toast?''

"No thank you.'' She'd trained herself not to eat much. Ray
was always holding help sessions with skinny coeds who didn't
know the difference between Plato and Pluto but who hung
breathlessly on his tweedy good looks, gushing, "Oh, aren't you
just too clever, Dr. Kocurek,'' as if he were the philosophy
department's answer to Indiana Jones.

"American women,'' teased Michael, "always slimmin'.'' He
dangled the toast rack temptingly before her.

Ah, so much for Ray and his coeds, too. Rebecca took another
piece and defiantly slathered it with butter. The cat reappeared.
To Michael's wheedling, "Eh, kittlin?'' he responded with a
baleful glare and wrapped Rebecca's ankles, his sleek body vi-

brating with a purr. The narrow kitchen windows, chutes in the thickness of the lower walls, brightened a bit. Maybe it would be another pretty day. Maybe she'd find the Erskine letter right off the bat. Coming here was the best idea she'd had in years.

She was just drawing breath to tell Michael about her own background, such as it was, when the phone rang. It squatted on the counter at her elbow; she lifted the receiver. "Hello, Dun Iain Estate."

The voice on the line was like Darnley's purr translated into a velvet baritone. "Good morning. Is this Ms. Reid?"

The American accent seemed flat after Michael's lilting cadences. "This is she."

"This is Eric Adler, Ms. Reid. We exchanged letters. I'm an attorney, the executor of James Ramsey Forbes's will."

"Yes, of course, Mr. Adler."

Michael shoved his chair back so abruptly it thunked against the wall. He swept the plates and mugs off the table and dumped them into the sink. The Scotch mist fell again over his face, congealing his expression into something resembling an outcropping of conglomerate rock.

Adler's voice said, "I was planning to drive up from Columbus about noon to bring you and Dr. Campbell the inventory that James Forbes had on file with us. Would that be convenient?"

"Yes, it would," Rebecca replied.

"What does he want?" asked Michael.

Rebecca said, "Excuse me," and covered the mouthpiece. "To bring us Forbes's inventory."

"Why didna he bring it last week?"

How the heck am I supposed to know? Rebecca retorted silently. She turned her back on Michael. And when he was bad he was horrid. "We'd be delighted to have you visit, Mr. Adler."

"Eric, please," he told her.

She'd pictured an old family retainer, white-haired and bespectacled, but the voice belonged to a younger man. "Eric. And I'm Rebecca."

"See you about noon, Rebecca."

She replaced the receiver, Adler's dulcet tones still caressing her ear. At least someone around here had good manners. She shot a glance from under her brows at Michael. He had a long, limber, eloquent mouth when he wasn't clasping it tightly shut.

Right now it looked like the door of a safe. Whatever had got his goat this time was something about the lawyer, the inventory, or both.

Michael scooped Darnley off the counter as the cat stalked a foil-covered dish. "Time for a recce, then."

"I took a quick look around earlier this morning, but I . . ."

"A' by—all by yourself?" He stared at her with exasperation and puzzlement mingled.

She stared back. Darn it, he was just as much a hired hand as she was. "I am old enough to be out without a nanny, Dr. Campbell."

With the noble forbearance of martyred William Wallace on the way to the scaffold, he turned and walked away.

Keep it up as long as you want, Rebecca told him silently, but I won't let you or anyone else spoil this adventure for me. Stubbornly she folded her arms and followed.

Chapter Three

MICHAEL LED REBECCA to the door through which Darnley had fled. "The larder," he announced. Below a sloping ceiling a window the size of a tea tray was set deep in the wall. A broom and a mop stood next to bowls of water and cat food. One wooden shelf was scattered with cans and boxes; the others were filled with dim plastic-draped shapes. Rebecca peeked. It was Royal Doulton china, untouched for years, like relics of Sleeping Beauty's castle.

Past the vinyl floor of the kitchen and the stone flags of the entry, between the main staircase and the front door, was another door. "Lumber room," Michael said. "Formerly the butler's pantry and wine cellar, back when John Forbes gave house parties for the posh set."

"Vanderbilt, Frick, Mellon. But never Carnegie—Forbes loathed him."

"If it wasn't for my Carnegie scholarship at Edinburgh, I'd no be here."

Nice historical irony. Nodding approval, Rebecca squinted through the gloom in the low, dungeonlike room. It was stacked with crates and chests, loot never even opened, perhaps, after one of John's obsessive buying sprees in the old country.

John Forbes's parents had emigrated from Sutherland with his infant self some years before Andrew Carnegie had left Dunfermline. Carnegie had shared the fortune he made in steel; no wonder he was lionized back in Scotland. The fortune Forbes had made in railroads, oil, and various sharp practices on Wall Street he'd never shared, and it had bought him only contempt.

Rebecca didn't feel particularly sorry for him. Wealth can buy happiness, she told herself, if you use it the right way.

When Carnegie had built a home in Scotland, Forbes had built Dun Iain here, truculently copying Craigievar, the seat of Forbeses who disdained all relationship with a brash American who simply happened to have the same name.

"Forbes had a muckle great ego," Michael continued, with a sly sideways glance, "to name the place after himself."

He was testing her. "Dun Iain means 'John's Fort' in Gaelic," Rebecca responded sweetly.

But Michael had already taken a few steps along the narrow passageway that ran between the boxes. He ran his hand over a dusty and cobwebby trunk and then rubbed his fingers together thoughtfully. The mark he left on the trunk was almost as clean as the smudges around the unlocked catch.

Someone had opened the trunk very recently. And the dust on the lid of the box next to it was also smudged with several fingerprints. "You didn't waste any time opening these up," Rebecca remarked.

Michael shied like a skittish horse. "I hivna been in here. I hivna had the inventory, have I? I've been muckin' aboot wi' old receipts and lists."

"Oh. Then I bet it was Mrs. Garst and the caretaker and gardener—the Pruitts—looking for the treasure."

"Treasure?" His smile glittered. "Have you been heedin' the old woman's gossip?"

"Have you?" Rebecca retorted.

Shrugging, he led the way upstairs to the Hall. The lantern-shaped chandelier dangled from a plaster thistle like a spun-sugar stalactite. Dining and easy chairs were upholstered in green Forbes tartan. Beneath its ornate plaster coat of arms the fire-place gleamed with oddments of brass. Antlers hung on the walls among antique swords and muskets. On one sideboard was a chess set, its pieces ivory Celts and Norsemen. A short-necked guitar, its inlaid wood carefully polished, and a small harp were enshrined on another.

"David Rizzio's guitar," said Michael, "that he was playin' the night he was murdered. Or so says a receipt. I haven't es-tablished provenance yet, mind you. The inventory will help, when Adler troubles himself to bring it."

"And Mary's harp, I suppose?" Rebecca touched the guitar. The wood was strangely warm and the strings vibrated gently beneath her fingertips. Her thought reverberated in response. She saw the small supper room at Holyrood Palace violated by Lord Darnley's bravos—Mary and her ladies staggering back, aghast, and poor harmless Rizzio dragged out screaming, until the flash of daggers cut his screams short . . .

Rebecca snatched her hand back from the guitar. She could have sworn the strings of the harp sounded a small, querulous note in some harmonic of memory. "Stupid Mary?" she asked, more breathlessly than she would have liked. It was early in the day to get carried away by the fascinating associations of the artifacts. "Last night you called Mary romantic and stupid."

Michael was staring at the harp. He blinked. "What?"

"Stupid Mary, you said. Surely you were just pulling my leg."

The dark, level line of his brows crumpled, appalled at the very idea. "Takin' the mickey out of you? No at all. Mary's heart ruled her head. She let herself be used by the men around her, like the mewlin' and greetin' heroine of some tatty novel."

"I imagine she did quite a bit of crying. Given the time in which she lived, she had little choice but to ally herself with men."

"Didn't she, then? What of her cousin Elizabeth, who ruled England with the heart and stomach of a man, as she said herself? Now, there was a woman."

"Well, yes," murmured Rebecca, "there's no higher compliment you can give a woman, is there, than that she acts like a man?"

Michael's hair was starting to lose its sleekness. He scooped it off his forehead with the impatient gesture she'd already noted as characteristic. He fixed Rebecca with an aggravated frown. This time it was she who turned away, shaking her head. It wasn't worth arguing over.

The sun really had come out, brightening the Hall and the landing. A quick glance into the study showed Rebecca the suit of armor that had frightened her the night before gleaming guilelessly in the corner amid the jumble of furniture. A large framed document proved to be a copy of the fourteenth-century Declaration of Arbroath. A small door in the paneling led to a tiny chamber with a rolltop desk and several metal filing cabinets.

"At Craigievar this was 'Danzig Willie' Forbes's private study," said Michael. "There it's called the prophet's chamber."

"Because Willie was a prophet of commerce?" Rebecca asked.

Michael chuckled humorlessly. "I would imagine 'profit'—with an 'f'—is closer to the proper meaning."

"You've seen Craigievar?"

"Aye. For a copy, this one's no bad." He bounded lightly onto the bottom step of the spiral staircase and padded upward. For someone who moved so catlike during the day, he was certainly heavy-footed at night. Rebecca followed, telling herself she could afford the extra toast; these stairs were as good as her aerobics classes.

Michael diverted into his bedroom and returned slapping his denim-clad thigh with his spiral notebook. The whine of the vacuum cleaner filtered faintly down the staircase. "Pay attention. Here's where we start separatin' the coal from the dross."

Yes, your grace, Rebecca thought again, as he led the way into the large bedroom down the hall from his small one.

Now, her second time through, she was able to focus on individual items. "Flemish tapestries," said Michael with a flourish of his notebook. "Excellent condition. Portraits by Raeburn and Lawrence. A Rembrandt cartoon. A Meissen clock."

Rebecca went from object to object, crooning appreciation. This was wonderful, everything she'd anticipated and more. "Graham of Claverhouse," she said, identifying one portrait.

"Died of old age in London in 1707," Michael returned.

She shot him a scornful look. "He was killed in the battle of Killiecrankie in 1689, as you well know."

"Mm," said Michael, aggressively noncommittal. "Who's that?"

Rebecca eyed an illuminated manuscript page. "Saint Margaret, I think. She of the chapel in Edinburgh Castle. Right?"

"Right enough."

The other small bedroom on that floor had evidently belonged to James. An aluminum walker and other bits and pieces of sickroom equipment lay jumbled beside a Sheraton wardrobe. Heck of a place to be stuck when you're old and sick, Rebecca thought, up three flights of stairs. The man must have loved Dun Iain to have resisted moving to the nursing home Dorothy had mentioned.

Rebecca reached for the doors of the wardrobe. "Careful," said Michael brightly. "If you go about keekin' into cupboards, you're askin' for things to fall out on your head."

She opened the door. Nothing fell on her but the stale scent of lavender, underlain by a slight acrid reek. The wardrobe was crammed with long dresses with puffed sleeves, hatboxes, prim high-button boots, and lacy garments shrouded in yellowed tissue paper. "Elspeth's things, still here?"

"They're from the right time," replied Michael. "She died in 1901."

Rebecca gave the cradle a quick rock as they went on to the next room. By its door was a pen-and-ink drawing. "Dunstaffnage Castle," she said. "Built by the MacDougals and appropriated by the Campbells."

"Where Mary Hamilton was imprisoned in 1571."

"Where Flora MacDonald was imprisoned in 1746. Will you stop that?"

"Stop what?" Michael eyed the drawing. "Poor daft Flora. If she'd handed Bonnie Prince Charlie over to the authorities, we'd have been spared a lot of romantic twaddle."

"Spoken like a true Campbell," she teased.

"So the Campbells had the gumption to see which way the wind was blowin', and sided wi' the Hanoverians."

"And were richly rewarded for doing so."

"It always comes to money in the end," he stated, with the finality of a period at the end of a sentence.

She wasn't about to dispute that. She waved airily at yet another portrait. "There's Prince Charles Edward himself. Take it up with him." And she walked on, leaving Michael to make a sardonic bow before the handsome if arrogant features of the Young Pretender.

Rebecca felt as if she were inside a kaleidoscope, bits of Scottish history from Robert Bruce to Robert Burns, from Saint Columba to Harry Lauder, shifting and sliding before her eyes. From the sublime . . . A Covenanter's Bible. A chain-mail gauntlet. A broken bit of statuary from Scone. Sir Walter Scott's inkwell. Scrapbooks filled with old postcards, neatly labeled in what Rebecca had already come to recognize as James's copperplate hand.

To the ridiculous. Jelly jars lined the windowsills, filled with scraggly bits of ivy. Candy wrappers were neatly spindled on old nails. Stacks of lurid detective novels teetered atop cabinets.

On the wall of the fifth-floor corridor was a portrait of John Forbes himself. The old tycoon's eyes were expressionless onyx marbles, his mouth a thin, suspicious fissure above an outthrust chin. Lush white sideburns and moustache could not soften a face dehydrated by a lifetime of resentment. On a little table below the portrait was a leather-bound copy of *Man of Iron*, by James Ramsey Forbes, its gilded embellishments cracked and tarnished. "Did James mean the title to be ironic?" Rebecca wondered aloud. "Iron rusts. Carnegie was the man of steel."

"Hard to say," said Michael. "How'd you like to be the only bairn of such a man?"

"Better than being his wife," Rebecca said emphatically. On the dresser in the big bedroom was a set of ivory-handled hairbrushes. They were flanked by several cut-glass bottles labeled with the names of expensive Paris perfumeries. "Also Elspeth's? John and then James kept her things out, as if expecting her to return any moment?"

"They were more than a wee bit mad, the both of them." Michael fluffed up a pillow on the sumptuously draped and canopied bed, removing the imprint of a resting head, then turned and regarded the full-length portrait of Mary Stuart. Rebecca, too, was drawn again by the tragic queen's serene expression. The crucifix she held gestured as calmly toward an inset scene of her execution as though she were a conductor sounding the downbeat of a symphony, "Scots Wha Hae" played in counterpoint to "Rule Britannia."

"I wonder," Michael mused, "whether yon face peerin' into his bed put old John on or off the job." He turned aside, disallowing his smirk.

That, Rebecca suspected, had been a salacious double entendre. She shouldn't acknowledge it. She smothered a smile at both John Forbes's necrophiliac tendencies and Michael's undisciplined mouth.

Footsteps clicked across the floor above. Michael's face tilted abruptly upward. He stood very still, very quiet, staring so intently at the plaster ceiling she thought for a moment he could see through it.

Before she could catch herself she spun about and looked toward the stairwell. Nothing appeared but Dorothy and her vacuum cleaner, heralded by thumps and crashes. Of course, Rebecca told herself. What did you expect?

"There you are!" the woman cried cheerily. "Found the treasure yet?"

Michael emitted a long exhalation and rolled his eyes.

"There's some fascinating things here," returned Rebecca. And yet they were lonely things, objects in exile stripped to the barest emotional resonance. Like the guitar and the harp, they exchanged quick notes of terrible reminiscence . . . Getting fanciful in your old age, she told herself. No wonder you got carried away with that guitar. Next you'll start believing in the Forbes treasure. The Erksine letter would be treasure enough.

"Checking out the bedrooms, I see." Dorothy rolled her engine of cleanliness into the room, plugged it in, and laid down her basket. She fixed Michael with a stare over the top of her glasses. "So the two of you will be spending a lot of time alone here together, hm?"

Michael glanced first at Mary's painted features and then at Rebecca, just as Rebecca, to her horror, felt her cheeks grow hot in a blush.

"I know how young people behave these days," Dorothy continued with a ghastly simpering grin. "Everything's so casual. Sleep around, have a good time, and never mind the consequences. Well, repent at leisure, I always say."

Time for a dignified exit. As one, Michael and Rebecca started for the hall, collided in the doorway, and lurched away from each other like magnets touching negative poles. They didn't stop until they'd gained the airy, whitewashed expanse of the ballroom. Blocks of sunlight danced a slow and stately minuet across the floor and a suggestion of rot hung on the air.

Michael seemed undecided whether to laugh or to swear. He said at last in a rather choked voice, "So then, what do you think?"

"About the house?" Rebecca asked, smothering a rather warped grin. "The collection is more idiosyncratic than I'd imagined."

"About the house," affirmed Michael, settling on laughter. He sauntered down the room, floorboards squeaking, to a semicircular window seat snugged inside a turret. "It's a right mixtie-maxtie. I wager old John didna ken the half of what he had."

"Do you think he has Admiral Nelson's glass eye around here somewhere?"

Michael leaned his elbow against the window frame and looked out. "He has the Earl of Montrose's heart."

"What?" Rebecca creaked down the room and looked out the other side of the turret. Below the window the driveway streaked the lawn like a line on a map and disappeared into trees. She felt as if she were in the crow's nest of a ship sailing a sea of maple leaves.

"Charles II sent Montrose to Scotland in 1650 . . ."

"I know that. But his heart?"

Michael cocked an eyebrow—squeamish? "There's a receipt for it among James's lists, signed by some retired brigadier in Swansea, of all places."

"Well," said Rebecca gamely, "people in the Middle Ages used to venerate the body parts of holy men and women."

"Montrose was hardly a saint. Well kent, aye."

"Like as not some soldier there beneath the scaffold simply helped himself to a souvenir."

They considered each other for a moment. Michael essayed, "Rumor has it that Elizabeth Curle . . ."

"Mary's lady-in-waiting who commissioned the portrait downstairs."

". . . rescued Queen Mary's severed head and took it to Antwerp."

"Wouldn't John have loved that? He could've carried it around with him like Walter Raleigh's wife carried her husband's head in a velvet bag." Rebecca shivered, a cold draft sliding through the window and tightening her shoulders. "I'll tell you one thing Forbes doesn't have: Mary's death mask. I saw it at Lennoxlove, outside Edinburgh, last summer with Ray." The name clunked as heavily as the nocturnal footsteps into the silence.

"The bloke in your photograph?"

If she'd peeked into Michael's room, he'd peeked into hers. "Yes," she answered. Interesting how her mouth didn't add, "my fiancé." Michael gazed out the window, Mary and Montrose much more relevant to him than Ray Kocurek. Rebecca rushed on. "Not that the death mask looks much like the effigy downstairs, but I guess that was idealized."

"Supposedly the one was modeled on the other."

She crossed her arms. "A sarcophagus in your front hall, even a half-size one. John must've been one of the great nineteenth-century eccentrics."

"Not so much as you'd think. The rich can afford to be slightly daft. In fact, they're expected to be. John was quite mindful of his social status. I'll show you some of the newspaper cuttin's when we go back down."

There was a distinct draft along the floor as well, wrapping around Rebecca's ankles like a cold purr of a reptilian cat. She hugged herself. "If I had any money, I'd be glad to act crazy and amuse the peasants."

"They say money can't buy happiness, although I'd like to give it a go." Michael straightened, his fingers rippling the pages in his notebook. The tiny whirring sound complemented the rustling of the trees. "Speakin' of which, there's a particularly interestin' series of cuttin's about Elspeth's death. I doot there's more to that than ever made the dailies. The verdict of the inquest was suppressed for a time, you know."

"No, I don't know. The book just said that she died."

"Oh, aye," exclaimed Michael. "Something you dinna ken?" He paused for effect. "She jumped or fell from this very window."

The cold in Rebecca's shoulders wriggled down her spine to splash against the cold in her ankles. "Suicide?"

"Apparently. But John would've preferred bein' up for murder, I wager, than admittin' his wife killed herself rather than live wi' him."

"It wasn't murder, though?"

"No one else was in this room when she fell, or there might've been some suspicion."

"The young woman married to the old man," said Rebecca. "A classic story. Poor Elspeth—that was the only way out of her trap."

"They laid her out on her own bed, there in front of Mary's portrait. After she was gone," he concluded wistfully, "there were no more parties."

Rebecca remembered how Michael had fluffed the pillow. He wasn't completely immune to Elspeth's mysterious charms. "In 1901 James was nine. And he fell down the stairs two months ago."

"Aye, the family seems to have had a right problem wi' gravity." He would have been completely deadpan, but the corner of his mouth twitched.

"Michael," Rebecca began reprovingly, and then, "Dr. Campbell . . ." Despite herself, she, too, smiled.

"Well, then, Miss Reid," he said, "it's awful cold up here. We should be gettin' . . ." A pickup truck was coming up the driveway, the roar of its engine and the crunch of its tires on the gravel muted by distance. "The Pruitts," said Michael. "I'll let them in, shall I?"

Rebecca watched him until he disappeared down the stairs. For a moment they'd almost been comrades, sifting the ashes of old scandals. He knew his history. He'd accepted that she knew hers.

She stepped closer to the window and considered the relentless ground far below. She imagined Elspeth falling, skirts fluttering madly, hair flying from its pins. It had taken courage to step out into the empty air. Not as much courage, though, as it would have taken to stay flat-footedly anchored to the stone and wood of Dun Iain.

Crimson maple leaves whirled across the window. The wind was rising. Maybe there would be a storm.

Chapter Four

THE SUNLIGHT ON the floor thinned and faded as clouds raced across the sky, damping its blue to gray. From her sixth-floor eyrie Rebecca looked down at the foreshortened shapes of the Pruitts. The middle-aged man wearing a checked shirt, sleeveless quilted vest, and a baseball cap must be Phil. Therefore the younger one was his son, Steve. He was dressed in black, half his head only stubble and the other sporting a long lock of greasy hair almost covering one eye. The earphones of a Walkman were affixed like the antennae of a sci-fi monster to his ears.

A huge Labrador bounded out of the back of the truck and sprinted across the lawn in pursuit of a fleeing wisp of butterscotch and white fur.

Rebecca's breath fogged the glass. "Darnley! Run!" But the cat was already up a tree, perched on a branch, no doubt wishing himself a leopard, as the dog capered beneath. Frenzied barking echoed like gunshots.

"Aw, shaddup!" shouted Phil. He plodded toward the front door, lopsided from the weight of the toolbox he carried. Steve ambled toward the shed, his limbs jerking in response to the thankfully inaudible music.

And here came another car up the driveway, a gray Volvo gleaming like mother-of-pearl in a brief ray of sun. Rebecca glanced at her watch. Noon already. That must be the lawyer.

The window gave abruptly and she jumped back.

Oh, it hadn't been latched. The top sash had slipped a couple of inches. Shaking her head at herself, Rebecca shut the window, latched it, and rubbed the steamy patch of her breath from it with her sleeve. No screens, she noted, true to British prototype.

Her jaw dropped at the gorgeous figure stepping from the Volvo. He wore a dark blue suit and a maroon tie, and his black hair was trimmed just so, conservatively close to the head. His sunglasses turned this way and that, looking from castle to dog to the ludicrous figure of Steve Pruitt. Not that she was familiar with designer clothing, but Rebecca swore the man was plastered with labels like a steamer truck after an around-the-world voyage.

Eric took a briefcase from the car and turned toward the front door. Steve stood clutching hoe and pruning shears, staring after him. Envious, Rebecca thought. Or perhaps scornful of the classy business suit and tie.

The dog was gone. No, there he was, sniffing among the trees like the Hound of the Baskervilles. Darnley was scampering for the house.

A vague fluttering came from the ceiling, blackbirds probably roosting in the chimneys. The wind whined around the turrets and cupolas of the roof. Rebecca seemed to be watching an old movie with the volume turned down, the images moving among eerie suggestions of sounds. Maybe this was how Elspeth had felt, looking down from her gilded cage at scenes irrevocably beyond her reach.

Rebecca walked sedately down to her room and looked at Elspeth's painted face with new interest. What tragic eyes, contrasting curiously with such a sharply honed chin!

Comb and lipstick—there, Rebecca thought, she was as presentable as she would ever be. In the edge of the mirror she saw the door of her wardrobe standing open. The smell of lavender had ebbed overnight, and she had left the door shut. Surely she had left it shut. A couple of blouses lay draped over the rim of the opening. Frowning, she replaced them, vowing to have a word or two with Dorothy about going through her things.

Voices came faintly from below, Dorothy's high-pitched yammer, a deep bassoon drawl that must be Phil, and the impeccable baritone, even richer now than it had been over the telephone. Michael's lilt was clipped of its diphthong extravagances like a sheep shorn of its fleece.

Rebecca passed Phil Pruitt on the stairs, shrinking to the side to avoid being scooped up by his box of tools like a cow caught by a locomotive's cowcatcher. Dorothy's voice clung to his heels,

"Children have no self-respect anymore, they just can't be bothered to dress properly."

"Aw," Phil shouted back over his shoulder, "leave the boy alone, he's just playacting with those friends of his. They all look like that. Don't hurt nothing." He turned, saw Rebecca, and didn't startle in the least. "Afternoon," he said, with a laconic nod, and climbed on by. His back pocket was distended by a can of snuff and a grotesque Grimm Brothers key, the twin of the one Michael had used to lock the front door.

Michael was seated at the table in the Hall, his notebook open before him, a porcelain teapot upside down in his hand. Narrowly he inspected its maker's mark, set it down, made a notation in his book. Eric Adler stood beside him, just slipping his sunglasses into his jacket pocket. "Sèvres china? That's quite valuable. You'll have to pack it very carefully to get it back to Scotland without breaking it."

"There's an allowance for professional packin'," replied Michael, never raising his eyes from the page.

Eric looked over Michael's shoulder at the book. "You're choosing all the best things, I see."

"That," said Michael, "is what they hired me to do. No sense in payin' a fortune to have a bloody jumble sale shipped back to the Auld Country." His brows tightened over his eyes like the proscenium arch of a theater.

"Yes, of course." Eric raised his hands as if calming a rabid dog. He saw Rebecca standing in the doorway and his wary expression broke into a smile. His teeth were crowded together awkwardly, an engaging flaw in an otherwise strong, square, classically handsome face. "Ms. Reid? Rebecca, isn't it?"

Oh, my, she thought. She stepped forward, hand extended. "Eric. Nice to meet you."

He shook her hand. His clasp lingered perhaps a moment too long, but his smile was openly, honestly appreciative. Maybe, Rebecca thought, he'd been expecting the stereotypical dried-up academic with wire-rimmed glasses, just as she'd been expecting someone along the lines of Marcus Welby.

Michael inspected a pewter candlestick and made another note in his book. Dorothy dusted the chess set, every line of her back alert to the conversation taking place behind her. Rebecca was surprised her ears didn't swivel like a cat's.

"There are the inventories." Eric indicated several rusty black notebooks next to his open briefcase. "James typed these up in the forties, and I'm afraid the ink has faded over the years. I'm sorry I wasn't able to get them here any sooner than this." He glanced across the table.

"No problem," muttered Michael to the candlestick.

"We appreciate your bringing them now." Rebecca picked up one of the books and leafed quickly through it. The paper was yellowed on the edges and scalped by erasures. The darkest areas of type were those with overstrikes and crossed-out words. She chose a page at random. "Portrait of William, eighteenth Earl of Sutherland. By Winterhalter. Purchased from Lord Alistair Sutherland-Leveson-Gower, London, 1899." Yes, she remembered that particular portrait, a lantern-jawed individual wearing a scarlet jacket and kilt. It was in the fourth-floor hallway outside the door of Michael's room.

Eric asked, "Satisfactory?"

"Oh, yes. Very helpful." She shut the book and laid it back on the table. Bits of the black paper cover stuck to her hand.

They stood smiling at each other; his eyes, she saw, were smoky gray. Michael set the candlestick down with a thunk. Dorothy turned around. Darnley squeezed through the railings of the piper's gallery, leaped onto the sideboard and then to the floor, landing just beside Eric. Eric jumped.

"Got you, too." Rebecca laughed. "The house likes to startle people."

The cat twined around his ankles, sniffing curiously at his shiny shoes. Eric's face went ashen. Dorothy, puckered with disapproval, seized the little animal and tossed him out onto the landing. "Shoo," she stage-whispered. "You know Mr. Adler doesn't like cats." Darnley trotted away, his tail an exclamation point of disgruntlement.

For just a moment Rebecca thought a cold sweat glistened on Eric's forehead. Some people had a phobia about cats . . . He collected himself and laughed a slightly forced laugh. "Please forgive me. I—I have nothing against the animal, you understand, but I have bad allergies."

"What a shame." Rebecca shot a severe glance at Michael's simpering expression, evidently meant to imitate a Victorian lady having the vapors.

Eric, tanned complexion and equilibrium restored, pulled a long, narrow sack from his briefcase. "Here's a small housewarming gift. Surely, in your profession, you've enjoyed single-malt Scotch."

Rebecca accepted the bag and pulled out a bottle. "Laphroaig! My favorite brand! What a treat—how thoughtful. Thank you."

Eric's smile broadened into a grin, savoring the effect he was having.

In the bowels of the castle the telephone rang. Dorothy bustled out, muttering about whiskey being the last resort of the alcoholic. Michael's eyes fixed upon the bottle with a thirsty gleam and then, catching Rebecca's jaundiced look, bent hurriedly over a set of silver spoons. She set the bottle down well out of his reach.

"Becky," called Dorothy up the staircase. "You're wanted on the phone. Jan Sorenson."

Rebecca's brothers were larger than she was; they could call her "Becky" and live. Through gritted teeth she said, "Excuse me, please, Eric." and when she passed Dorothy on the stairs, "I prefer Rebecca, Mrs. Garst."

Dorothy shrugged. "It's just a nickname. People call me Dottie, and it never hurt me none."

Rebecca grabbed a dry piece of toast from the kitchen counter and picked up the receiver. "Jan? Hi!"

Her friend's voice sounded a continent away. "Sorry to interrupt, I know you must be busy, but Peter and I were wondering if you'd like to come for dinner and some human companionship tomorrow. Bring the Scottish prof, if you think he'd be comfortable with the kids."

"Love to," replied Rebecca, snapping off a bite of toast. "I haven't decided yet if Dr. Campbell fills the bill as human."

"Oh? One of those shriveled-up little characters like the old major on *Fawlty Towers*?"

"Oh, no. Not at all." Rebecca sighed. "If he's as grateful for the invitation as he ought to be, you can see for yourself. Thanks."

"I'd go nuts slaving away in the dust all alone out there."

"I'm not slaving, it's not very dusty, and it's like Grand Central Station. The lawyer, the gardener, the handyman, the housekeeper."

"I know Dorothy," said Jan. "Peter works with her son Chuck down at the plant."

Rebecca flicked crumbs from her sweater and decided she'd kill for a cup of real coffee. "Really?" she asked, encouraging the friendly voice.

"Chuck had a great story last winter about the night his mother spent out at Dun Iain."

"She told me she didn't spend the night here."

"Not anymore she doesn't. She came home carrying on so about how the place was haunted, Chuck and Margie had to give her one of her Valiums."

"Haunted?" asked Rebecca. She turned so that her back was to the kitchen counter, the doors innocently open in front of her.

"She claimed there were footsteps going up and down the stairs all night long, and things disarranged, and shapes in the shadows. I'm surprised she didn't pull the one about a bloodstain that can't be washed away."

No, Rebecca thought, the bloodstain's under the gravel outside the front door, beneath the fatal window. A chill like a snake slithered down her spine and the crumbs in her mouth turned suddenly into sand.

Jan's voice caroled on. "She probably had a nip of Mr. Forbes's Scotch. Or didn't take her prescriptions properly, or something."

"Or something," croaked Rebecca. She coughed, and managed to say, "There were probably branches banging against the windows, or the cat knocking things over. Unless it was James himself." She remembered the aluminum walker laying abandoned upstairs. She remembered the green lawn stretching between the walls of Dun Iain and the closest tress. She remembered Darnley gliding noiselessly up the stairs.

A yelp sounded from the receiver. "Mandy, put that down!" And, "Sorry, gotta go! See you both tomorrow at six."

"Jan?" The line was dead, as dead as James, and John, and Elspeth, and the Good Lord knew how many others whose belongings now lay caged within the thick walls of the castle.

No. It couldn't be. Ghosts and haunted houses belonged in movies, not in real life. There was a reasonable explanation, birds in the chimneys, or bats in Dorothy's belfry, or just the spooky atmosphere of the old house. Yes, that was it. Anyplace that had rumors of buried treasure had to have a few ghost stories as well. Maybe James had planted them himself, just to keep the locals away from his hermitage.

Rebecca slapped the receiver into its cradle so emphatically the telephone's bell dinged a protest. "Thanks, Jan," she said aloud. "That's just what I needed." She left the kitchen, cast a glance at the invitingly open front door, and stamped back up the stairs. A breath of fresh air would steady her nerves. She'd go get her typewriter.

As she passed the door of the Hall she heard Michael pontificating on Rizzio's guitar. Who, where, when, what—his dry manner made the dramatic scene sound like a police report. "Interesting," said Eric, politely but without conviction.

A hammer tapped away upstairs as Phil mended something. Rebecca went into her bedroom and retrieved her car keys. A narrow glance showed her that everything was where she'd left it, right down to Ray's impassive smile. Of course—Dorothy was downstairs.

Below her window, Steve, his lock of hair concealing his downturned face, was sitting behind the wheel of Eric's Volvo inventorying the dashboard. The lights flashed off and on. Well! Rebecca exclaimed to herself. She understood how the boy would be intrigued by the car, but to actually climb inside took a lot of gall.

She went back down again. In the Hall Dorothy was saying, "—just put it in the oven at three-fifty for about an hour."

"Very kind of you," replied Michael tentatively.

"You bachelors think you can survive on a few cold cuts and a can of fruit cocktail. You have to learn to take care of yourself, you know."

Michael didn't reply. By this time he'd no doubt learned resistance was useless.

Rebecca broke free into the outside world. The wind, if cold, was wonderfully fresh. It found and yanked free several locks of her hair, which began waving around her face like sea anemones in a current. She pulled the strands aside and saw Steve standing beside the Volvo, his hand on the door as if he'd just closed it. "Hi!" she said.

He shot a furtive look at her and scurried away, in his black garments and Walkman appearing unappetizingly like a cockroach.

Mustn't judge him on how he dresses, she chided herself. Phil's right—a kid's clothing is his admission into a circle of friends. Rebecca herself had suffered agonies wearing a cousin's hand-me-down bell-bottoms when all the other girls were wearing smart narrow-legged jeans. That was when she'd learned how to sew, even though she had to take a part-time job after school to buy the sewing machine.

She opened the trunk of her car and extricated the typewriter.

The gale made her wool sweater feel like chiffon, but it was preferable to the sneaky little drafts in the upper room. She turned to see Eric striding across the gravel. "Let me help you!" He slammed the trunk, gave her her keys, took the typewriter, and escorted her into the lee of the building.

Very smooth, she thought; in taking the typewriter he brushed her fingertips so lightly with his own a pleasant tremor rippled up her arm.

Eric set the typewriter inside the door and pointed toward the stone fretwork structure across the lawn. "Did you know that that's the mausoleum where the Forbeses are buried?"

"Here? On the grounds?" Again she crossed her arms and hugged.

"John thought he was too good to mingle with the peasantry in the Putnam cemetery, I suppose. At any rate, he had a vault dug to accommodate his wife. Do you know about her? Very unfortunate." Eric's jaw twitched, as if he'd clenched his teeth.

"Yes," Rebecca murmured. She scuffed the gravel with her toe. These particular pebbles wouldn't have been here then.

"Later on John built the dovecote behind the vault, to camouflage it, perhaps. If he'd been at all a romantic soul, I'd say he was equating doves with the goddess of love—the usual Victorian sentimentality. But he probably just wanted an inexpensive source of fresh drumsticks."

Rebecca grinned. How gracefully he'd smoothed over his macabre revelation. "If John could stand having Queen Mary in his front hall, I guess he could stand burying his wife in his front yard. He became a recluse after she died, didn't he?"

Eric nodded, his eyes fixed on the structure that was Elspeth's only memorial. As if to dramatize the scene, a ray of sun peeked out and the stone sparkled. It must be Connecticut granite, Rebecca thought, like the house.

"He lingered on another thirty years," said Eric, "without speaking to anyone but James and the servants. I'd feel sorry for him, except . . ."

"He brought it on himself?"

"Yes." Eric made a precise about-face and offered Rebecca a grin of his own. Glancing at his watch, he said, "I have some business in Putnam this afternoon, but I should be finished by five. Would you like to have dinner with me before I go back to Columbus?"

His unfortunately crowded teeth made his grin look like a cartoon wolf's. Rebecca had to laugh. "I'd love to."

"Great. In Putnam most of the places are franchises or hole-in-the-wall diners suitable only for a truck driver's stomach. Unless you're a Big Mac freak I suggest Gaetano's, a new Italian restaurant."

"Sounds much better than a Big Mac. I ate altogether too many of them when I was putting myself through school."

"So did I," Eric confided. He pulled out his sunglasses, considered the sky, replaced them in his pocket. She half expected him to kiss her hand, but he only nudged her shoulder toward the door. "Go back inside before you get a chill. I'll be here at five-thirty."

But the inside is as cold as the outside, she thought ruefully. I'll have to get some long johns. "See you then," she called.

He responded with a jaunty wave. She watched the gray car until it had disappeared among the trees, following it in her mind as if it were a camel caravan traversing trackless wastes. Dun Iain seemed as isolated as a desert oasis, thousands of miles from civilization. Not that there was anything wrong with that, she assured herself, she was just used to the bustle of the campus.

The wind and the trees danced a Highland fling, the rush of air around the turrets providing the *skreel* of the pipes. Rebecca strolled toward the dovecote thinking, when the state turns Dun Iain into a museum, or a youth hostel, or a scout camp, or whatever they're going to do with it, they need to move the parking area away from the house. Rather ruins the facade to have all these old heaps parked below it. Not counting Eric's Volvo, of course.

Steve's pruning shears lay half in, half out of the marigolds, draped by the tangled cord of the Walkman. A faint thumping and whining emanated from the tiny machine. He was nowhere in sight.

The dovecote loomed under the dark red eaves of the forest, larger than it had appeared from the door. Now Rebecca could see that only the side facing the castle was perforated with openings for the birds. In several places the narrow, undressed stones had pulled loose, leaving gaps the size of her typewriter case into the black and featureless interior. She followed a path around the circumference of the building, the grass brittle beneath her feet. The back looked much more like the mausoleum it was.

Beside a door glistening with the mottled green patina of copper was a brass nameplate that read, not surprisingly, "Forbes." Above it the rough granite blocks climbed in uncompromising tiers, contracting at the top to make a domed roof like an Irish monk's beehive cell. Or, in keeping with John Forbes's ambitions, an ancient tomb of a king of Mycenae. Close under its archaic bulk Rebecca could no longer see Dun Iain's Scottish baronial splendor.

She stepped onto the top of a short flight of steps that cleft the turf before the entrance. The lock that secured the door required a key even larger than the one for the castle. Its hinges were streaked with copper grooves; it had been opened two months ago for James, the last of the line. John had probably intended many generations of his descendants to be interred here. He must be looking down—or up, as the case may be—with a very bitter eye at his dynasty's premature demise.

Here beneath the trees the air was still, heavy with the fetid odor of mold. Rebecca drew back, her limbs prickling. She had thought it was quiet in the upper room of the castle, but here it was oppressively silent. The rush of the wind among the leaves seemed to be filtered through the stone of the mausoleum, as if she stood not outside but inside, enveloped by the dark tranquillity of the grave.

No, not tranquillity. Not Mary Stuart's serene smile. A brooding silence, as though something or someone waited on the other side of the massive door. The hair on the back of her neck lifted, drawn by a subliminal static charge. Rebecca whirled back up the step onto the path and hurried around the side of the building. There was the castle, raising its whimsical turrets toward the sky. Whimsical, not sinister, never sinister . . .

A huge black shape leaped from the trees. Rebecca gasped. The dog barked, shattering the silence so abruptly that Rebecca felt the noise slice through her head. Don't run, she ordered herself. He'll chase you. She planted her feet in the grass and stood her ground as the huge animal came to a halt just in front of her, barring her way back to the castle.

"Hi, there," she tried. "Nice dog. Good boy."

The dog's head seemed as large as a lion's, its ears reaching to her waist. It stank that peculiar doggy smell of wet dirt and raw meat. Slowly she raised her hand and offered it to the gargantuan muzzle. "Nice dog." It regarded her with liquid brown eyes scummed by suspicion, and sniffed.

"Hey, Slash!" yelled a voice. Steve emerged from the forest. For a moment Rebecca thought she glimpsed another human shape among the tree trunks. "Get away, Slash," Steve ordered. "Can't you see she's scared of you?"

"I think he can," Rebecca said. "Good boy, Slash."

Slash licked her hand with a hot, wet tongue the size of a dish towel. She jerked away and suppressed an automatic "Yech." When Steve reached around her to grab the dog's collar, she saw he was wearing a gold stud in his ear. His black T-shirt reeked of sweat and something else, an elusive scent of sweet smoke that reminded her of a certain passage in the student center at Dover. Marijuana. That was why he'd been weeding the marigolds with pruning shears.

He dragged the dog into the trees. It whimpered—Gee, boss, I was minding my own business and this crazy woman jumped out at me!

"Thanks," said Rebecca, and made tracks to the castle. She stood on the threshold catching her breath. A breath of fresh air would steady her nerves. Sure.

The front door, the only door, stood open before her. A coat of arms carved in the stone above, three bears, was the arms of Danzig Willie of Craigievar. Somehow she was surprised John Forbes hadn't had his own arms carved here, three locomotives, maybe, on a field of stock certificates. Above the coat of arms, at the base of the turrets, the small gargoyles concealing the shot holes leered down at her. The holes themselves had been filled with glass, so that each bizarre creature seemed to be holding in its mouth a diamond chip like that in her late, unlamented engagement ring.

Odd how she wasn't cold anymore. Nothing like fear to get the circulation going. Even if the fear was only partly based on reality. For years she'd tried to deny her imagination—perception hurt. But all it took was a spooky old house and her fancies returned to haunt her. No pun intended, she assured herself.

Her thoughts cycled into their usual rhythm. All right, then. Time to start earning her keep. With a wry smile Rebecca walked back into Dun Iain.

Chapter Five

REBECCA PAUSED INSIDE the door to inhale the already familiar must and dust scent of the castle. Compared with the reek of mold behind the tomb, the odor was not unpleasant at all. The enclosing walls seemed snug and almost peaceful. Dun Iain, she decided, had its moments of *Alice in Wonderland*, but a version that had been annotated by Edgar Allan Poe.

Dorothy came out of the kitchen door, coat buttoned, head swathed in a scarf, handbag securely under her arm. "Are you all right?"

What do I look like? Rebecca wondered, and smoothed her hair. "That humongous dog of Steve's startled me. I'm not a dog person, I'm afraid."

"That dog was the cutest little pup you've ever seen. Skippy, Steve called it then. That's before he dropped out of school and started hanging out with those punkies and their loud music—if you can call it music. The company you keep tells a lot about you, you know."

Ray, Rebecca thought. Dover's all-star couch potato. "I know."

"I keep telling Steve that animal will end up in the pound," Dorothy persisted. "He lets it run loose and it tears open garbage sacks waiting on the curb. But kids! You try to help them and their ears fold up on you."

"Steve's mother," said Rebecca, leaping into Dorothy's inhalation, "must be very patient to put up with the dog."

"Oh, she ran off with an auto parts salesman from Cleveland six or seven years ago. Right after Chuck died—my husband, that is. Went into the hospital for gallbladder surgery and the next thing you know, pffft!''

Rebecca's head swam. "Steve's mother's gallbladder . . . ?''

"No, no, my husband. Would've done better to have lived with the gallstones.'' The lines in Dorothy's face deepened, her expression settling like a house on uncertain foundations.

"Oh. I'm sorry,'' said Rebecca. And after an awkward pause, "Steve has no mother. I see.'' The two women briefly met on common ground.

Dorothy's expression lightened from grim back to merely dissatisfied. "Have to run. I promised my son Chuck I'd help them get settled in their new house. Just between us, Margie's a dear, but no housekeeper. I hope she'll improve now they've got the nicest new place in the development out toward Dayton. Savoy of Nob Hill Ranch. Real brick veneer fireplace in the family room.'' She swept the stone walls, the huge wooden door, the queen's effigy, with a withering glance. "This place makes you appreciate a real house.''

"Yes, it does,'' replied Rebecca, but she meant the opposite. She'd grown up in a series of tract houses and apartments so similar she couldn't remember which was in Denver and which in Atlanta. Dun Iain had character—if maybe a little too much character.

"I told Dr. Campbell about the tuna casserole I left you for dinner.''

"Why, thank you. I didn't realize your duties included cooking.''

"They don't, but I thought you might be too busy to eat properly.'' Her glance started at the crown of Rebecca's head, traced a path to her toes, and moved back up. "Some women believe those fashion magazines with the models who look like they'll blow away in a strong wind.''

"I never read fashion magazines,'' Rebecca replied, and added to herself, I'm not that far gone. She found her keys in the pocket of her jeans but had no memory of having put them there. That was Eric's blinding effect. "Actually I won't be here tonight. I'm going out to dinner with Mr. Adler.''

"Oh?'' Dorothy's pale, drained eyes lit with a conspiratorial smile. "He'd be a great catch, wouldn't he? Such manners. The kids today think manners are old-fashioned—they just honk their horns at each other. Good luck to you. Just remember not to act too smart. Men like their women decorative.''

Rebecca knew for a fact that she and Dorothy were from different planets. She picked up her typewriter. "Thank you," she said with finality.

"See you next week." Dorothy at last left.

It took Rebecca a moment to remember that today was Friday. She set the typewriter down again, went into the kitchen, and washed her hands.

That casserole had better go into the refrigerator; already there were punctures along the rim of the foil, made, most likely, by cat incisors. In the refrigerator Rebecca found additional odds and ends of food provided by Dorothy's culinary altruism. She took enough pressed ham for a quick sandwich and completed her lunch with vile instant coffee and a stale Oreo she found in the pantry. One of the wooden shelves, she noted, was rickety.

Judging by the dishes in the sink, Michael had been in here calmly eating crackers, cheese, and tea while she'd been outside running an emotional gauntlet from elation to terror. Fine. She didn't need a champion.

Out of habit she started to wash Michael's dishes, too, then caught herself and washed only her own. She hauled her typewriter upstairs. Again the cloying reek of lavender hung on the air of her room. She looked again for an air freshener, still couldn't find one, and opened the window.

Michael was in the Hall, down on his knees scrounging in a sideboard. Bits of crystal and cutlery were scattered on the floor around him. At her step he said to the depths of the cabinet, "Good of you to come back."

If he was implying she hadn't been working, she'd concede the point. By way of explanation she asked, "Have you looked at the bizarre mausoleum/dovecote combination out there?"

"Technically it's only a tomb, not posh enough for a mausoleum. Only a miser like Forbes would've thought of addin' a doocot. Like feastin' on his own dead." Michael sat back on his heels and inspected a decanter.

"Yeah." Even here in the brightly lit Hall Rebecca's nape crawled.

"Gave me a cold grue." He shivered, suiting action to word. "So austere. When I go I want to be planted in Tomnahurich, the firth gleamin' beyond the yew trees and fairies pipin' beneath the sod."

"The big cemetery in Inverness built on a fairy mound? That's an awfully romantic image for a skeptic like you." Caught him,

but his quick glance and dismissive gesture wouldn't admit it.
He didn't have to. It was a relief to know she wasn't the only
one affected by the atmosphere of the tomb.

She eyed the stack of black notebooks on the table. "Do you
have any preference where I start?"

Michael stood up, dusted his hands, and started to stack his
booty on the table. "I did the kitchen, the lobby, and the sittin'
room when I first got here. Not much there. Been spendin' most
of my time here. Startin' at the bottom and workin' up seems
as good a plan as any. There's no order to this rat's nest."

"I noticed. What about the store—er, lumber room?" She
wondered if he was dragging matters out just to irritate Eric, or
if he was more meticulous in his working habits than in keeping
his room tidy.

"Take more than one pair of hands to fetch and carry around
that lot. I was thinkin' of savin' it for last."

Rebecca wouldn't have minded saving the cold, quiet upper
room for last, but it wouldn't seem so daunting after she'd grown
used to the place. "Because the lumber room might have the
most valuable things?"

"No." He tossed a yellowed linen tablecloth onto a paper and
twine package that might have contained anything from a Tupperware canister to the Holy Grail. "I doot it has the least value.
Wouldn't John have put his dearest things out where he could
show them off?"

"But you said this morning he probably didn't know what he
had."

"We'll never ken what he had if we dinna look at it!" he
retorted, a little louder than was necessary. Rebecca felt a prickle
of shame; she'd been baiting him. Odd, she never acted like this
normally; she was always Miss Meek and Mild, the harmless
drudge. With a sudden laugh that made Michael's brows knit,
nonplussed, she chose a notebook labeled "Prophet's Chamber"
and asked, "There?"

"Be my guest," he said, bowing her out the door.

In a chair in the study Rebecca found Dun Iain's presiding
genius, Darnley, curled up in the feline version of the fetal position. He acknowledged her entrance with his usual salute, a
blink of the eyes and a stiffening of the whiskers. She paused a
moment to stroke his sleek, warm head. Give me, she thought,
an animal smaller than a bread box.

Just inside the door to the prophet's chamber were two snuff-

boxes and a miniature portrait of a Tudor lady. Hilliard? Rebecca flipped open the notebook. Hilliard it was. That was a
valuable piece the museum would want. She found a pencil on
the desk and checked it off.

A faint gurgling and rumbling must be water pipes. Above
the desk a brown stain spread like a Rorschach blot across the
plain plaster ceiling. A pipe had leaked, or else someone had let
the tub in what was now her bathroom overflow. Rebecca found
a sheet of paper and made a list of repairs: shelf in pantry, stain
on ceiling.

The armchair in front of the desk was a dilapidated affair of
heavy varnished wood, the kind of chair Rebecca associated with
bank presidents in prewar movies. It was not only not an antique, it probably wouldn't even make a decent pile of firewood.
She perched on its edge, opened the rolltop of the desk, and
winced. The jumbled contents threatened to spew into her lap.
Sparring with Michael and flirting with Eric were all well and
good, but now it was time to prove herself. She dug in.

Three hours later she sat back with a sigh. She had scrounged
through the desk and the filing cabinets, searched the walls and
the floors, and uncovered two other alcoves. No, Michael wasn't
dragging the inventory out just to irritate Eric. He was being
remarkably efficient. It would take at least a forty-hour week
just to catalog the papers in this room, let alone decide what
was valuable, what was useful, and what could be used to wrap
the garbage. And she had envisioned herself spending quiet evenings typing away at her dissertation. As usual, reality fell far
short of fantasy.

So far Rebecca had found three snuffboxes and the Hilliard
miniature that were mentioned in the notebook, and a yellowed
letter written in the spidery script of the eighteenth century that
was not. Of the two small daggers, the one the notebook labeled
an eighteenth-century sgian dubh looked promising. The other,
a nineteenth-century fish-cleaner, didn't. A sheaf of letters and
military orders signed by various historical personages was also
duly listed, although several, including James of Monmouth and
Robert Louis Stevenson, were missing. But it wasn't surprising
that some things would have been moved around in the forty
years since James typed up the inventory.

She'd even found the typewriter itself, in its case in the corner.
Its age and decrepitude made Rebecca's tired machine look positively opulent.

What she hadn't found was the Erskine letter. She'd have to search the inventories for it. The records of its sale to John in 1900 had percolated into academia; it had existed then. Fortuitous that Arabella Erskine, Countess of Mar, had defied discretion and written her sister about trading her newborn child for Mary Stuart's suddenly and shockingly dead one.

Well, Rebecca thought, if I were giving up my child to be king of Scotland, and later England as well, I'd want someone to know it.

The file drawer of the desk was crammed with more black notebooks, James's diaries, apparently. These were handwritten in faded sepia ink and shed newspaper clippings like a maple sheds autumn leaves. She'd have to go over those some other time.

As she struggled to wedge the one notebook she'd removed back into the drawer, she glimpsed a bit of white at the far back corner. She pulled it out. It was a scrap of James's handwriting, maybe an abandoned draft of a letter: ''—ever problem you are having you have brought upon yourself. I cannot help you any more than I already have. Your threats are . . .''

Useless? Rebecca concluded. Interesting. Maybe James's life hadn't been quite as dull as she'd thought. She put the scrap inside one of the diaries, shut the drawer, and looked up.

Above the desk was the most striking item in the room, a four-foot-long claymore dated to Bonnie Prince Charlie's final defeat at the battle of Culloden in 1746. The sword looked lethally heavy, if far from sharp.

Rebecca cleared a spot on the desk, propped her feet on it, and unfolded the eighteenth-century letter. Inside was a curl of hair almost the color of her own, a light tawny brown. She held the paper to the light. Oh—another lock of Prince Charlie's hair. So much of his hair was in the stately homes of Scotland that the Young Pretender must've worn a powdered wig for more than fashion. Unless, like modern Hollywood stars, his flunkies handed out hair only purporting to be his.

It would be easy enough to check the handwriting on the paper against proven samples of Charles Edward's. He was—Rebecca counted back—Mary's grandson's grandson's son, heir to her feckless grace. If Charles really were Mary's descendant. If James VI and I had been her son, not an Erskine . . .

Rebecca yawned. In this warm, snug room counting crowned heads seemed only slightly more stimulating than counting sheep. A beam of afternoon sun shone in the window, faded, and shone again, teasing gleams from the sword on the wall. The sound of the wind was muted into a gentle lullaby. The subtle gurgle of water was as soothing as the rush of a mountain stream. The lock of hair was soft in her hand.

The gurgling changed in timbre, becoming the swish of rain. The wind filled with voices growing first into shouts and then screams, blended with a staccato rattle of guns and the flat reports of cannon. Rebecca frowned, turning her head from side to side, struggling against the images, but still the sounds buffeted her ears and ricocheted across her skull. She felt the sting of sleet against her skin. She smelled gunpowder, cold steel, and the warm stench of blood.

The claymore above her head flashed. It wrenched loose from its brackets and drove right at her breast.

Metal rent, and the world turned upside down. With a short, strangled scream Rebecca crashed backward onto the floor. She lay stunned, her heart fluttering against her ribs, blinking as stupidly at the walls and ceiling as though she'd never seen them before.

Then she focused her mind and caught her breath. Weird! The sword hung innocently in its brackets. The room was quiet except for the rustle of papers and the background murmur of wind and water. And yet for a moment she had been someplace else: Culloden, 1746.

"Oh, for heaven's sakes," she exclaimed, abjectly embarrassed. She'd dozed off, had a brief, if extraordinarily vivid, nightmare, and upset the chair. She was wedged against the wall in an inverted "V," the lock of hair crushed in her hand.

Nothing seemed to be damaged except her dignity. But she couldn't get up. She had no room to maneuver; she didn't dare struggle too violently, she might break something. Something other than the chair, that is.

A movement in the door was Darnley, sitting with his head cocked to the side as if wondering what amazing gymnastic feat she would attempt next. She could, she thought dizzily, send Darnley for help, like Rin Tin Tin. No, she'd be mortified to have Michael help her, let alone see what she'd done. Even if she had to lie here all afternoon.

No, that wouldn't work, either. Eric was picking her up at five-thirty. She held her wristwatch before her face and swore. It was almost five. She wriggled, trying to turn herself on her side. The thick arms of the chair seemed almost malevolent the way they clutched at her.

The sound of footsteps reverberated in the floor beneath her head. Darnley whizzed away. In spite of herself she drew her knees close to her chest and tensed. The steps came down the staircase, through the study, to the door. A vast pair of work-boots stopped by her eyes, and hands the size of scoops on a steam shovel picked her up and set her on her feet.

"Thank you, Mr. Pruitt," she said. She carefully peeled the royal lock of hair from her damp palm.

"I was just coming to fix that chair when I heard you go over," Phil said. "Almost dumped Dorothy last week when she was dusting the desk. Looking through it, more likely. None of her business."

So Dorothy was a snoop. After finding her wardrobe open Rebecca wasn't surprised. She restored the hair to its paper wrapper and tucked it away. "Maybe one of the ghosts thought I was her," she said, not sure just how funny she was trying to be.

Phil was inspecting the metal contraption that had hinged the seat of the chair to its base, turning it over and over in his hand. Sheared through, Rebecca saw. Just old and fragile . . . Wait a minute. The jagged rim of the break stopped suddenly at a shining straight edge.

Phil thrust the hinge into his rear pocket and picked up the two pieces of the chair. "The ghosts out here are pretty peaceable ones. I'll take these out to the shed." He tramped away, the rhythm of his boots going out not varying from the calm cadences which had brought him in.

Rebecca shook her head. That was an awfully precise break, almost as if the metal had been filed through. Had Phil set a trap for Dorothy? He didn't look like a practical joker. He didn't look like the fanciful type, either, and yet he agreed matter-of-factly that there were ghosts in Dun Iain. She followed Phil through the study and onto the landing. Considerate of him, to destroy only something that was worthless, anyway. That's the kind of consideration Michael would show.

In the Hall Michael was smearing white paste over a bowl, completely absorbed. He was the more likely candidate for practical joker, and yet if he were, surely he'd show some interest in the results of his joke. Maybe he hadn't counted on Phil playing cavalry, maybe he'd been waiting to play the gallant rescuer after she was thoroughly flushed and flustered.

You're getting paranoid, Rebecca chided herself. It was an accident. There was simply no reason for it to be any more than that.

The front door thudded shut behind Phil. Rebecca turned and hurried up to her room. Almost five o'clock, she wouldn't have time to wash her hair.

The telephone jangled. An odd ring, in stereo. Oh—there was an extension on the fourth floor. It was probably a salesman, a computer selling aluminum siding, and she hadn't even decided what to wear. "Hello. Dun Iain Estate."

"Rebecca!" said a familiar voice. "There you are!"

Her mind hiccuped. She knew who it was—who was it?

It was Ray. "I've been worried about you, Kitten. You never called to tell me you'd gotten there safely."

"You never told me you wanted me to call," she replied, trying to ignore the accusatory tone in his voice. The man's timing was incredible, calling her just as she was about to step out with another man. She tapped her fingernails against the table, the rapid *tic tic tic* displacing the quiet creaks and settlings of the house. But that was the protocol—while she was gone, they were to date other people. They were to give each other space. And here he was already violating hers.

"How's it going?" Ray asked.

"Fine."

"Have you found that letter of yours yet?"

"No." She grimaced at her own impatience and tried not to peer through the adjacent door at the clock radio beside Michael's bed. "There's an incredible amount of material to sift through. We didn't even get the inventories until a few hours ago."

"We? Oh, yeah, the guy from England."

"Scotland," corrected Rebecca wearily. She straightened and walked the length of the phone cord to look into James's room. Here, too, was a strong odor of lavender. One of the cut-glass perfume bottles from Elspeth's dressing table sat on the window-sill.

"I'll bet he's one of those funny old guys like our tour guide."

First Jan, then Ray. Didn't anyone realize that people were still bearing children in Scotland? It wasn't all one big museum. "No, he's about our age." Rebecca took another step and almost yanked the phone off the table. That bottle hadn't been there earlier. Dorothy or Phil must have moved it.

"Oh, I see. Good-looking?"

"I don't know. I hadn't noticed." Liar, she said to herself. He has red glints in his hair, his eyes are as blue as a loch in the sunshine, and he has a tartan chip on his shoulder.

"Oh. Well. I see." Rebecca pictured Ray settling back in his chair, pipe in hand. "So, then. What have you had to eat?"

"Not much. I didn't come here to cook, I came here to work."

"The leftover meat loaf is gone," he said. "I ate it last night. I was thinking of having spaghetti sauce tonight, but there's no spaghetti. You must not have put it on your list."

Rebecca stifled an impulse to throw the phone against the wall. I'm busy, she wanted to blurt. I'm finally doing my own work, not yours. Inspiration struck. "Ray, this phone call must be costing you a fortune!"

"Oh, yeah. Well, drop me a letter," he said briskly. "I miss you, Kitten."

"Take care," she replied, and hung up feeling absurdly guilty, as if she'd been kicking a stuffed animal. She'd never suspect Ray of filing through a desk chair when he couldn't buy a package of spaghetti.

No, that wasn't fair. It was her own fault he'd come to depend on her efficiency to smooth his path, just as she'd depended on his cozy banality to smooth hers. He'd provided security, she'd contributed stimulation. He did miss her, she was sure of that. It was startling to realize she didn't miss him. She felt like a character from *Invasion of the Body Snatchers*, someone entirely different from the woman who'd once loved him.

She seized the glass bottle, whisked up to the fifth floor, and restored it to its place on the dresser. The pillow on the bed was hollowed again. Someone had decided to sneak a nap. She fluffed it up and catapulted back down to her room.

The odor of lavender hadn't dissipated. Rebecca hoped it hadn't permeated her clothes. Rejecting a frilly pink dress and her tweed skirt, she seized a dark blue skirt and white blouse topped by a colorful paisley jacket. As she tried wielding her curling iron with one hand and her mascara with the other she heard voices raised outside. Now what?

A ray of sun, slanting below the teeming clouds, washed the landscape in bronze. The Pruitts' pickup looked oddly yellowed, like an unbrushed tooth. Slash, the monstrous Labrador, sat in the back with his chin draped over the toolbox. Steve lolled on the passenger side, addressing his remarks to the ceiling, while Phil hung on to the open door. The two voices, Phil's bassoon and Steve's nasal twang, reached Rebecca's ears in bursts, fly balls batted by the wind. ". . . tie up that dog . . . only friend I have . . . dig flower beds over again . . . who cares, the old man's dead anyway . . . honest day's work for honest day's pay . . . give me a break . . ."

Rebecca shut the window. That was the same chapter and verse her father had repeated with her brothers. Her mother would make placatory sallies into the fray and be repulsed again and again. Her only weapon had been instant accession to every request, if you could call that a weapon.

The engine of the pickup roared. Gravel spattered. The thick metallic light winked out, plunging the house into twilight. Rebecca turned on the bedside lamp, collected her purse and coat, and went down to the Hall.

Michael stood stretching. The bowl-like object he'd been polishing lay shining before him, revealed as a large silver goblet. "Look!" he said to Rebecca. "A copy o' the Craigievar Mazer. A fancy drinkin' cup. Accordin' to the receipt in the package, John had it made in Edinburgh when he couldna buy the original from the Marquess o' Bute. Worth a packet in the right places, even as a replica."

"So not everything valuable is on display," said Rebecca, and braced herself.

"Aye, I was wrong aboot that." He beamed at his handiwork, rocking back on his heels.

Rebecca's expression hung between a grimace and a grin. If Ray was aggravating because he was so predictable, Michael was aggravating because he wasn't. "I'm going out," she said. "I don't know when I'll be back."

Only then did he notice her change of dress. "Ah?"

She couldn't tell whether his intake of breath was an interrogative or approval of her grooming. "With Mr. Adler."

"Oh. Well, there's no accountin' for tastes." With a slightly off-center grin he added, "Don't do anything I wouldn't do."

"How should I know what you're capable of doing?" she retorted with mock indignation. The bottle of Scotch Eric had brought her still sat in pristine condition on the end of the table. Again she thought of hiding it. But she'd been petty enough for one day. "Help yourself to the Laphroaig."

One of his brows quirked. "Oh, aye?"

"Unless you'd rather I brought you some beer. Moosehead, was it?"

"The best is McEwen's ale, but if you can get it here at all, it's much too dear. I'll content myself with the whiskey." And he added belatedly, "Thank you."

"No problem," she told him.

He laughed. "Take the key hangin' by the door. I'll no be goin' anywhere. Someone has to stay wi' the house bogles."

His laughter was just a bit forced. He had, Rebecca remembered, been here a week by himself. A spooky old house, and the imagination could do strange things. She glanced back to see him in the same position, his face framed by the gleaming strands of his hair, looking at the silver goblet as though appraising it.

"See you later," she said, and walked down the stairs. As she lifted the huge iron key from its hook by the door she heard a car on the driveway. Five-thirty exactly. She would have known Eric would be on time. Ray would have been early, and while she hurried to dress, would've passed the time reaming and filling his pipe, dribbling bits of ash and tobacco on her carpet.

"See you later!" she called again.

"Have a good time," came the reply, echoing in the stairwell.

Rebecca wrenched open the door and once again escaped to the outside world.

Chapter Six

THE GRAY VOLVO was a phantom shape in the dusk until Eric opened his door and a cheerful puddle of light spilled onto the gravel. "Hello!" he called. "Ready for dinner?"

"Am I ever," Rebecca replied. A cold gust of wind almost knocked her over and she huddled in her coat. With a fumbling clatter she found the keyhole, locked the door, and stowed the key in her purse.

Eric helped her into the warm interior of the car. She closed the seat belt and settled back into the embrace of the upholstery, inhaling the delectable odor of leather.

"I took the liberty of picking up the mail," said Eric as he slid behind the wheel and slammed his door. The light went out and for a moment Rebecca couldn't see a thing. "The mailbox is down by the road," his marvelous voice continued in the gloom. "All that was in it were some advertising circulars addressed to James Forbes."

"Immortality," said Rebecca, "is your name on a mailing list." Her eyes adjusted, and she could see the castle looming with surreal frailty above her. A lamp cast a feeble glow over the door. The window of her room was a dim rectangle, barely illuminated by the light she'd left on. The rest of the windows were dark, absorbed by the enigmatic walls of the house. She let her head drop back onto the headrest and exhaled in a soundless shiver.

Eric turned the car and it purred down the driveway past the dark bulk of the mausoleum. "Tired? Is Campbell working you too hard?"

"Probably not hard enough." She assumed a more ladylike position. "This place takes a bit of getting used to. I think I'm suffering from too much input, overexcitation of the brain cells or something. I dozed off this afternoon and had a nightmare about the battle of Culloden."

"It's a creepy old place. If it were mine I'd exorcise it by putting in modern furniture and accessories. I'd hire a jazz ensemble to play on the minstrel's gallery and invite lots of people to troop in and out."

"The state is planning to make it a youth hostel or a scout camp. That should do for the troops, anyway."

"Assuming the state gets it."

"Didn't James will the estate and the remaining furnishings to Ohio?"

"He did, but only if no relatives are found by the first of January. His property taxes kept getting higher, and he kept getting angrier, until finally he came up with that scheme, hoping to keep the state from taking it all. Except your and Campbell's and the servants' salaries, of course—those are covered in any event."

And your no-doubt tidy fee, Rebecca added silently. "James didn't know whether he had relatives?"

"John Forbes had an elder sister, Rachel, but she went her own way well before the turn of the century. James made up his mind about the will just a few days before he died, unfortunately. But I'm working on it. Odd to think that's one of the last duties I'll be doing for Dun Iain, finding someone to give it to."

"Mmm, the unexpected inheritance, just like in a movie."

"Life follows art," Eric said. "Except in life there's more paperwork." The car stopped at the end of the driveway. In a field across the road a pair of eyes, caught by the headlights, glittered and vanished.

"Do you need me to get out and close the gates?" Rebecca asked.

Eric turned onto the road. "The gates haven't been closed for years."

So much for Rebecca's image of Michael considerately opening them for her. "I thought James wanted to keep people out."

"John did. By the time James took over no one was particularly interested in coming out here, anyway. Except for teenagers looking for a place to party, and they climb in over the fence. They're harmless enough; they stay away from the house. Dun

Iain's outside the city limits of Putnam, in the sheriff's jurisdiction, and he keeps a close eye on the area.'' The headlights swept a stretch of brick wall that was partially collapsed, overgrown with underbrush between whose limbs peeked bits of spray-painted graffiti. "I saw a car parked over there today. Probably friends of Steve's come to keep him company while he doesn't work.''

"Yes, I think I saw one of them.''

Eric nodded. "Subtlety is not Steve's strong suit, I'm afraid.''

"The house is safe enough,'' Rebecca continued. "Craigievar may have been an example of seventeenth-century conspicuous consumption, but it was still built for defense. Scotland had a few wars yet to go.''

"Who? Oh, the castle in Scotland that John copied.''

Rebecca considered Eric's profile, illuminated by the faint lights of the dashboard, and reminded herself that most people wouldn't even be aware that Dun Iain was a copy, let alone what it was a copy of. So the man wasn't a historian. Historians didn't wear suits that expensive.

She had seen that profile on a Roman coin. Maybe his nose was a bit prominent, like an eagle's beak. But then, "Adler'' meant "eagle'' in German; that nose was the sort of characteristic that could become a family name. Like her grandfather's red hair, appropriate for a Scot named Reid.

Eric realized she was looking at him, caught her smile, cradled it a moment in one of his own, and returned it. Oh, my, she thought, clearing her mental throat. He is good at the game of the sexes, isn't he?

A few minutes later the car passed under the interstate and entered Putnam. There was the Burger King. Several doors down was a shabby pizza place lit with neon beer advertisements. Despite the cold, a dozen or so teenagers of indeterminate sex lounged amid the cars in the parking lot, pinpoint lights of cigarettes hovering like fireflies among them. Rebecca, gliding by in her cocoon of warmth and comfort, looked at them only casually. Then she looked again. That insectlike figure had to be Steve Pruitt, nursing a bottle of something that, she bet, wasn't a soft drink.

Suddenly red and blue lights flashed simultaneously from a side street and from the main road. A siren wailed and then died on a piercingly flat note. Some of the dark figures in the parking lot jumped and scattered; others stood their ground with non-chalant attitudes.

Eric slowed and edged toward the curb, evading the approaching police car. "This place has a reputation for selling booze to underage kids."

"Wasn't that Steve over there?" Rebecca asked.

"Probably. He's only nineteen; he's a disaster area."

"What about . . ." Rebecca cut herself off. Maybe she'd smelled marijuana on the young man, maybe she hadn't.

"Illegal drugs? Putnam's kids still get their kicks from beer. So far."

The lights of the police cars converged on the mass of shouting, gesticulating figures in the parking lot. Faces whirled by, at one moment painted harshly by the glare, at the next swallowed by the rim of darkness. Eric eased back into the traffic lane and accelerated.

"You're not going to rush over there and start handing out business cards?" Rebecca inquired sweetly.

"Thanks," replied Eric, with a quick sarcastic glance.

One dim form broke loose from the tangle of bodies. It sprinted across the sidewalk and into the street. "Watch out!" shouted someone, and another voice cried, "Hey, you! Come back here!"

Rebecca gasped. Her foot made futile pushing motions at a nonexistent brake pedal. Eric spat a four-letter word that clashed with his suit and tie. His foot succeeded where hers had failed. The car skidded, fishtailed, and stopped. The fleeing figure spun through the headlights, eyes and mouth gaping; a fist pounded the hood of the car and then vanished. The face was branded on Rebecca's retina—eyes and mouth smeared with makeup, delicate features almost erased by the glare of light. A girl.

"You all right?" asked one of the policemen, running up to the car.

"Yeah," snapped Eric, his voice, if not his body, showing evidence of whiplash. He turned to Rebecca. "Are you?"

Her hand was pressed over her mouth as if she were keeping her tonsils from leaping out in a scream. Surely the lines of the seat belt would be engraved on her body. She blinked and managed to say, "I'm fine, thank you. Only a dent in my composure."

She'd had to start kidding him just then. If he'd had slower reflexes, he'd have hit that—that child—while he was looking at her. She didn't know him well enough to be kidding him like that, anyway.

"Better go on," advised the officer. "Traffic's backing up."

With infinite care Eric straightened up the car and crept off down the road. "You're sure you're all right? I'm sorry, I . . ."

"Good Lord," she said. "I distracted you. I'm the one who's sorry."

She could see his frown in the barred light of the streetlamps, the black arch of his brows furrowed. The car accelerated beyond a turtle's pace. "At least let me apologize for swearing like that."

"You're entitled," Rebecca told him. "If I'd had a voice just then, we would've had a duet."

He shook his head and allowed his face to smooth. In silence they passed through the old downtown district, storefronts divided among boutiques, feed stores, and boarded-up windows, skirted a residential area, and emerged on another highway. The topmost of a tier of signs before a strip shopping center proclaimed in fancy script letters, "Gaetano's."

"Here we are." Eric pulled into a parking place and stopped. Rebecca, used to letting herself in and out of a car, hesitated a moment and was rewarded by Eric's handing her out with the self-mocking gallantry of a Regency beau. She returned the pressure of his hand before releasing it.

The interior of the restaurant was all subdued lighting, tasteful pastels, and the occasional impressionist print. The maître d' recognized Eric and bowed them into a banquette. This is living, Rebecca said to herself. She opened the menu and tried not to gulp at the prices. It might be a shopping center on the outside, but inside it was strictly uptown.

"May I?" Eric asked. Rebecca murmured something polite, too embarrassed to admit she didn't know what half the things on the menu were. Tuesday nights with Ray and his everlasting olive pizzas were beginning to look pretty thin indeed.

Eric turned to the hovering waiter. *Gnocchi con pomodoro e rosmarino, focaccia*, salad, veal *alla pizzaiola*, something hideously expensive from the wine list. Rebecca's composure crumpled even further. She and Ray would treat themselves to glasses of what Dover's Pizza Paradise optimistically called wine, but a whole bottle? And she was sure her palate wouldn't appreciate anything so exclusive. "Are you trying to get me drunk?" she whispered.

"Now why would I want to do that?" Eric replied with a smile. Oh, Grandmother, she thought, what lovely teeth you have.

He sat close enough to her that she could sense his presence, far enough away to preserve her personal space. She could just sense the spicy aroma of his after-shave, probably only available at upscale department stores.

His hands smoothed the intricate folds of the napkin on the table. For someone exuding wealth and sophistication his hands were those of a laborer, blunt, sturdy, oddly prosaic. But on one finger he wore a thick gold ring, set with a diamond suitably discreet but still twice as large as her chip of an engagement stone, and monogrammed "EFA." "F?" she asked.

He looked up, startled. "What?"

"The 'F' on your ring. What's your middle name?"

"Oh. Frederick. Nicely Germanic. Fits with the Eric and the Adler."

"It's nice to meet someone who isn't of Scottish ancestry."

"It takes all kinds."

The wine came, was approved, and poured into her glass in a sparkling crimson stream. Eric waited, glass poised. She lifted hers and clinked it against his. "To Dun Iain," he said.

"Yes," she replied. "By all means."

By the time the antipasto arrived they were well into polite cross-examination. Rebecca had three older brothers, Eric was an only child raised by his grandmother. Rebecca's undergraduate and master's degrees were from the University of Missouri, Eric had attended law school at the University of California at Los Angeles, his hometown. Like her, he'd worked his way through college, his grandmother's Social Security checks barely covering their rent. Now she understood why he'd never had his teeth fixed—as a child too poor to afford braces, as an adult too vain to wear them.

Rebecca envied his state as an only child, and envied even more his current financial security. But then, unlike her, he'd chosen a profession that offered financial security. She toyed for a moment with daydreams of fiscal hedonism, clothes, cars, and wine lists.

Judging by the current events that appeared in the background of his biography, Eric was about thirty-five. Rebecca wondered if there was a divorce in his past, and whether his frank admiration for the feminine had contributed to it. She contented herself with the innocuous, "And what brought you from California to Ohio?"

"I was offered a position with Birkenhead, Birkenhead and Dean, in Columbus, just about the time my grandmother died. There was no reason to stay in L.A., and I'd never been in this part of the country."

"You were handed the Dun Iain account, I suppose, as the older members of the firm were getting too dignified to drive up here."

"Spot on," said Eric, "as your Scottish friend would say."

"He's not necessarily my friend. He came with the job."

"Want to file a complaint with OSHA, the occupational-hazard people?"

Rebecca laughed. The waiter whisked away empty dishes and deposited full ones. To Rebecca's slightly glazed eyes each plate was haloed with oil and cheese. She wondered if Italian food could be considered a sacrament.

"Did you tell Michael about wanting to put a jazz ensemble on the piper's gallery?" she asked. "I'll bet he threw a rampant lion of Scotland gold and crimson fit."

"Not exactly. He is pretty touchy, though. Can't say as I blame him. He knows I'm supposed to be checking up on him." Eric's jaw tightened; in his body language, Rebecca told herself, that signaled suppression of stress. "I also made the mistake of telling him you were coming. And he didn't like that at all. Sorry."

"I hate to think what kind of reception I'd have gotten if he hadn't been expecting me."

Eric twirled a strand of linguini around his fork and contemplated it a moment. "Actually, though, there's more than that . . ."

"Yes?" Rebecca urged.

"Campbell's fully aware that he's a scholar and I'm not. I think he's been—well, not to put too fine a point on it, overestimating the worth of some of those old things. And putting some things down as valuable that aren't at all. I can't help but wonder if he's doctoring the books, in other words, trying to get a little extra for himself after the dust of the insurance and shipping costs settles. I hate to accuse him of . . ." He stared glumly at the tangled strand of pasta, as if it were a noose dangling at Michael's neck.

"Skimming the cream?" Rebecca suggested.

"I beg your pardon?"

Rebecca discovered that her wineglass was empty. She regarded it sadly. "Just something he said. Embezzlement is the word, isn't it? I must admit he doesn't seem the sort." The red drop remaining at the bottom of the glass shone like crystal, but she saw nothing in it. Michael had a distinct secretive streak, yes. But if he had criminal secrets, surely he'd be a lot more poker-faced, less charming and less obnoxious both.

"Ironic, isn't it?" Eric went on. "If I had more technical knowledge, I'd probably find my suspicions are all wrong. I'm sure he's quite honest, and simply resents your and my breathing down his neck."

"I'll be keeping an eye on him. He's already tried to get a few things by me. Jokingly, you understand; I figured he was testing my knowledge just to flatter his ego. But you never can tell."

"Thank you," said Eric. "I really appreciate your help." He patted her hand where it rested on the table. She could feel the print of his fingers glowing on her skin even after he picked up his fork again.

Was that the deal, then? A fancy dinner for her services as—well, as a spy? But that wasn't all he wanted. Every feminine antenna she had was quiveringly alert, responding to the nuances in his voice, his face, his body.

Rebecca was mellowing fast. The rest of the restaurant seemed as hazy as a scene photographed through a gauzed lens; the conversations of the other diners and the clink of cutlery reached her ears in slow, indistinct eddies. Only the banquette was completely tangible. The candlelit plates and glasses and Eric's face with the intensity of stained-glass windows lit from behind. Rebecca grimaced at her descent into unashamed sensuality and cut another morsel of veal. She was eating olives, she realized, and enjoying them.

"So you've been handling Dun Iain's legal matters for several years," she said. "Does that take up a lot of your time?"

"Not really. I'm the one-man Putnam branch of the firm, so I have to be here at least once a week, anyway. There's usually something to attend to over at Golden Age Village, for example—wills, trusts, various financial and legal matters to sort out."

"Dorothy was saying that James resisted going into the Village."

"He certainly did. Dun Iain was his home and that was where

he was going to stay. A shame he had to fall down those stairs, but, well, he had had a long life. Not like his mother when she died." This time it wasn't Eric's jaw that tightened, but his mouth, its deep curve thinning into a narrow line.

"That must have been a real tragedy for James, losing his mother like that . . ." Rebecca bit her tongue. She didn't know how Eric had lost his own mother. Or his father, for that matter. No wonder the thought of Elspeth's death distressed him.

But his voice was smooth as always. "I'm not saying James wasn't a little crazy. He was. And yet in many ways he was perfectly sane. He loved his books, and his writing, and all those artifacts were his babies. Even though he felt guilty over them."

"Guilty?"

"He said they shouldn't have been brought here. He said they wanted to go home." Eric gazed off over the restaurant as if seeing the old man pottering among the portraits, the letters, and the cut-glass bottles.

"Not that he wanted to send them home, but that they wanted to go?"

He turned to her with an apologetic smile. "I said he was a little crazy. But he's getting his wish now. They're going back."

"I suppose, then, that James resisted selling off the more historically interesting objects?"

"There's not much of a market for that kind of thing. He sold some decorative items to support the place, yes. 'De-accessioning,' I guess you'd call it. But they didn't lose their entire fortune in the Crash of '29."

"De-accessioning." Rebecca chuckled. "That's good museum-speak. You're learning fast." Eric grinned and bowed over his wineglass. "I assume," she continued, "that the readily salable pieces are in the bank."

"Some bonds, a certificate of deposit or two. That's about all. James sold his mother's jewels, if that's what you're wondering. You'll notice the erasures in the inventories."

"Rats," she said. "I was hoping to find Elspeth's diamond choker, the one in the Sargent portrait."

"Already gone. A shame; you'd look lovely in it."

"I'll ignore that," Rebecca chided him, without really meaning it. "How do you suppose the rumor of treasure got started?"

Eric threw his head back and laughed. "Good Lord, Dorothy didn't waste any time filliny you in on the local gossip, did she? Treasure?" He leaned conspiratorially toward Rebecca and lowered his voice. "I think part of it is the normal human love for a mystery—the recluse in his castle—and part of it was fostered by James himself. He would carry things around and hide them and then forget where. I found his father's signet rings in an old coffee can one time. Rescued them just before Dorothy threw them out."

"The ones in the prophet's chamber?"

"You've already seen them? Yes, those. I had my own ring modeled on them. Not that I had any intention of flattering him, you understand."

"I should hope not," sighed Rebecca. Again her glass was empty. There was a wonderful taste of garlic, basil, and red wine in her mouth. Eric was still leaning close to her. The candlelight made his eyes look like polished smoky quartz—cairngorm, in Scotland . . . All right, she ordered herself. "Poor John, and Elspeth, and James," she said. "They just never found how to buy happiness, did they?"

To her surprise Eric straightened. "Money can buy happiness," he said quietly. "What it can't buy is justice."

For a long minute she looked at the somber line of his profile. A lawyer with a conscience. Maybe he'd rather be in criminal law but doesn't have the stomach for it, and feels guilty . . . Her head was swimming. So James had thought the artifacts wanted to go back. Did he, too, imagine Rizzio's murder and the terrible battle at Culloden?

The waiter was hovering. Eric was smiling and nodding as if he'd never made a serious statement in his life. "I'm stuffed," Rebecca protested laughingly. "I can't eat another bite. You'll have to roll me out of here. Except I'll be so huge you won't be able to lift me."

"You're barely even a handful as it is," Eric replied in mock reproof, and ordered chocolate mousse and espresso.

Odd, Rebecca thought, how everyone seemed to suddenly think she was too thin. And she thought, a handful, huh? What part of her anatomy was he considering handling? She giggled helplessly, and Eric regarded her with indulgence that was far from platonic.

The dessert and coffee were as delicious as the rest of the meal, and the jolt of caffeine helped to keep Rebecca from falling comatose in her plate. All too soon the day of reckoning came; the waiter appeared with the bill. Eric produced a pen and began to refigure it.

She seized the opportunity to pull out her compact and renew her lipstick. Circumscribed in the mirror's tiny circle, her face glowed and her eyes shone in the candlelight. Tendrils of hair softened the often too-crisp lines of her features. If Ray could only see her now . . . It was because Ray couldn't see her now that she was so splendidly flushed and tipsy. Yes, the engagement was over, all but the shouting. Not that there'd be any shouting, not with Ray. Rebecca made a face at herself and returned her compact to her purse, where it clinked against the huge door key.

Eric summoned the waiter and consulted over the new, improved version of the bill. The waiter bowed and scraped. The ceremony moved to its conclusion, the ritual presentation of the American Express card.

When all was completed to his satisfaction, Eric tucked the receipt into his wallet and turned to Rebecca with an engagingly self-deprecating smile. "Sorry to take so long. But it's the principle of the thing, isn't it?" He captured her hand from her lap and this time really did hold it briefly to his lips. Amazing how the man could get away with gestures that would be ludicrous in another. The kiss tingled all the way to her toes.

When she stood up, her knees were hardly steadier than her linguini. The rush of cold air and the chilly seat of the car cleared her head somewhat Eric checked the gauges on the dashboard with the careful scrutiny of an astronaut preparing for launch.

When they returned down franchise row, the neon lights of the pizza place shone innocuously over a few parked cars, but no living figures were in sight. Rebecca asked Eric to stop at the convenience store on the next block; she wasn't going to spend one more day in that house without coffee. Eric not only stopped, he bought a can for her and assured her there was a coffee maker in the pantry. "I brought it out there myself," he told her. "James preferred tea for his elevenses, but I don't think anything beats a good cup of coffee."

"Amen," agreed Rebecca, and crinkled the bag happily in her lap between similarly happy if speculative glances at Eric.

He was, she thought, orchestrating an old-fashioned seduction. Slowly, one day at a time, none of this "Hi, pleased to meet you, your place or mine" business. An affair might be just the ticket. No more commitments, not now. There was nothing wrong with simple mutual pleasure.

Not that she was an expert on seduction. Ray was the only

man she'd ever slept with. And he'd been the professor next door, a trusted friend, well before he ever became her lover. Once that placid quasi-domestic Friday night arrangement had been established, engagement had been the logical next step.

Every now and then Ray would hint about how repressed she'd been before he came along. She supposed she had to allow him that brief glint of machismo. So it had taken her awhile to discover the opposite sex. Once her caution would have been commended, not condemned.

In the darkness she bit her lip and then smiled ruefully, wondering what had happened to that caution; she was considering this stranger as a potential lover. Her singed fingertips must be extraordinarily sensitive.

All too soon the car turned into the driveway. There was Dun Iain, lit up like a Christmas tree. You can tell he's not paying for the electricity, Rebecca said to herself. He's left every light in the place blazing. The windows were squares of brilliance against the black invisibility of walls, ground, and cloudy sky. They looked even more like eyes than they had in the daylight. Considering all that she had seen from them, they *were* eyes.

Pellets of rain struck the windshield in a brisk fusillade as Eric stopped the car and turned off the engine. He peered rather quizzically up at the house, then released both his and her seat belts and gently but firmly pulled her across the seat into his embrace.

Not that she had any idea of resisting. The kiss sent static hissing down her nerve fibers. She wondered abstractedly if she'd frizzle up like a cartoon character caught in the throes of G-rated passion. But this was not G-rated. She melted against him.

The can of coffee fell off her lap and cracked against his ankle. "Ow!" he exclaimed. "You could've just said no."

"I'm so sorry—I didn't mean . . ." They both scrabbled after the can, cracked their foreheads together, and subsided laughing against the seat.

Eric escorted her to the door, took the key, and unlocked it. "If I were you, I'd get a locksmith out here to put in a new lock."

"This contraption lends it character, though, don't you think?"

He smiled and said, "I'll be appearing on your doorstep again soon. I'd like to look over James's papers one more time for

news of Rachel Forbes's descendants. If you don't mind sharing
the space."

"Of course I don't mind."

"And we'll have to do another dinner, or maybe a concert,
soon."

"Yes. Definitely." They kissed again, quickly but not superficially, and Eric ushered her inside. But not before her damp
lips turned abruptly cold in the chill of the night.

Just as the lights of the car flashed on, the rain came down in
sheets. Rebecca slammed the door, locked it behind her, and
stood with her back against the wood waiting for her red corpuscles to stop pirouetting like bubbles in champagne. Slowly
her idiotic grin ebbed to an introspective smile.

Eric was certainly a class act. How long had it taken him to
smooth the sharp edges of his background—ten, fifteen years?
But his manner wasn't a seamless whole. His occasional somber
abstraction suggested depths beneath the surface gloss. He held
something back, kept something in reserve.

Rebecca asked the marble features of Queen Mary, "Were
any of your husbands like that? Francis, the gallant? Darnley,
the dandy? Or Bothwell, the warrior? As if he were waiting, like
a cat at a mouse hole?"

The serene face of the queen, all passion spent, did not reply.

Chapter Seven

REBECCA WAS TEMPTED to creep up the stairs and leap into the Hall screaming "Boo!" But that would be a cheap trick. She shouted "Hello!" toward the light gleaming on the landing and walked into the kitchen.

Even the light in the hood over the stove blazed away. The casserole dish sat on the counter, almost full of noodles and what looked like the flour paste children use in kindergarten. Dishes and cutlery were propped in the drainer, clean, and an empty can of beans lay in the trash can.

So Michael had given up on Dorothy's cooking. While she stuffed herself with enough Italian food for three: herself, Michael and . . . Rebecca put the coffee in the cabinet, folded the sack, and wondered if Ray had ever gotten any spaghetti. She visualized him leaning against the kitchen counter in his apartment, spooning food off a paper plate, all alone.

Dammit, she wasn't his keeper. She'd heard that breaking off a serious relationship entailed a certain amount of guilt. All right, if that was the price, she'd pay it. Tomorrow she'd write him and get it over with. The misty glow cast by her senses dissipated, revealing the hard edges of reality. A shame that glow had barely lasted past the front door.

When she put the sack in the pantry, she found Darnley's dish filled with noodles; Michael had made every effort to get rid of the evidence. But Darnley had probably gone mousing. In fact, there was a mouse now. Rebecca bent and peered into the darkness beneath the wobbly shelves. No, she'd thought for a moment she'd seen tiny glittering eyes, but none were there now.

Turning off lights as she went, she returned to the entry and again shouted "Hello!"

"In here," called a voice behind her, and she jumped.

Michael was in the sitting room, stretching and yawning. That was it, he'd dozed off and hadn't heard her come in. He looked comfortable enough, lying back in a recliner, the whiskey and a glass on the table beside him. The bottle wasn't too badly depleted. The television wasn't on, but the cassette player was. "Turn that off, please," he asked.

She turned it off. The cassette was one of the Scottish folk-rock bands she herself enjoyed, pipes, tin whistle, accordion, and electric guitar.

Michael's lap overflowed with a pile of cloth and wooden tubes that looked like—that was an eviscerated set of bagpipes. "If you canna beat them," he said, "you can always join them." With a tiny brush he began to ream what Rebecca recognized as the chanter.

"Where'd you get the brush?" she asked.

"It's amazin' what you can find if you take a turn tae yoursel'."

And in ransacking the place he'd turned on all the lights. She shrugged off her coat and yawned.

"I see your evenin' was a success."

"Yes, I had a good time."

His eyes glinted briefly up at her. "He must be a dab hand at the chattin' up. Your lipstick's a' smudged."

Touché. Hastily she reached into her pocket for a tissue. "What do you have against him, anyway?" she asked.

"He's fair taen wi' himsel', nae doot aboot it. Poncin' aboot wi' yon fancy claes, fancy car, fancy manners."

"Nothing wrong with good manners," said Rebecca. "Or with clothes and cars, for that matter."

Michael discarded Eric's manners with an abrupt gesture that almost sent the brush flying across the room. "Treats me like a bluidy dogsbody. Always flytin' and bletherin' aboot, what's this worth, allow for extra insurance, can you no leave this or that behind."

"That's his job," Rebecca protested.

Michael glared at her. As though his words were a cork popping from a champagne bottle, he blurted, "That's as may be, if that's a' there was. But he tried tae gie me the sack. What the museum and the state dinna ken'll no hurt them, he said. A little extra here and there, set aside the pretty things tae sell tae collectors and never gie a cheep aboot it. I pretended I dinna ken what he was on aboot, but I took a scunner tae him, right enough."

Michael's accent had thickened almost to incomprehensibility. Rebecca registered the rhythm but had to struggle for the meaning of the words. "Please," she groaned. "You're laying it on awfully thick. I've heard you talking what your Southern neighbors would call proper English—would you mind giving me the benefit of the doubt?"

His hands stopped dead at their task. Expressive, probing hands that moved as if they searched for rabbits in hats. Long elegant fingers, and slender wrists that seemed almost fragile . . . The blue flare in his eyes dragged Rebecca's gaze to his face and focused her thought.

"I can talk just like a Beeb newsreader," he said in a clipped Oxbridge accent. "Excuse me, BBC announcer to you. I've lived in London. I've had an English lass. Lady friend, except she was no lady." He rammed the brush so violently into the chanter that Rebecca flinched. "I'm no ashamed o' bein' a Scot," he concluded, sliding back into the rich tones of his native brogue. "I'll no call my country 'North Britain,' or talk like a toffee-nosed twit just tae please the absentee landlords bleedin' the land dry, thank you just the same."

Rebecca inquired, "How much did you have to drink?"

"I'm perfectly sensible. I just took a wee drap, for which I'm properly grateful tae you." He raised his chin with exaggerated dignity. "You're none tae sober yoursel'."

No, she wasn't. She collapsed into a chair, kicked off her shoes, and closed her eyes. Her mind was filling with a glutinous substance like cotton candy, across which memory left slow, sticky prints. Ray's smile. The claymore. Eric's eyes in the candlelight. A perfume bottle on the windowsill. Michael's hands. She peeked through her lashes. "What did you say?"

"Too much," Michael replied sheepishly. "Sorry."

Rebecca opened her eyes the rest of the way. She'd accepted that when a man was drunk he was aggressive, blustering around looking for a fight; her father and her brothers always did. Her mother got sloppy and pitiful when she'd had too much.

That was Michael, apologizing just when she'd thought she had him typed. "I'm sorry, too. I talk about manners and then criticize your speech. I don't know what's come over me. Everything here's so—so intense."

Michael nodded. "Just that."

A curl at one corner of his almost-sensitive mouth reminded her of the tissue in her hand, and she scrubbed at her lipstick. What had she intended to ask? Oh. "You said Eric tried to give you the sack? Get you fired?"

"The state'll no take kindly tae my doctorin' the books for him."

"You're sure that's what he wanted?"

So much for that hint of tenderness. Again his mouth tightened in irritation. "I'm no sure. He only implied, he said naething direct. He's a lawyer, him and his silver tongue."

Rebecca tensed, waiting for Michael to make some awful joke about the manifest abilities of Eric's tongue, but he nobly resisted.

"I think he tried tae buy me," he concluded, "and I must've gie him the pip when he couldna. Probably never found anything money couldna buy."

"It won't buy justice," said Rebecca.

Michael looked up at her from under his brows. *"He maun hae justice, or faith he'll take it, man,"* he sang in an untrained but agreeable tenor.

Yeah, Rebecca thought, it's his word against yours. She opened her mouth to tell him what Eric had said about him and then clamped it shut. No sense in lighting his fuse again. "You gave him the pip?" She pictured some arcane British version of an obscene gesture.

"I annoyed him. Wi' any luck, half as much as he annoyed me."

"I think you did." She frowned, squeezing thought from her mind. Assuming anyone had an embezzlement scheme was one heck of a leap. If Eric was the shady party, then he could've told her it was Michael just to shunt suspicion away from himself. If it was Michael, he could be throwing suspicion on Eric. But how could he know Eric had even brought up the subject? It would've been easier just to keep quiet. And how, for that matter, would Eric have known Michael would mention it?

Maybe Eric was slick as well as—well, physically compelling. He was also the trustworthy family retainer. If he'd wanted to embezzle or steal anything, he could've done it a long time ago.

Each thought dissolved, airy and slightly sickening. Eric and

Michael had had trouble communicating, Rebecca told herself. That was all. No one was trying to embezzle anything.

The silence was tangible, the rush of wind and rain muted here behind the thickest walls of the castle. When Michael lay down the brush, it sounded as if he'd struck the table with a two-by-four. He picked up a rag, started polishing, and sang, *"The news frae Moidart came yestereen, will soon gar mony ferlie, for ships o' war hae just come in, and landed Royal Charlie."*

"Seventeen forty-five," said Rebecca. "But you don't like Charlie."

"What I like are the old songs. *We hae tint our plaid, bonnet, belt and swordie, how they'll skip and dance ower the bum of Geordie."*

"Seventeen fifteen. Also a disaster, for the Highlanders at least."

"Ye'd better kiss'd King Willie's loof, than come to Killiecrankie-o."

"And more civil war. Are there any songs for Bannockburn?"

"There's always 'Scots Wha Hae,' if you dinna mind the gore." Michael considered the bottle of whiskey and shook his head. *"The flowers o' the Forest are a' wede away."*

"Flodden Field, 1513. Utter catastrophe." Rebecca's stomach muttered unhappily beneath her ribs, sending a revolting taste of chocolate and garlic into her throat. Justice, perhaps, for having eaten or drunk, flirted or fought, for having felt more than she'd let herself feel in years. Not that it mattered. If justice couldn't be bought, it couldn't even be defined. And Michael had to sit over there singing about lost causes.

That was it. When he was drunk he was maudlin, a typical Celt. Just like me, she told herself. She struggled to her feet and was mildly surprised the heaviness of her skull didn't flip her head over heels like a baby's toy.

"But pith and power, till my last hour, I'll make this declaration: we're bought and sold for English gold, such a parcel of rogues in a nation. Even though some o' my ancestors were doin' the sellin'." Michael glanced up. "You look fair clapped oot. Get on wi' you."

"I think I will. Can you get all the lights?"

His hand stopped moving on the chanter. "What lights?"

"Every light in the place is on." She spoke with exaggerated enunciation; why was he always denying such stupid insignificant things? "Will you please turn them off?"

"Every light in the place is on?"

Rebecca moaned under her breath—spare me—and gestured toward the entry. Michael put down his work and went to look. He stood a long moment gazing up the stairs, stiff and still, his hands clasped at his sides. "Oh. I see. Aye, then, I'll do the lights."

Rebecca muttered something she hoped he'd interpret as thanks and started upstairs. She had a bottle of aspirin up there, a goal as tempting as the gold of El Dorado. She took a step, and another. The landing. The study on one side, the Hall on the other. Rain beating against the windows.

Behind her Michael was singing, *"She's just a Kelty Clippie, she'll no take nae advice, it's och drap deid, away bile your heid, I'll punch your ticket twice."* So he'd had an affair with an Englishwoman which had come to a bitter ending. Something to do with that tartan chip, maybe.

Darnley sat in the corridor outside the door of Rebecca's room, hunched and bristling, his yellow eyes focused on the next flight of stairs. Rebecca stopped dead, her arm holding her coat and her purse tightening in a spasm of—no, not fear. The cat was just watching for a mouse or something. She stepped around Darnley, her neck and shoulders cramping with the effort it took her to not look up the staircase.

She stood in the doorway of her room. Her brain detonated inside her skull. Her eyes bulged. Now she knew what Michael was capable of. She shouted his name. No reply. She tried again, her rage adding so much volume she recoiled from her own voice. "Michael Campbell, get yourself up here!"

Far, far away she heard his voice. "Ah, dinna get your knickers in a twist." His footsteps scuffed with agonizing slowness up the staircase. When he at last appeared, he stopped abruptly, eyeing the cat.

Darnley arched like a Halloween mascot, looked up with a disinterested air, and glided away. Michael said, elaborately nonchalant, "He just sits like that sometimes. I dinna ken why. What're you on aboot?"

"Damn the cat," said Rebecca. "Look here." She flapped her hands toward her room and its contents, bathed in the uncompromising blaze of the ceiling light she had not left on.

Michael stepped forward and looked.

Underwear lay strewn across bedcovers so tangled they might as well be tied in knots. The wardrobe gaped, vomiting blouses, skirts, and slacks. Shoes lay on the dressing table, and oddments of jewelry and cosmetics lay on the floor amid upturned drawers. The postcard from the mirror was stuck jauntily in a corner of Elspeth's picture, while Ray's picture lay face downward on the carpet amid a spatter of broken glass. The clock and the tape player were tied together by the ribbon from the typewriter, all three in a disconsolate pile. The old copy of *Man of Iron* spewed torn pages across the mess.

Michael's brows were question marks across his forehead. His mouth hung open. "I take it you dinna leave it like this?"

"What kind of fool do you think I am?" she demanded. "You think you can just waltz up here and do this and I wouldn't know it was you?"

His mouth clamped shut and his eyebrows plummeted. His face snapped around to hers. "What kind o' fool do you take me for? I didna do this."

"Then who? The odd passing poltergeist?"

A page or two from the book stirred restlessly in a draft. The lights emitted white auras of glare. The words hung between them, twisting as slowly as corpses from a gibbet.

"Ah, bugger it!" exclaimed Michael. He flung his hands wide, as if throwing away something distasteful, and then brought them to his chest protectively clenched into fists. "I'll help you sort it oot." He bent and scooped up the curling iron, its cord a dead snake across the threshold.

"Not so fast," said Rebecca. "Answer my question. Who?"

Michael threw the curling iron onto the bed. His hand seized Rebecca's forearm. The fingers that had appeared so fragile doing delicate work now crushed her with uncanny strength. "You answer my question. Do you think I'm a fool? Tell me why I'd do this! Tell me why I'd bluidy bother!"

She stood staring up at him, her neck craned back, shivering with fury. His eyes were as sincere as she'd ever seen them; his amazement at the state of her room seemed perfectly genuine. And yet liars and salesmen looked right at you, openly and honestly.

Her hands were knotted in a double handful of his sweatshirt, either pushing him away or holding him to steady herself, she couldn't tell. He exuded a faint aroma of whiskey, not at all unpleasant; Rebecca herself must reek of garlic. Why would you

bother? Because you want me out of here, she shouted silently.
Because if you can get rid of me you can embezzle the Forbes
money. "Because if you didn't do it," she said, "then someone
else was in here tonight. Either someone or . . ."

"Something." He gave her a frustrated shake, as though she
were a malfunctioning appliance, and looked over her shoulder
at the staircase.

He was frightened. That was why he hadn't answered her. She
didn't want to know what scared him. "Let me go," she said.
He did.

Wearily, kneading her aching temples with her fingertips, she
walked into the bedroom and started picking up her scattered
clothes. Michael began to gather the pages of the book. "I fell
asleep in the sittin' room," he said. "The music was playin'. I
didna hear a thing. You took my key, but Dorothy has one. So
does Phil."

"It was in his pocket," Rebecca agreed. "You don't suppose
he and Dorothy have been helping themselves to the goodies all
this time, and are trying to get rid of us so they can continue?"

Michael's face suffused with horror. He dropped the pages of
the book and they scattered in his wake as he bolted from the
room and up the stairs. Rebecca waited, ready for anything. A
moment later he returned and began to pick up the pages again.
"Naething wrong wi' my room," he announced.

How can you tell? she wanted to retort, remembering what
the room had looked like this afternoon. But that kind of remark
wouldn't help. "So who did it, then? And why?"

"Well, it wisna Eric, was it? He was wi' you."

"An alibi?" she asked sarcastically. "Come on—it's only on
Columbo the best-dressed suspect is automatically the villain."

Michael shrugged. He found and contemplated a lace teddy,
noting the discrepancy between her fantasies and her prim public
demeanor.

She snatched the garment away from him. "Maybe some of
the local punks decided to indulge in a little vandalism. I did
have a difference of opinion with Steve over his dog. But then,
I saw him in town, too." She slumped onto the threadbare carpet and sorted her earrings and cosmetics into their respective
containers. Her contact lens case was safe. So was the earring
snagged in the fuzz of the bedspread. Nothing was missing.

Michael rescued clock, tape player, and typewriter and separated them. After a good five minutes' meditative silence he said, "Rebecca?"

"Mm?" She got up, hung her skirts beneath their corresponding blouses, and returned them to the wardrobe.

"Is it worse to think o' vandals breakin' in, or to think o'— well, the poltergeist you mentioned?"

Every nerve ending in her body went numb. "What?"

Michael dropped on the edge of the bed. He spoke hoarsely, as if the words were forced through a sieve of pride and fear in his throat. "Why do you think I jumped when you caught me up in the Hall—yesterday, was it?"

"I startled you." Don't, she wanted to order him. I don't want to hear it.

"You thought you'd seen me in the window."

"Yes."

"I wisna in the window. I'd been in the Hall at least an hour. Listenin' to the footsteps on the stairs like I listen to them at night."

Rebecca sat beside him, her head in her hands, pressing her poor overstuffed mind back into her skull.

"This mornin' you asked me when I'd got to bed; you were listenin' to them yoursel'. The bluidy great tackety boots goin' up and doon, up and doon, until you're fair mad wi' the noise." He dropped his voice even lower. "And the lights. I didna turn on the lights the night. I didna turn them on three nights ago, when I was here alone and a' the lights came on."

"It's a dream," she insisted, "it's a hallucination, it's only imagination. There's some logical reason!"

"It's a flamin' adventure just tae go tae the loo!"

Through her teeth Rebecca said, "If it's that bad why don't you leave?"

He snorted in humorless laughter. "Gie up my job, go home wi' my tail between my legs, and tell everyone I was scairt of ghosties and ghoulies? Are you daft, woman?"

Oh, all right. She wouldn't insult him by asking him why he hadn't told her this yesterday. At least it explained his reaction when she'd told him she'd already been through the house. Some of his reaction. It didn't explain his resentment.

Rebecca forced herself to sit up straight. Outside the bedroom, the ceiling light in the corridor illuminated the closed door into the piper's gallery. Her mind was, it seemed, shedding wisps of nasty pink stuff over all her preconceptions. Those edges of reality she had thought so hard and sharp fuzzed disconcertingly out. "I thought any good Scot would grow up believing in ghosts," she said.

"Admittin' strange things happen, aye. But no runnin' away from them." Michael sat with his elbows propped on his knees, also staring out the door. "There's something goin' on here, whether by supernatural or human agency I dinna ken. If it's supernatural I'm inclined to think it'd happen, anyway, like that philosophical tree fallin' in the forest. We're just here to acknowledge it. If human—well, that's another matter." He paused, and then asked rather too carefully, "Will you be leavin' the noo?"

And back we come to where we started: you want me gone. With a profound sigh Rebecca got up, put Ray's picture in the depths of the wardrobe, and began picking up shards of glass. If Michael registered her disposal of the photo, he didn't react.

Did you saw through the chair in the prophet's chamber? she wanted to ask him. *Are you counting on all this nonsense about ghosts and intruders and Loch Ness monsters in the bathtub, for all I know, to run me off?*

It wasn't nonsense. That was about the only thing she knew for sure.

Her mind was too tired to think anymore; frustrated anger thinned into weary bewilderment. Silently she and Michael sorted out the bedcovers and made the bed. "Well, then," he said, "I'll turn off the lights, shall I?"

"You're a braver man than I am, Gunga Din," she told him.

He grinned. The grin was stretched fine and taut, but it was a grin. "I'm hopin' the museum'll no mind my puttin' in for combat pay."

"Haunted-house shell shock," she agreed, and gave him the key from her purse. She stood listening while he turned off the lights in the lower stories and locked the door with a grinding and clanging like sound effects from "The Fall of the House of Usher." When he came back up the stairs, he threw her a quick, wry salute before going on to the fourth floor. His quiet steps echoed for a few more minutes. Apparently he'd survived the expedition to turn off the lights. Or else something had sprung out on him from the sudden darkness.

Rebecca shook herself and walked to her window. She shaded her eyes with her hand and looked out into the wild night. The trees and lawns were pitch-black except for spills of light from her room and Michael's. And for a quick glint that she might have imagined, close to the forest. From the dovecote, maybe, headlights reflected from the road as the trees thrashed in the storm. She drew the curtains, hurried into her pajamas, turned off the lights in the bathroom and hall, and slammed the bedroom door firmly behind her. It had no lock. Great.

She sat on her bed brushing her hair, hoping the aspirin she'd taken would quell her headache. But even her chest seemed to be filled with cotton candy; each breath she took felt fluffy and sticky. Rain pattered against the window and the wind sobbed around the turrets. A thunk from overhead must be Michael dropping his shoes; yes, there was the other one. At least there was someone in the house with her. Of all the things she had to be frightened of, surely she didn't have to be frightened of Michael. Irritated, annoyed, scunnered, as he would say, but not . . . Her hand clenched on the hairbrush.

He seemed perfectly rational. So, probably, did your average mass murderer. Maybe she should be frightened of him. Just because he went all misty over the old songs didn't mean he wasn't a liar. He could be faking his mercurial manner, even the ebb and flow of his accent, to hide cold calculation. He would have to be a superb actor, but stranger things had happened. He'd said so himself.

The room was damp and chill. Rebecca left the bedside lamp on, the shade focusing the light into the corner, and mummified herself in the bedclothes with only her eyes and nose emerging. Her bones crawled with dread. She'd wanted an adventure but this wasn't what she'd had in mind.

Michael couldn't be staging an elaborate charade to get her out of the house. If he'd trashed her room, he'd have had to trash his, too, to make her think it was an outsider. Unless he meant for himself to be so obviously the only suspect she wouldn't suspect him . . . The end of her thought snapped her mind. He couldn't. She'd be a prize chump if he was.

She moaned; aspirin was simply inadequate for a headache of these dimensions. A flamethrower might have helped.

Ray would've nodded sagely and told her yet again that her imagination was pathologically overactive. But it wasn't her imagination. Something *was* going on here. Even if Dracula and a team of werewolves were living in the lumber room, she wouldn't go crawling back to Ray.

If Eric had been here tonight, he might have seized the opportunity and offered to spend the night with her, just to protect her. Although even his slightly overenergetic hormones would realize that would be rushing things.

Next to the bed, her face glossed by the light of the lamp, Elspeth Forbes looked out into nothingness. Social morality had changed since her day. Now recreational sex was acceptable. Rebecca writhed under the blankets and discovered that outside the warm print of her body the linens were the temperature of a marble slab. She jerked her toes and elbows back into the cocoon.

Was that a footstep outside her door? She lay, straining every sense, trying to hear beyond the tick of her clock and the torrent of wind and rain. She could always look out and see if it was Michael. Yeah. She might as well fly as open that door. It wasn't a footstep. No. It wasn't.

The question was whether whatever was happening here, supernatural or not, was threatening. The question was whether she should cut her losses with Dun Iain, research, education, academic brownie points, and run away. But that was no choice. Her self-respect hinged on her staying here.

Rebecca's nostrils flared. Odd, the scent of lavender was completely gone. The theoretical vandal must've taken the air freshener from the wardrobe. But if she had never been able to find it, how had he, she, they . . . Someone giggled. The sound was gone as soon as she heard it, but she had heard it. Someone in the hallway outside her door had giggled.

Don't be childish! It's just the old house talking to itself! Rebecca pulled the covers over her head and started counting crowned heads—Duncan, Macbeth, Malcolm, Donald Ban— desperate for the unconsciousness of sleep.

Chapter Eight

THE SAUCE WAS thickening nicely. Rebecca stirred it with one hand and arranged the broccoli in the baking dish with the other. Meowing pitiably, Darnley wove himself in and out of her legs, his eye on the chicken breasts simmering on the stove.

"Oh, all right!" she exclaimed, and peeled off a portion of the meat. As the cat trotted away with his booty Michael's voice shouted, "Good mornin'!" Rebecca was not at all surprised the final syllable had the upward twist of a question. "Good morning," she called. "In the kitchen."

The night had lasted, it seemed, well into eternity. Rebecca had dozed fitfully, waking again and again to find the rain still pouring and the wind still blowing through the darkness. At least, she told herself, if there had been footsteps, she had not been able to hear them.

When at last a blessed glimmer of dawn lightened the overcast, she had ventured out, only to discover the window in her bathroom was open. The lid of the toilet, which she had left lowered, had been raised, so that the seat was covered with icy raindrops. She had not been amused.

Rebecca poured herself another cup of coffee and set the teakettle on the burner. She'd also not leaped to the assumption that the open window had been Michael's doing, despite his comment about the adventure of going to "the loo." Ghosts must be capable of practical jokes; she'd heard a giggle outside her door. She suppressed the quick ripple of her spine.

Today Michael was wearing a "Monty Python" sweatshirt. He approached the stove and observed, "You're cookin'," with the diffidence he might have accorded Lucrezia Borgia. Maybe, Rebecca told herself, he'd spent half the night wondering if he should be afraid of her.

She took the saucepan off the burner, wiped her hands on her apron, reached for her coffee mug, and took a long grateful swallow. The cobwebs in her mind shriveled and disintegrated. Eric deserved a medal for providing Dun Iain with a coffeepot. "Yes," she said, "I'm cooking. We have to eat the food I brought day before yesterday, but we're going out tonight."

"We are?" Michael asked, with a bright blue sideways gleam. He checked the temperature of the kettle and dumped tea leaves into the pot.

Oh. She'd never told him. "My friend Jan in Putnam invited us to dinner tonight. If you'd like to come." Rebecca poured sauce over the broccoli, arranged the chicken, finished with a dusting of cheese. "Move," she ordered, and as Michael skipped aside thrust the baking dish into the oven.

"Ah," he said. "Americans, are they?"

For a fleeting moment she thought he meant the chickens. "Jan and Peter Sorenson? Americans are mostly what grow around here."

"I'd like to meet some normal Americans," he said wistfully.

Rebecca laughed. So far the poor Scot had met only the occupants of Dun Iain, who probably reminded him of the cast of *Arsenic and Old Lace*.

Michael deftly poured boiling water into the teapot. "You don't think they'll be servin' tuna casserole?"

"Jan's a good cook, never fear. I was supposed to warn you, though, that they have kids."

"I have three nephews. My sister and I call them Huey, Dewey, and Louie. If I can put up wi' them, I can put up wi' anything." He poured a mug of tea, added milk and sugar, drank. His expression went as blank and mellow as Ray's did after successful completion of a page in *The Joy of Sex*.

She had to think of that. Grimacing, Rebecca warmed up her coffee. She and Michael leaned against their respective patches of counter, exchanging wary glances over their individual mugs of restorative. In the cold, gray light of morning her suspicions of him the night before seemed absurdly paranoid. "So you think the house is haunted?" she asked, taking the plunge.

He shook his head. "It could be that Steven Spielberg's set up a special-effects lab in the attics."

"Cognitive dissonance. Your mind isn't equipped to deal with unfamiliar input. So you try to familiarize it."

"Telling yourself it's all in your imagination. I don't know," Michael confided, "whether I was more frightened of the unfamiliar, as you say, or of goin' mad. But when it happened to you, too—well, that was all right."

"Thanks," she replied dryly. "Although having ghosts in the house does add flair to the proceedings. If there weren't any, we'd have to make some up, just to spice up the state's advertising brochure."

"Old things do have an air about them. Rizzio's guitar, for example; you can just feel what it must've been like, can't you?"

"Oh, yes." He was a closet romantic, no doubt about it. She'd have to stop teasing him about it. "James used to say the things wanted to go home."

"They wanted to, as if they were alive? Aye, I think they probably would have done."

Plunging even further, she admitted, "I dozed off in the prophet's chamber and dreamed I was at Culloden."

"Culloden," he repeated sadly. "What a waste."

Rebecca sipped her coffee. That had been more of a vision than a dream. Dreams didn't move objects around and turn on lights.

"The question," said Michael, "is whether there are ghosts, spirits, psychic forces—whatever you want—or just bloody-minded humans. And whether it really matters. We still have to live with it."

"I'll tell you what would help with the human element," Rebecca said. "Changing the lock on the front door and being very careful who gets a key."

Michael topped up his mug. "Good idea."

"Eric's idea. He mentioned it last night."

"Eh? Timely suggestion, what?"

She ignored his implication. "And as for the ghosties and ghoulies, maybe I can work them into my dissertation." That didn't come out quite as lighthearted as she'd intended, but it would do to serve notice she was staying. If she had to pretend the supernatural existed in order to get her Ph.D., so be it.

Michael fished a cat hair out of his mug and didn't respond.

"Here." Rebecca picked up the bread and handed it to him. "Make some toast. The chicken's almost ready."

"Chicken and broccoli?"

"Chicken Divan. Not quite up to Mrs. Beeton's specifications, maybe, or even Betty Crocker's, but it's what we had on hand."

"For breakfast?"

"You can't live forever on eggs and pork," Rebecca told him, thinking of the identical breakfasts in every hotel on her British tour. "Be adventurous. Be daring." She pulled out the baking dish.

Michael set the toast to attention in the toast rack. A slightly rueful, slightly calculating glance made Rebecca wonder if just putting up with her was as daring as he wanted to be. It rankled, that he'd rather be alone with assorted spooks than have her around. But they weren't being paid to like each other, just to work together without bloodshed. Even though he was, every now and then, actually likable.

Darnley sat in an empty chair washing his face while they ate. Or rather, while Michael ate. Not only had Rebecca not quite finished digesting last night's sumptuous repast, she was so fascinated with the way he mashed his food onto the back of his fork with his knife that he finished long before she did. She gave him the rest of her portion and he ate that, too. "Very good," he pronounced at last.

"Thank you. You go on. I'll get the dishes—this time."

Michael refilled his mug and wandered off, looking more like the laid-back academic than Rebecca had ever seen him. Funny how food acted as a tranquilizer. Not that physiology was her field.

She'd barely piled the dishes in the sink when his bellow reverberated down the staircase. "Rebecca! Get yoursel' up here!" Well, she thought with a roll of her eyes, peace had been nice. She took off her apron, tempted to shout back, Ah, don't get your y-fronts in a twist!

Even with the chandelier shining, the Hall was a murky gray, reflecting the morning outside the windows. At least the rain had stopped pouring and was now reduced to a dispirited drool. Michael stood staring at the long table as though a cobra lay coiled next to his mug. When Rebecca stepped over the threshold, he demanded, "Where did you put the mazer?"

That big silver goblet? "I didn't put it anywhere. The last I saw, it was right there. You were looking at it." As if you were appraising it, she added to herself.

"It's gone missin'," he said.

"You didn't put it back in the sideboard for safekeeping?"

"Why? This is a castle, no a news kiosk. It's quite defensible . . ."

Rebecca waited while the horrible comprehension washed over him, draining the color from his face. As if on cue his carefully smoothed hair collapsed onto his forehead. "Damn," he snarled.

"I didna check the place last night. Whoever broke in had plenty o' time tae do a flit wi' the mazer."

"I didn't check it, either. I must've assumed thieves wouldn't call attention to themselves with vandalism. Unless it was meant as a distraction. Nothing of mine was missing." The coffee that had a moment ago been so delicious was now acid eating away Rebecca's esophagus. No one would want anything of hers, anyway. "You're not blaming this on ghosts?"

Michael pounded his fist on the table, then lunged and grabbed the pile of cups that threatened to fall over at his blow. "Is that why . . ." he started to ask, and then stopped, his face hidden, holding the cups.

"Is that why what?"

The words came in a rush. "Is that why you gie me the whiskey, sae I'd fall asleep and you and your toffee-nosed boyfriend could . . ."

"Trash my own things and steal the mazer?" she demanded. "Don't try that on me. You had every opportunity while I was gone to do it yourself. We're both suspects in this, whether you like it or not."

For a long moment the room was silent. A gust of wind rattled the tall windows. Michael and Rebecca stood staring at the jittery teacups. "All right, then," he said at last. "We'll search the hoose. First, to see if the mazer's been moved aboot by the spooks. Second, to see if anything else has gone missin'. I dinna suppose it would've helped if we'd reported the theft last night. We do have to report it."

"Now you're talking sense. I'll call Eric. He's the executor, isn't he?" she added hurriedly, to forestall explosions.

But even though Michael's eyes flared, all he said was, "Aye, that he is. Ring him and tell him what's on."

Rebecca stamped irritably into the kitchen and consulted the list of numbers posted by the phone. Garst, Pruitt, Adler, work and home. She dialed. Darnley, still curled on a chair, opened an eye and closed it again. The door of the lumber room opened with a crash that reverberated through the entry. Rebecca turned her back on the kitchen door. If it wasn't Michael making the noise, she wasn't going to acknowledge it.

"Hello!" With just the one word the velvet voice smoothed the hair bristling on the back of her neck.

"Eric, it's Rebecca. We've got a problem out here."

"What's happened?"

"We had vandals last night. At least, we think we had vandals last night. And this morning we're missing an artifact. Or we think we are, at least—Michael's looking for it now." That sounded really incisive and vigilant, she scolded herself.

"What's missing?"

"A thing called a mazer, a big silver goblet. I was wondering if you could find a locksmith who'd work on Saturday . . ."

"The mazer? It's been stolen?"

Rebecca wondered if the faint static echo on the line was Eric grinding his teeth. "We don't know for sure yet," she repeated. "We're checking to see if anything else is gone, too."

"Rebecca. I'll be right out. And I'll bring Lansdale, the sheriff. I'll bring a locksmith, too, if I have to tie him up in the backseat. And you, you take care. Keep an eye on Campbell." He hung up.

Now, there was incisive. Rebecca nested the receiver tenderly in its cradle. Poor Eric, he was probably envisioning lawsuits with the museum, the state, and any heirs extending into the next century. In a way it was comforting to know that his polished veneer could be scratched.

The mazer, he'd said, knowing what it was. The newspaper it'd been wrapped in was dated last spring. Maybe he'd wrapped it up himself and tucked it away, thinking it would be safe.

Good grief, people were coming and she hadn't cleaned up the kitchen! Rebecca wrapped the apron around her sweater and jeans and started juggling dishes. Somewhere between the cutlery and the saucepan Michael charged through into the pantry and back out again. "I'm up to the top," he said. He hadn't found it on the lower stories, then.

Rebecca arranged the clean dishes in the drainer, ran to her room to tidy both it and herself, then went up one more flight. Judging by the slams and crashes, Michael was looking in the storerooms on the sixth floor. She had the fourth to herself—she hoped. She stood outside Michael's door, her hands clenched at her sides, arguing with herself. I have a responsibility to my employers. I have a responsibility to myself. I have to live with this man.

Feeling less like Mata Hari than Gomer Pyle, Rebecca took a deep breath and walked into Michael's room.

Even though her hands itched to make the bed, she simply patted down the tangled blankets. Two empty suitcases were beneath the dusty box springs. She slid open the dresser drawers, wincing at each squeak, peered into the wardrobe, checked the bathroom. She found nothing she wouldn't have expected to find: shirts and jeans, toothpaste and comb, a pair of the green rubber boots called wellies that Britons are born wearing. The mazer was too big to be hidden just anywhere.

Books lay scattered on every surface. Textbooks, a travel guide, paperback science-fiction novels. There was the spiral notebook. She opened it. Every page was filled with the columns of items and numbers prefaced by pound signs she'd already seen. "Coalport vase. £50. Acquire." Sounded good to her. If he was into double-entry bookkeeping, she'd never notice it.

On the bedside table an envelope was tucked behind the clock radio, a newspaper clipping dangling like a cigarette from its lip. The headline said something about a firebombing in the Western Highlands. Goodness, Rebecca thought, and hoped no one Michael knew had been there at the time.

Footsteps. Her face flaming with embarrassment, Rebecca catapulted through the bathroom into the big bedroom and started ransacking the cabinets there. The only thing out of place was a cut-glass perfume bottle on the bed. It was icy to the touch.

She trudged up the stairs and returned the bottle to the dresser. The chandelier in the big bedroom, set amid plaster garlands on the ceiling, glared off the windows in the turrets as if each pane of glass were a mirror backed by mist instead of silver. Michael bounded in the door just as she was counting the other perfume bottles. "Did you find it?"

Five, six. There had been seven yesterday. "No, I haven't found it. Is there a bottle missing?"

"This one?" He set down a small crystal decanter. "They move aboot on their own. Subduction currents or something."

"I've put this one back twice now. I guess you could be moving them around. So could I, for that matter."

"And who's been sleepin' in the bed? Goldilocks?"

Rebecca turned. The pillow was hollowed as if by the print of a head. They had each smoothed it out at least once. "That might be . . ." she began, but her voice trailed off. The house creaked and the windows rattled.

"Elspeth?" asked Michael. "It's the bed where they laid her oot."

Rebecca wondered, in a sort of dispassionate horror, if she was going to scream or faint or be sick. But even though her skin crawled, all she found herself doing was folding her arms and setting her jaw obstinately.

Michael's eye moved from the pillow to Rebecca's stubborn expression. "That's all right, then. Keep your pecker up."

Rebecca disintegrated in laughter. "I wouldn't use that expression quite so loosely around here."

He grinned. "Has a double meaning, does it? I'll remember that."

Neither of them moved to fluff the pillow. As they began opening and shutting cabinets and drawers Rebecca decided he knew perfectly well that expression had another meaning on this side of the Atlantic, and had used it to make her laugh. Maybe it was time for her to do some tension-breaking, too. She asked, "Did you search my room?"

"Oh," he said faintly. He turned on his heel and stalked off. She followed him down the stairs quickly enough to see him pause in the door of his own room and survey the contents. Then he shrugged and loped on down the next flight. Rebecca called, "Put everything back where you found it." His reply was some muttered idiom she didn't try to decipher.

She went into James's room and poked desultorily around. The clothes in the wardrobe were even more heavily scented with lavender than they had been the day before. Elspeth's hatboxes contained nothing but Elspeth's hats, the feathers disgustingly molted. The tissue-wrapped garments turned out to be a baby's long lacy dresses and tiny caps. A hundred years ago even baby boys wore dresses.

Rebecca was sitting back on her heels admiring the fine stitchery when Michael returned. "Naething's there that wisna there last night," he announced. "You're clean. Am I?"

"You will be as soon as you tell me why you don't want me here."

He sat down so heavily in a rocking chair he almost went over backward. Catching himself, he said, "Excuse me?"

Well, that chair wasn't sabotaged. "Why don't you want me here?"

For once he was at a loss for words. "It's no that—I mean, I dinna mean—I . . ."

"Count to ten," she told him caustically. "Then try again."

He rocked back, the chair squeaking in protest, and fixed the wall above her head with his most candid gaze. "The state sent you to check on me."

"My instructions were to work with you. That I was to look

out for my own country's interests was merely implied. Not to mention my own interests."

"I already had Adler breathin' ower me. He should've been enough."

"But he's not living here. And he doesn't have the background to do more than glance superficially at what you've been doing, which is probably why . . ." She bit her tongue, but it was too late.

"Aye?"

"He's a little suspicious of your accounting. Just as you are of his."

"Damn cheek!" Michael said to the ceiling.

Rebecca took a deep breath that didn't quite fill her lungs. "You haven't been setting up any little practical jokes, have you? Like fixing the chair in the prophet's chamber?"

"What aboot the chair in the prophet's chamber?"

"It broke in half when I leaned back in it. The connecting piece, the bracket, it was sawed through."

He looked at her in disgust. "Now, why would I do that? It was probably dickey from old age."

"I don't have the pieces to show you—Phil took them away."

"Aha!" exclaimed Michael. "That might be significant!"

"Or it might not." Rebecca began to fold the baby clothes back into their brittle sheets of tissue. Michael rocked briskly back and forth, mouth crimped. She glanced up at him. His reply to her questions had merely confirmed her original suppositions, not told her anything new. No telling what, if anything, he was up to. She laid the crinkly bundles in the wardrobe and said, "I'd thought this was going to be an interesting job, but I didn't bargain for just how much!"

"Interestin' is an understatement." Michael bounced out of the chair, offered her his hand, and hauled her to her feet. "No matter if the yobbos who're causin' the trouble are human or supernatural or both—and I incline to think they're both—they're keepin' us from doin' our jobs."

Accepting the existence of either human or supernatural malefactors in her life was a dizzying leap of perception. Rebecca wondered how long she could postpone brain meltdown. "All the more reason to get on with those jobs," she replied staunchly. "Right?"

"Right," he said, equally stalwart, and they shook on it.

Chapter Nine

THE SILENCE WAS shattered by the slam of the front door. Michael's and Rebecca's handshake turned into a convulsive clutch. As one they raced to the stairs. When Michael shouted "Hello?" the word echoed into the depths of the house as though down a well.

"Hey," called Steve Pruitt's nasal voice. "Anybody home?"

Rebecca and Michael met him on the landing between the Hall and the study. Today he was wearing a shabby black vinyl jacket. His lock of hair hung lank as a piece of seaweed over his face, and instead of a gold stud in his ear he wore a dangling silver skull. "Didn't get finished yesterday," he said to Rebecca's feet. "Came back."

You mean your father sent you back, Rebecca said silently.

"Fine," said Michael. "Can you find everything you need?"

"Mm," Steve replied, and shuffled back down the stairs. This time it was his back pocket that was distended by the massive key.

"We should tell Steve to knock, not let himself in," Rebecca said.

"Next time he comes he'll no be able to let himself in, remember? In fact," Michael added with a grimace, "there's no point to startin' anything, Adler'll be here any minute."

"I'll mull some cider." Rebecca went down the stairs thinking, Poor Steve. His persona, instead of being tough, was that of a pathetic little boy. Well, what future did he have? That was one thing Rebecca had to say for her father—he'd insisted each of her brothers attend junior college and learn a skill, auto mechanics, food processing, electronic repair. "History?" Joe Reid had demanded when Rebecca told him of her academic ambitions. "Can you get a teaching job with that, to tide you over until you find someone to marry?" His assumptions had been so different from hers she hadn't bothered to say more than "Yes, Daddy. Don't worry about me."

Her family had thought Ray was a good catch—they'd be shocked she'd broken up with him. They'd think Eric was an even better one, except that marriage was hardly what Rebecca wanted from Eric. Proof of her independence, mostly. Except she hadn't written to Ray yet . . .

The front door was standing open. Someone was in the cab of the pickup outside, a girl with hair like a dust mop and hula hoops in her ears. She was gazing apathetically at Steve as he pecked at the marigold bed with his hoe, her eyes so heavily outlined in black they seemed to be holes torn in the pallid skin of her face. Rebecca paused, her hand on the huge doorknob. That might be the girl who'd run in front of Eric's car last night, looking like a hapless mouse or vole caught in the spotlights of a PBS nature special.

If Slash was here he'd run into the woods. Rebecca knocked at the window of the pickup. "Hi! I'm Rebecca."

The girl started violently, recovered, and whispered, "I'm Heather."

She couldn't be more than sixteen. "Would you like to wait inside? It's awfully cold out here."

"No," said Heather. "Thanks." She huddled into her shapeless black clothing, her tights-clad legs knotted together. Steve watched them expressionlessly. Blackbirds exploded like shrapnel from the trees, whirled overhead, and disappeared toward the roof. There was Slash, emerging from behind the mausoleum. On the whole, Rebecca would rather have Heather than Slash hanging around. She hurried back inside.

The drizzle had become a thick Scotch mist. Michael must feel right at home. So, she thought, shutting the door and eyeing the marble tomb, must Mary. Except for the insistent peal of the telephone in the kitchen. Dutifully she ran to answer it.

"Miss Reid, this is Phil Pruitt. Is my son Steve out there?"

"Why, yes. He's finishing up the flower beds."

The line hummed expectantly. "Oh. I see. Well, thank you."

Rebecca hung up and found a large saucepan for the cider. So Phil hadn't sent Steve; the boy had come on his own. She'd had students who went through these spasms of responsibility. She

found a can of cinnamon, sprinkled some into the cider, set out
a row of cups.

The front door snicked and her ears perked like the cat's. She
heard a patter of feet on the staircase. No one was in the entry.
If I stay here until January first, she thought, and then corrected
herself: by the time I stay here until January first, I'll have a
nervous system so sensitive I could sell it to the CIA.

She walked upstairs. Michael was in the study, eyeing the
copy of the Declaration of Arbroath. A floorboard creaked in
the hallway above. Maybe it was the Ghost of Christmas Past.
But this time Rebecca was pretty sure just who it was. As Michael turned and registered her presence she held her finger to
her lips and beckoned. Getting into the spirit of things, he tiptoed to the door. Together they started up the staircase.

Car doors slammed outside. Eric. Maybe the sheriff. Even the
locksmith. Great, the more the merrier.

Heather stood at Rebecca's dresser, inspecting a tube of lipstick. Michael chuckled under his breath. Rebecca exhaled—
right, for once.

Downstairs the door crashed open. Heather spun around and
saw the two people watching her. Her face went even paler, the
whites of her eyes glinting below the black rims. She slapped
the lipstick onto the dresser and sprinted between Michael and
Rebecca from the room and down the stairs. The rapid fire of
her steps against the stone mingled with shouts of surprise and
warning not only in Eric's voice but in two unfamiliar ones.

Rebecca collided with Eric on the landing outside the Hall.
"What's going on? What was she doing?" he demanded, clutching her shoulders.

"She was just poking around. We frightened her; that's why
she ran."

A stocky middle-aged man in a brown uniform and a jacket
whose insignia read "Harding County" stood in the entry,
Heather dangling like a kitten from his massive hand. "You're
sure, ma'am? She wasn't taking anything?"

Michael skidded to a halt beside Eric and Rebecca. "She'd only
been upstairs for a minute, lookin' at Rebecca's pretty things."

"Please let her go," Rebecca asked.

"She almost fell," the sheriff explained, releasing the girl.
Heather fled out the door.

"Pathetic kid," said Eric. "Wait here." He freed Rebecca
and strode back down the steps and out through the front door.

She flexed her shoulders experimentally; no, Eric's fierce grip had not left bruises.

"Warren Lansdale," said the sheriff. He took off his broad-brimmed hat and nodded affably. Probably he smiled, but it was hard to tell what was happening beneath his broom-sized and -colored moustache. "I hear you've had some mysterious goings-on out here. Wouldn't be the first time."

Rebecca and Michael exchanged a knowing look—not the first time?—and introduced themselves.

Eric's voice wafted in the door past the cadaverous little man who squatted on the stone flags amid an array of tools and metal pieces. In the parking area the pickup was boxed in by the Volvo, by Lansdale's squad car, and by a van labeled "Kwik-Fix Hardware." Steve and Heather stood like identical bookends, hunched, arms crossed, faces sullen, while Eric's admonitory forefinger counted out the riot act, his tone compelling attention even though the words were unintelligible from inside. Slash loped up and nudged Eric in the side. Absently he fondled the dog's ears.

Michael leaned negligently against the sarcophagus. Lansdale commented, "I figure Eric will take off for New York or someplace now." Yes, thought Rebecca, a goldfish like Eric might find even a city like Columbus too small a bowl. And his work here was almost done.

Eric opened his hand, palm up. Steve laid the door key in it. Eric gestured. With inspiring briskness Steve picked up his hoe, Slash gamboled away, Heather scrambled into the truck and crouched so far down only the spikes of her hair showed over the dashboard.

Eric came in the door and stopped dead, realizing four pairs of eyes were fixed on him. The locksmith quickly picked up his tools. Eric grinned at the other three. "Did the cavalry arrive just in time?"

Rebecca eyed him appreciatively. The fine rain had silvered his dark hair and sheened the burgundy leather of his jacket. His idea of casual clothes was an open-necked knit shirt and loosely cut canvas slacks. If lawyering hadn't paid off, he could have been a model. With his smoldering Heathcliffian looks he didn't need to smile and reveal the awkward teeth.

Michael spoke and her bubble of admiration popped. "Do you think they were the ones who mucked us about?"

"We saw them in front of that pizza place on our way into town," Rebecca answered. "I suppose they could've had time to get out here and get into the house with Phil's key. Seems awfully well timed, though, for kids that scatterbrained. And why?''

"A lot of them get real perturbed," offered Lansdale, "when they find out the world doesn't owe them a living.''

"Even if they didn't have the key," Eric said, putting the item in question into his own pocket, "they might have been able to pick the lock. Dorothy and I told James over and over he needed a newer lock on that door, but he hated for anything to change.'' He looked suddenly down at his feet.

"Hard to believe he's gone," Lansdale said. "I used to mow the lawns for him when I was just a kid back in the forties. For years we played chess every week. Fine old gentleman. A little strange, but we all have our quirks.'' He looked up the stairs as though he expected the old man to come hobbling around the corner. "It was a real shocker when Phil called to say James was dead. He hadn't been out of bed alone for months. The Good Lord only knows what he was up to, trying to get around at night. Dorothy certainly earned the little legacy he left her, nursing him for so long.''

Rebecca asked quietly, "Who else did he leave money to?''

"Phil," Eric replied, still distracted and somber. "A few local tradesmen. The mail carrier. Me.''

"Even me," said Lansdale. "He said we were his family. But we're not talking large amounts. I took the missus out to a fancy place in Columbus and we went to the opera; that pretty well blew it all.'' He cleared his throat. "What we're concerned with now is who broke in and stole the—the thing.''

Michael patted Mary's cheek and stood up. "I'm no so sure that whoever messed Rebecca's room stole the mazer.''

"Your room was vandalized?" exclaimed Eric, focusing abruptly.

"Everything was thrown around but nothing was destroyed.'' Except the glass on Ray's picture, but she wasn't going to complain about that, especially to Eric.

"I suppose you've already picked everything up," he chided gently.

"Yes, we did . . .'' Oh. But she couldn't see the Putnam forensics lab dusting her underwear for fingerprints.

"They didn't leave any clues lying about," Michael said.

"Let's let Warren decide about that," retorted Eric.

The sheriff made soothing noises in his moustache.

"But," Rebecca said, "it may not even have been . . .'' Michael quirked the outer end of an eyebrow as though watching a trapeze artist do a death-defying trick. ". . . human beings," she finished. And added to Michael, "You brought it up, remember?"

He grimaced reluctant assent. "Oh, aye, there's something none too couthy about the place."

Lansdale, surprisingly, nodded. "James wasn't the only one convinced there were—what do you call 'em—poltergeists out here. But they don't send around Wanted posters of ghosts. I'm not sure how to deal with one."

"Me either," said Rebecca.

Eric looked annoyed and uncomfortable, as if he had a rock in his shoe.

Michael shoved his hands into his pockets and shuffled his feet. "Come up to the Hall. I'll show you the drawin' of the mazer in the inventory."

"I'll bring something to drink." Rebecca found a tray in the pantry and poured out the fragrantly steaming cider. When she returned to the entry, she found Eric lingering at the foot of the staircase. "Are you all right?" he asked. "I'm not only worried about the house but about you. I don't like the thought of people breaking in."

"No more people are going to break in," said Rebecca. She diverted to the front door long enough to offer a cup to the locksmith. "Why, thank you, ma'am," he said.

In the Hall Michael was walking Lansdale through the inventories. The sheriff watched him with the fixed stare of the linguistically bewildered. Michael, taking pity on him, had lapsed almost into his BBC accent, except for the burred r's that clung to his words like thistles to a sheepdog.

"Do you think there'd be a market for that, that mazer?" Lansdale asked. "It's sure not something you could fence easily."

"Collectors," said Eric, pulling up a chair. "If you were familiar with the museum and antiques trade, it might not be too difficult to find a buyer. Under the table, of course." He sipped from his cup and did not look at Michael. He hadn't heard Michael say the mazer was "worth a packet in the right places," but he might as well have.

Michael eyed the lawyer as though he were a worm in a half-eaten apple. Rebecca handed Lansdale a cup and set one down before Michael. He included her in his aggrieved glare. "The thief needn't have a market in mind," she said hurriedly. "It looked like something expensive, so he took it."

"If the thieves had simply wanted valuables," said Lansdale, "they would've taken the silver cutlery, too, wouldn't they?" He drank, managing not to trail his moustache in the cup. His skull glistened through sparse strands of sandy hair—the moustache was probably compensation.

"You said that this wasn't the first time there'd been mysterious doin's out here," Michael said to the sheriff.

"Over and beyond James's talk about ghosts, and his idea that the papers and things wanted to go back home . . ." Lansdale glanced at Eric and Eric gestured encouragement. ". . . he was convinced things had been stolen—old letters, bits of jewelry, artwork—his stories were never the same twice."

"What happened," Eric said, "was that he resented having to sell a few items to help keep up the estate. And he forgot about the things he sold years ago. That's why you'll probably find things listed in the inventories that aren't here—he refused to mark them off."

Rebecca's heart sank. He couldn't have sold the Erskine letter. Michael leaned his chin on his hand and his elbow on the table.

"But I think there really were some things taken," the sheriff went on. "After all these years half the people in Putnam probably have keys to the house. Had keys, that is." He drained his cider and drew his clipboard across the table. "All right. Let me take down the information. Dr. Campbell said something about you and a chair, Miss Reid."

Rebecca filled the sheriff in, concluding, "—so Phil took the pieces to the shed." It all sounded foolish now, almost as much as stories of footsteps, objects moved around, and lights going on and off by themselves.

"The way I see it," said Michael into his fist, "a few odd bits of hauntin' are happenstance. A broken chair and a room mucked about might be coincidence. But the missin' mazer—now, that's enemy action."

Rebecca grinned. "Very tidy summary. Thank you."

"Sounds good to me," Lansdale commented, scribbling away.

"Dr. Campbell," said Eric, plunking his cup down on the table, "why don't you take care of the formal reports? I'd like Rebecca to show me her room, just in case you—she—missed anything."

Michael's eyes gazed unblinkingly out over his knuckles, hard and cold as blue arctic ice. "Very well, Mr. Adler, why don't I do just that?"

Eric seized Rebecca's elbow and whisked her out of the room.

"Is Campbell always like that?" he hissed when they were half-way up the stairs.

"No. Mostly to you, I think. How do you expect him to act when you practically accuse him of taking the mazer? Why didn't you accuse me as well? I had almost as much opportunity as he did."

"You don't have the museum background he does," Eric reasoned. He glanced around Rebecca's room, spending a moment or two inspecting smudges on the typewriter and clock.

"Yes," she said, "there're probably fingerprints. You know typewriter ribbons—the ink gets all over everything. But it was Michael who tidied them up . . ." She stopped in midphrase. "All right, even if you got any good prints off those smudges, half of them would be Michael's."

Eric's lips thinned. He seized her coat from the wardrobe and bundled her into it. "Come on. I want to talk to you. Up here."

She buttoned the coat, feeling both gratified and betrayed that his polished veneer could not only be scratched but gouged. He steered her to the sixth floor, then up the steps to a tiny room just beneath the roof platform whose broken windows were lined with birds' nests. Even in the chill draft the room smelled of droppings and decay. When the trapdoor in the ceiling slammed open, a brief riot of chirps and flutters erupted from above. Then there was only the moan of the wind.

Guided by Eric's hand, Rebecca climbed the ladder onto the roof. Fine raindrops struck her face like a slap. And yet the view from the platform was spectacular. She could see all the way to the rooftops of Putnam, brown and green smeared into a uniform gray. The dark crimson of the trees below her was muted by the mist. Shadowed land and overcast sky blended so subtly at the horizon that Dun Iain seemed to be encapsulated in a huge murky crystal ball. It was frightening and exhilarating at once—just like the last few days.

She stood cautiously in the very center of the platform, her ponytail flapping like a banner, and considered Eric. He was certainly masterful, the proverbial iron fist in a velvet glove. She wasn't sure she appreciated that. She'd have to see how he handled this crisis.

He stood right at the low balustrade, surveying the landscape laid out at his feet like Napoleon plotting new conquests. "Sorry for the bum's rush," he said. "The walls inside have ears." One corner of his mouth tucked itself into his cheek, acknowledging that he wasn't quite joking.

"They have eyes and noses, too, I think," Rebecca returned.
"But aren't you overreacting just a little?"

"Probably. Making a living in the law courts doesn't do much
for your opinion of human nature."

"Whose nature? Michael's?"

"I ought to call Edinburgh and make sure he is who he says
he is."

"But you wrote to him just like you wrote to me!"

"I wrote to a Michael Campbell, yes."

"Sure, the international art thief bumps off the old professor
and takes his identity," she groaned. "Michael knows his history too well to be an imposter, for one thing."

"He's a foreigner . . ." Eric stopped short at Rebecca's frown.

"Then we should give him the benefit of the doubt. I have."

"Oh, I see that you have," Eric said softly. "How did he
manage to convince you of his sincerity?"

Rebecca turned her back on him, planted her hands in her
pockets, pulled her head like a turtle into her collar, and looked
out across the lawn behind the house. A few scraggly flower
beds showed where once had been a formal garden. Surely she
wasn't defending Michael just because he liked the maudlin old
songs. "Like I said last night," she answered, grasping at some
reason, any reason. "Intuition. He can be pretty obnoxious, but
he just doesn't seem to be any more a criminal than anyone else
around here. And it's not fair to pick on him because he's not
an American."

The wind wept and wailed. Rebecca shivered, her entire body
clenched like a fist; she'd contradicted him, now he wouldn't
like her anymore.

"You're right," Eric said, and she spun back around. His
stern, arrogant mask cracked into a rueful grimace. The wind
tousled the dark strands of hair across his brow, making him
look less formidable. "Keep reminding me that I can act pretty
obnoxious, too. There're hazards to having been trained in ad-
versarial relationships."

"Oh," said Rebecca. "I see."

"I suppose a real international art thief would expect a better
return on his efforts than some old bric-a-brac from a Victorian
folly."

"Unless the stories about treasure are true, and the mazer was
taken just for an appetizer."

Eric stiffened. A tiny flame flickered deep in his eyes. "Rebecca,

I worked for James Forbes for three years. If there were anything to that treasure rumor, don't you think I'd know about it?''

She contemplated that flame. "Would you? Or are you denying the existence of a treasure because you're hurt he wouldn't tell you about it?''

He stared at her the same way Lansdale had stared at Michael. She could almost hear the gates opening and closing in his mind, computing comprehension.

"Who does know about it?'' she went on. "Phil? Steve? Warren? What better cover than being the sheriff? What if Dorothy didn't think her legacy was enough payment for all her work? How do I know you don't have some scam going to rake off more than your fair share of the Forbes money?''

She stood with her mouth open, the damp, earthy wind scouring her teeth. My God. She'd actually said it. She snapped her mouth shut—too late, dammit—and waited for the deluge of contempt.

The flame in Eric's eyes sparked and went out. He threw his head back and laughed. "You're the devious one, aren't you? Should we, just for the sake of argument, assume there is a treasure of some kind? Should we suspect everyone, even ourselves, of being after it?''

"Probably,'' she replied. She felt as if she'd picked up a brick and found it to be papier-mâché.

Still laughing, he opened his arms. She went into them. His jacket was freezing; shocked by her own boldness, she opened and dived beneath it to embrace the warmth of his shirt. His mouth wasn't cold at all. Amazing, she managed to think, how comforting a hug and a kiss could be.

"Did James ever say that the place was haunted?'' she asked at last, when Eric's warm breath migrated to her ear.

"He was convinced of it. I'll admit I never believed him. None of the ghosts ever performed for me.'' He drew away, brows puckered. "Do you believe there are ghosts here?''

"I'm not sure. Michael has seen and heard some of the same things I have—if you'll accept the consensus of a couple of social scientists, not parapsychologists.''

Eric shook his head, confused, she judged, and irritated at being confused. "Look, Rebecca, if you're scared to stay here, maybe you could stay with your friend in town.''

"No, if I'm going to work here I need to be here. I'm not going to run away just because the place makes me a little nervous.''

He clasped her even more tightly. "But what if there's real danger?"

"It's probably dangerous standing up here! What isn't dangerous? Driving on the freeway, eating pesticide-laced foods . . ."

A catcall wavered on the wind. Eric and Rebecca looked at each other, then over the balustrade to the ground. Far below, Steve leaned out of the pickup, hooting some thankfully muffled remark as he started the engine.

Rebecca blushed, her face burning against the cold leather covering Eric's shoulder. Eric's eyes narrowly followed the pickup along the driveway and into the trees. "Sorry," he said when the vehicle had disappeared. "This is hardly the time or the place, is it?"

He was implying there would be a time and place. "I never made a public spectacle of myself before. I'm having all sorts of new experiences."

"Like being in danger." He helped her back through the trapdoor.

Rebecca made a mental note to ask Phil to fix the broken windows. Leaking rain wouldn't help the plaster ceilings, that was for sure.

The ballroom seemed oddly close and quiet after the airy platform, except for a cold draft. The window that had slipped when Rebecca leaned against it was partially open again. She shut it and checked the locking lever, even though it would probably open itself again as soon as they were gone. She returned to Eric's side, grateful for his presence.

"Rebecca," he said, guiding her past the storerooms to the back stairway, "last night you offered to keep an eye on things here. Is that offer still good?"

"Of course."

He planted a grateful kiss on her nose. "If you say Campbell knows his business, then he does. Just—well—make sure everything's on the up-and-up. You have the historical expertise. You'll know if something's wrong."

Rebecca smirked into her coat collar. So Dorothy thought Eric liked his women decorative. And here he was complimenting her intelligence.

Michael was alone in the Hall, looking over a carbon of the sheriff's report. He glanced around, his jaundiced eye making a silent comment on Rebecca's pink cheeks. No lipstick, she told him silently. No smudges. Nyah.

Michael scooted back his chair and stretched elaborately before

Eric's scrutiny. "The sheriff's gone to see if he can find the broken chair. We were wonderin' if you'd happen to know where the key to the mausoleum is. Lansdale hasn't seen it since James's funeral."

"It's in the Chippendale secretary in the study," replied Eric. "Would you like me to show you?"

Michael waved toward the door. Eric strolled off. As Rebecca passed the staircase the locksmith called, "Ma'am?" She changed course toward him.

"I can't remove the mechanism of the old lock without leaving a hole in the door. I've disabled it, though. And the new lock is all fixed."

Rebecca checked it over. It was a sturdy bolt that could be slipped back from the inside, but that, if closed, could only be opened from the outside with a key. She took the four keys the man handed her and hung them beside the door. "Did Mr. Adler pay you?" she asked.

"Sure. Gave me a check when he came by the store this morning."

Voices echoed down the staircase, Eric's intense velvet semi-monotone contrasting with Michael's rhythmic swing and sway, like the hem of a kilt. Both tones were crisp with exaggerated courtesy. "Thank you," Rebecca told the locksmith.

As he was going out the door Lansdale came in. "I can't find that chair in the shed," he announced, hanging that key, too, by the door. "Phil must've taken it away with him. James usually let him have broken things. Are you sure it was deliberately sawed through?"

"No," Rebecca admitted. "And no one else saw it, either."

Eric and Michael appeared at the foot of the stairs. Eric held out his hand. "I'm sorry I implied you were suspect number one. I'm responsible for the place, you understand."

Michael looked from Eric to Rebecca and back as if unsure whether this was some kind of trap. Rebecca shook her head— if Eric was not quite as smooth as he pretended, neither was Michael as prickly. Michael shook Eric's hand and said, "Oh, aye, I understand. You're just earnin' your screw."

Eric gaped incredulously. Lansdale stopped writing and started wheezing. Rebecca, wavering between mortification and hysteria, said brightly, "Here the word is salary, Michael. Pay packet. Wages."

Michael, his complexion ruddier than usual, backpedaled toward the kitchen. "I'll fix some tea, shall I? We still have work to do the day."

"Please," Rebecca called after him. Since the stones of the floor weren't going to swallow her, she brazened it out and grinned sheepishly. Eric, slightly cross-eyed, muttered something about work in town, since he was here, anyway, and escaped out the door.

Rebecca realized Lansdale was waiting for her to sign the report. She signed. The sheriff settled his hat on his head and zipped up his jacket. "Miss Reid, if you have any more problems, you let me know."

"Thank you. I will." Rebecca shook his hand, her fingers disappearing into his voluminous grasp, and then he, too, was gone.

Eric waited by his car, equilibrium restored. He said, "The key's in the secretary. I guess it's safe there. If anyone breaks into the mausoleum, we'll know we have a bunch of weirdos on our hands."

"True enough." Just as they turned to look at the tomb a fluff of butterscotch and white emerged from the dovecote and settled down to wash its paws. Rebecca laughed. "I bet that's great mouse territory."

Eric shuddered. He leaned over and gave her a perfunctory kiss, missing her mouth by an inch. "I'll be back out on Monday to look through some papers, if you don't mind. Sorry to have to rush off." He was in the car, the door locked, the window rolled up, almost before he finished speaking.

She watched with affectionate exasperation as the Volvo zoomed past the mausoleum and vanished. Why, she asked herself, doesn't he just admit he's afraid of cats and have done with it? But no, he wouldn't, would he? Endearing, to know he had more than one chink in his burnished armor.

She looked up the dizzying height of the castle, to the platform where they'd stood looking like the lurid cover of a paperback romance. She laughed at the absurdity of it all, and went back inside laughing, to the warm kitchen where the teakettle was whistling merrily.

Chapter Ten

MICHAEL WAS SLICING cheese onto pieces of bread arranged on a cookie sheet. Rebecca's laughter withered into a rueful grimace. "I'll give you the benefit of the doubt: that comment to Eric didn't come out like you intended."

He slipped the cookie sheet under the broiler, poured boiling water into the teapot, and didn't look at her. "After all the American books and films I've seen you'd think I'd remember just what the four-letter words are. And there he was apologizin', too. Made me look a proper twit."

"Freudian slip?" she inquired dryly.

"Oh, aye." His voice was strangled by amusement or contrition or both, she couldn't tell. "Mind you, that comment about things gone missin' from the inventories was very instructive."

"Michael Campbell, you are incorrigible."

"It's a national trait," he assured her. "Sit down."

Rebecca took off her coat and sat down. He plunked sandwiches and tea onto the table. The slice of tomato sunk into the hot cheese of her sandwich looked like a red smiley face. She smiled. "It's a shame we can't work in here all the time. It's the warmest room in the house."

"The house is no so bad," replied Michael, joining her at the table.

"You're used to a cold climate. A good thing Dun Iain isn't in Texas. A hundred and ten degrees in August—you'd shrivel up and die."

He rolled his eyes in horror and gulped scalding tea. "You're from there?"

"I'm not from anywhere, really. My dad's a machinist, and was always chasing the pot of gold at the end of the lathe. Never found it, though. He and my mother are in Florida now."

"Florida. Disney World. When I first got here, I told Dorothy I'd be drivin' down to Disney World for the afternoon. She laughed at me. Then she told me how far it was."

Rebecca grinned. "To an American a hundred years is a long time. To a Britisher a hundred miles is a long way."

"Just that," Michael replied with his own dazzling grin.

When the dishes were empty, Rebecca began clearing them away. "I'm not so sure anymore," she said, thinking aloud, "that there isn't something in those rumors of treasure."

Michael, caught halfway between seated and standing positions, finished straightening as if his joints had suddenly rusted. "You're gettin' carried away by that again?"

Rebecca stood balancing the plates, suppressing an impulse to hurl one at his head. Every time she was ready to take him at face value, he turned another version of that patronizing face. And she had defended him to Eric. "Even if there isn't a treasure, someone—Phil, Dorothy, someone—believes there is."

"No necessarily." Michael started running water into the sink, accompanied by a robust squeeze of the detergent bottle. Suds billowed. "Whoever's been creepin' about probably doesn't have such a nice, tidy motive. And there's no law sayin' it has to be someone we've met, either!"

Damn him, he had a point there. "All right, Dun Iain's really an ancient cult center and everyone within a hundred-mile radius is a Satanist and Darnley is their familiar."

"Maybe it's an alien invasion," Michael countered, "and the place is filled with bug-eyed monsters in invisible space suits."

No ploy she had ever learned for dealing with a man worked with this one. And they called women unpredictable! Rebecca tramped upstairs, collected the sticky cider cups, carried them back down, and slipped them into the sink. "I'm going to work in the study," she announced.

"I've one more cabinet in the Hall. What time is your friend expectin' us?" Michael slopped dishes in and out of the sink so briskly soap bubbles swirled around him.

The man could cook *and* wash dishes. Truly mind-boggling. "Be ready at five-thirty," Rebecca told him, and left.

She opened the front door. Sure enough, Darnley was waiting on the doorstep. He yawned, showing every indication he was doing her a favor by coming inside. "I'm beginning to understand," Rebecca said to Queen Mary's marble face, "why James named the cat after one of your husbands. Men!"

Forget about Michael. Forget about Eric, tempting as it was to indulge in a daydream or two. She hadn't yet written Ray. Not that there'd be any point in writing a letter today, it wouldn't go out until Monday. And there was work to do.

Rebecca collected a notebook from the Hall and saluted the suit of armor in the study. It was supposedly Charles I's Dutch-made jousting attire, but without provenance Michael had had to leave it to the state. The first thing she saw on the secretary was the huge, ornate mausoleum key. She took it into the prophet's chamber, opened the desk, chose a diary at random, and thrust the key inside. It caught on something.

Rebecca pulled out the entire book. The serrations of the key were hung on a photograph of a young woman taken sometime in the 1920s, judging by her bobbed and waved hair. Although she had a pretty, if rather plain, face, there was a discontented curve to the painted mouth that reminded Rebecca of Dorothy. Although Dorothy, she calculated quickly, probably hadn't even been born when this picture was taken. The eyes were different, anyway, large and dark and oddly furtive. Had the girl sneaked out to have her hair cut despite her parents' wishes, the typical adolescent rebellion of the period?

She turned over the thick cardboard. On the back was the stamp of a Columbus photography studio and a faded pencil scrawl. "Gemmell," she thought it said. A last name only. Some lady friend of James's? A relative? She scanned the page in the diary where the picture had been. It was an account of Warren Harding's election in 1920. No help there.

Rebecca tucked the picture and the key inside the book and returned them to the drawer. She added "Windows below platform" to the list of repairs she was making for Phil. Back in the study, she pulled a chair up to the secretary and went to work.

A portfolio of illuminated medieval manuscripts would repay preservation. Several Roman coins rattled in an old cigar box, neatly labeled "Ardoch Roman Fort." A flint arrowhead might be prehistoric.

Darnley leaped into her lap and thrust his tail up her nose. She did a record-breaking sitting high jump and then, ashamed of herself, patted the enticingly purring creature until he settled down on her lap, snagging her jeans with his claws.

A Neolithic chert axe head. A copy of *The New Yorker*, war-time edition 1944. A rolled strip of Aubusson tapestry. "Okay," said Rebecca, "where's the rest of it?"

Her voice boomed in the afternoon silence. Darnley looked up at her disapprovingly. Despite herself, she glanced over her shoulder at the empty doorway. Nothing. She might as well be alone in the castle with the cat and the spattering sounds of her frying nerves.

There was a medieval "healing stone," a ball of dark quartz mounted in tarnished silver. Rebecca held it up, watching the mysterious play of light and shadow in its depths. Superstition, she told herself. It couldn't really heal a hangnail. Although strange things happened in your mind if you believed—whatever. She thrust the stone into the back of the desk and checked it off the inventory. The cat's sleeping weight was putting her legs to sleep.

More books, more papers. No Erskine letter. She considered a Caithness glass paperweight, a modern version of the trans-lucent healing stone, but the museum could buy itself a hundred of those. The room was warm, and the cat was purring as he slept. Rebecca's eyelids went down for the third time.

She was suddenly yanked into wakefulness by the sound of footsteps. Darnley leaped from her lap, his claws stabbing into her thigh. She gasped. She was awake, all right.

The steps plodded down the staircase just outside the door. For a moment she sat paralyzed, every follicle on her body dis-tended, while the cat crouched bristling at her feet.

"Darn it," she whispered, "if that's you, Michael . . ." Darnley sped between her legs. She threw herself toward the door, knowing if she hesitated one instant she'd barricade herself in the prophet's chamber instead.

Watery sunshine illuminated the landing and the stairwell. Nothing was there, not even a shadow. But still the footsteps continued, one after another, ringing hollowly on the cold stone.

Perception shattered and its shards sliced bloody grooves in Rebecca's mind. She had had nightmares like this. She tried to move, but her muscles wouldn't work. Her lungs burst and her face empurpled itself with a shout that wouldn't come. But this wasn't a nightmare. It was real.

The steps stopped. "Rebecca?" said Michael's slightly slurred voice from the Hall. "Is that you?"

Galvanized, she spun across the landing and into the room.

He was sitting at the table, his head lying on his crossed arms, one of a stack of books open before him. She collapsed in the nearest chair and stared at him, feeling as if her eyes extended from their sockets on stalks.

He sat up. "I thought I was dreamin' footsteps. I wisna, was I?"

Wordlessly she shook her head.

"You went to look? What did you see?"

She shook her head again and forced out, "Nothing. I heard the steps but nothing was there."

"Ah, bugger it," he exclaimed. "If you'd only had a video camera, we could've sold tapes to the telly!"

Something snapped in Rebecca's chest. She inhaled raggedly, thought for one ghastly moment she was going to disgrace herself by crying, then burst into laughter that had more than a trace of hysteria in it.

Michael's crazed smile crumpled. He looked around, as though considering making a break for it, then stood and patted her clumsily on the shoulder. "Are you all right?"

"Intellectually," Rebecca gasped, "you can talk about ghosts and the supernatural all you want, but when it hits you emotionally—Christ!" She seized her wits, gulped, mopped at her eyes. "Yes, I'm all right." This was ridiculous. She stood up so quickly her head cracked Michael's solidly on the chin.

He staggered back, face contorted with pain, hand cradling his jaw.

"I'm sorry," she moaned, rubbing the dent out of her skull.

Michael said between his teeth, "Is it time to go yet?"

"It's past four-thirty."

"Good. I'd like to be ootwith Dun Iain for a time."

"Even if it means going with me?"

He removed his hand from his chin and tried moving it from side to side. It still worked. "I never was brave enough tae go chase the footsteps," he told her. "Even in broad daylight."

"Darnley pushed me," she said, ducking the question of whether he meant that as a compliment. "I'd better go get ready."

Rebecca fled upstairs. The front door opened and shut. Michael bounded past her room. From her window she saw Darnley frisking across the lawn. She envied the cat's simple life; this roller coaster of temperament she'd been riding made her feel as if she were possessed by a demon chameleon.

By the time she'd washed her hair and put on her makeup she was so limply drowsy she could barely keep from collapsing on the bed. She forced her eyes open far enough to examine her packet of birth-control pills. She really should keep taking them and forget her vague notions of giving her hormones a vacation. Which was a pretty cold-blooded calculation. But since those who equated romance with hot-blooded spontaneity ended up not with doctorates but with babies, she could live with it.

So having an affair will proclaim your independence of Ray, she said to herself. Are you sure it won't cut your nose off to spite your face? What if Eric turns out to be the average mass murderer?

Eric couldn't be a criminal. Any more than contradictory Michael, or laconic Phil, or garrulous Dorothy, or affable Warren. Michael was right. Whoever was responsible was someone they didn't know, with motives they couldn't fathom. With a frustrated snort she threw the packet back into the drawer and opened her jewelry case. Those hoops would go well with her tweeds. Or maybe those gold posts . . .

She stared dumbly for a moment, the gears of her mind failing to mesh. Two gold posts lay in one compartment, one in another. The odd one was larger and heavier. She picked it up and held it to the light.

Steve had been wearing one like this when she'd met him beside the mausoleum. One like this had been caught in the bedspread last night, last week, whenever the room had been trashed. And today Steve had come back without Phil's knowledge, wearing a different earring, and Heather had sneaked not to just anywhere in the house but to Rebecca's room. Just as if she'd known where the room was. And what she was looking for.

Michael's voice filtered down the stairs. He was singing something depressing about homesickness, defeat, and death. "Thanks a lot," Rebecca said to the ceiling.

Steve and Heather had problems enough without her calling the law down on them. If it had just been her room, she might have let it go. Even though she wondered why they'd attacked only her room. Surely the smashing of priceless antiques would better have relieved whatever fit of resentment had come upon them than simply throwing around her ordinary things.

But they'd taken the mazer. They had to have taken the mazer. She had to tell Lansdale—she had no choice. Knowing that Michael was wrong, that it was someone they knew, brought no satisfaction at all. And as for their motive . . . Pathetic kid, Eric had said.

Rebecca put the earring in a twist of tissue and tucked it into the bottom of her stocking bag. She looked back into the mirror to see Elspeth Forbes's reflection gazing over her shoulder. The postcard was still tucked into the corner of her portrait, the rim of its shadow lying across her chin so that she seemed to be smiling knowingly at Rebecca.

"Yeah," said Rebecca. "I'll call Warren tomorrow. Tonight I'm going to get away, have fun, clear out the old gray matter."

She left on the light beside her bed and the one in her bathroom as well, and was in the entry separating the new door keys from their ring when Michael came bounding down the stairs. His hair was meticulously combed and his faintly bruised jaw shaved. The off-white fisherman's knit sweater he wore over a blue button-down shirt emphasized his rangy build, all sinew and synapses. Rebecca pounced. "What a gorgeous sweater!"

"My mum made it for me," he said, recoiling.

"Let me see." Warily he extended an arm. Rebecca traced the intricate pattern with her forefinger. "I learned how to knit when we lived in Denver, but then we moved to Houston and we didn't wear sweaters anymore. My mother does crewel embroidery, beautifully, but she moans all the time about how it's not anything worthwhile. Keeps her sane, though."

His eyes crinkled with that peculiar cynical gleam. "Aye?"

"Nothing. Just yammering." Rebecca handed him one of the keys. "I'll drive."

"No, no. I need practice drivin' on the wrong side of the road."

"Do you have insurance?" she teased.

He sniffed, pretending offense. "I've been drivin' here for a week."

"All right, then—it's all yours." She turned on the light in the kitchen, made sure there was food in Darnley's dish, and helped Michael find the quilted coat he'd left in the sitting room.

Darnley was chasing a moth on the lawn. Rebecca, at first alone and then with Michael's help, tried to herd him inside— with predictable results. "He'll freeze out here," she said at last.

"He has a nice little fur coat," Michael told her, locking the front door. "He can bide in the doocot till we get back. Don't worry about him."

"Hey, he deserves his fair share of my worrying time," Rebecca protested. Michael laughed.

After a moment's confusion as to which side the steering wheel was on, they sorted themselves into the Nova. Rebecca snugged the seat belt across her lap and winced as Michael slammed his left hand into the door, reaching for a nonexistent stick shift. "Real men dinna drive automatics," he proclaimed, resignedly attending to the lever on the steering column.

"Right," said Rebecca. In the thin gleam of dusk the few lighted windows of Dun Iain shone innocently. The castle was like a child dressed in pristine pinafore and sailor hat, waiting until the parents' backs are turned to go make mud pies. Already a few stars pricked the depths of the cobalt sky, and the damp grass and leaves sparkled frostily. The tang of woodsmoke hung on the wind. They were in for a hard freeze.

Rebecca laid her head against the seat and snuggled into her coat, turning the collar up around her cheeks. The cloth smelled faintly of Eric. Bemused, she allowed herself a few moments of reverie as the car glided slowly through the darkness.

Chapter Eleven

WAVING HER HANDS, Rebecca directed Michael past the Burger
King, past the sleazy pizza restaurant, and through a complicated intersection where he stopped briefly to debate his right
and his left. Just beyond was the narrow tree-lined street where
the Sorensons lived. "Very good," said Rebecca as they stopped.
"In the dark, too."

"It helps that the steerin' wheel's on the other side."

The porch light of the tall clapboard house shone with welcome. "Don't expect anything fancy. Jan and Peter are on a
strict budget."

"I've been cheese-parin' for years," Michael assured her.
They emerged from the car, he opening his door, she opening
hers.

There was Jan herself. She said goodbye to a dim shape who
retreated into the house next door and rushed forward to meet
her guests. "Rebecca! Come on in. And you must be Dr. Campbell."

"How do you do, Mrs. Sorenson," he said, shaking her hand
as politely as Rebecca even at her most punctilious could have
wished. Peter stood silhouetted in the screen door, his burly
form looking like the colossus of Rhodes with the two children
clinging to his legs.

The porch light caught the rich gleam of Michael's hair and
the brightness of his eyes, the long, expressive mouth, and the
wiry body. Jan glanced at Rebecca, saying, "Ooh," under her
breath.

"Not necessarily," returned Rebecca.

Peter and Michael introduced themselves. Brian inspected from his three-year-old's vantage point Michael's Reeboks and jeans. Mandy, the five-year-old, said, "Mommy, he isn't either wearing a dress."

"Uh-oh." Jan explained, "We looked up Scotland in the encyclopedia. I think they expected you to look like the picture of the Gordon Highlander."

Michael smiled at Mandy. "It's called a kilt. When I played the pipes for a band, I wore one. And to my sister's weddin'. But few people wear one every day the now. We save it for best, you see."

Mandy continued to stare. Brian decided the stranger was incoherent but harmless and set off on a search-and-destroy mission. Peter sat Michael down on the couch and handed him a can of Budweiser. Jan said, with a nod toward the house next door, "Sue says there was a drug bust at the Pizza Shed."

Rebecca's ears pricked. "When?"

"Last night. Everyone kept saying it couldn't happen here."

"It's everywhere," Peter said gloomily. He took a swig from his beer.

So Eric had been wrong; the local kids hadn't been confining themselves to booze. Rebecca knew marijuana when she smelled it.

Jan headed for the kitchen. Peter leaped forward to extract a pencil from Brian's mouth. Michael peered dubiously into his can of beer. "Like it?" Rebecca asked.

"I've had water wi' more gumption to it," he whispered. But when Peter sat down and began talking about his job, Michael not only managed a good pull at the can, he conveyed the impression that wiring prefab houses was the most interesting work he'd encountered in years. He was showing more consideration than Rebecca would have thought him capable of. But then, he wasn't competing with the Sorensons.

She followed Jan into the kitchen and found her pouring glasses of wine out of a jug. Rebecca chuckled. Eric would be appalled. He probably only drank from bottles cobwebbed by genuine French-speaking spiders.

"He's not as nice as he looks?" Jan asked.

Eric? Oh, no, Michael. "He's all right. Moments of schizophrenia, though. Now I know why *Dr. Jekyll and Mr. Hyde* was written by a Scot."

"Oh?" Jan stirred a pot of stew redolent of onions and bay leaves. "Not like good old predictable Ray."

Rebecca slumped. "Good old Ray," she said sadly.

"So that's the way it is. I thought I smelled a breakup on the horizon. Is that why he's lurking around town?"

Rebecca stared at Jan as if she'd suddenly spoken Swahili. "What?"

Jan blinked. "Oh. Well, maybe that wasn't him I saw outside the mall. Sure looked like him, though. Waiting for the green light to cross the street even though there wasn't another car in sight."

"That sounds like Ray."

"Wearing an old flannel shirt and a knit cap."

"That doesn't sound like Ray."

"Unless," Jan suggested, "he disguised himself in order to follow you."

"That isn't Ray at all." Rebecca groaned. "Don't scare me like that, Jan—I get enough melodramatics at Dun Iain."

Jan stood over the salad bowl, paring knife poised. "What did I say?"

Rebecca was so far gone she was being rude. "Sorry," she told Jan, and between sips of wine told her of the mysterious happenings. "And the last person I thought to suspect was Ray."

"Ghosts, burglars—everything but secret passages in the library. I thought you were looking a little twitchy." Jan tossed the salad so vigorously bits of lettuce plopped out onto the counter. She scooped them back into the bowl. "And I hear you had a hot date with Eric Adler last night."

"Dorothy broadcasting on the grapevine network?" Rebecca asked. "I figured he'd already worked his way through the female population of Putnam and needed fresh prey."

"I've only said hello to him up at Golden Age Village myself, but as far as I know, he keeps a pretty low profile. I guess a lawyer has to be discreet. Or is he?" Jan handed over the salad.

"Yes. No. I don't know." Rebecca carried the bowl into the dining room and placed it on the table. Peter was asking questions about Scotland. Michael's brogue, unthickened by the beer, expounded on the tartan revival—"mostly laid on for the tourists"—and took a slap at absentee landlords.

"I read somewhere about Scottish nationalists," said Peter. "I thought they were like the Irish IRA, you know, bombs and guns."

"Most of our wounds are self-inflicted to begin with. Why make more?"

A remarkably live-and-let-live statement from Mr. Thistle, thought Rebecca as she returned to the kitchen. But he had saved that clipping about the firebombing in the Highlands. It must be an issue that interested him.

"Yes?" teased Jan. "You don't know whether Eric is discreet?"

The pit of Rebecca's stomach tingled delectably at the memory of their mutual indiscretion on the roof of the house. "He's human. He brought me a bottle of hideously expensive whiskey, but he didn't bring any to Michael. Out of spite, I guess, although to look at him you'd think he didn't know the meaning of the word. But he and Michael don't get along too well."

"Michael must be the only one. James just loved Eric, I hear. At least until right before he died, when he went kind of soft in the head. And Dorothy treats Eric as if she'd thought of him herself."

Rebecca laughed. "She does seem rather at a loss for criticism."

"Maybe she's got a crush on him. Don't laugh—when she was young and wild she had boys all the way from Columbus on her string."

"Dorothy? Wild?"

"Oh, yes. Back in the early fifties, Margie tells me, she was the town scandal. Boys and cigarettes, drinking and dancing. Funny, isn't it, how she goes on at poor Steve Pruitt about his clothes and his beer when she's puffing Virginia Slims and popping Valiums as if they were candy."

Rebecca drained her wineglass and rinsed it out in the sink. She hadn't told Michael about the earring. Poor Steve, indeed. Poor Phil. The egg would hit his fan, too. Unless he knew all about it already.

Jan installed the children at a card table and gave them bologna sandwiches. The adults she seated around the dining table. Rebecca tasted a forkful of stew appreciatively; Jan could do amazing things with ground beef.

"I take it you're finding some valuable things out at Dun Iain," said Peter. "That old furniture is much better quality than you can get today."

"Except for desk chairs," muttered Rebecca.

"Oh, I don't know," Jan said. "I'm rather partial to early

Sears Roebuck myself.'' She waved her hand airily around her house.

Michael and Rebecca laughed. Peter looked pained. "Actually," said Rebecca, "we're more interested in historical artifacts."

"Have you found your letter yet?" Jan asked.

Michael glanced up curiously. The children, losing interest in his dextrous manipulation of knife and fork, ran into the living room. The sound track of *Teenage Mutant Ninja Turtles* blasted through the door. "Turn it down!" bellowed Peter.

Rebecca explained about the Erskine letter and the rumored exchange of babies, Queen Mary's for the Countess of Mar's. "Of course, Ray," she added, "thinks it's politically incorrect to question the antecedents of the royal family. He was really put out when the committee accepted my proposal." She looked across the table at Michael, expecting indignation at the least.

But he was wickedly amused. "I've seen footnotes about that letter. I never knew old John had made off with it. Wouldn't it be grand to pin back a few English ears? I'll help you. You could use some expert help."

"Thanks." If he heard her slightly acid tone, he ignored it.

Jan and Peter shared a speculative look at that exchange. Jan said, "You know, Michael, you have us to blame for Rebecca's being at Dun Iain. When she was here a couple of years ago, we drove by the place, and we almost had to tie her up to keep her from marching up to the front door and demanding admittance. Then, after James died, Margie told me the state wanted a historian to balance the one the museum was sending—you, it turns out—and I tipped off Rebecca before the advertisement was published."

Michael nodded. "You do what you can to get your work."

A fine point Ray had never really understood. "I appreciate your help, Jan," said Rebecca. "I think." The dining room was a bubble of light and warmth filled with friendly voices. It was cramped and stuffy compared to the Hall at Dun Iain, where voices echoed in darkness and solitude. She blinked rapidly. What an odd feeling, to watch her own perceptions flapping in her mind like fish in the bottom of a boat.

Jan was saying something to Peter about the Dun Iain ghosts. Rebecca started to add, "I'm not imagining things. Not only Michael but the cat sees them, too," when she caught the impact of Michael's savage glare. All right, admitting to ghosts threatened his manhood. She said instead, "Peter, you've been inside Dun Iain, haven't you?"

"Sure. I've done some subcontracting for Phil. He's good at carpentry, plumbing, that sort of thing, but he gets me to do the electrical work. Some of that antique wiring could curl your hair. No pun intended."

He sat innocently deadpan while everyone groaned, then snapped his fingers. "By the way—Jan, where's the key?"

Jan leaned back, lifted a huge iron key from the china hutch, and presented it to Rebecca. "Better late than never. Phil got this for Peter before James died, and we've been forgetting to give it back."

The key was heavy and cold in Rebecca's hand. She intercepted Michael's keen glance toward Peter. No, she told him silently. Ray isn't the last person I'd suspect, Peter Sorenson is. She said, "You might as well keep it as a souvenir; there's a new lock on the door."

Jan put the key back on the hutch. Peter never so much as blinked. Michael shrugged very briefly and asked, "Would bad wirin' in the fuse box or wherever make all the lights come on by themselves?"

"No way. That box is the first thing I fixed."

"Oh," said Michael. He leaned his chin on his fist, winced, shifted his hand to the corner of his jaw, and contemplated his empty plate.

Sorry, Rebecca thought. I'd have liked a logical explanation. I have to go back to Dun Iain tonight, too.

"In fact," Peter went on, "I've done so much work out there the last couple of years James left us a hundred bucks in his will. Touching, how he regarded half the community as family."

"He even left a legacy to Louise O'Donnell, Phil's grandmother, out at Golden Age," chimed in Jan. "She worked at Dun Iain for years. She was a maidservant there when Elspeth died."

"That was in 1901!" Rebecca exclaimed. "She must be . . ."

"One hundred years old next month. We volunteers have a surprise party planned for her. You ought to come meet her—she's a lot like you, she remembers the old days better than last week."

"Occupational hazard," Rebecca explained.

"And," Jan continued, "she has lots of good gossip. She was the only one there when the baby was born, for one thing. Can you imagine having no one but a thirteen-year-old girl to help you give birth?''

Michael's forefinger moved in midair, calculating, ''But wasn't James born in 1892?''

''Yes, he was. Louise was there for the other baby.''

''What?'' Rebecca asked. Those tiny frilly clothes so tenderly tucked away—Elspeth had had another child?

''You didn't know about the daughter?'' Jan sighed heavily. ''I'm not surprised. The poor little thing died. I guess she's in the mausoleum. It was only a few days later, you see, that Elspeth threw herself out that window. Louise was in the house then, too, although not in the actual room.''

Michael whistled and shook his head. ''I read the cuttin's, but they didn't say anything about a child. So that's why she killed herself.''

''What a soap opera,'' said Peter.

''What a tragedy,'' Rebecca stated. Poor Elspeth. No wonder she haunted the house. If whatever entity moved there could be said to have a personality. ''Louise's name is O'Donnell, not Gemmell?''

''Now it is. Her maiden name was Ryan, I think. Her daughter married a Pruitt; he begat Phil, who married some shady Sadie and begat Steve.'' Jan stood and started stacking the plates. ''Aren't small towns wonderful? You get genealogy along with your Cheerios.''

Laughing, Rebecca collected the salad bowls.

Michael cocked his head. ''Gemmell?''

''That was the only name on the back of a photo of a girl in James's diary,'' Rebecca told him. ''I thought for a minute there maybe I'd read 'O'Donnell' as 'Gemmell.' But even if I had, the picture's from the 1920s—Louise would have been too old and her daughter too young.''

Michael nodded. ''And the Erskine letter wasn't by any chance folded in the back of the frame?''

''No frame. Just another miniature mystery, like the scrap of a letter. When did I find that?'' It seemed as if she were looking down the wrong end of a telescope. ''Apparently someone had been making demands on James and he was telling them where they could go.''

''That's interestin', but not anything the museum would want.''

Jan said to Peter, ''While the scholars here discuss their work would you check on the kids? I think they've turned on *Miami Vice*." And to Michael, "I've made a pound cake; would you prefer coffee or tea? The coffee's unleaded. Decaffeinated," she added to Michael's puzzled look.

"He's a tea drinker," said Rebecca.

"Coffee after dinner, thank you," Michael said, smiling amiably.

Rebecca rolled her eyes upward and caromed off the kitchen door. Only her experience as a waitress kept her from dropping her clattering burden of dishes. "Careful," said Jan. "Although I see how he might have that effect."

"What?"

"Michael. He's delightful."

"Every now and then. He's on his best behavior tonight."

"I don't have to work with him," Jan conceded. "But, hey, that remark about your needing expert help was just male chest-thumping. Peter always gripes about the furniture; he's upset because we can't afford better. At least with Michael there you don't have to catalog everything yourself. Or be alone with the ghosts."

"Not funny," Rebecca told her. But her thoughts fastened not on ghosts but on Peter, who wanted to buy new furniture for his wife. Motive and opportunity for prowling around Dun Iain?

No. If the man cared enough about his family not to move them all over the country chasing some mythical pot of gold, he cared enough not to get involved in monetary mischief. Unless he thought such mischief was evidence of his caring. The principle of the thing, justice, whatever.

The snug kitchen contracted as if pressed inward by the night. The delicious aroma of coffee acidified. The voices of the children, raucously singing the words to a McDonald's commercial, smeared into meaningless noise. Jan rinsed the dishes, unaware that her best friend stood just behind her, figurative dagger posed to stab her in the back.

No. Not Peter. Never. And that, as far as Rebecca was concerned, simply had to be that.

Chapter Twelve

SOMEWHERE BEYOND THE white noise in Rebecca's ears the telephone rang. Jan lay down her dish towel to answer it. "Hello?" Then, with a sharp glance at Rebecca, "Oh, hi! Yes, she's here." She extended the receiver. "Speak of the devil. It's Ray."

Rebecca stared numbly at the mouthpiece while the all-too-familiar voice percolated through her head. "I tried and tried to call you at the castle, but no one answered the phone. I was really worried."

"Ray, where are you?"

"What do you mean, where am I? Right here in Dover, where else?"

Where indeed? She slouched against a corner of the refrigerator like a boxer in his corner between rounds.

"I was really worried," Ray went on, not to be detoured from his set statement. "After that card you sent I didn't know what to think."

"Card?"

Michael appeared in the doorway, helping Jan to carry the rest of the dishes. He cast an inquisitive glance toward Rebecca. Jan clued him in. His brows arched. Rebecca turned her back on him.

"The postcard," Ray was saying. "About how vandals had broken in and smashed a bunch of stuff. I warned you about going there, out of state and all. We don't know these people!"

And she'd once thought him profound simply because his IQ approached hers . . . Someone had sent him a card. Not that his address was a state secret. But her room alone had been vandalized. If he were in Putnam picking up the local news, he could've made up the card. And yet Ray had always been as devious as a drink of water. He had his moments of possessiveness, but Rebecca simply couldn't see him skulking around Putnam.

"Rebecca, are you there?"

"Ray, if you got a card today, I'd have to have sent it the day I got here, but nothing happened until last night, and nothing was smashed."

"You're in danger!"

"No, no. Just someone trying to be funny. We've changed the lock on the door, it won't happen again. I'm not in danger."

"Kitten, you really ought to stop this foolishness and come home."

Her spine stiffened. "No, Ray, I have work to do. Important, interesting work. I sublet my apartment and stored my books and dishes, remember?"

"Then you'll have to move in with me."

Now he was having delusions of himself as father knows best. Enough was enough. This was it, D day. Just like Ray to ambush her before she'd been able to script a graceful exit. "I appreciate your worrying about me," Rebecca said. "But I'm all right. I've been working and I've been thinking, too. About us."

"About us?"

"It's time to call it quits, Ray. Lay the engagement to rest permanently. Break up."

Silence.

She bit her lip, released it. "Ray?"

"Rebecca," said the calm, reasonable, hurt voice. "What a thing to say. We've been together three years!"

"It's been a good three years. It's been . . ." She groped for a word. ". . . very comforting. But we've grown apart, and it's time to stop."

"I haven't grown anywhere," he said plaintively.

"I'm the one who's changed. I'm sorry." This was like squeezing a pimple: painful, messy, and humiliating.

Apparently Jan and Peter were trying to herd Mandy and Brian to bed; screeches of outrage emanated from the living room. Michael scurried into the kitchen like a man escaping Devil's Island, helped himself to the coffee, and opened the refrigerator door at Rebecca's elbow. He found the milk and poured some into his cup. "So you're goin' to gie him the elbow?" he stage-whispered, and sneaked back into the dining room as the front rolled upstairs.

Rebecca shot a glare at his retreating back that missed by a mile.

"Let's not rush into anything, okay?" said Ray. "I mean, we can go ahead and date other people, and when you get back here in January you'll see things differently." He was no doubt polishing his glasses. Stuffing the pipe was for contemplation, polishing the glasses was for agitation.

"I won't be seeing things differently. Let's just make a clean break. It's easier that way."

"Rebecca . . ." No, he was too dignified to argue. "If that's what you want, Kitten. You know where I am if you need me."

"Take care, Ray."

"No, no, you're the one who needs to take care. All right?"

"All right, I will. Goodbye."

"See you around, Rebecca."

She stood looking at the phone after she hung up. If they were both teaching at Dover they would be seeing each other around. That would be awkward, but not as awkward as shoring up a relationship whose timbers had rotted out. Rebecca allowed herself a quick sniff. No, the three years hadn't been wasted. Odd, though, that what she felt now wasn't sorrow but relief.

She poured herself a cup of coffee and drank. Strong and smooth, dark and aromatic, like Eric . . . She swallowed the wrong way, coughed, and for one quick moment wondered just what would've happened with Eric by the time January rolled around.

Judging by the distant sounds of water splashing and children being tortured, Jan and Peter were washing their offspring. Impressive how Peter waded in, too. And he must really be wading—Rebecca looked cautiously up at the ceiling. No spreading water spots. Fathers, she thought, had changed since she was a child.

She carried her coffee into the dining room and collapsed in her chair. Maybe she should abandon her idea of a dissertation on the Erskine letter and instead explore the varieties of tension headaches.

Michael leaned on the table, cradling his cup. His expression was candid, maybe even sympathetic. "What was her name?" Rebecca asked.

"Who?"

"The Englishwoman to whom you gave the elbow."

The blue eyes grew brittle. They looked through her, seeing someone else. For a moment she fully expected him to say, "None of your business," even though he'd thrust that mouth of his into her business. But he sighed and said, "Sheila-bluidy-Fitzgerald, that was her name. I was tempted to gie her the back o' my hand, but that would've said more aboot me than aboot her."

Rebecca's eyes widened. At least she hadn't ended up hating Ray. "What happened?"

"Ah, she thought I was the most precious noble savage she'd ever had. And I do mean 'had.' She was bletherin' to her friends aboot me, what does a Scotchman—she couldna even get that right—wear beneath his kilt? Proper little bitch, she was."

"Ouch." Rebecca winced. How on earth had he ever gotten into a relationship like that to begin with? Galloping male hormones, probably.

Michael dropped his eyes to his cup. Rebecca rubbed her aching temples.

Jan and Peter returned, damp and disheveled, escorting the children. Mandy and Brian shone as if they'd been polished in their little robes emblazoned with Big Bird and Cookie Monster. "The urchins thought we were sending them to bed without any cake," Peter explained. "I think we have it all cleared up now."

Jan swathed the children with dish towels and gave them their rewards, which they proceeded to mash onto their clean faces. She plumped down beside Rebecca. "Should I ask what that phone call was about?"

"He got a card, supposedly from me, about vandals at Dun Iain."

"But the post isn't fast enough," Michael said.

"Spot on," said Rebecca. "Our mysterious prowler has become our mysterious poison pen. And I think . . ." She told them about Steve, Heather, and the extra earring. "Although how a kid like Steve could realize any money out of a decorative piece like the mazer I don't know. That's why I don't think we need to rush to report the earring. The mazer's probably gathering dust in his garage while he wonders what to do with it."

Michael swore softly under his breath. "So now we know."

Jan shook her head. "Not necessarily. Steve and Heather

could've been up there making out. You said you found the earring caught in the bedspread.''

"Makin' out?'' asked Michael. And then, "Oh, snoggin'.''

"Snogging?'' Peter queried.

"In my bed?'' Rebecca felt slightly queasy.

Michael shrugged. "People have probably died in that bed.
It's two hundred years old, at the least.''

Rebecca offered him a savage glare of her own. Jan smothered
a laugh.

"Maybe,'' said Peter, "I can see Steve and Heather committing vandalism, though theft is hard to swallow. And I'll allow
that it's rather gilding the lily to assume two different sets of
people were there that night. But I hate to jump to assumptions
about those kids just because they look like extras in a horror
movie. They've never been in trouble before.''

"And for Steve to write Ray,'' Michael said, "doesn't make
sense.''

Jan steepled her fingers in her most Sherlockian pose. "Look
at it from another angle. Who stands to gain from your not doing
your job?''

"James's will,'' answered Rebecca, "leaves the estate to any
relative who can be found before the January deadline, because
he was mad about paying such high taxes. If we don't get done
sorting everything out, then the relatives—or Ohio—get what's
left. But the state wouldn't go in for such skulduggery. And if
there're people who know they're related they would have stepped
forward by now; if they didn't know, how can they be plotting?''

Michael's teeth showed in a humorless grin. "And how does
Mr. Adler benefit from that wrinkle about the relatives?''

"The only way I can see him profiting,'' Peter said, "is to
charge for searching for the heirs. Hardly a scam. None of us
work for free.''

Rebecca put down her fork. Jan's pound cake was feeling like
just that, a pound of flour paste in her stomach. Couldn't get
away from the public or the private melodramatics long enough
for a friendly meal.

"I hate to say it, Rebecca,'' said Jan, "but as long as you're
being singled out I do wonder if it isn't Ray.''

"But plotting like that, picking locks, throwing things
around—it just isn't like him. He wouldn't break the glass on
his own picture!''

"Famous last words?" Michael inquired. "Oh, my, Mrs. Ripper, and little Jack was always so squeamish about blood."

"Michael!" protested Rebecca.

Unfazed, he went on, "Besides, I'm the one takin' away the most valuable things."

"Valuable to you," said Peter. "But ordinary things would help someone who just needs a little butter and egg money. The plant's had some cutbacks recently, and there're people around here who've run up pretty hefty debts."

Rebecca eyed him, mollified by his words. That was certainly that—he wouldn't be calling attention to himself if he were the guilty party. This was a democracy, let everyone in town be a suspect.

"Phil Pruitt," said Jan, "is on a disability pension from the plant—asthma, I think. That's how he and Steve can support themselves with part-time work at Dun Iain."

"Chuck and Margie Garst just bought that new house," put in Peter. "And with three kids, too. You know Dorothy's helping them out. I'd say housekeeping at Dun Iain must earn a prettier penny now than it did in Louise's day."

"Considering the fringe benefits?" Rebecca asked. "Warren did think some things had been stolen." And she said to herself, here we go round and round, digging ourselves in further and further, learning nothing.

Michael yawned. It was contagious—everyone yawned. Jan realized Brian had fallen asleep with his cheek pillowed on his cake while Mandy was industriously writing the alphabet by pressing crumbs onto the wall. The evening was over.

"Thank you, it's been wonderful," said Rebecca, piling her napkin on her plate. "I'm stuffed."

Michael snapped to attention, and without missing a beat said, "Oh, aye? And when did this happen?"

Rebecca groaned. Asked for that one—Freudian slip, indeed. "No fair," she said cordially, "hitting below the belt."

Michael lay back in his chair and howled. Jan and Peter looked as if they were ready to send for the butterfly nets until Rebecca explained, in a censored version suitable for Mandy's ears, just what that bit of slang meant on the far side of the Atlantic.

All too soon she had to hug Jan, Peter, and merciful normality goodbye. She crawled flinching into the frigid car where her breath and Michael's made little cumulus clouds against the windshield. They pulled away from the warm lights of the house, the car's engine stuttering like the chattering of Rebecca's teeth.

"Here," she said at the next corner. "All-night pharmacy. Let me get a new typewriter ribbon and a newspaper."

Obligingly Michael stopped, wondering aloud just why a chemist's shop would have typewriter ribbons. She ignored him, made her purchases, returned. The newspaper affirmed that the world had continued on its bloody path while her back was turned.

"Do you want to call Lansdale tomorrow, or shall I?" Michael asked.

"I will. I found the earring. Let's hope he can get some straight answers from Steve."

"Let's hope he can find the mazer. I suppose it's insured, but . . ."

"While a check is all very nice, it's no substitute." Rebecca tried to contract herself into her coat. By the time the heater warmed up the car, they'd be back at Dun Iain. Thank goodness she'd left some lights on.

Even her thoughts were cold, jostling in her mind like ice floes. Maybe she shouldn't have confided in Jan and Peter. Maybe she shouldn't have told Michael about the earring, about the postcard, about the Erskine letter.

But it was incredible that Michael could get a scam going in only a week. If he were a crook he was a lousy one, jumping down her throat whenever she mentioned the conjectural treasure. Unless he were acting suspicious as a cover for being suspicious.

As she glanced over at him he emitted a gaping yawn—he probably hadn't slept since he got here. He had no Roman nose for the lights of the dashboard to illuminate, just even features made remarkable by the strength of personality in the brows and mouth. And the clean line of his jaw had been sculpted, no doubt, by being so frequently jutted forward.

Why had he come here, anyway? He was hardly as idealistic as she'd first thought. The attraction of the artifacts, maybe. Or the attraction of outlandish America. Or to forget Sheila-bluidy-Fitzgerald. It was possible to escape a relationship, even though it meant leaping through a ring of fire so hot you carried scorch marks on your heart.

Michael concentrated on his driving, clinging doggedly to the right-hand side of the road, never suspecting he was being psychoanalyzed. The headlights of the Nova bit arcs from the road. The dim shapes of the trees slipped by on either side.

Rebecca's head fell forward. She caught herself, sat up straighter. Eric. Just to be fair, consider Eric. He'd readily admitted why some objects were missing; he had nothing to hide. Even if he was trying to milk as many fees as possible before the Dun Iain cow ran dry, well, no one could expect him to do cut-rate work.

Rebecca squirmed uncomfortably. Then there was Ray. Good old Ray.

Michael slowed and turned in the driveway. He leaned forward over the steering wheel. Rebecca pulled her coat tightly around her chest. The stars were only visible straight overhead, the trees on either side of the driveway blotting out the ones close to the horizon. They should be able to see the house. But it wasn't there. Only darkness loomed ahead. "No lights," said Michael quietly. "The electricity's gone oot. Or it's been turned off. How convenient, wi' the both o' us gone."

"But the new lock . . ." Rebecca's voice died away. And she had said so bravely to her gallant protector there on the roof, "I'm not going to run away just because the place makes me a little nervous." A little nervous? Her nervous system was shooting sparks like a Fourth of July Roman candle.

The headlights swept across the facade of the castle. It looked more secretive than ever, blank-faced, a black bulk in the starlight. The Nova stopped. Michael killed the lights and the engine. The trees stood shivering with the barest perceptible murmur, pressing as closely around the house as spectators at an accident.

"Do you want to go back to Jan's?" Michael murmured.

"Run away?" Rebecca steadied her voice. "Are you daft, man?"

Michael threw open his door, leaped out, slammed the door behind him. The ceiling light flashed like a flashbulb. The crash resounded across the lawn. Rebecca forced herself out her own side. In the darkness Michael's bulbous jacket and slender legs gave him the silhouette of a stork. "Surely you have a torch in your car."

"A flashlight? In the trunk." Rebecca fished out her keys, fumbled with the lock, retrieved the flashlight. "It's got fresh batteries."

"I widna be expectin' you to have stale ones." She gave a

weak laugh. Michael took the flashlight in his right hand. His left secured Rebecca's arm just above the elbow, his fingers squeezing so tightly through her coat and sweater that she grimaced. But she wasn't about to shake him off. "Unlock the door," he ordered, shining the light on the lock.

She unlocked the door. And it was locked—she noted that. She tucked the key ring into her left hand with the keys protruding between her fingers, the closest thing to a set of brass knuckles she could provide at the moment.

The grumble of the door's hinges could have been heard back in Putnam. A bird protested sleepily among the trees. "A' right, then," Michael said. "No exactly the Charge o' the Light Brigade, but it'll have to do."

"Just remember what happened to the Light Brigade," Rebecca whispered.

"Hush."

Together they stepped into the entry. No, the light switch just inside the door didn't work. The marble sarcophagus was a pale implication to the left. The stairway was a dark suggestion to the right. The narrow beam from the flashlight crept across the open doors of the sitting room and the kitchen, picking glints from objects inside. Rebecca wondered if she had gone suddenly deaf, the silence was so deep.

Something moved on the staircase. Blood surged in a sparkling tidal wave through Rebecca's head, roaring in her ears. Her windpipe stuffed itself with feathers. The keys fell from her hand and jangled harshly on the stone floor. So this is what fainting feels like . . .

Michael held her upright. "Dinna you dare!" He swung the unsteady pencil of light onto the staircase. Darnley sat on the center tread, front paws set primly side by side and wrapped with his tail, his eyes shining like tiger's-eye gems. Yes, his attitude seemed to say, May I help you?

"How did he get in?" demanded Michael.

Rebecca inhaled, clearing away blood and feathers both, and seized her wits like an acrobat seizing a trapeze. "Someone must have let him in." She turned, pulling Michael around with her. The two other keys still hung by the door. Not that that proved anything.

A tremendous clattering crash reverberated through the house. Darnley sprinted up the stairs. The light beam swooped wildly across the ceiling, down the walls, across Queen Mary's imperturbable features. "The pantry," Rebecca gasped. "The Royal Doulton. Do we really want to corner someone in there?"

Michael snarled, "We have to find oot what the bluidy hell is goin' on!"

Like Siamese twins they plunged into the kitchen. Automatically Rebecca reached for the light switch. The bank of fluorescent lights blazed out, blinding them both so that they recoiled and stood shielding their faces. "Damn!" said Michael.

Rebecca extricated her by now almost numb arm. Do it now, before you break . . . She threw open the pantry door.

The rows of dishes sat in their neat shrouded piles. Not even so much as a saucer was broken. The air in the tiny room was icy cold, turgid with the scent of lavender. A dim phosphorescence swirled against the ceiling. Maybe it was a face, eyes and mouth gouged, gaping holes in the flimsy light. Maybe it was just a luminescent cloud.

It was gone almost before Rebecca realized she'd seen it. Only the scent lingered. She wrapped her arms around herself, but that did nothing to quell the bone-racking shudder that shook her from head to toe.

Cracks widened in her mind, in her senses. Any port in a storm. Rebecca spun around and bounced off Michael's chest. Clutching a double fistful of his coat, her voice muffled by the fabric and the body beneath, she lost her grip on her wits and with one long scream fell into terror.

His arms tightened around her, crushing her. His voice, husky with fear, reverence, and a hint of hysterical mirth, worked its way in profane litany from A to Zed.

Darnley slipped in between them, inspected his empty dish, and meowed for his supper.

November

Chapter Thirteen

MICHAEL SHOVED ASIDE the stack of diaries and set his mug of tea on the kitchen table. He asked Rebecca, "Would you like a biscuit?"

"Not right now, thank you." She smoothed her pink dress across the bath towel she'd arranged on the counter and tested the iron to see if it was hot. "Anything you need pressed?"

"Why?" Michael settled down with his box of Walker's shortbread liberated from the specialty coffee shop in the mall. Maybe his offer of a cookie was her reward not only for refraining from helping while he laboriously counted out the price, but for commenting on how confusing American money was.

Rebecca grinned. "Why press anything? That's Jan's philosophy. When I asked if I could borrow the iron, she wasn't sure she had one."

"Intelligent woman, Jan." Michael shoved again at the diaries, gaining another inch or so of space.

The small clothes dryer whumped away in the corner of the kitchen. The pot of broth destined to be soup simmered on the range. Dorothy's vacuum cleaner whined like a giant bee through the upper reaches of the house, punctuated by the thuds of Phil's hammer. A vicious screech through the partly open window was Steve and his hedge clippers. Rebecca winced. But just because Steve and Heather had admitted trashing her room didn't mean either of them was capable of violence. Or even theft, for that matter.

Darnley trotted purposefully through the room, hoping that the odor of broth translated into food in his dish. Michael and

Rebecca, cookie and iron upraised respectively, watched him slip into the pantry and sniff beneath the shelves. Nothing jumped out at him.

Rebecca laid the iron down. "I really am sorry . . ."

"You've been apologizin' every day for the last month."

"I shouldn't have cracked up like that," Rebecca persisted. "Especially all over you." She imagined the jeers of her father and brothers—just like a girl, scaredy-cat. At least she was honest, unlike her mother, whose stiff upper lip was deeply seamed with stress fractures.

"And what was I doin'?" Michael asked. "Takin' a rise oot o' you? Hell, I was ready to pack it in, cut my losses, and push off home."

"No," said Rebecca, "you didn't make fun of me. I appreciate that." She hefted the iron again. It might make a good weapon against a living assailant, but there didn't seem to be any living assailants, not anymore. They were certainly getting Eric's money's worth out of the new lock on the front door—as she'd be sure to tell him when he picked her up for the concert tomorrow night. She ran the tip of the iron around the placket of the dress, nipping her fingertips with its heat.

Michael opened a drawer beneath the telephone and hefted an inexpensive palm-sized flashlight, one of the half dozen they had chipped in to buy at the Wal-Mart. "Well, we're ready for the bogles the next time."

"Don't give them ideas. It's been so peaceful around here. The dishes haven't done their crashing routine for at least a week, and it's been longer than that since the lights went squirrelly. Except for the cut-glass bottles—they were moved around again this morning."

"It'd be unusual to find them keepin' still," Michael said. "Like the footsteps. Those nights there were none, I started missin' them. Strange what you can live wi', when you must. A' this hokery-pokery, bogles or no."

Rebecca smiled. Michael's accent was as personable as his eyebrows. In moments of stress or excitement or, like now, domestic indolence, it thickened like syrup. She had a feeling he wouldn't be pleased if he realized how much his speech revealed of his still secretive inner self. "In other words," she said, "if you've made your bed, you have to lie in it."

"I intend to. No more nights in the recliner in the sittin' room."

Rebecca laughed. Now she could laugh. That night four weeks ago when they'd found the ghost, the apparition, the cold lavender-scented entity, neither of them could've laughed any more than they could have brought themselves to go upstairs—or to retreat into Putnam. They'd passed the bottle of Scotch back and forth, waiting for the lights to go out again and something horrible to leap out of the darkness. Only when dawn had thinned the threatening night had they staggered upstairs to find that not one single object had even been moved, let alone stolen. Their only visitors had been supernatural. Darnley must have gotten into the house through the tiny pantry window—assuming it had been left unlatched.

Michael gazed reflectively into his mug. "I suppose there's room in the hoose for Elspeth and James."

"The scent of lavender is Elspeth," said Rebecca. "So is the print on the bed, and probably the moving bottles. The footsteps and that shape in the window is James. I'd sure like to know why they're still here, instead of—well, disappearing onto another plane or whatever you do when you die." She arranged her dress on a hanger dangling from a cabinet doorknob.

"James might be guardin' the artifacts. Makin' sure they get to go back, like they wish. And do they ever wish!"

Rebecca glanced at him. "What got you this time? That curl of hair in the prophet's chamber?"

"Oh, aye. For a moment there I was ready to pick up that claymore and kill the nearest Englishman. Last time I felt like that I was pipin' 'Scotland the Brave' at Bannockburn."

"Swept up by Bonnie Prince Charlie's charisma, after all," she teased.

Michael snorted. "Can objects have charisma?"

"The ones here certainly do. Kind of like music, as you say—gut reaction. Like the background static you get on the radio. Always there, just louder at some times than others." She poured herself some tea, sat down, and accepted her cookie. Darnley settled on another chair and began grooming himself with little slurping licks.

"Aye, that's a good simile." Michael opened one of the diaries. He extracted the massive mausoleum key, laid it on the table, and inspected the photograph of the young woman labeled "Gemmell." "We finished the study and the prophet's chamber last week, and there wisna anything on your floor. The museum'll no be wantin' these—why are you lookin' at them?"

"For the Ohio State Historical Society. Remember—I wrote them last week. Actually got to use my typewriter."

"I was sure the Erskine letter would be in the study." He leafed through another volume. "Will you be far behind on your dissertation?"

"I don't have a schedule. And my dissertation director is the patient sort." A good thing, too; she'd started imagining her typewriter was looking at her in silent reproof. Frustrating to have laid so many plans around that letter and then not be able to find it. "Maybe when I get back to Dover, I'll write a best-seller about a haunted castle in Ohio. That was always one of Ray's get-rich-quick schemes, except his best-seller was going to be a hot and heavy romance about the affair between Jean-Paul Sartre and Françoise Sagan."

Michael looked up skeptically. "Aye?"

"Probably with the hot and heavy parts copied from *The Joy of Sex*," she added, and bit her tongue. That was a cheap shot at Ray. Eric didn't need a reference book to make her purr like Darnley. When he kissed the back of her neck, she wanted to roll belly-up, just like the cat. Not that she had—yet.

Michael struggled and failed to quell a grin, part amused, part exasperated, which escaped as a lopsided parody of itself. "Well, then, when you're makin' a fortune, remember I get ten percent to put my chin back together and to repair the claw marks in my anorak."

"That bruise on your chin is all healed, and your coat isn't damaged in the least," Rebecca retorted.

Michael didn't hear. He was staring at a loose sheet in the back of a diary. "Here you go—the Gemmells."

"Oh?" It was, she saw, a page out of a ledger book, dated 1912.

Michael pointed. "Expense sheet, see? John's handwritin'. Servant's pay packets. There's Louise—she was still Ryan then. And there's Rudolph Gemmell, butler, and Athena Gemmell, cook. Could this picture be Athena?"

"How old would you say this girl is—early twenties?" Rebecca took the photo. The dark eyes gazed impassively, almost resentfully, out at her. "Unless Athena was a child prodigy cook, she would've had to be at least in her thirties when this picture was taken. Nineteen twenties, isn't it?"

"Aye, that's flapper era, all right. Not that she looks as if she has much o' a taste for flappin'. Do you suppose she's the Gemmells' daughter?''

''That's it! James was sweet on her, but since she was the servant's girl, John didn't allow them to marry, and so she married someone else and he kept this picture all his life and never married himself!''

Michael pried her fingers from the photo and put it and the account sheet back in the diary. ''Save it for your book,'' he told her.

Rebecca laughed. The hedge clippers stopped abruptly and a thunderous hammering reverberated through the house. Michael and Rebecca started for the front door, only to encounter Dorothy already there. They exchanged a quick look—how long had she been in the entry listening to them talk? Not that they had anything to hide. But her insistence on having a finger in every conversational pie was more than a little irritating.

And the housekeeper was holding one of the extra keys that had been dangling from the hook beside the door ever since the lock had been changed. Rebecca grimaced; they'd already been over that.

Dorothy threw open the door to reveal the stocky form of Warren Lansdale outlined against the sunshine outside. Over his shoulder Rebecca caught a glimpse of Steve Pruitt warily eyeing the squad car. Not surprising that he hadn't enjoyed his ride to the Putnam Police Department, Heather beside him and his earring tucked away in Lansdale's pocket.

''Good morning,'' said the sheriff, his affable smile breaking through the underbrush covering his mouth. ''Sorry to interrupt your work.''

''They were taking a coffee break,'' Dorothy said. Her glasses glinted with reflected sunlight, and Rebecca couldn't see her expression.

''Mrs. Garst,'' she said, ''you won't be needing a key. Someone will always be here to let you in.''

''I've worked here for thirty years,'' replied Dorothy, as much to the air as to Rebecca. ''A lot longer than some people have. I've always had a key. Just like the world today, the experienced workers get no respect.''

Rebecca looked appealingly at Michael. It would take someone with a lot more brass than she to remind Dorothy that since no one but Michael and Rebecca herself had had keys, no one had broken in. But Michael, his brass suddenly tarnished, turned and clicked shut the door of the lumber room as if its being open a crack were of earthshaking importance.

"It's not that, Dorothy," Lansdale said, stepping into the breach. "It has to do with the division of the property, and the insurance, and James's will. Just legal red tape. You know, Eric explained it to you."

How clever! Rebecca thought. At the magic name, Dorothy's sour expression grew sugary, like oversweetened lemonade. She handed Rebecca the key. "Oh, of course. Not for us mere mortals, is it, to understand the law? Here, honey, you make sure Mr. Adler knows the key is safe."

Michael had been practicing his response-to-Eric poker face for some time now. He didn't turn a hair at that statement.

"Thank you," Rebecca told the older woman, and slipped the key into the pocket of her jeans. This time she would hide it.

Dorothy exuded an aroma of hair spray, stale cigarette smoke, and alcohol. "I already gave the other key to Phil," she continued. "You'd better go up and get it. If I can't have one, neither can he."

"I'll take care of it," said Rebecca.

"I don't need to be standing around here passing the time of day." Dorothy started up the staircase, carrying herself as though she were a porcelain vase that might break. Rebecca glanced after her curiously.

Warren hung his hat on Queen Mary's toes. Leaving the door open, Rebecca and Michael escorted him into the kitchen, seated him at the table, and offered him a soft drink. Michael opened a can of Coke, tossed an ice cube into a glass, poured. Rebecca took can and glass out of his hands, filled the glass with ice, handed them with a napkin to Warren. Michael put on his "Americans are crazy" expression and perched on the end of the cabinet. Warren eyed Michael's "Disarm today" T-shirt, assumed his "Europeans are nuts" face, moved aside the mausoleum key, and nodded his thanks to Rebecca.

"I take it," said Michael, "that if you'd had any news about the mazer you'd have said so by now."

"That's right. Afraid it's still missing. The Putnam police took out a warrant and searched both the Pruitts' and Heather Hines's houses. Sandra, her stepmother, had hysterics. But the mazer wasn't there. Neither was any dope."

Rebecca almost wished she hadn't told the sheriff about smelling marijuana on Steve, but she'd figured if she was coming clean, she might as well come spotless. "They haven't broken up the mazer, have they?" she asked, sitting down beside him.

"We wondered if they meant to sell it for scrap. But Chief Velasco in Putnam agrees with me—it's not that Steve and Heather are too dumb to know what to do with it, but too smart to take it to begin with. Especially Heather. You wouldn't know to look at her, but she's got more than air between her ears. She's still in school, and on the honor roll."

Lansdale stroked his moustache. "I've known these kids since they were babies. Pretty wild, yes. But they have no records. And Heather's only sixteen, a minor. Without finding the mazer actually on them, all we could do was slap them on the hands for tearing up your room, Miss Reid. Even if they've never really come up with much reason for picking on you. Maybe they had no reason—your room was there, like Mount Everest. My advice is to stop worrying about Steve and Heather and start looking for someone else."

Rebecca nodded. "Yeah, I know. There were two sets of male-factors in the house that night. That story is just unlikely enough to be likely."

"And there I was takin' a snooze in the sittin' room," Michael moaned.

Warren glanced speculatively at him. So it has occurred to him, too, that Michael might have taken the mazer himself. Just likely enough to be unlikely. "Surely you've decided to let Ray off the hook," said Rebecca.

"Well," Lansdale said apologetically, "you never can tell what someone will do when their emotions get in a tangle." He peered into his glass. Michael eyed the ceiling.

Rebecca hid her frown by getting up and pouring more hot water into the teapot. God, she hated airing her if not dirty at least slightly smudged linen in public. She hated having smudged linen to air. Michael and Warren had to be exchanging one of those knowing masculine looks behind her back. She wouldn't be surprised if even Darnley was smirking. She turned. Darnley was gone. Michael was swinging his feet back and forth like a child. Warren was inspecting the mausoleum key.

"I'm just an innocent bystander," Rebecca said, more testily than either man deserved. "Someone wants to get their hands on the artifacts, that's all. Money's a better motive than . . ." She almost said "sex," but swallowed the word in the nick of time. ". . . coming in from left field with all these theories about Ray," she concluded awkwardly.

Michael looked at her with his favorite analytical expression, as though she were a bacterium on a slide and he were peering at her through a microscope, safely removed from return inspection. "Left field?" he queried.

She explained the baseball analogy.

"I'm a Glasgow Rangers fan myself," he said. "Football—er—soccer."

Lansdale laughed. "Yes, I think we are going to have to eliminate Dr. Kocurek as a suspect. Have you heard from him recently?"

Despite her following up their conversation at Jan's house with a letter, Ray still fondly believed he could win her back. Rebecca felt as if she'd stepped on bubble gum in July. "Another sentimental greeting card last weekend. The most recent batch of flowers I gave Jan to take to Golden Age. I haven't talked to him, no."

"Has he gotten any more postcards?"

"Not that he told me. Just the three 'Visit Ohio' cards last month, typewritten, signed with a fair approximation of my signature. He did send them on to you."

"Oh, yes. He was very helpful, putting them in a cardboard-lined photograph mailer and everything."

"The package was postmarked Dover, was it?" Michael asked. Rebecca shot him an indignant glare, which he returned with a shrug.

"Yes," said Warren, "it was. And all of the cards were postmarked Putnam. I think we've pretty well proved he was never here, ever since we found that drifter Mrs. Sorenson saw outside the mall. He did look a lot like Dr. Kocurek, I'll admit."

Rebecca nodded. Giving Ray's picture to the police had been the low watermark of her month. When she'd gotten it back she'd burned it, full of remorse for ever suspecting him.

"The first card did predict the vandalism and the theft," the sheriff went on, "but the other two were frankly imaginary. One said there'd been a fire, the other something about more thefts."

"Who around here would have your signature to copy?" Michael asked.

"I wrote to Eric about coming here. I've been writing to Jan and Peter for years. I even wrote James Forbes after I first learned about Dun Iain, asking for information. Even though he never answered, my letter could still be here somewhere."

Warren made water rings across the table with the bottom of his glass. "And someone could have found one of your letters to the Sorensons in the trash, for example."

"Dorothy said something about Slash tearing open garbage bags. But to take a letter from the trash argues an awful lot of premeditation, doesn't it?"

"Maybe that's what we're supposed to think," said Michael darkly. "You thought some things had really been stolen, Sheriff. What about Dorothy?"

Lansdale made a dismissive gesture. "Don't worry about Dorothy. Her bark's a lot worse than her bite."

"The cards, then?" asked Rebecca.

"We don't know that who took the mazer had anything to do with the cards."

"Occam's razor," muttered Michael. At the sheriff's puzzled look he explained, "The simplest explanation is the most likely—the same person did both the theft and the cards."

Warren drained his glass, the ice cubes tinkling together. He delicately wiped his moustache. Rebecca's dress turned slowly in the draft. The place always has a draft, she thought. Funny little breezes licking the back of her hypersensitive neck.

Steve sauntered in the door. The only indication that he was aware of the three pairs of eyes watching him was his exaggeratedly relaxed walk. He got a glass, ran water in it, drank, sauntered out.

"I'm sorry, Miss Reid," said Warren as Steve's footsteps passed through the entry and out the front door. "I know this has been real upsetting for you. But until something else happens, we're just going to have to leave it where we are now. Not that anything else should happen. Chances are you'll be able to finish out your work in peace and quiet."

"I hope so," said Rebecca.

Michael leaped down and headed for the door. "Speakin' of which, all I've done the day is turn out some cabinets."

"I'd better be going, too," Warren said. "Keep me posted." Rebecca escorted him to the door and stood watching him drive away.

The sunlight of the cool Indian-summer morning was so rich she could almost gather it in her hands. She'd have to collect Michael and go for another walk. On yesterday's jaunt into the woods they'd found an old mill; after exploring that for an hour she'd had to wash her Nikes. But all Michael had had to do, grinning condescendingly, was hose down his wellies.

Steve was raking the drifts of sodden red leaves into piles on the lawn. If Rebecca squinted she could make out the interstate, the cars moving pricks of light beyond the bare branches of the trees. Odd how at night the headlights from the farm road outside the gates would reflect on the dovecote. She'd seen it several times now.

Darnley prowled through the bare sticks tufted with an occasional orange petal that had been the marigolds. Slash sniffed around the mausoleum. Wouldn't it be nice to be an animal, Rebecca thought, and have no worries?

Slash spotted Darnley, emitted a bass woof, and churned his long legs into a gallop. Darnley jumped straight up, spun in midair, and streaked for the house. Rebecca danced out of his way. On second thought, she told herself, at least she wasn't in peril of her life. She slammed the door in Slash's face, locked it, and went back into the kitchen for her dress.

Chapter Fourteen

REBECCA TOOK HER dress to her room and collected her own spiral notebook filled with notes and sketches. If she didn't have the Erskine letter, she could at least study Mary's needlework, letters from contemporaries, and Rizzio's guitar with its odd harmonic of memory. Her dissertation wasn't on the letter specifically, after all, but on the Queen of Scots's role in sixteenth-century politics. And yet she needed bells and whistles, like the proof of King James's ancestry one way or the other.

Michael was sitting cross-legged on the carpet in the large fourth-floor bedroom, leafing through a photograph album. The shorter strands of his hair framed his face that in contemplation seemed less sharply angled; the longer strands lay with deceptive softness over the neckband of his shirt.

Dorothy was in the fifth-floor bedroom fluffing the haunted pillow so forcefully she must've been trying to exorcise the impression of Elspeth's body. On the sixth floor Phil was replacing a bit of wood paneling that had shrunk away from the bricks of the fireplace. "I'll paint it tomorrow," he told Rebecca. "By January it should blend right in."

"Looks great," she told him. And, with a deep breath, "Mr. Pruitt, I'm afraid Dorothy wasn't supposed to give you a key to the front door."

He blinked at her, giving her no help.

"What with all the legal considerations," she blundered on, "only Michael and I can have keys. So if I could have yours back again, please."

Wordlessly Phil pulled a key chain from his pocket and detached the door key. Dangling from the chain was a plastic photo holder displaying a picture of a chubby-faced baby and a woman with the straight, parted hair of the late sixties. The mysterious Mrs. Pruitt and Steve, no doubt. "Thank you," Rebecca said, and put the key into her pocket with the one she'd wrested from Dorothy.

"Miss Reid," Phil began. He glanced at his worn workboots, jangling the key chain. "Miss Reid, was that the sheriff downstairs?"

"Yes."

"Has he found that fancy cup thing yet?"

Rebecca took a step backward; he should've been staring resentfully at her. She'd called the police down on his son and a search party into his home. "No," she said, and added, "Warren doesn't think Steve took it."

"He didn't. But if the boy needs to make some restitution for what he did to your room . . ." Phil ducked again, embarrassed but forcing himself to see it through.

Rebecca visualized Washington with his little hatchet, "Papa, I cannot tell a lie." "No," she said. "That's all over and done with."

He looked up. Those basset hound eyes made her feel like he'd caught her pushing old ladies into gutters and stealing candy from babies. "He was just playing a prank. He and his little friend—they didn't mean no harm. Kids will be kids, you know. He wouldn't hurt no one. He didn't saw through that chair. I showed it to the officers who came to the house." He stopped for breath, an entire paragraph of speech almost too much for him.

"It's all over and done with," she repeated, wising desperately for something she could say that would comfort the man.

Unless Phil was acting, burbled that irritatingly analytical part of her mind. He could be attacking with pathos before he could be attacked with facts. Maybe he was plotting with Steve, or with Dorothy, or with little green men from Mars. "Thank you," Rebecca said, and rushed for the staircase.

Dorothy was arranging the cut-glass bottles. Michael hadn't budged. Rebecca returned to the kitchen, gave the broth a quick stir, and pulled the laundry from the dryer. She put the door keys in the drawer beneath the phone.

The diaries sat on the table. If she stopped to read them, on the off chance they mentioned the Erskine letter, she wouldn't be working on anything else. If Michael found the letter, he'd give it to her, if only so he could strut his knowledge.

There was the book with the photograph and the ledger sheet. There was the one that contained the scrap in James's handwriting she had found in the desk: "—ever problem you are having you have brought upon yourself. I cannot help you any more than I already have. Your threats are . . ."

What was not there was the key to the mausoleum.

Rebecca stood, her hands on her hips, staring at the tabletop. She bent and studied the floor. Neither offered any answers. Warren had been looking at the key. Michael had left the room first. She'd shut the door behind Warren and had seen both Phil and Dorothy upstairs. Steve had only been in the kitchen when they were there, too, and that was the only time the front door had been left open all day. She hadn't the foggiest idea whether the key had been there when she came in to get her dress.

Michael might have taken the key. So might Warren. But why? Eric had said, "If anyone breaks into the mausoleum, we'll know we have a bunch of weirdos on our hands."

Rebecca shoved the chairs against the table. First thing to do was to ask Michael. Then—well, she'd already included Warren on her list of suspects, just on general principles. For all she knew Dorothy and Warren were really Heather's parents, or were conspiring to sell her into white slavery, or had manufactured both Heather and Steve in some basement laboratory.

She was suddenly very aware of being the outsider. "I knew it'd been too quiet around here," she said aloud, "like the calm before the storm." She stamped out of the room and up the stairs.

Michael was surrounded by scrapbooks, folders bulging with papers, a mail gauntlet, a miniature of Mary of Guise, and a cream pitcher shaped like a cow. "Guess what?" called Rebecca as she strode into the room.

He looked, his expression partly annoyed, partly amused, but not at all surprised. "I'd really rather not."

"The key to the mausoleum is gone." Rebecca cleared several squashed cardboard boxes from the bed and sat down. "I don't suppose you took it."

Michael look at her with his patented guileless gaze. "I don't suppose I did. Did you?"

"Then why would I be asking you about it?" He shrugged, as if to say her plots were unfathomable. She really ought to be flattered, she reflected wryly, that at least someone suspected her of having a plot. "Did you see either Phil or Dorothy go downstairs?"

"Neither of them came down these stairs, at the least."

"Maybe Warren took the key."

"Maybe he wants to keep it safe. We've no good record about the keys here, mind you. And his friend James is planted there in the doocot."

True enough. Rebecca said, "Did you get the impression he was trying to cover up for Steve and Heather, not to mention Dorothy?"

"He's known the kids since they were weans, and he's probably an old school pal of Dorothy's. Why shouldn't he protect them? As long as he's told them to leave us alone, he can do what he wants wi' them."

Rebecca exhaled. "All right. Say I stop wondering why they picked on me and let it go. What about the mazer?"

"Let Lansdale and Adler decide," Michael said. "They're the ones responsible. We only have—what? Six or seven weeks left to go through this mixtie-maxtie. The museum is keen on gettin' it all, not just the mazer."

"But we're missing another key. What next? Is the mysterious perpetrator going to back a U-Haul up to the door and cart away Mary's sarcophagus? Has he or she already found and absconded with the Forbes treasure and the Erskine letter?"

"Come off it. The museum'll no be wantin' the sarcophagus. There is no treasure, and there's no guarantee there's a letter."

"So you have it all compartmentalized?" asked Rebecca. "You worry about your own territory, let everyone else worry about his?"

He offered her his sweetest, most irritatingly condescending smile. "You're always tongue-waggin' about me doin' my job. So I'm doin' it."

"Give me the pip, why don't you?" Rebecca demanded.

"I'm no chargin' you for it, am I?" His smile broadened into a grin, every gleaming tooth a testament to the British National Health Service.

She bounced to her feet, stalked out of the room and up the stairs. As soon as she was around the bend in the stairwell she stopped, swearing and laughing at the same time. Such confrontations were as much a part of the background static as the undercurrent of the supernatural. Their skirmishes always ended the same way, a cloud of dust and verbiage but no conclusion. She had to admire him for protecting his territory so fiercely.

So they'd inadvertently glimpsed the vulnerable bellies hidden beneath each other's spiky shells. She hadn't had enough glimpses beneath his shell to keep her from wondering if it also concealed harassment, embezzlement, and theft. Michael had said he'd been frightened enough that night in the pantry to cut his losses and push off home. But what losses did he have to cut? His job at the museum was waiting. Unless he expected some greater return on his investment of time and energy than a visit to the United States.

Rebecca walked on past the fifth floor and John Forbes's painted glare. Probably it was simply the same obstinacy that had made her persevere through the alarms and excursions of her first days here that had kept Michael here, too. His pride would never let him return to the museum empty-handed.

"What is it?" said Dorothy from the sixth floor, and Rebecca jumped.

Phil said, "A loose brick. A hidey-hole. I'll go tell them."

"No, keep your voice down. Let's see what's in it first."

"What if it's some kind of artyfact thing?"

"What they don't know won't hurt them," said Dorothy.

Time for reinforcements. Rebecca was not the only outsider here. She skimmed back down the stairs and into the bedroom. "Phil's found a secret cache in the fireplace," she said to Michael. "Want to see?"

He dumped the scrapbook and was out of the room so quickly he would've mashed her against the door frame if she hadn't dodged. She clung to his heels all the way up the stairs.

The ballroom's white walls and pale hardwood floor glistened in the sunlight. A cold draft moved like a sluggish ocean current about ankle height. As usual, Elspeth's window was open. The air was fresher now that Phil had fixed the windows and cleared away the birds' nests in the tiny room below the platform. Now the occasional blackbird coasted by the ballroom windows, its beady eyes staring indignantly but futilely inside.

Dorothy stood in front of the fireplace, arms crossed, a dust rag dangling from one hand. Phil squatted, prying at a brick about two feet above the hearth. It inched painfully away from its neighbors with a shrill sound like chalk scraping across a blackboard.

Rebecca said, "Can you get it out?"

Dorothy spun around, her hand clutching at her heart, eyes bulging.

"I was just outside on the stairs," Rebecca said, tempted to imitate Michael's sweetly condescending expression. Michael himself bent, his hands resting on his knees, so close to Phil that he almost got an elbow in the eye. The fringe of his hair hung over his face, but Rebecca was ready to swear his expression was more intense than simple curiosity.

With a patter of dust Phil levered the brick far enough away from the others so that his fingers could get a grip on it. He jerked it out. He and Michael bumped heads looking into the aperture. Dorothy craned over their shoulders. Rebecca hung back, arms crossed, toe tapping on the floor.

Michael reached into the hole. He extracted a string of beads and a crumpled piece of paper. Dorothy took the paper from his hand and smoothed it out on the mantelpiece. It was an advertisement from a magazine of the turn of the century, an elegantly dressed woman touting soap.

Michael blew on the beads and rubbed them with the hem of his shirt. Flakes of red paint adhered to the fabric. "Cheap clay," he pronounced. "For these you could've bought New York, back when prices were somewhat less." He tossed the beads to Rebecca, turned on his heel, and walked away.

The necklace was cold and gritty. A toy, probably, stuffed behind the loose brick with the picture in some childish magic ritual. Louise was an adolescent when she first worked here, and had probably lived in the rooms just off the ballroom. "May I have the clipping?" Rebecca asked Dorothy.

Dorothy, her face curdled with something Rebecca suspected was disappointment, handed it over. She turned to inflict her dustcloth on the closest piece of furniture. Phil laid the brick on the hearth. "I'll bring some mortar tomorrow and fix it," he said tonelessly.

Rebecca nodded. Glancing sharply at Dorothy's back, swathed in a shapeless pink sweater, she headed for the stairs. "What they don't know won't hurt them," the housekeeper had said. Very helpful. What weren't they supposed to know—about items listed but missing from the house?

Just as Rebecca walked past the fourth floor the phone rang. Michael reached out of his room to answer it. "Hello? Aye, she's here. It's your boyfriend," he told her, holding out the receiver.

She said to him, "I thought you didn't believe in the Forbes treasure. Your body language speaks better English than you do, you know.''

His eyes flashed, his lips thinned, his chin snapped up like a shield. She ducked toward the staircase, calling, ''Hang up the phone in just a minute, please.'' No Forbes treasure, huh? Not that it mattered whether he believed in it or not, but his inconsistency was unsettling.

Leaving the necklace and the clipping in her room, she picked up the phone in the kitchen. An emphatic click on the line assured her that Michael had not only hung up the extension, he'd probably slammed it through the table. ''Hello!'' she said.

''What was all that about?'' said Eric's velvet baritone.

''What was what about?''

''Something about the Forbes treasure speaking English.''

''No, no. Michael's always been adamantly against there being any such thing as a treasure, and then when Phil finds a loose brick upstairs he practically tramples me to get there. All it was, was a cheap necklace and an old ad. Louise's, I bet.''

''We'll ask her on Sunday, at her birthday party,'' Eric said. ''So Campbell is doing his 'dog in the manger' routine? I tell you, he's up to something.''

''Well, he's damned lousy at it, whatever it is.''

Eric laughed. The sound smoothed Rebecca's feathers. The last time she'd seen Eric was last Saturday night when they'd returned to Dun Iain after visiting two other castle follies near West Liberty. They'd sat under this castle's enigmatic facade, the lamp beside the door and the window of her room shining, the stars cold and still overhead, until the car windows were opaque with the steam of their breaths.

She'd gone inside glowing with pleasure and frustration. Fortunately Michael hadn't stayed up, honing his armory of snide remarks and amused glances, to see her blouse misbuttoned. Well, it had been dark in the car, Eric's sturdy hands had done their best—which was very good indeed. She was always embarrassed after such an encounter, not during. Like indulging in a sophisticated meal and then getting indigestion.

Eric was saying something about the mazer. ''Oh,'' Rebecca replied, grateful he couldn't see how hot her cheeks were, ''Warren's already been here. Nothing this week at all about the mazer, about the cards, about anything. Except that now the mausoleum key is gone.''

''What?''

"I put the key into one of the diaries, and had that one in the kitchen when Warren was here, and now the key's gone. I'm afraid it looks like Warren took it, although I guess Dorothy or Phil or Michael could've rushed down the stairs when my back was turned. Not that Dorothy or Phil knew the key was here."

Eric said, "Great. Now what? I'll call Warren about the key and tell you about it tomorrow night. Five o'clock?"

"Yes, with bells on. I even ironed my dress, I'll have you know. I haven't been to a real symphony concert in ages."

"You'd look lovely in a gunnysack, Rebecca." She smiled; that was a line, but she enjoyed swinging on it. He went on, "I thought we'd go to a special place to eat. My condo. I'm pretty good with a wok, if you don't mind my cooking Chinese for you."

Rebecca's chest went fuzzy. She leaned against the cabinet, trying to keep herself from hyperventilating with trepidation or delight or both. They were going to his place. She'd have to wear the lacy teddy that had survived the night of the vandals . . . God, she was acting as if going to bed with the man was as casual as ordering dessert; I'll have one silver-tongued lawyer, please, with a dusting of habeas corpus. Giddily she asked, "You can cook?"

"I refuse to live on fast food and TV dinners. I thought something out of the ordinary would be in order since I have to leave town for a few days next week. I've finally turned up something about Rachel Forbes."

Grateful he'd changed the topic—chicken, she said to herself—she asked, "Have you contacted Rachel's children?"

"No," he answered, "I don't do séances. John was born in 1847, remember? And since Rachel was the older of the two, I'll be lucky if I find her grandchildren still alive."

"I should've figured that out." Rebecca sternly ordered her corpuscles to stop doing backflips through her brain. "Where are you going?"

"Nebraska. A Rachel Forbes Dennison is listed in the census for 1890. I'll have to hit several county seats, checking property records and that type of thing. Every other courthouse has had at least one major fire that's wiped out the relevant information."

A horn honked outside. "Oh! Eric, the Sorensons are here. Peter's going to do some work for Phil and they brought the kids along. I have to run."

"And I'm doing lunch with the district attorney. Keep me posted if anything comes up. I'll check with Warren about the key. See you tomorrow."

"I can hardly wait." She hung up, wondering whether she could wait or not. Anticipatory fantasy was so enjoyable it might be difficult for reality to compete. Reality did have its hard edges.

One of reality's harder edges, Michael Campbell, strolled into the kitchen. "The Sorensons are here. Steve's puttin' the Hound of the Baskervilles into the shed. Wi' no good grace, but I doot he has his orders."

Rebecca nodded abstractedly. She leaned against the counter, smoothing the tousled edges of her libido with little strokes of self-discipline. Michael began cutting vegetables into the pot of broth. A good thing he hadn't heard her exclaiming over Eric's ability to cook when he'd been capably shouldering his share of the cooking duties all this time. Even though she did have to dump pepper into everything but the raspberry trifle.

A tap-tap-tapping sounded from the entry. Poe's raven, no doubt . . . Rebecca wrenched herself into coherence. That's right, she'd left the door locked, fending off vandals in U-Haul trailers. She hurried into the entry, absurdly grateful for Jan, someone she'd known for ten whole years.

Chapter Fifteen

THE SORENSONS LOOKED refreshingly like Beaver Cleaver's next-door neighbors. Jan had a firm hand on the back of each miniature T-shirt; Mandy's sported a unicorn, Brian's read "Here Comes Trouble." The children's scrubbed faces peered upward at the height of the castle.

"Thank you for coming out on a weekday," said Phil, clomping down the staircase. "I want to fix the stain on the ceiling tomorrow so the plaster can dry over the weekend."

"No problem," Peter returned, hoisting his toolbox. "I had some comp time." The men went off talking about wiring and water damage.

Rebecca left the door gaping and settled with Jan on the stone wall where she had first seen Darnley. The children chased a ball across the lawn. Steve crept around the side of the building, rake held like a halberd over his shoulder. Slash whined, his feelings hurt, in the toolshed. Dorothy shook her dust rag out of a fifth-floor window.

And there was Darnley himself, ejected through the front door. "Get on wi' you," Michael said to him. "You'll no be gettin' the soup bone quite yet." Then, going back inside, "Aye, I'll take it down."

"How are you getting along with yon braw lad?" Jan asked. "Been listening to the tapes he lent you?" returned Rebecca.

Jan grinned, producing a couple of Battlefield Band cassettes from her duffel bag of a purse. "It's contagious. You should hear me when we're at Peter's grandparents in Minnesota. Ya, it's a fine lutefisk, huff da," she said, perfectly mimicking a Norwegian accent.

Rebecca laughed, and answered Jan's question. "Amazing—if I'd said to my brothers some of the things I say to Michael, I'd have been mincemeat. That wee tartan chip on his shoulder can take it as well as dish it out."

"Sounds as if you can be honest with him."

"I guess so. The question is whether or not he's being honest with me."

Jan tilted her head curiously. "At least his chip isn't a giant four-leafed green one. Louise got a letter the other day from a group in Belfast wanting money from Americans with Irish ancestry. For Irish orphans, they said, but I told her to forget it, they were probably buying guns to create more orphans."

Brian and Mandy linked hands and sang, "Ring around a rosy, pockets full of posies, ashes, ashes, we all fall down." They collapsed giggling onto the lawn.

"Didn't I hear once," said Jan, "that that song is really a grim little ditty about people dying of the pox or something equally nasty? You now, the rosy ring is the rash, and you leave flowers on a grave, and it's really 'achoo, achoo, we all fall down dead.' "

"Yeah, I heard something like that, too. Except I thought it was the Black Death, and it really was ashes, because they had too many bodies to bury so they burned them. And the Great Fire of London in 1666 finally wiped out the Plague—there, at least."

Jan shrugged. "Whatever. The point is that nothing is really what it seems to be, nursery rhymes or anything else."

"You can say that again," replied Rebecca, with a sideways glance at the inscrutable face of the castle.

Michael appeared in the doorway, carrying the claymore from the prophet's chamber. He struck a pose, declaiming, "Once more into the breach, for Charlie, Scotland, and Saint Andrew!"

The children goggled at him. Rebecca laughed. Jan applauded. Michael lowered the sword and rested its tip on the ground. "How'd they carry these things about? No wonder they adapted so quickly to firearms."

Jan called, "He who lives by the sword dies by the sword."

"I'm no livin' wi' one," Michael returned. "I'm takin' it to the ballroom, so Peter'll no drop the ceilin' on it." He vanished into the house.

"Honestly," Rebecca said, "every time I'm ready to roast him over a slow fire he about-faces and does something appealing. His bad moods blow over instantly. But then, so do his good ones."

The children, scratching their heads dubiously at the weirdness of adults, swarmed forward demanding food and drink. "I got some animal crackers yesterday," Rebecca told them. "Come on in the kitchen."

Jan resumed her clutch of their T-shirts. Rebecca left the tapes in the sitting room and explained that the pile of cloth and polished wooden tubes on Michael's chair was a set of great Highland pipes under renovation. "The reeds came in the mail last week," she concluded.

Jan plunked the children at the kitchen table and started counting out the cookies. "What smells so good?"

"Michael's making soup. With garlic and onions, even. He thought the mustard and catsup on the Whoppers we ate the other day was spicy but no bad."

"Went to Burger King, huh? Dutch—or should I say Scotch—treat, I suppose. You're really big spenders."

"Neither of us has money to heat up, let alone burn."

"Speaking of money to burn," Jan said, "Eric was telling me out at Golden Age that he took you to the Velvet Turtle last week. Wow! For the price of a meal there I could have that new living room suite."

"Not quite," replied Rebecca. "But I've never seen so much silverware. I kept waiting until Eric chose a piece and then I picked up the same one. I figure if he can rise above his humble origins, so can I."

"And what do you two have planned for this weekend?"

Oh. Rebecca blushed, tried to duck, and turned positively scarlet. Either she was going to have to learn better self-control, she told herself in disgust, or wear a ski mask all the time.

Mandy and Brian began clamoring for the bathroom. Jan herded them up the stairs and past the study, where Phil's and Peter's earnest voices were interrupted by the patter of falling plaster. She deposited Brian in Rebecca's bathroom just as Dorothy came down the stairs. The housekeeper had already lit a cigarette and trailed smoke like a crashing plane. "I don't know how I'm supposed to keep this place tidy," she said without preamble, "when things are piled on the floor. Mr. Forbes would never have approved of his things being left on the floor. He was very particular, believe me."

"We won't damage anything," Rebecca assured her yet again.

"Thirty years I've worked here." Dorothy went on down the next flight of stairs, her monologue trailing like the smoke behind her. Mandy coughed.

"Last month," Rebecca said to Jan, "she was asking why James didn't throw out all this junk and get some nice things from Wal-Mart."

"She's probably going to be out of a job soon. After thirty years you'd expect her to be a little possessive."

"Oh, yes," stated Rebecca. "You're sure Dorothy was a flaming youth back in the fifties? She certainly flamed out."

Jan laughed. "All right, explain that blush. What do you have planned with Eric? An intimate dinner at his condo?"

Rebecca made a throwaway gesture. "It seems like a good idea."

"I'll bet it does. He's a charmer, isn't he? I've been wondering about you two—I mean, you've always been so cautious about relationships. Ray must've worked on you for ages before . . . Oh, I'm sorry."

Brian came out of the bathroom and Mandy went in. The little boy started up the stairs while the women played goalie at the bottom. "It's nothing I haven't thought about," Rebecca assured Jan. "When you grow up hearing your brothers talk about women as if they were baseball diamonds, you get a bit apprehensive. Ray never hounded me, he was just there. Eric's not hounding me, either, even though he does come on a lot stronger."

"He has his talents, definitely." Jan peered upward. Her son had disappeared around the bend. "Brian?"

"I'll check on him." Halfway up the stairs Rebecca heard Brian's voice in James's old bedroom, not words, just the bright polite tone the boy used when speaking to adults. Who was he talking to? Michael's footsteps loped down the stairs above her, returning from stowing the claymore.

Brian stood in the middle of the room, alone, looking at the rocking chair. He must've just climbed out of it; it was rocking gently. He turned as Rebecca entered and said gravely, "The man's scared."

"What?"

"The man's scared."

The nape of Rebecca's neck chilled. Michael rounded the angle of the staircase and she gestured at him to keep quiet. "Who's scared?"

Brian pointed at the chair. It rocked twice more, then stopped. "That man there. The old man, like Great-grandpa."

Rebecca shot a sharp significant glance at Michael. He blinked. She asked Brian, "How do you know the old man was scared?"

"He said," the child answered, " 'no, don't push me, help.' "

"Don't push me," Rebecca repeated. God Almighty. Don't push me.

Michael muttered something that was either Gaelic or profanity, and added, "The wean's scared o' the staircase, Rebecca."

"Yeah, that's it. Just an imaginary situation. Kids don't have preconceived ideas of how things should be." No, children see things the way they are. They speak to ghosts, and we only hear their steps. I only saw James the once, before I started watching for him.

Michael shied away. "The weans brought a ball, did they? I'll get the broom from the kitchen and teach them to play shinty. Show Jan yon scrapbooks. Photos o' the old days."

"Okay," said Rebecca. She stood, fixed to the floor, while Michael ushered Brian down the stairs, collected Mandy, sent Jan up. That's all they needed, she told herself, to imagine that poor James had been murdered. On the garbled evidence of a three-year-old. Even Eric would be laughed out of court with nothing better than that.

"I'm hallucinating," Jan announced. "I thought I heard a bachelor say he wanted to play with my kids."

"He misses his nephews," explained Rebecca.

"You sure are pale. Did you run into one of the local ghosts?"

Rebecca forced a laugh. "Brian was talking to some imaginary playmate. Gave me a chill, that's all. This place does get on your nerves."

"He does that all the time." Even so, Jan looked over her shoulder. "It is kind of chilly in here. Michael said you had some pictures to show me?"

"Yeah, sure." Shaking herself, Rebecca opened the top scrapbook.

The first photograph was of a garden scene. John and Elspeth sat in lawn chairs at the side of the castle. Beside them the child James in his sailor hat and short pants clutched a disgruntled ancestor of Darnley's. John's face was that of a hawk, beady-eyed, stern, and keen. Elspeth was smiling, a coquettish laugh frozen in time, her eyes turned toward the man standing behind her. He wore a black suit and was proffering a tray with a cup and saucer on it. His dark good looks were no less keen, but much warmer. He, too, was laughing, secretly.

"Ooh," said Jan. "How'd you like to have that for a butler? The man looks like Valentino. And he knows it, too."

"So does Elspeth—look at the way she's eyeing him. And she was so much younger than John. I bet he was jealous of her."

"If he was he kept it quiet. Louise says he lived for the opinions of his neighbors. We'll ask her if there's any juicy gossip from back then."

"Great." Rebecca turned the page. There was a casual picture of the girl in the studio photograph, the dark face younger but no less petulant. "Katherine Gemmell (Katie)," read James's neat handwriting. "There's a formal picture of her in a diary," she told Jan. "So she is the Gemmells' daughter. There goes my story of a tragic love affair between her and James."

"Why?"

Rebecca laughed. "I only had time to glance at the diaries, but I do remember references to a 'KG.' And they weren't flattering. Apparently she took advantage of the expansion of female horizons in the twenties and did some work as an actress. James disapproved."

"A man of his generation would."

"Afraid so." Jan and Rebecca sat turning the pages, wandering among the static images of long ago. Athena Gemmell, it turned out, was a plain, rather dour woman with a white apron. Pairing her with the elegant Rudolph was like mating a pigeon to a falcon, Rebecca thought. I'd be dour, too.

Michael's and the children's shouts echoed from the lawn, Phil's hammer tapped away downstairs, and Dorothy's vacuum cleaner emitted its banshee wail. Some time later Peter called, "Jan? We need to be going." Just as Rebecca closed the album she caught a faint whiff of lavender. If Brian were here, would he start talking to the beautiful lady?

Jan was already out the door. Rebecca followed precipitately. They and Peter met Michael on the main staircase. He was flushed and out of breath, and the wind had made the shorter strands of his hair stand on end. "The bairns're pettin' the moggie," he said to Jan, and as her face registered alarm, amended, "The cat."

"Oh," Jan said. "Poor little critter. I'd better go rescue it."

"Here," said Peter, pulling a wrinkled, legal-sized envelope out of his pocket. "This was under the desk. Just saw a corner of it when I was packing my tools. Fell off the top, I guess, maybe months ago."

Rebecca took the envelope. The paper was grainy with dust. It was sealed, but nothing was written on it, even though some kind of paper was inside. "Probably soup-can labels or coupons for candy bars," she said. "I've found both in that desk. Thanks, anyway."

She laid the envelope on Queen Mary's marble bodice as they trooped out onto the lawn. Darnley had managed to escape Brian's and Mandy's attentions and was disappearing into the dovecote, the children in hot pursuit.

Jan, Peter, and Rebecca followed the children around the side of the dovecote to its alternate, paradoxical face. Here, on the north side of the structure, the bright afternoon winked out and they plunged into shadow. Brian, unperturbed by the grim ambience of the place, ran up and down the steps while Mandy knocked on the door of the tomb calling "Anybody home?"

Jan snatched her away. "What if somebody answers?"

That was a real possibility, Rebecca thought. Every time she'd come out here she'd had that same sense of being watched, although never as intensely as the first time. Maybe if James's and Elspeth's spirits still moved in the house, John's was trapped in the mausoleum, his raptorial gaze fixed on his part-whimsical, part-lunatic castle, waiting possessively for his family. She looked narrowly at the lock. No new scratches. Whoever had the key hadn't used it.

Back in the sunlight Michael was putting Peter's toolbox into the Sorensons' station wagon. The adults strapped the children into the car and said their goodbyes. "Keep me posted," whispered Jan to Rebecca. "About Eric, you know." She grimaced, attempting a lascivious leer. But her good-natured features simply couldn't achieve such an expression.

Rebecca ignored her implication and called, "See you at Louise's party Sunday," as they drove away and disappeared.

Michael said from the corner of his mouth, "That's all right, sweetheart, I counted the silver."

"That's the worst Bogart imitation I've ever heard." Rebecca retorted. "Where do you get off going through Peter's things, anyway?"

He looked at her indignantly. "I thought everyone was a suspect in this little caper. Includin' you and me."

"But they're my friends!"

With a pitying smile Michael shrugged and turned away.

Today Dun Iain was wearing its guise of fairy-tale castle. The afternoon sun slanted through the bare branches, turning the beige harl of the castle to rose and gilding the roofs and dormers. Even the telephone and electricity lines shimmered like dewy spiderwebs where they looped through the trees. The resident ogre, Steve, materialized from wherever he had been lurking and let Slash out of the shed. The dog cavorted around him like some grotesque shadow, then sped off into the trees. The white mail truck advanced up the driveway.

Michael took the mail, handed it to Rebecca, and stood chatting with the young, blond mail carrier. Ever since the woman's first encounter with the blue eyes and the enticing accent, she'd started bringing virtually everything up to the house. Today it was a package. Rebecca would have recognized those precise letters printing her address as Ray's even if the postmark hadn't been Dover.

With a sigh she flipped through the letters. Several ads, an official-looking envelope addressed to James Forbes from the Bright Corporation, and a note from Rebecca's oldest brother, Kevin. Or from his wife, to be exact. Her family, steady and virtuous people, hadn't the foggiest comprehension why she was spending three months at an old castle in Ohio, and had been stunned to hear she'd broken up with Ray.

Three blue British airmail envelopes peeked out below the others. The Sheffield postmark was Michael's sister Maddy, whose husband had been reduced to one of those soddin' great factories in England. The Fort Augustus was Michael's chum Colin MacLeod. The third envelope was printed, "Tighnabruaich, 10 Ness Bank, Inverness," his parents' hotel.

The mail carrier drove away, Michael waving. Rebecca handed over his letters. "You've hit the jackpot today."

"All right!" he exclaimed.

Steve, absorbed in rewinding his Walkman as he strolled toward the pickup truck, almost collided with them. With muttered apologies everyone dodged. Steve climbed into the pickup, clamped on his earphones, and closed his eyes, effectively raising a Do Not Disturb sign.

Rebecca went into the house wondering whether Phil had ever

noticed the distinct odor of marijuana clinging to his son. Maybe he thought it was after-shave, like Eric's sandalwood scent.

She picked up the envelope she'd left on the sarcophagus and found Michael in the kitchen chuckling over his letters. "You'll like this," he said, handing her a snapshot. "Only my mum would think of sendin' it on."

Oh, my, she thought. There he was, kilt, stockings, and sporran, brass buttons on his high-necked jacket, plaid over his shoulder. It wasn't his contemporary haircut that was incongruous, but the ease of his pose. The camera had caught him striding forward, hand upraised, starting to speak some pleasantry. She'd seen him laugh, and his grin was dazzling, but never this open and unaffected, hiding nothing. Body language indeed—here was an honest, happy man. "I'm impressed," she told him, handing the picture back. "You have very handsome knees. When was this taken?"

"Thank you kindly. At Glenfinnan last August, my farewell appearance wi' the band. You have to settle doon sometime, you see."

"I see." Maybe she should urge the mail carrier to take him out some evening and loosen him up a bit.

She opened the package. Inside were layers of sprigged tissue paper emitting a flowery perfume that clashed with the odor of soup. Inside that was a lacy semitransparent black negligee. Rebecca held it up, gaping. Ray, spending good money on something like this? Not counting the recent spate of flowers, the last present he'd bought her was a toaster oven.

She crushed the negligee back into the box and glanced at Michael ostensibly reading his sister's letter. He didn't betray by so much as the flick of an eyelash he'd seen the filmy garment, but she knew he had. She ransacked the package. No letter. Nothing except the suggestive and damning garment. She jammed the top onto the box.

"Here's another," said Michael, with downright malicious nonchalance. She looked blankly at the photo he gave her, then focused. Michael and a wavy-haired man stood on a rocky snowfield wearing parkas, heavy hiking boots, and backpacks. "That's Colin. I go hill climbin' wi' him, he listens to my music. Though I prefer hikin' and he prefers Bruce Springsteen."

"Compromise," Rebecca agreed, "makes the world go 'round."

On the remaining envelope James's name was typed, not on a

mailing label. The Bright Corporation. Sounded like business, not an ad. She'd give it to Eric.

And there was the packet of coupons or whatever Peter had found beneath the desk. Rebecca slit open the envelope and pulled out the one long paper folded within. The letters, typed on the same ancient manual as the diaries, strobed before her eyes. "I'll be damned," she murmured.

"What is it?" Michael asked, tucking his snapshots away.

"The last will and testament of James Ramsey Forbes."

"What!" He peered over her shoulder. His breath would've raised gooseflesh on her cheek if she weren't already chilled with bewilderment. "His will was probated months ago. That's why we're here."

"Look." Rebecca indicated the bottom of the paper. There was James's shaky, almost illegible signature. Below it were lines for two witnesses, only one of which was filled with firm letters reading, "Warren H. Lansdale." "If the sheriff knows about another will, why hasn't he told us?"

"Either none o' our business, or no important," answered Michael. "This will isna legal, is it? Dinna you need two signatures?"

"I think so. It's dated August twenty-four; when was the legitimate will dated, do you know? Maybe this is a rough draft of it."

"No." Michael pointed at a block of type. "Naething aboot passin' the goods onto relatives. They all go right to the museum and the state."

Rebecca's mind felt like her stomach did when she skipped a meal. "Eric said something about James changing his mind right before he died because he was fed up with paying taxes. I guess this is the version he started out with, and then made the other one once he'd decided."

"The probated will's on file somewhere."

"Of course it is. I'll ask Eric. He'll know all about it."

"Oh, aye," Michael said. He began stirring the pot of soup so vigorously broth splashed over the sides and sizzled on the burner.

"Is something burning?" asked Dorothy from the doorway.

How long had she been standing there? Rebecca shifted her jaundiced gaze from Michael to the housekeeper. "What day did James die, Mrs. Garst?"

"August twenty-seventh. And yes, he made a new will right

before he died. Eric was such a help to him. Don't know how we'd have managed without him.''

At least she wasn't pretending she hadn't eavesdropped. ''This will is different from the one that was probated,'' Rebecca told her.

Dorothy pulled her shapeless sweater more closely about her shapeless body. ''Those taxes were eating him alive. He'd had to sell some things, and that hurt him terribly, you could tell. He loved his things so much. They were his children.''

Michael banged the spoon on the edge of the pot and laid it down. Phil loomed in the doorway behind Dorothy. ''I'm leaving the sheet over the furniture in the little room,'' he said.

''Thank you,'' Rebecca called.

''I don't know,'' said Phil, with a sidelong glance at Dorothy, ''about that lawyer fella being such a big help. James was kind of down on him there at the end.''

Dorothy bristled. ''Just because he was old and confused and got it in his head Eric was to blame for the high taxes. In spite of that, Eric helped him work out the compromise in the will. He's always the perfect gentleman. Right?'' She fixed Rebecca with her dreadful simper. Apparently, as far as Dorothy was concerned, whatever Eric wanted Eric could have.

Rebecca said to Michael, ''The barley's in the pantry. I'll get it for you.'' The door was open a crack; inside Darnley sat licking his whiskers.

''I'll be back tomorrow to finish the ceiling,'' called Phil.

''Thank you,'' Michael said. ''Much obliged.''

''I'll be leaving as soon as I get my things.'' Dorothy followed Phil into the entry. Rebecca emerged from the pantry in time to overhear her say to him, ''I hope you're going home by way of Ed's Clip Joint. Steve needs a haircut. He doesn't have to look like a foreigner; we have standards here.''

Phil didn't reply. The front door slammed. Dorothy's loafer-clad feet slogged up the main staircase. Michael stood, one arm braced against the counter, his other akimbo at his hip. ''Was she talkin' aboot me?''

''People of her generation tend to exaggerate the sociopolitical connotations of hair,'' Rebecca told him, handing over the barley. ''Yours is long, therefore you're some kind of revolutionary.''

Michael tossed his head defiantly, setting the brown strands dancing onto his forehead. While Steve, Rebecca thought, needed his hair not only cut but washed, Michael's was always scrupulously clean. Just went to show you couldn't predict a person's personal habits from the tidiness of his bedroom.

Michael turned to the soup. Rebecca dialed Eric's office, only to have a polite conversation with his secretary. "No," she said, hanging up, "he's not there. He does have more than Dun Iain to worry about, after all. I'll tell him about the other will tomorrow. It's curious, but no big deal. We'd have our funding even if this were the legal one."

"True enough," Michael said. He strolled into the sitting room.

Rebecca gathered the box with the negligee, the letter from her sister-in-law, the missive from Bright Corporation, the will. And there was her notebook, abandoned on the table. She hauled everything upstairs to her room. From the window she saw the Pruitts' pickup, the huge Labrador hunkered in the back, departing up the driveway. A distant screech and wail must be the vacuum cleaner protesting its trip downstairs.

Rebecca sat at the dressing table. Maybe she was the one who should get her hair cut, or color it red instead of plain-Jane brown, or something. She looked twitchy, as Jan would say. Something about the wary lines at the corners of her eyes, or the smoke coming out of her ears. Too much input, she thought. Brain error.

A scream echoed up the staircase. Maybe Darnley had caught a mouse. Maybe Slash had caught Darnley . . . Rebecca was already out the door before she remembered she'd seen the Pruitts leave with the dog.

She shot into the Hall from the landing just as Dorothy, carrying her basket, thumped in from the back staircase. There, backlit by the gold-tinted luminescence of a window, stood Michael playing the old pipes. Except they weren't old pipes anymore. Now the chanter emitted a high clear note underlain by the bass hum of the drones like silver underlies the glass of a mirror. The sound filled the room and overflowed. A hush fell on Dun Iain, as if the stones themselves were trembling in some subtle harmonic of the music.

Rebecca recognized the melody and her mind sang the words. *I was forced to wander, because that I was poor, and to leave the hills of Caledonia seemed more than I could endure. And when that I was travellin', oh a thought came to my mind, that I had never seen her beauty 'til she was far behind.*

The music was piercingly sweet, piercingly sad. Rebecca's nerves shivered with a delight so profound it hurt.

Dorothy clamped her available hand over her ear, hurried across the Hall, and brushed by Rebecca, exclaiming, "What an awful noise! Sounds like he's skinning that poor little cat!" Her steps rushed down the staircase. The front door slammed.

Rebecca stood enchanted, watching the dust motes dance in the sunlight. *The foreign winds cry Caledonia, it's time you were goin' home.*

Her presence didn't matter any more than those motes of dust. Michael's eyes were shut. His deceptively delicate fingers moved on the chanter as though he were making love to it. The drones lay trustingly against his shoulder and moaned in response.

Rebecca folded her arms. He was wearing the open face of the pictures, charged with intense emotion. She didn't want to see that much feeling, that much vulnerability, in him. It was like opening a box of cornflakes and finding it filled with gold dust, startling and disturbing.

And should some young man ask of me, is it brave or wise to roam, I'll bid him range the wide world over the better to know his own home.

The song squeezed Rebecca's heart until it ached. She was desperately homesick for Scotland, for Alba, for Caledonia, even though she'd been there only briefly. Now she understood why, after Culloden, the English had banned the pipes as instruments of war. Their song was gut feeling expressed in rational precision, right brain and left in a formidable, terrifying union.

Ferry me over, ferry me there, to leave the hills of Caledonia's more than my heart can bear.

She wanted to go to Michael and tell him he wasn't alone. But he was alone. If she interrupted him, she'd only embarrass them both.

Rebecca trudged to her room and shut the door. The portrait of Elspeth looked abstractedly down, as if the painted woman, too, were drinking in the song as potent as whiskey. Home. Home.

Abruptly the music stopped, leaving an odd hollow echo hanging in the air, emotion unfulfilled, love unrequited. Rebecca wanted to scream to fill the empty silence. She was alone, and she hurt. Tears filled her eyes and she dashed them away. Damn Michael. She hated a man who made her cry.

Slowly the light faded and the shadows of evening filled the room.

Chapter Sixteen

THE WHIR OF the can opener filled the kitchen. "Have you seen the moggie?" Michael asked. He plopped a couple of spoonfuls of brown goo into Darnley's dish. "This one's liver. Right muck, if you ask me, but he probably thinks that about shortbread."

Balancing her mug of tea, Rebecca peered through the pantry door. No cat. "Last time I saw him was in the ballroom when Phil was mortaring that brick. He was sitting on a windowsill surveying his territory."

"I'll leave it for him, then." Michael put the dish in the pantry, looking at the piles of dishes at his shoulder as doubtfully as a soldier on a bomb-disposal squad.

"You heard them go again this morning?" asked Rebecca. "Six A.M., wasn't it?"

"Oh, aye. I decided they'd had me on once too often. If they'd really broken this time, there was naething I could do. I went back to sleep."

"Nerves of steel." Rebecca gathered up her sandwich plate and mug.

"Did you come doon?"

"Good heavens, no. It's cold enough in the mornings without chasing ghosts. But I didn't go back to sleep, either." She'd lain there weighing the possibilities of her date with Eric tonight, but she wasn't about to admit to that. Briskly she rinsed off her lunch plate. Five times now they'd heard the dishes crash to the floor, only to rush in and discover them sitting innocently on their shelves. Like everything else around here, the Royal Doulton was innocuous and unnerving at once.

"I'd better get back to work," she announced. "I have to leave at five." She took a moment to leave the front door ajar—Dorothy was expected momentarily—and fell into step beside Michael on the main staircase.

"Who's playin' at the concert tonight?" he asked.

"Cleveland Symphony."

"That was one compensation for livin' in London, the concerts at the Royal Albert and Saint Martin's in the Fields."

I'll bet, Rebecca thought, the Royal Albert didn't have pipers wringing the heart out of your chest. She'd never again hear "Ferry Me Over" without thinking of Michael. Typical, to ruin a perfectly good song for her. Not that he'd volunteered over his bowl of soup last night that he'd played it. And she hadn't volunteered that she'd heard him, let alone how she'd reacted. He'd think she was a real sob sister—one of her brothers' favorite epithets.

They hadn't discussed anything else, either. Not Brian's apparent conversation with James, not the odd second will, not the supposedly nonexistent Forbes treasure. They'd debated what to get for Christmas for their respective nieces and nephews—Michael's three, Rebecca's seven. "Populatin' the world wi' Reids?" he'd asked.

"My brothers are very traditional," she'd replied. "Marry young and make sure you get your money's worth out of your school taxes."

Rebecca switched on the chandelier in the large fourth-floor bedroom. Michael considered the objects strewn across the carpet and the bed. The doors of the George II bureau gaped open, revealing a variety of tiny drawers and shelves all crammed with artifacts, intriguing and otherwise. So were the shallow drawers of the apothecary's chest. So were the cheap plywood bookshelves. It had taken all morning just to sort out the scrapbooks, decide they should go to the Ohio Historical Society along with James's diaries, lug them all down to the Hall, and arrange them in the cardboard boxes Eric had brought.

Michael picked up the inventory. "Have you seen the Pratt ware coo?"

"The what?"

"The creamer shaped like a wee Guernsey. Hard to believe what people collect. Although John would buy a thing just because someone else had it."

"Oh! The gaudy nineteenth-century Staffordshire cow, right? It was here yesterday. The Pratt Toby jugs are upstairs."

His finger on the page in the book, Michael said, "I need the coo."

The front door slammed. Dorothy advanced up the staircase with her basket, intent, apparently, on Michael's bedroom. He headed her off. "Mrs. Garst, there were some things on the floor in yon room . . ."

"Yes, there were. Shameful way to treat Mr. Forbes's nice things. That little cow pitcher, now—cute, isn't it? But a silly thing to have in a bedroom. I took it down to the kitchen and put it away."

Michael assumed his martyr expression and headed back down the stairs. Dorothy stood in the doorway of his bedroom like a scuba diver getting her last breath of real air. She was looking even paler and more tightly wound than she had yesterday, as if she had a permanent stomachache.

Rebecca got a tumbler of water for the scraps of ivy growing in an assortment of Keiller's marmalade jars on the windowsills. Phil and Steve were sitting on the granite step of the toolshed, eating their sandwiches and chips from Phil's rusty lunch box. Above them clouds gathered; yesterday's warm sunshine had become today's chill wind.

Michael returned with the cow and sat down at the bureau. Dorothy ran a Niagara Falls of water into the bathtub next door. The phone rang. "I'll get it," Rebecca called, as Michael didn't look up and the water kept running.

It was Eric. She settled into a comfortable slump against the wall, cradling the receiver to her face. "My secretary's off today," he said. "I just now found the memo saying you called late yesterday. I'm sorry—I was playing racquetball."

"Nothing important," Rebecca assured him. "Just wanted to ask you, out of rank curiosity, when was James's will written and who were the witnesses?"

"Curiosity killed the cat," he said with a laugh. "It was written August twentieth and witnessed by Phil and Dorothy. What on earth brought that up?"

August 20. The will Peter had found yesterday was the newer one. She hadn't expected that. "Eric, Peter found another will when he moved the desk in the prophet's chamber. It's dated the twenty-fourth, and doesn't have the provision about relatives. Warren's the only witness."

"Oh, that!" Eric exclaimed. "I'd wondered where that one had gone. Beneath the desk? I guess James left it there waiting for another witness and it got knocked off. I'll have to tell Warren it turned up."

The water stopped running. Michael was humming something under his breath that sounded suspiciously like "Ah, sweet mystery of life, at last I've found you." Rebecca grimaced; throwing something at him would only acknowledge that she heard him. She straightened and paced down the hall. There was one of the crystal bottles in the cradle in James's room—Elspeth, remembering her infant daughter?

"So James resigned himself to leaving Dun Iain to the state, after all?"

"Poor old James," Eric answered. "You know how some people think if they don't make a will they'll never die? With James it was if he made lots of wills he'd never die."

"I'm sure he had no idea the end was so near." Rebecca stood at the top of the stairs and looked down. No. Don't push me. Help.

"No one does," said Eric. "A mercy, that."

Rebecca shivered. She turned to see Dorothy right at her elbow, dusting the frame of Michael's door.

Eric went on, "I talked to Warren this morning. He didn't take the mausoleum key and doesn't know who did. Frankly I can't imagine why anyone would want it, but it does belong to the property. If nothing else we'll have that lock changed, too."

"I'll let you worry about that," Rebecca said. "I'm worried if we're going to get through all these little treasures before January first."

"You can do it if anyone can." Rebecca laughed; she felt like Tarzan swooping through the jungle on those facile lines. "Bring that copy of the will with you tonight, please," Eric continued, "and I'll put it with the other ones. A different Forbes collection, a memorial to indecisiveness."

Poor old James. "All right, then. See you at five."

"See you at five, Rebecca."

She hung up with a smile and a pat to the receiver. Michael was singing, "Some day my prince will come." Dorothy was smirking at her. Damn it, she wasn't staging a show for their entertainment! Rebecca stamped into James's bedroom, rescued the perfume bottle, and took it upstairs. The fifth-floor bedroom, John and Elspeth's room, was thick with the odor of lavender. The depression in the pillow on the bed was deeper than ever. Rebecca hurried away without looking behind her.

Back on the fourth floor Michael had shut up and was absorbed in a book. Rebecca sat on the bed, opening the first box she came to. Inside was a mound of intricate hand-stitched lace. "Wow!" she gasped.

Michael looked up. "What?"

"Irish lace. And . . ." Carefully she unfolded the top layer, revealing a latticework basket made of porcelain so fine it shone like pearl in the light of the chandelier. "Irish Belleek."

"Here we go." He flipped through the inventory. "John bought them from the Perth Moncrieffes in 1921. Limerick lace, is it?"

Rebecca's fingertips smoothed the almost microscopic stitching. "No way. See the appliqué, and the layers of tulle and organza? Carrickmacross."

"Aye, then. Carrickmacross it is."

At least he was man enough to admit he was wrong. Rebecca said, "John didn't restrict himself to specifically Scottish goods, did he? A lot of these things are just typical collectibles of the period—the Meissen clock upstairs, for example. The Pratt ware. This."

"But he nicked them from someone in Scotland. That was what mattered. It was all a game to him."

"Like James writing wills," Rebecca said.

Michael swung around. "What did Adler say about the other will?"

"He said he'd been wondering where that one got to. It's only one of several, I gather."

"He wasn't surprised?"

"No." Rebecca smoothed the lace back around the basket and labeled the lid of the box. "The legal will, by the way, was dated August twentieth. If the one Peter found had been signed by two witnesses, it would be the legal one."

"Takin' away Adler's tidy fee for findin' relatives, eh? How nice that it was never signed properly. Mark my words, Rebecca, he's up to something." With this pronouncement Michael turned back to his stack of books.

His back was, as usual, uncommunicative. Why the two men had to be so suspicious of each other Rebecca couldn't fathom. It must be some kind of territorial imperative. If Eric hadn't known about the August 24 will, she'd wonder why James hadn't told him. But he had known.

The next box she opened contained yellowed rolls of paper.

Gingerly she pried one open. "Maps! Copies of General Wade's eighteenth-century surveys. When the English were building roads and bridges so they could get at the natives to 'pacify' them."

"And the first effective ground transportation in the Highlands," Michael said to the bureau. "An economic blessin' to those same natives. The museum'll want those maps, right enough. You can set them aside."

Not one flicker of patriotic indignation. Rebecca stuck out her tongue at his back, said "Yes, my lord," under her breath, and set them aside.

Dorothy vacuumed the corridor. Phil slapped plaster downstairs. Darnley padded in, sniffed, padded out again. Michael's chair creaked gently. Before long the little Tompion clock beside the bed said four o'clock. Rebecca slipped away, leaving Michael with inventory, spiral notebook, and a pile of papers that looked like letters and receipts. So much to do, and here she was leaving. Of course she'd worked every evening this week. And Michael was a full Ph.D., they were probably paying him more.

Her bedroom, despite its white walls, was already dusky. Before she plunged into the ritual of shampoo, hair curlers, pink dress, she stuffed Ray's negligee into the bottom of her wardrobe. At least the odor of lavender had never returned. Steve and Heather must've frightened Elspeth away.

In the dim light the garnet, jet, and diamond of Elspeth's pictured necklace seemed to sparkle. while the woman's face was obviously only paint, sad, sensitive expression and all. But the woman in the photos had been a vivacious flirt.

Shaking her head, Rebecca touched her throat with the Chanel No. 5 Eric had given her and plugged in her earrings. She packed her toothbrush in her purse, took it out, packed it and took it out again. Any man as well organized as Eric had to have an extra toothbrush. It just seemed, well. so calculating to actually plan to spend the night. Rebecca put her contact lens case in her purse, popped out the day's birth-control pill and swallowed it, even though her throat was dry.

She emerged from her room to encounter Michael strolling by, and waited for him to say something about her being "tarted up." He said, with his appraising look, "That's the frock you made, is it? Awful posh."

"Why, thank you," she replied.

They passed the study in time to see Phil bringing out the white-stained plaster bucket, and the entry in time to see Dorothy open the door and go out. "What culinary time bomb did Dottie bring today?" Rebecca asked, following Michael into the kitchen.

He unrolled one end of a foil bundle. "Looks like a petrified haggis."

"Oh, no." She could've cried. That gray brick had once been a lovely little rump roast. "Maybe I can shred it and serve it with a sauce."

"At least she didna bring those sausages filled wi' yellow glue."

"The hot dogs stuffed with American cheese? Pretty bad, I agree. The meat loaf was okay, though, even with the catsup smeared on top."

"My mum makes the best shepherd's pie you ever ate," Michael said wistfully. He opened the box of shortbread. "And her black bun . . ."

"Oh, Becky!" warbled Dorothy from the entry. "Eric's here."

Michael extracted a cookie without so much as rustling the paper wrapper. Rebecca went to the door. "In here!"

Eric was wearing the charcoal three-piece suit that made his eyes look like onyx. All he needed was a pocket watch and chain with fobs dangling across his vest. He greeted Rebecca with a wink and shook hands with Michael. "How's it going? Making any progress?"

"Just about," Michael replied, butter not melting in his mouth. "Do you know anything about an English book cover inset with rubies and diamonds, circa 1630? Or a decorated English agate perfume bottle, circa 1540? From Hopetoun House and Drumlanrig, respectively. The list doesn't say if there was a book in the cover—I assume there was no Shakespeare folio."

Eric smiled. "I asked James about those same pieces. He de-accessioned them about ten years ago, I think, before my time. Showy things like that sold quickly when he needed cash."

"They're still listed in the inventories." Now Michael smiled. Rebecca watched, fascinated. They were just like dogs—a border collie and a Doberman, possibly—sniffing each other out.

"I warned you that James didn't always record a sale," Eric said. "Somehow he thought if he didn't mark an item sold, he'd still have it."

Michael said lightly, his smile becoming a lazy grin, "Convenient, then, that you know the inventories so well. I thought cheap lawyers didn't bother with things like that."

"Oh," said Eric, voice perfectly moderated between a laugh and a polite protest, "but I'm a very expensive lawyer."

"*Touché,*" said Michael, and ate his cookie with an emphatic crunch.

Eric turned to Rebecca. "Shall we go?"

"Let's," she said. Really—men were absurd.

"Have a good time, children," called Michael. "Don't forget to write."

The toad. She'd been worried about leaving him with more than his fair share of the work and he was glad to get rid of her.

Phil was waiting in the parking area, his Cincinnati Reds cap shading his hangdog face. "Mr. Adler, here's an expense sheet. I hope it's made out all right."

"I'm sure it's fine, Phil. Let's see—nails, plaster, glass panes, caulking."

Steve, Slash at his heels, slouched across the gravel. "I'll put the leftover gas in the pickup."

"No, you won't," said Phil. "That gas belongs to the estate. We'll save it until we start the lawn mowers up again in the spring. But," he added apologetically to Eric, "I will have to get a new gasoline can."

Assuming Phil and Steve had jobs here in the spring, Rebecca said to herself. She looked at Slash. He looked at her, nostrils flaring.

Eric said, "Get a good one. You don't want gasoline to be stored improperly." He pulled out a pen, jotted "Gas can" on the list, put both paper and pen in his pocket, and shook Phil's dirty hand with his clean one. "Thank you. I'll see that you're reimbursed quickly."

Eric turned to Steve and Steve spun away, one corner of his mouth twitching in a barely suppressed sneer. Swells like Eric, he seemed to be thinking, didn't have to know gasoline from Perrier. A shape moved in a fourth-floor window. Rebecca shot a sharp, wary glance upward. It was Dorothy, her bulbous form outlined by the ceiling light. She stood, arms crossed before her, impersonating a waxwork figure.

Michael's voice echoed through the door, singing lustily, "There's many a wean wi' the red locks of the Campbells who's ne'er seen the coast of Argyll." If he grew a beard, Rebecca thought, it'd be red. Wasn't the Campbell who was murdered in *Kidnapped* called "The Red Fox"?

"Earth to Rebecca," said Eric.

She started. "Sorry. I haven't been quite with it all day."

"Then it's time for an evening out." He opened the door of the Volvo and Rebecca climbed out of the chill wind.

The limbs of the trees along the driveway were black brush strokes against an overcast sky that shimmered like sifted ashes, touched with mauve where the sun sank invisibly toward the horizon. "The days are creepin' in, right enough," she said.

Eric started the car. "You've been working with Campbell too long. You're starting to talk like him."

"Dialect is insidious," admitted Rebecca. "Especially that one. I've been reading British all my life."

"And whatever is a nice girl like you doing in a field like that?" But he touched her cheek as he spoke—just kidding, no criticism implied.

"My great-grandfather emigrated from Ayrshire a hundred years ago. My grandfather taught me the old songs his father had sung to him. 'Loch Lomond,' for example."

"The one with the high roads and the low roads?"

"Do you know the story behind that?"

"I have a feeling I'm going to hear it," Eric said with exaggerated patience. He guided the car out of the driveway.

Rebecca batted affectionately at his shoulder. "There're two Scottish soldiers—or drafted crofters, most likely—in prison in England. One's going to be released, the other executed. Taking the low road means to go along the fairy route, underground, as a ghost. So he'll be home, but he'll be dead." Like James, she added to herself. Like Elspeth. But maybe she had never considered Dun Iain home.

"I'd always thought," said Eric, "it was a happy little tune."

"Typical Scots, making lemonade out of lemons. Irrepressible."

"I've noticed," he said dryly.

Eric would never have believed the expression on Michael's face when he played the pipes. His astringent manner had been peeled like a lemon, the raw pulp exposed. But she didn't have to think of him tonight.

"I'm rather partial to 'Music from the Hearts of Space' myself." Eric reached to the dashboard and inserted a tape. Synthesized New Age harmonies emanated from the speakers, soothing and nondemanding.

Rebecca relaxed into the upholstery. "So," she continued, "when I was being carted around all over the countryside as a child, British history seemed exotic enough to be interesting but familiar enough to be safe. Make sense?"

"Perfectly. When I was a kid, I was partial to automobile engines—rationality, you see. When I wasn't down at the beach. But you can't make much of a career out of cars or surfboards."

No, Rebecca thought, those meticulously clean fingernails hadn't touched engine grease in years. The motherless child had found his rationality.

They turned onto the access road, gained the interstate, and accelerated smoothly toward Columbus. The music murmured, its subtle rhythms blending with that of the car wheels on the road. The lights of passing cars threw Eric's face into sharp relief and then swept on, leaving him in twilight. Carefully controlled features, noted Rebecca, framed by an exact haircut. And yet, that afternoon on the roof of Dun Iain, she'd glimpsed the flame that burned within. His sophistication had probably been hard-won, layer after layer of shiny lacquer applied to both enhance and protect the fiery core. She admired him for that, even as she was amused by it. Well, Eric was in a profession that rewarded smooth edges.

"A penny for your thoughts," he said.

She laughed. "Have you ever considered politics?"

"No. Much too demanding."

"Have to keep your nose too clean?"

"My nose is clean, thank you. I take my lumps on the stock market like everyone else, and there's not a single messy divorce clouding my record."

"Divorce doesn't matter these days like it did back in Mary Stuart's," said Rebecca. "Or in Elspeth's."

"Divorce wasn't even an option for her."

"Or John. Although I daresay she was the injured party, not him."

"You'd better believe it," Eric murmured, so quietly Rebecca wasn't sure she'd heard him.

"So Warren says he didn't take the mausoleum key," she said.

"If he did take it, he can have it. In some ways Warren's too soft to be a law officer, but he'd protect John, James, Elspeth, and the baby."

Rebecca regarded Eric's profile thoughtfully. James must have told him about the baby. Or Louise. It was no secret. "He wouldn't have had to lie about the key, though. That bothers me."

"People sometimes lie for perfectly innocent reasons."

"If they're innocent they can be honest," Rebecca persisted. "Did you know Warren was the only witness on that will?"

Eric looked over at her. Passing headlights reflected in his eyes, making them glint like the gold ring on his hand. "Yes. James told me on the phone. Last time I talked to him before he died. Poor old guy. As far as he was concerned, state or relative, it'd still be some stranger who took over Dun Iain. Can you blame him for wanting to stay longer?"

He meant living, not as a ghost. But no, she couldn't blame him. "What do you mean by Warren being too soft? Do you think he's covering up for Dorothy? She's been lurking around like Bela Lugosi."

"Dorothy?" Eric's features flickered with sardonic humor. "The uncertainty about her job is eating her. Not surprising. Phil, too, although with him it's harder to tell. But we have no proof that either of them has done anything dishonest."

Central Ohio slipped by on either side of the highway, clumps of trees, farmhouses, and stores all fading into the evening obscurity. The occasional lighted window or neon sign seemed like a hole cut in a gray backdrop.

Rebecca sighed. Her suspicions sounded so melodramatic. And she wasn't even talking about the ghosts. "It's like trying to follow a railroad timetable in an Agatha Christie thriller. Who signed what will when? Where were Steve and Heather when? Who had what key when? You've solved the problem of the front door, but now the mausoleum key is lost. Return to 'Go,' do not collect two hundred dollars."

"Steve," Eric snorted, "could use a stint in the Army."

"And Heather?"

"Get her away from Steve, she'll be fine. She just needs to do a little growing up."

Don't we all, Rebecca thought. "You didn't answer my question. Do you think Warren is covering something up?"

"Inquisitive tonight, aren't we?" he teased. "What's to cover up? Surely you don't think Warren, Dorothy, and Phil are planning a heist? If you ask me, it's Campbell . . ."

"I didn't ask that," she said, and then bit her tongue. Michael, too, was an outsider. But if dishonesty meant guilt . . . No, he could be annoying enough when she was with him. Now she wasn't.

Eric glanced narrowly at her but said nothing.

"What's to cover up?" she repeated. "That's what's so irritating. Nothing I can put my finger on." Of course there was Phil's comment about "that lawyer fella." Someone else had said that James had soured on Eric there at the end. Warren? Jan? She wriggled uncomfortably. She was starting to sound like Dorothy, an obnoxious voice in a loop. But she asked, anyway, "Why would James blame you for the taxes?"

"What?" Eric asked incredulously. "Who said that?"

"Phil, I think."

"Oh. Probably some comment James made about my filling out his tax returns for him. Bet you didn't know I do accounting, too, did you?"

"And leap over tall buildings in a single bound?"

He laughed, crooked teeth flashing unashamedly.

Rebecca was beginning to appreciate just what it would be like opposing Eric in court. If he was being deliberately evasive, that would mean there was something to evade. Maybe he was simply confident that matters were under control. Or else . . . If anything infuriated her, it was a man's condescending "Don't worry your little head about it."

"So you don't want me to worry about anything?" she asked. "The whereabouts of the mazer, or the key, or whether someone—Jan's kids, anyone—is planning a heist, or whether I'm going to find Steve's and Heather's fingerprints all over my room when I get back tonight?"

"I think you shouldn't worry about anything, but if you want to, that's up to you. Besides . . ." He tickled her ribs with that admonitory forefinger. "What if you don't get back tonight?"

The look he gave her would have ignited tinder. With a nervous laugh she sank back against the seat, glad the darkness concealed her pink face. She'd never believed men like him really existed; compared to him every other man she'd met was an irredeemable clod. Yes, he had to keep throwing that stardust in her eyes. That was part of the bargain.

The traffic grew heavier. They were swept along in the stream, past residential areas and businesses, below glaring yellow streetlights that made Rebecca's pink dress look as sepia as the old photographs of Elspeth. Soon they eddied into the Veterans' Memorial Auditorium parking lot and stopped. When she got out, Rebecca's hair whipped in a gust of chill wind off the river.

She leaned appreciatively into Eric's protective arm, and together they hurried into the building.

Chapter Seventeen

How BLISSFUL TO spend a couple of hours not worrying, not thinking, just feeling the glorious music of Handel, Beethoven, and Vaughan Williams. Rebecca had hardly even noticed Eric holding her hand. It was almost painful to stand up and register the auditorium and the departing crowd.

In the lobby they encountered Benjamin Birkenhead. Eric's boss, and his wife. Rebecca made a quick mental inventory of her appearance. She was presentable. Eric said, "Let me introduce Rebecca Reid. She's been cataloging the artifacts out at Dun Iain."

"Ah," boomed Birkenhead. "The lady historian. Isn't she a pretty little thing, though? How do you find them, Eric?"

He did have a pocket watch and dangling fobs. And the massive belly to display them. Next to him, his wife resembled a bird searching for insects on a hippo. She looked from Eric to Rebecca and back as if Rebecca were applying for a position at the firm.

"Nice to meet you," Rebecca said tightly. So there were real historians and then there were lady historians. And her job description included being an attractive artifact herself. She wished she had a run in her stockings or lipstick on her teeth.

Safely in the parking lot, Eric whispered, "Never mind old Ben. He's—well—unreconstructed."

"How can you tell?" Rebecca returned.

He laughed, unlocked her door, bowed her into the car. She lay back against the seat, feeling almost drunk with music. But the accompanying melancholy wasn't exactly pleasant; it was the same yearning she felt when seeing a distant airplane, or when hearing the music of the Highland pipes. Yes, sex could assuage that longing, temporarily. Ray, in his own correct manner, had proved that. Eric could probably prove it, too. But the yearning, it seemed, was chronic.

Eric's condo was several floors up a high rise. A wall of glass in the living room revealed a breathtaking view of downtown Columbus, the lights of the city reflecting in a gauzy glow off the lowering sky. He relieved her not only of her coat but of her shoes, and she gave him the will and the letter before stowing her purse beneath the coatrack.

"The Bright Corporation," he said, inspecting the letter first. "They've already contacted Ben. Very tidy offer they've made for Dun Iain. I'll advise the Dennisons—assuming I find them— to accept it. Only corporations and governments can afford to keep estates anymore."

"Just as long as they keep it, not tear it down."

"That'll depend, won't it?" He unfolded the will. "Yes, this is a version of the others. See, these bequests to his 'family' were in every one. And he always meant for the historical artifacts to go back to Scotland."

"I'm not surprised," Rebecca said. Living among the haunted objects would get to anyone. It had certainly gotten to two people living there.

For all Eric's continental airs, she thought, Michael was the European. And while he could be polite, he was not smooth. He bristled like a porcupine. He'd been pleased she was leaving tonight. What was he doing while she stood wiggling her toes in Eric's carpet—playing the pipes, his shoes planted solidly on chill stone? Or cuddling the mail carrier? That was only fair. Lonely people needed someone to hold. How do porcupines make love? Very carefully. Rebecca smiled and the image of Michael shattered.

Eric put the letter and the will in his desk and headed for the kitchen. "It's late. You must be hungry."

"Starved. But first . . ." Rebecca detoured through the bedroom, noting that Eric had a king-sized bed, and found the bathroom. Compared to the basic fixtures at Dun Iain it was a Cecil B. deMille set. The lights spaced along the top of the mirror made halos in her slightly dazed eyes. She wet a tissue, mopped at a crumb of mascara, threw it away. The wad of tissue missed the wastebasket and landed under the rim of the cabinet.

When she bent to retrieve it, her fingers touched something metallic and cold, a tube of flame-red lipstick.

She visualized the woman with the bold red lips, a lobbyist from the Capitol downtown, or a corporate lawyer every bit as smooth as Eric himself. Cool and collected in her pin-striped suit, but an animal clawing at him as he . . . Rebecca put the lipstick in a drawer and the tissue into the basket, and grimaced at herself. Her flushed reflection grimaced back.

A rhythmic tapping issued from the kitchen. Eric had shed his coat, vest, and tie, rolled up his sleeves, and was chopping vegetables. The red and greens of peppers and broccoli shone brightly amid glass, chrome, and leather. Rebecca, feeling as if she'd been magically transported from 1890 to 2001, stopped in the living room to survey the bookshelves.

Geological specimens shared space with best-sellers, a collection of the classics, and books on popular physics and train journeys through India. The magazines—*The New Yorker, Atlantic Monthly, National Geographic*—were slightly crumpled; they were for reading, not decoration. Nothing changed Rebecca's impression of Eric as a man determined to improve himself.

On the desk was the only photograph, a tiny, unfocused picture of a woman and a child. Rebecca held it to the light.

The woman was about sixty, her hair pulled away from her face in a ringleted perm of the late fifties. Her eyes were dark smudges made even larger by the weary circles under them. But her mouth was a thin line of tenacity. She was a fighter. And so was the child. His hair was a caterpillarlike crew cut above his small, somber face. Even at the age of five or six, his black eyes had been burnished with intelligence and a certain sad perception.

"Find anything?" Eric called.

"It's lovely. Awful posh. And no ghosts—what a treat."

He glanced up at her from beneath his brows. She wasn't sure he'd ever believed her account of the lavender-scented entity in the pantry. There was no reason to make him even more skeptical of her common sense by telling him what Brian had said about James.

She went on, "This is you and your grandmother?"

"Yes. She was quite a woman to raise me alone. She always pushed me to make something of myself."

"So I see." Above the desk was a copy of *MacKay's British Antiques*. No wonder Eric knew the inventories so well. Rebecca pulled the book off the shelf and flipped through it. A photograph of a Chippendale secretary like the one at Dun Iain was marked by an envelope whose return address read "Sotheby's, New York." Sotheby's, the classy antiques dealer.

Eric's arms came around her from behind and she jumped. "Now what?" he murmured into her hair. "Oh. I wrote them to check on some of Campbell's valuations. And to see if the mazer was on the market. Outside chance, I'll admit, and sure enough they'd never heard of it. But if they did know of its whereabouts, and I retrieved it for you, you'd have spoiled your surprise, wouldn't you?"

"We already know I'm too curious for my own good." She couldn't tell whether the undertone of irritation in his voice was genuine or pretend. Ray had had a knack for playing with irritation, as if she couldn't be trusted with the real thing. "Isn't that above and beyond the call of your duty? I thought Warren was making inquiries about the mazer."

"He has his channels, I have mine."

So Eric wanted to show off by finding the mazer. To make up, no doubt, for the galling fact that Michael's valuations were correct . . . Eric took the envelope from Rebecca's hand, replaced it in the book, turned her around, and kissed her. Her senses flared like sparklers in the July dusk. She wheezed, "Can I help?"

"Cook, or look for the mazer?" He laughed and released her. "Neither. Just relax." He went back to work, and in a moment the delectable odors of onion and soy sauce filled the room. Rebecca consoled herself by finding the silverware and setting the glass-topped table in its alcove by the window. "Technically we should be having plum wine," said Eric, producing a bottle from the refrigerator. "But you just can't beat champagne for a special occasion." The cork popped. He poured, sipped, nodded, and handed the glass to her.

The food was delicious. The champagne bubbled in Rebecca's head with prismatic sprays of sensuality. Was there anything Eric did, she wondered as she chased the last grains of rice around her plate, that he didn't do well? When he pulled her away from the sink, wrested the dishcloth from her hands, and led her to the sumptuous leather couch, she settled down happily for a demonstration of yet another of his skills.

How much more comfortable the couch was than the seat of the car, she thought. It invited licentious activity. Then she didn't think at all, but floated on sensation as she'd float on music, the song her body sang leaving her more intoxicated than the champagne ever could.

She curled against him, one of his arms across her knees, the other supporting her shoulders. Her hand splayed inside his shirt against the scratch and silk of his chest. The hem of her dress rode two thirds of the way up her thigh. Eric's hand was even higher, his ring sliding over taut nylon, making its slow but resolute course toward what her brothers would have called home base. Her lips felt delightfully bruised.

Rebecca groped after her wits. Not that she wanted her wits, but it didn't seem right to abandon them at the side of the road like unloved kittens. The ring and the hand stopped at the lace-trimmed edge of her teddy.

"Would you like to change clothes?" Eric asked. His voice was now brushed velvet, slightly husky.

So was hers. "I didn't bring anything else."

"There's a robe on the back of the bathroom door."

With her lips Rebecca traced the tense line of his jaw. All she had to do was go to the other room, undress, and put on the robe. He would take the robe off, hold her, and make love to her. She could cling to him and make stupid little vocalizations into his shoulder. She was guaranteed one complete orbit of the earth and side trips to the moon and Venus as well.

Bubbles of champagne and sensuality spattered across her mind like raindrops across her face. Then it would be morning. In the cold light of dawn he'd drive her back to Dun Iain. Back to reality, and Michael Campbell's mocking gaze.

She didn't move. His fingers began tapping gently but impatiently at the angle where her hip met her thigh.

Eric's masculinity flared around his armor like the corona around an eclipse. When the barriers were down he'd incinerate her, as Zeus did some hapless mortal—not Europa, not Danaë, she'd have to look it up.

If the barriers came down. She wanted to hold that part of him that was the child in the picture and tell him it was all right. But the man he was now didn't need her to tell him anything. Even in the most intimate of moments he was perfectly capable of remaining so slick she'd slide off him.

She didn't move. She was still in his arms, but she was no longer touching him. The song she'd been singing thinned and died into a sour resonance in the back of her mind. His armor was so brightly polished it reflected odd, evasive shapes. She might never be able to see inside.

Items listed in the inventories were missing. James hadn't liked Eric anymore, there at the end. A letter from Sotheby's marked a page in *MacKay* . . . Just once, Rebecca demanded of herself, can't you trust someone?

She couldn't see his face; her face was buried in his throat, her nostrils filled with his salt and spice scent. His hand clenched on her teddy, twisted, and released it to retreat down her thigh. Beneath her hands his breath slowed and deepened, the tension ebbed from his body, his skin cooled.

That's all? But men were mortally insulted at being thwarted—especially at such a moment.

Rebecca looked up. He was gazing not at her but at the window across the room. With his hair tousled across his forehead he seemed almost vulnerable. Tired. Certainly disappointed. He would hit her not with anger, then, but with sarcasm. No fair, she pleaded silently, to talk about wasting the concert tickets, the fancy dinners, the bottle of champagne.

He exhaled, pulled the hem of her dress to her knee, and stroked her hair back from her face. His eyes were the black cairngorms she remembered from that first night, a hint of smoke drifting in their depths.

"I'm sorry," she said. "I'm being pulled in so many different directions right now. I've been leading you on all this time, I know."

"Then continue to lead me on. I'm enjoying it." He kissed the tip of her nose. "After the first of January, after all the sound and fury at Dun Iain is over, would you like to come on a cruise with me?"

She stared. "Do what?"

"Come on a cruise with me. The Caribbean in January. A vacation after all your hard work. My treat, of course."

She relaxed against him. Thank God for Eric's self-control, for his almost frightening maturity. If his hand had taken the plunge, she'd have been Jell-O; he could have carried her into the bedroom like Rhett Butler. And would probably have thrown out his back, halting the proceedings in an even more embarrassing manner.

A cruise. That might work. After she'd survived the ghosts, the artifacts, the maudlin music of a set of pipes. After her damned suspicious nature had burned itself out for lack of fuel.

They could have that brief, intense encounter, after all, made nice and tidy by a beginning when the ship sailed and an end when it docked. She'd bring fire-fighting equipment and grappling hooks, just to be prepared. "Why, yes," she said. "Let's try that."

"It's a date, Rebecca." Eric levered her off his lap. "Would you like to go home now? You can stay, if you like." He held his hands to the side—see, I'm unarmed and not dangerous.

"Dun Iain? Home?" She laughed wanly. "It's the closest thing to a home I have right now, isn't it? Yes, I would, please."

He put on his burgundy jacket, helped her collect her coat and shoes, and walked her down to the car. It was after one A.M. Even so they were in traffic almost all the way to Putnam. They sat not talking, quiet music emanating from the speakers, Eric driving with one hand and holding her hand with the other. Passing headlights swooped out of the darkness like flak, burst, and died. Rebecca slumped, aching, tied in knots of unrelieved desire. The pain would eventually dull. It always had before.

The drive was a tree-lined tunnel. At its end every light in the castle blazed. No cars were in the parking area beside the Toyota and the Nova. So much for her fantasies about Michael and the mail carrier. Unless the woman had been and gone. Well, he was a grown man. He could manage his own affairs. Rebecca clambered wearily from the car.

"The lights were on like this the night your room was vandalized?" Eric eyed the ranks of glowing windows. "I'd better come in with you."

Rebecca unlocked the door and pushed it open. Her steps on the flagstones sounded like gunshots. "Michael?"

A sudden pounding shattered the silence. She whirled around. Eric was staring at the storeroom door. "Hello!" said Michael's voice. "Would you mind terribly unlockin' the door?"

"What the hell?" asked Eric. He tried the knob.

"Use the key," Michael called.

"It's not in the lock."

"Then look for it!"

It took Rebecca only moments to find the key, lying in a rim of shadow just where the white marble of the sarcophagus met the gray stone of the floor. She thrust it into the lock and threw the door open.

Michael leaned against a packing crate, two cans of Moosehead, his notebook, a crowbar, and a heavy screwdriver beside him. Other crates stood open, their lids strewn all the way back

into the shadows where the ceiling curved toward the floor.
"Welcome home," he said to Rebecca. "I was afraid you'd no
be back the night." He inspected her up and down and added,
"You're a wee bit peelie-wally."

"Peelie-wally?" asked Eric.

Michael's eye shifted to him, taking in the absence of vest,
coat, and tie. "Thin and pale, like a plucked chicken," he explained. Something in his expression glinted not so much with
amusement as with a furtive satisfaction.

Eric turned one way, rolling his eyes upward. Rebecca turned
the other, looking down at the floor, smothering a grin and a
groan. The turkey, that was exactly how she felt. But if it was
none of his business what she had done this evening, it was none
of his business what she hadn't. "What on earth are you doing?
Did you open all those boxes?"

Michael closed his spiral notebook and tucked a pencil into
the wire. "It's a fair cop. Caught me workin'."

"At this hour?" Eric asked.

Michael yawned. "I was goin' to quit hours ago, mind you.
But the door slammed and locked itself. Or at least I never heard
anyone leave."

"Here we go again," said Rebecca. "Every light in the house
is on. Human or supernatural malefactors?"

Eric scoffed, "You could've locked the door and scooted the
key underneath it. It was just over there."

"Oh, aye, I was right keen on spendin' the night in the lumber
room."

"You could've used that stone to smash the lock."

He was pointing at a three-foot-high piece of sandstone whose
surface rushed with carvings of hunters on horseback. Michael's
face suffused with horror. He stepped back and patted the artifact protectively. "This is a Pictish sculptured stone, I'll have
you know. Resembles the one at Aberlemno. And look at that
one there."

Oh, my, Rebecca thought. She followed him like a child following the Pied Piper. "Is that what I think it is?"

"Roman milestone, probably from Hadrian's Wall. See?" His
forefinger traced the inscription. "*Imp Caesar Hadrianius Leg
III*. Third Legion."

Eric, still in the doorway, hiked back his jacket, stuck his
hands in his pockets, and rattled his change.

"John must've bought oot some grave robber's entire store,"

continued Michael. "Look—a bronze figurine, a stone bowl, and Samian ware from Gaul. Legionary Tupperware, eh?"

Rebecca picked up the smooth red-slipped bowl. It had come from France to Britain and now here, over the miles and the centuries. It thrummed very faintly next to her skin, transmitting some inchoate memory of the other hands that had held it.

"A glass flask for oil." Michael indicated a small tissue-wrapped object. "Very rare. And here . . ." Another stone, carved in a faint image of a seated woman. "An altar. *Deo Sancto Juno Caelestis.*"

"Look!" Rebecca called to Eric. "Isn't it great?" He smiled faintly, his eyes glazed. Whether at the flood of information or at a Scot speaking Latin Rebecca couldn't tell. She turned back to Michael. "*Juno Caelestis.* That means Brigante territory. What's the provenance?"

"That's just it." Michael dropped the lid of a case with a thud and turned to Eric, scowling. "Your bleedin' inventories dinna have Sweet Fanny Adams aboot these things. They're taken oot o' context. It's criminal!"

"They're not my inventories," retorted Eric.

Michael gesticulated. "Forbes should be hanged for scarperin' wi' this lot. They're soddin' useless the noo!"

"He's already dead," said Eric. "Has it occurred to you . . ."

Rebecca started toward him. Michael jogged her elbow, pulling her back. "Just look at this."

He put into her hands a metal casket about the size of a loaf of bread. The silver trimming was tarnished, but bits of enamel showed faintly through the dust. An inscription ran along the rim of the lid. She held the casket up to the light and squinted. "James Graham, Earl of Montrose. Michael, you don't mean this is the man's heart!"

"I told you it was here." he replied. "The one thing I do have provenance for. Open it up and take a keek."

"Bloody hell I will!" Rebecca thrust the casket at him so quickly he almost fumbled it. She dusted her hands. "The last thing I want to look at is someone's mummified heart. Especially when you consider how it left his body!"

Michael grinned. "Dinna get the wind up. You dinna have to look. Noo if John really had Mary's severed head around here somewhere . . ."

"Is he always this gruesome?" asked Eric.

Rebecca retreated toward the door. "Not really. Pardon him

his enthusiasms, will you? Most of them are mine, too." And to Michael, as he stood unrepentant, holding the casket, "No wonder you didn't hear anyone lock the door. You wouldn't have heard a brass band. You've made quite a dent in the pile, haven't you?"

"Well, since I was locked in . . ." His eyes slid slyly away from hers. He wrapped the casket with a cloth and tucked it into a box.

No wonder he'd wanted her to go away. But Rebecca didn't have enough energy for a real head of rage. With Michael rage was wasted effort. "You've been in here every night I've been gone, haven't you? Trying to get all the goodies for yourself."

"For the museum," Michael corrected. "It's my job."

"If you say that one more time, I'll scream!"

Eric smiled at Rebecca and Michael both like a teacher at slow pupils. "Has it occurred to you that someone could've been out here looting the entire house?"

Rebecca sagged. Michael swore, charged past her, and ran up the stairs. They went through the house, from the room beneath the platform on down, Michael at point, Eric and Rebecca following warily behind. Nothing was gone. Nothing was moved. Darnley sat impassively washing his face on the bed on the fifth floor, the impression of Elspeth's body beside him.

One glimpse of the cat and Eric sidled back downstairs. "You lucked out this time," he told Michael when they regained the entry.

"You make it sound as if I let someone in," Michael replied. "For a' I ken it was the bogles again, bein' more creative this time oot."

"Sure," said Eric.

Michael turned abruptly and stamped into the kitchen—as well as he could stamp in Reeboks.

"Innocent until proven guilty?" Rebecca suggested to Eric. "Surely it's our same malefactor. But he—she—would need a key."

"The keys are still here," called Michael. "Is that evidence for or against me, Mr. Expensive Lawyer?"

The tight line of Eric's mouth relaxed. He didn't demand why Rebecca was defending Michael. She wasn't sure herself, except that she lived in Dun Iain, too. "As long as nothing's missing I'll have to assume you're innocent, won't I?" he called. And, with a shudder as if something cold had traced his spine, "God, I'll be glad when all this is over." He wrapped his arm around Rebecca. "Walk me to the car?"

He might well be glad when it was over with her, too. He looked, she thought contritely, exhausted. His eyes were brittle smoked glass, the parallel lines between his eyebrows cut deep. And he had to drive back to Columbus. "Would you like to stay here?" she asked. "We have plenty of beds."

A sardonic spark lit his eye and winked out. Sure.

The night was utterly dark, utterly silent except for the dissatisfied mutter of the wind in the trees. On the neutral ground of the parking area Eric and Rebecca kissed with more rue than passion. "I hadn't intended the evening to end like this," he told her.

The best laid schemes o' mice an' men gang aft agley, Rebecca said to herself. The best laid schemes to get laid, that is. Aloud she said, "I'm sorry. I don't think I did, either."

"Well, now we have our cruise to look forward to."

"Yes, we do." Just keep letting me see those chinks in your shell, she thought. Even for a brief encounter I want a man, not a knight in shining armor. She stood shivering in the cold until the red taillights disappeared into the trees.

Just as she was locking the door Michael wailed, "Damn and blast!"

Rebecca wasn't sure she was capable of caring about anything else tonight. The echoing clarity inside her head was worse than any headache. She looked into the sitting room. "Now what?"

He held one of his cassettes. The tape spilled from it, tangled around the lamp, the chair, the shelf where the stereo equipment sat. "It's one o' my Runrig tapes. You canna get them here!"

"Oh, no! Not the live album, the one with 'Loch Lomond' on it?"

"Aye, that one." He tried to reel in the tape. It was knotted beyond repair. "Damn," he moaned, and laid the cassette as reverently down as if it were the mangled body of a pet.

"I love the way they do 'Loch Lomond,' " Rebecca protested. "They have such a gestalt going with the audience, the song tarted up into pop rock and yet with the bloody heart still beating."

"Oh, aye," Michael said softly. He glanced around, just long enough for her to glimpse the anguish in his face. For once the psychological warfare, whether perpetrated by man or spirit, had been directed at him.

"I'm sorry about the tape."

He had already turned away. "Thank you."

"You're welcome." She turned, dragged herself up the stairs to her room, and shut the door on the complications of the night.

Chapter Eighteen

REBECCA SCURRIED THROUGH the rain toward the car. Michael leaned across the seat and opened the door for her. "Did you find Darnley?"

"Asleep upstairs, intelligent creature. What a day for Louise's birthday party."

"It's no so bad," said Michael. He rubbed the fog of his breath off the window. "You should be in Stornoway on a dreich and dreary Sunday, when they're takin' their religion like a dose of cod liver oil."

"No thank you," Rebecca told him. She started the car. It stuttered, balked, and crept down the driveway. Rain rattled on the roof and the wheels hissed through puddles. The windshield wipers muttered like Dorothy grumbling about some fancied slight. The house dwindled in the rearview mirror, pouting in the rain, walls colorless and windows blank. Maybe, Rebecca thought without a great deal of hope, Dun Iain will mind its manners while we're gone.

"Did Warren ever phone back?" Michael asked.

"No. What could he have found out? It's worse than it was last time. Who or what locked you in the storeroom and why didn't they take anything?"

"They murdered my tape," he growled.

"I daresay that was sheer spite, human or otherwise."

"It was no ghost. Someone was in the house wi' me Friday night."

He slumped, his hands in his pockets, his head turned so that Rebecca couldn't see his face. If she felt like an outsider here, he must feel like an astronaut on an alien planet. "It's possible that someone else has a house key," she said. "I don't believe you locked yourself in, like Eric suggested."

"Much obliged," Michael returned. "I don't believe you killed the tape. Or came back early and locked the door."

"Thanks." She shot him a dubious glance. If she asked him if he was up to something, he wouldn't answer.

Yesterday Michael had been his usual professional self. They'd spent hours struggling to correlate the items unearthed from the storeroom with the inventories, and had at last agreed James had bothered to open only a few of his father's crates and boxes. Maybe that's why James was still at Dun Iain. Unfinished business was an accepted motive for haunting.

The Toyota chugged beneath the overpass and into Putnam, the sound of the rain suddenly stopping and starting again. Rebecca's hands were so cold on the steering wheel she could hardly feel her fingers. "All right," she said. "Someone was in the house. It wasn't Eric."

"I'm sure you were right on top of him."

Red light. Rebecca hit the brake with a jolt and frowned at Michael's reflection in the window. "As a matter of fact I wasn't."

"Woman, you've a bad influence on my tongue. You know what I mean."

"I know what you mean." But she hadn't mistaken the quick glint of satisfaction he'd shown when he realized what hadn't happened Friday night. "You don't like Eric, therefore I shouldn't, either. Is that it?"

"It's the clever ones like us who fall arse over tit for smarmy swine."

"What?"

Michael stretched, his knees colliding with the dashboard, and turned the astringent blue glow of his eyes toward her. "Women have no monopoly on self-delusion. I fooled myself once, right and proper. We clever ones, we're the ones who fall for gilded weeds. Too unworldly, I suppose."

He was comparing Eric to Sheila. "I'm under no illusions about Eric," Rebecca asserted. "I've spent too much of my life already repenting at leisure." An impatient toot from the car behind jerked her attention back to the traffic light. She accelerated through the intersection.

Men! she thought. And, just to be fair, added, Women! There

she'd been, champagne, king-sized bed, no doubt silk robe, and she'd frozen up. "Okay," she said, as much to herself as Michael. "Graft is fashionable these days, and Eric has expensive tastes. What if he—as well as half the people in town—is picking up a little extra from Dun Iain?"

"It depends on what you want from him, doesn't it?"

"A good time, some affection, a touch of class. I don't think I know what I want."

"You're settin' your standards awful low."

"Probably." Her baleful glare at Michael was deflected by his amused and quite sympathetic gaze. Her resentment shattered into laughter. "How did this conversation get started?"

Michael shook his head. "Damned if I know, lass."

Still laughing, Rebecca turned into the parking lot of Golden Age Village. The Sorensons' station wagon was just turning out. Peter waved, grinned, pointed toward the building, and mimed hysteria. Michael waved back. Rebecca parked next to the Pruitts' pickup, two cars away from Eric's Volvo. The lights in the windows of the sprawling brick building radiated warmth and welcome. When Michael opened the door and bowed her in with a flourish, she punched playfully at his jacket. Darn the man, honey and vinegar weren't supposed to mix.

The faint antiseptic smell of the hallway was eased by an aroma of coffee. A banner reading "Happy 100th Birthday, Louise" was strung across the door to a large sitting room. People of all ages milled around a long table set with a punch bowl, trays of cookies, and the coffeepot. Jan, wearing her pink volunteer's blouse, met Rebecca just inside the room. "Nasty out there, isn't it? You must feel right at home, Michael."

"No," he answered. "Any chance of a cuppa?"

"I have a pot of tea just for you and Mrs. West. She emigrated from some burg in Scotland lo these many years ago." Jan steered Michael toward an old woman propped up in a wheelchair, her bright beady eyes fixed hungrily on his sweater. "Here he is," Jan called, "one bona fide Scot."

"How do you do, Mrs. West," said Michael, engulfing the old lady's shrunken hand in his. Her face lit up with a smile so broad she looked like an advertisement for dentures.

"Lay it on thick," Jan whispered. "I'll keep you fortified with tea."

Michael took off his coat and pulled up a chair. "So you're from God's country?"

"Yes indeed," Mrs. West replied. "Glen Lyon."

"Perthshire! Ah, bonny airts."

The hills of Caledonia, Rebecca thought. Jan guided her back across the room. "There. I made the mistake of telling her about him last month, and she's been after me to produce him for her."

"I'll bet he doesn't talk to her like he talks to me."

"I hope not." Mandy, Brian, and a couple of other children went whooping by, right under the legs of an old man with a cane. "Mandy!" Jan called. She said to Rebecca, "Get some more cookies out of the kitchen, would you, please?" And she was off after the kids.

Admiring Jan's broken field running. Rebecca headed for the kitchenette at the corner of the room and picked up a platter of cookies. "You stay away from him." said a voice right beside her. She looked around. A second door, open only a crack, led into a hallway. A woman with permed blond hair and a jangling necklace over her pink blouse stood just outside. "He's no good, I tell you. Stay away from him."

"God, Sandra," said a sharp voice that only with difficulty did Rebecca recognize as Heather Hines's. "Get off my back."

"Don't you talk to me that way, young lady."

"You're not my mother. You just married my dad for his money. Leave me alone." A quick stamp of feet and Rebecca caught a glimpse of Heather's black-clad form skimming down the hall like a dragonfly.

With a graphic oath and a jangle Sandra threw open the door and strode through the kitchenette into the sitting room, high heels clicking on the tile. If she saw Rebecca she took no notice. Rebecca was just as glad the woman didn't know who she was. She shook her head; girls Heather's age were emotional accidents looking for someone to happen to.

"Eavesdropping, I see." said Eric's voice in Rebecca's ear.

"I plead innocent, Counselor. Merely a casual witness."

He grinned. "Come meet Louise."

"Let me put these cookies down." So, Rebecca thought as she placed the platter on the table, he wasn't going to turn up that Roman nose at her in retaliation for the awkward scene on Friday. When she'd talked to him on the phone yesterday, he'd been perfectly at ease—he'd even tut-tutted about Michael's tape. But you never could tell with men.

He tucked her hand beneath his arm and led her across the

room. As they passed behind Mrs. West's chair the old lady was saying, "—children from the village sixpence a day to run miles across the moor beating the grouse toward the English shooting parties."

"As if you were animals," said Michael, gesturing with his teacup. "It's no better the noo. We're still used and abused by the wealthy."

"Rebecca," said Eric, "this is Louise O'Donnell."

The old woman's hand felt like a cotton glove filled with baby powder. "You've hardly changed at all from your photos!" Rebecca exclaimed. Louise still had a turned-up nose and a round face, even though her rosy complexion was now the texture of a dried apple. Her hair, while sparse, was still red. A shade that owed more to artifice than to nature, but then, more power to her. "I think these may be yours," Rebecca went on, pulling the clay beads out of her purse. "They were behind a brick in the sixth-floor fireplace."

Louise's glasses were so thick her eyes were magnified out of proportion, as if she were a sketch by Picasso. "Thank you, dear. I'd forgotten all about those beads. You mean you're actually digging through Jamie's scrapbooks?"

"It's a real adventure," Rebecca assured her. "I'm sorry I came too late to meet any of the Forbes family. But that's archaeology, trying to piece together people's lives from what they leave behind."

Eric seated Rebecca and asked Jan, "Do you need any help?"

She said, "Peter's just come back with some more cookies, if you don't mind going out in the rain with that nice suit." Eric headed out into the rain, navy-blue suit, striped shirt, cranberry tie, wing tips, and all.

"Isn't he pretty?" said Louise. "If only I were eighty again."

Rebecca laughed and accepted a cup of coffee from Jan. "We were just looking at the photos of Rudolph Gemmell. He was very pretty, too."

"Much too pretty for his own good. And for Mrs. Forbes's."

"She seemed so flirtatious in the pictures I'd wondered if John was ever jealous of her. You don't mean he was jealous of his own butler."

Louise nodded sagely. "And with good reason, too."

"Really?" Nothing like good, juicy, harmless gossip about people who were dead and gone. History was little more than man's insatiable taste for gossip, after all.

"It was so long ago," Louise said. "I was too young then to understand what was happening. The voices in the night, the steps on the stairs, the stained linens. But I understand now. Mrs. Forbes and Rudolph were lovers."

"Well! The butler did it—how about that!" So Elspeth, the stranger in a strange land, had been so lonely she'd taken not an aristocratic neighbor but her servant to her bed. More than one ballad recounted such a story.

"And the baby!" Louise went on. "I was there all alone with Mrs. Forbes when it came, and believe me, that was a very sudden education!"

Rebecca remembered Prissy in *Gone with the Wind:* "I don't know nothing about birthing babies!" "It must've been rather a shock to Mrs. Forbes, too."

"The poor little thing was so small and frail. Now I see, counting back, that she might've been Mr. Forbes's daughter, just come early. He had been in Scotland on a buying spree the last winter, if you see what I mean."

"The plot thickens! There was talk of the baby not being John's?"

"If the baby was full-term, it couldn't have been his. But it was so small, it might've been early."

"But the baby died," said Rebecca. "Poor Elspeth. Mrs. Forbes. She must've been heartbroken."

Eric and Peter carried boxes into the kitchenette, their laughing and joking an odd counterpoint to Louise's tragic story. "Mrs. Forbes was beside herself. Especially since the Gemmells' baby was born just two days later, and she was fat and sassy."

"Ouch. I didn't realize the babies were born close together. Rudolph must've been busy that winter."

Louise cackled delightedly. "Oh, yes, I should think so!"

"How cruel, though, to have a healthy baby just upstairs." Rebecca visualized Elspeth languishing about the castle in pre-Raphaelite poses, like the Lady of Shalott.

"And Mr. Forbes going on at her about Rudolph. I don't think he knew for sure, but he certainly suspected. After the baby died Mrs. Forbes started railing at him that it was all his fault. She had a temper, that one. She'd scream at Mr. Forbes and the servants and throw dishes at them. Athena, the cook, Rudolph's wife—she had to keep the Royal Doulton locked up."

Rebecca's thoughts kaleidoscoped, settling in a new and different pattern. So much for her—and Eric's—idealized picture of the tragic put-upon Mrs. Forbes. Who still liked to throw dishes.

Louise bent forward. "Mr. Forbes brought home some letter, and Mrs. Forbes said it was because of the letter her baby died. Lost her mind, I'm afraid. Grief will do that."

"Letter?" Rebecca's ears pricked.

"Always kept it wrapped in an oilskin, he said."

Oilskin . . . "The Erskine letter!" Rebecca cried, so loudly heads turned and one old lady reached for her hearing aid. Even Michael glanced up, brows at the alert. "Do you know where John—Mr. Forbes—kept it?"

Louise shook her head. "That's what he called it, all right. The Erskine letter. But I never saw it, dear. Sorry."

With a sigh and a pat on Louise's hand Rebecca said, "That's all right. Just daydreaming. So Elspeth jumped from the window. Not in despair, I guess, but in some kind of black anguish. You and she were alone in the house?"

"Well, almost." Louise looked down at her lap, her gnarled fingers twisting the necklace. "I was watching Katie, the Gemmells' baby, in the kitchen. Mr. Forbes was in the study. Mrs. Forbes started screaming, 'I want my baby back!' Then I heard her fall."

"I'm sure it's still a very painful memory," said Rebecca. "I shouldn't have asked about it."

"No, no, it was so long ago. All I really remember is grabbing up Katie when Mr. Forbes ran outside. He came back in white as a sheet. And the funeral. Poor little Jamie holding my hand, not understanding, and Athena glancing over at Rudolph."

"I can imagine. A stiff wifely 'Are you satisfied now?' look. Athena knew about his relationship with Mrs. Forbes?"

"Looking back, I think so. But Athena was very practical. How was she going to support her own baby without a husband? Not that Rudolph ever admitted to a thing, you understand."

"Why should he? John Forbes would just have created a scandal by firing him."

Eric walked by, saying something complimentary to Jan. Her simper was a wicked parody of Dorothy's. Grinning, Rebecca visualized Dun Iain filled with family and servants. It had never been an ordinary home. But it had not always been the part-sinister, part-absurd structure it was today. She said, "I saw a photo of Katherine—Katie—all grown up. She became an actress?''

"She did some bit parts in Hollywood," Louise answered. "Then the talkies came in and her voice wasn't good enough. Back she came to Putnam. Rudolph and Athena left when Mr. Forbes died in the thirties, and I haven't seen Katie in ages. She's probably dead now. Most everyone is."

Michael's voice filled a lull in the conversational buzz. "As if the Clearances were no sae bad, noo they're fillin' the glens wi' great bluidy forests. Turnin' a quick profit on the lumber, they are, while the local people canna afford to keep their farms. The values have been driven up by incomers who dinna even live there. Look at the adverts for rental properties, all the phone numbers are south o' the border!''

Mrs. West nodded eagerly, hanging on every word.

"Oh, aye, it makes you want to pluck up sword and gun and fight it all ower again. All we're askin' is justice.''

Or faith we'll take it man? thought Rebecca.

Eric fished Brian Sorenson out from under the table and tied his shoe. Phil Pruitt appeared beside Louise's chair. "Happy Birthday, Grandma. And many more.''

"Don't be foolish, Philip," she replied. "I could go tomorrow.''

Phil was dressed in his Sunday best, a rusty suit that had come off a Sears Roebuck rack a good many years ago. Next to Eric's tailored wool he seemed like a scarecrow. "Hello, Mr. Pruitt," Rebecca said, but Phil was looking over her head toward the door.

She glanced around. There was Heather, staring intently at—me? she thought for a moment. It was hard to tell: the girl's eyes were so heavily encased in black makeup she looked like a raccoon. Oh. She must be staring at Steve, who was grazing among the punch and cookies.

Sandra Hines, fluffing a pillow for the occupant of a wheelchair, glared at Steve and gave the pillow an extra hard thump, her bright red lips turned down in a scowl. Eric released Brian and looked Sandra's ripe figure up and down. Sandra's red lipstick might be the same shade as the tube lost in his bathroom. Rebecca smothered a smile. No, Eric was not fooling her at all, either with the surface gloss or the carefully banked fire beneath.

She stood and kissed Louise's cheek. "Happy Birthday, Mrs. O'Donnell.''

"Thank you, dear. Come see me again sometime."

"I will."

Jan beckoned from the kitchenette and Rebecca headed through the crowd. "Did everything come off all right Friday?" Jan stage-whispered.

"That's terrible," Rebecca told her. "Nothing came off at all. Sorry to disappoint you."

"Just as long as *you're* not disappointed."

"No, actually I'm not."

Jan glanced over Rebecca's shoulder. Peter was poking inquisitively into the motor of a wheelchair, the occupant offering querulous suggestions. Eric exchanged pleasantries with Heather. Steve was gone. Michael was flirting shamelessly with Mrs. West.

"I invited Michael for Thanksgiving this Thursday," Jan said. "It's our duty to give him American lessons."

"Can I come, too?" asked Rebecca.

"Of course!" Laughing, Jan sped away after her offspring, dodging around Eric's approaching form. Eric cornered Rebecca behind the door of the kitchenette and stole a kiss. "I'm off to Omaha tonight. I should be back in time for Ben's Thanksgiving dinner—attendance required for us junior members. Are you going to be with Jan or would you like to come, too?"

Dinner at the Birkenheads'? "I'll be with Jan," Rebecca stated. "Good luck on your quest."

"Take care, then. I'll see you next weekend." He offered Rebecca her kiss back again, and she accepted it ruefully. This wasn't turning out as she'd expected a casual affair should. But she had only herself to blame.

The party was breaking up. Mrs. West and Michael parted with assorted diphthongs and expressions of good cheer. He and Rebecca plunged into the gray, damp afternoon. At least it had stopped raining.

Steve sprawled in the pickup, surrounded by a haze of sweetly scented smoke, his eyes half closed. "The lad's beggin' for trouble," said Michael.

"Want to go over and yell at him?" Rebecca asked.

"No." They sorted themselves into the icy interior of her car. "What was that shout aboot the Erskine letter?"

"Oh!" As Rebecca negotiated the rain-slicked streets she filled him in on Louise's story of Elspeth, the butler, the baby, and the letter.

Michael whistled. "She blamed poor old John, eh? Typical. You have to wonder whether he didna chuck her oot the window after all. Her death and the baby's solved a few problems for him."

"Sad to say. At least we know for sure he had the letter."

"Aye. I was beginnin' to think it was just rumor, like the treasure."

Rebecca glanced at him, but his face was noncommittal. "Not that Louise knew whether the letter said King James was Mary's baby."

"Hard to believe he was. He was ugly and intelligent, Mary and Darnley were beautiful twits."

"I think it was finding a baby's body in Edinburgh castle— when was that, 1830?—that's most damning. Wrapped in a silk cloth with the initial 'J,' yet. I don't suppose you have the bones in the basement of the museum?"

"That'd come a treat, right enough."

"Well, even if James were Arabella Erskine's son, he was still a Lennox Stewart, since everyone was intermarried, anyway."

"Did you ever think aboot the other woman at the birth, Lady Reres? She was James's wet nurse—she must've had a bairn o' her own." Michael poked Rebecca's arm. "You remember her name?"

It was . . . "Aha! It was Margaret Forbes!"

"Watch the road," said Michael, and Rebecca swerved back to the right. "That's why Johnnie wanted the letter."

"Like he modeled Dun Iain on Willie Forbes's Craigievar. Like James contributed when Hector Forbes bought Culloden for the National Trust in 1946."

"The National Trust for Scotland in 1944," Michael corrected. "Do you ken the English heiress who married into the Craigievar Forbeses was a Sempill? The Sempills fought for the Hanoverians at Culloden."

"Like the Campbells?"

"Like many Scots. The issues were no clearer then than noo."

"Sounded to me like you had the issues down pretty good for Mrs. West."

"Got a wee bit carried away." He shrugged. "Appreciative audience."

"Uh-huh," said Rebecca. "The Sempills got a title for their daughter, like the Bowes at Glamis and the Gilstraps at Eilean

Donan. But what did the Ramseys get marrying Elspeth to John?
He had the money."

"Grief," Michael said. "Ah, home again."

The maples drooped and wept over the driveway like the sentient trees of a Disney cartoon. The mausoleum crouched by the drive. The castle stood hunched as defensively as Michael with his hands in his pockets, the same bright, perceptive eye-windows gazing out under the brows of the parapets. When Rebecca turned off the engine, the only sound was the slow drip of water from the roof and the branches. Except for a meow. Darnley was sitting on the low stone wall. "How did he get oot?" Michael demanded.

"Oh, Lord. Who was here with their handy-dandy counterfeit key?" She picked up the animal. Only his paws were wet; he hadn't been out when it was raining. "Speak, Darnley. Who's your partner in crime?" The cat yawned.

"Who wisna at the party?" Michael asked. "Dorothy? Warren?" He unlocked and threw open the front door with a crash. "Come oot, come oot, wherever you are!" His voice echoed eerily. No one and nothing answered.

"Don't do that!" Rebecca hissed.

"No, ma'am," he said, chastened. "Sorry, ma'am."

The lights worked perfectly. Each blazed into life at the flick of a switch as Michael and Rebecca yet again slogged from room to room. "I'd feel better if something were gone," she said at last, throwing her coat over a kitchen chair.

"Amen," replied Michael. He opened the refrigerator.

Darnley headed into the pantry. He lapped daintily at his water, then crouched and peered under the slightly unsteady shelf. Rebecca watched him. She'd seen a mouse beneath that shelf. "Have you ever owned a cat?"

"Cats have lived where I've lived, but I canna say I've owned them."

"We were never in one place long enough for a pet." Rebecca knelt and looked where Darnley was looking. The shadow of the shelf was almost opaque; she couldn't see where the stone walls of the pantry met the stone flags of the floor. "But I've known plenty of cat lovers."

Michael laid a couple of plastic containers on the cabinet and glanced quizzically at Rebecca. "Worshippin' the Royal Doulton?"

"Don't be silly. It's just that cats are weaselly little critters."

She stood up, brushed off her knees, and got the flashlight from the drawer. She said to Michael with a grin, "Elementary, my dear Watson."

Down she went to her knees again, this time shining the light beneath the shelf. Sure enough, there was a cat-sized gap where one tier of stones had cracked and settled away from the floor.

Darnley parked himself next to his food dish and twitched his tail, sublimely unconcerned. Michael knelt beside Rebecca. "You dinna mean . . . Ah, how dense can you get!" He laughed. "Come on, let's find the exit."

The flashlight danced like a firefly along the castle walls where they dived into the damp darkness of turf and weeds. In several places the covering harl had chipped and flaked from years of weather, exposing the granite blocks beneath. On the opposite side of the building from the door the tiny gleaming square of the pantry window punctured the wall.

"Shine the torch doon here." Michael crouched beside several rather bedraggled rosebushes planted along the foundation and reached gingerly into the tangle of branches. "Looks like the builders tried to scrimp a bit by usin' stone scraps. One's pulled loose . . . Ouch!"

He stood. One hand had a long scratch across the back, the other held a tuft of butterscotch and white fur. "Castles usually have postern gates. Even if they're just moggie-sized."

They tramped back into the house. Rebecca anointed Michael's hand with antiseptic while he protested, "It's just a scratch, hen."

Hen? An affectionate pet name—for her? She looked up with a smile that was both bewildered and shy. He smiled similarly back. So he approved of the way things were, or were not, going with Eric. Okay . . .

She released his hand and said, "I don't know whether to give Darnley some extra liver or kick him. He really had us going, didn't he?"

"The night he did. But he didna lock the lumber room Friday night."

"No, he didn't." With a sigh she confronted the plastic containers. "I'll make something out of that pitiful little roast."

"Shepherd's pie?" Michael asked. "I'll mash the tatties." He picked up Darnley and scratched his ears. "So you were havin' us on, were you?"

Darnley, as much as a cat could, smiled.

Chapter Nineteen

REBECCA WAS ALMOST ready for bed, flannel nightgown, socks, and fifty strokes of the hairbrush. She plugged in a Tannahill Weavers tape and looked again at Elspeth's portrait. So she hadn't been the stereotypical victim. Rebecca decided she liked Elspeth better for that surprisingly hard edge.

Odd—that pipe solo had a depth she'd never heard on her inexpensive player . . . Michael was downstairs playing a pibroch. Apologizing to the Tannahills, Rebecca turned off the tape, closed her eyes, and drifted on the aching tranquillity of the songs. Men wouldn't cry, so they made music.

The pibroch slid into a reel and then into a modern ballad. When the songs ended, the last note vibrated in the hush of the lonely house. Rebecca pulled the cold sheets over her head and curled numbly into a knot, her thoughts eddying with the skewed imagery that haunts the frontier of sleep.

With one flick of his paws Darnley pushed aside a huge block of stone. Brian and baby Katie paddled like ducklings in the punch bowl. Young Louise and old Mrs. West danced a strathspey as Athena's cooking pots drummed accompaniment. Steve dropped his cigarette and smoke blotted his image.

Eric's eyes were smoky quartz. He cornered Rebecca and kissed her. But they weren't at Golden Age, they were in his condo. stretched across his bed. All Rebecca wore was Elspeth's jet, garnet, and diamond choker. Her skin was smoke and sweat against Eric's. She writhed, exultant. But his body slipped through her grasp and vanished. She was alone.

With a strangled gasp she awoke. For a moment she lay disoriented. Then she threw the smothering covers aside and scraped the damp strands of hair from her face. She could barely see the dial of her clock registering two A.M.; the dim light of the night-light was filtered through a mist, as if she really had been burning . . . She inhaled. The room was filled with smoke.

Rebecca catapulted out of the bed. The door wasn't hot. She threw it open. The corridor was thick with smoke. Yellow light flickered in the stairwell. Not pausing to grab her glasses, she hitched up her nightgown and scrambled up the stairs, her sock-clad feet slipping, her lungs burning. She dived into Michael's room, threw herself onto the bed, and pummeled the long lump beneath the covers. "Get up! Get up! We're on fire!"

Michael heaved, snorted, and mumbled plaintively, "I'm no even hot!"

She found an arm and yanked at it. "The house is on fire!" His chest and shoulders above the blanket were stark naked. That figures. He would have to be one of those men who don't wear pajamas.

His slightly blurred eyes clicked into focus. He swept Rebecca and covers aside and leaped to his feet. In the feeble, hazy light she saw that he was wearing a pair of soccer shorts. She didn't have time to be relieved.

Michael hurriedly wet towels in his bathroom. He slapped Rebecca's face with clammy terry cloth, ordering, "Put this ower your mouth." He wrapped his own face. They ran through the big bedroom, down the back staircase, out into the Hall. The high ceiling was matted with smoke. The light of the flames flickered on the walls.

The metal trash can from the kitchen stood on the landing. Already the flames shooting above its rim were subsiding and the thick black smoke dissipating. Michael slipped past the can, down the steps, and to the kitchen. A few soup pots of water later the fire was out.

The front door was standing wide open. Rebecca slammed it shut, hoping the eyes she felt watching her were only Queen Mary's marble ones.

Once again she and Michael trekked through the house, turning on lights, checking the artifacts, and opening windows on all floors but the sixth. There Elspeth's window was already open, not the inch or two it usually was, but flung wide. The door and the window had drawn the smoke through the height of the house as if it had been a chimney.

Michael adjusted the window to its usual crack. "Was Elspeth ticked off at your bletherin' aboot her the day?"

"Maybe she decided to help the fire along, but she didn't set it. Someone very real was in the house." Rebecca's voice arched suddenly and she steadied it. "Was he—she—were they trying to kill us?"

He glanced at her, raised his hand, and wiped his hair off his forehead, leaving a streak of charcoal across his skin. "It was another warnin'. Like lockin' me in the storeroom. Like murderin' my tape."

"A threat. An order to leave." Rebecca hugged herself, the cold draft slicing through her gown and drawing gooseflesh from the skin that had only moments before been hot and sweaty.

"Whoever it is," Michael said, "must've taken a proper scunner to us, to try and set the place on fire."

Back down they went, and considered the blackened trash can. The intricate white plaster ceilings of Hall and study were bruised with soot, but there was no other damage.

"Bluidy stupid way to give an order," said Michael. "These places may be built o' stone, but there's enough wood inside to make one—this one—go up like a torch. Especially when we're miles from the fire brigade. A good thing you woke up. See, the drapes on the window were singed by sparks."

Now that the excitement of both dream and fire was over, Rebecca felt hollow and slightly sick. She was much too embarrassed to tell Michael why she'd waked up. She uttered a four-letter word that surprised herself and made his brows shoot upward.

"Excuse me." Inhaling deeply of the cold but clear air, she peered down into the entry. Small chunks of mud like chocolate bits lay scattered on the floor and the steps up to the landing. "Look. The mud that squishes up beside the sole of your shoe and then falls off when you walk."

"Aye, Sherlock?"

They followed the faint mud track into the kitchen. The stone floor of the pantry was marked by one faint, smeared footprint. "Here's where they found their fuel," Michael said. "The old newspapers for packin'. Pasteboard boxes. Dorothy's dust rags."

Rebecca rubbed her arms briskly, wondering if her flesh was going to break off her bones, it was so cold. With a smothered groan she picked up the towels that were still lying on the floor, rose, and found she didn't need her glasses to appreciate Michael.

Smudges of soot looked like bruises on the fair skin of his arms and shoulders. The hair on his chest was indeed auburn, his legs below the shorts were lean and strong. If his waist wasn't as slender as it had probably once been, he still had a way to go before flab dulled his wiry lines. Nice, she thought, if grubby. With a corner of the towel she went after the charcoal smear on his forehead.

"I can bathe mysel', thank you," he said, fending her off with a forearm and a grin. "You're none too clean, either."

"A flannel gown isn't the most efficient of fire-fighting garments."

"Nor the most attractive."

"I wasn't dressing for an audience." She stooped to wipe the mud from the floor.

"Dinna do that! We'll have to have Lansdale oot the morn!"

"Oh, of course. Sorry." She folded the towels and laid them on the counter. The breeze nibbled at her with tiny cold teeth. She shivered, her own teeth starting to chatter. Shock, she told herself dispassionately.

"Cold?" This time when Michael raised his hand he locked his arm around her shoulders. "Or scared?"

The stubble on his jaw was at the moment his only concession to prickliness; she ran her arm gratefully around his waist. His skin was cool beneath her hand. "Both," she replied. "You would be, too, if your skin wasn't so thick."

"It's no sae thick as all that," he told her.

No, it wasn't, she thought, but she wasn't particularly surprised.

They turned off the lights, left two windows slitted open, went back upstairs. With bemused smiles they parted in Rebecca's doorway just as Darnley crept out from beneath the bed. His baleful look seemed to say, Life was much simpler before you got here.

Rebecca's thoughts hung suspended in the hollowness inside her, as if they were displays tucked away behind safety glass. A clean nightgown. A bath. Hot water to wash away soot and sweat both . . . Michael still stood in the door. She said, "It's been a long time since you've asked me if I'm going to turn tail and run. Now's your chance."

"A fine thrawn lass like yoursel', runnin' away? If the bogles canna get rid o' you, I widna expect a human bein' to do it."

"Stubborn, *moi*?" She laughed. "I'll take that as a compliment."

"It was meant as one. Good night, lass."

"Good night, lad. Thank you. And, oh, be sure to wash that scratch!"

"I will, I will." His bare feet padded up the staircase.

Half an hour later, when Rebecca was curled drowsily in her nest of blankets, it occurred to her Michael might have hesitated in the door because his not so thick skin had wanted to sleep next to hers. Platonically, of course. In the spirit of comradeship.

But you never could tell with men. Even the comradely ones were likely to have sex-saturated brains. Must be difficult for them, dealing with a handicap like that.

Dealing with dreams like the one that had wakened her to the fire. Rebecca looked at the shadowed canopy as though her look could penetrate it and ceiling both and see Michael alone in his bed. Dr. Campbell had no business turning attractive to her. None at all.

She drifted at last into a light but dreamless sleep. Monday morning dawned, as most Mondays seemed to do, cold, damp, and dismal.

Warren Lansdale and a forensics team from Putnam arrived within an hour of Rebecca's call, while she and Michael were still exchanging wry and wary glances over their breakfasts. The men crashed like a tidal wave over the house, collected various lumps and scrapings of mud and charcoal, boxed up the trash can, and with noncommittal shrugs ebbed away.

Michael leaned against Mary's marble effigy, his hands in his pockets. He was wearing his blue sweatshirt with the white Saint Andrew's cross, the emblem on the flag of Scotland, as though he had nailed his colors to the mast. Warren stood in the door with his hat in his hands. Behind him the rain drifted down onto lawn, dovecote, and the assorted cars in the parking area. Rebecca inspected the sheriff's face, trying to penetrate the shrubbery.

His concern seemed perfectly genuine. "I was sure you'd seen the last of the vandalism. But a fire—that's ugly. Would you consider leaving?"

"No way," stated Rebecca, despite the slightly sick feeling

still lurking in the pit of her stomach. "I'm not letting some nut push me around."

"Mr. Adler is out of town?" the sheriff went on.

"I left a message with his secretary, and she said she'd pass it on to him if he calls in. He couldn't do anything if he were here."

Warren shook his head. "Just the vandalism. Nothing else has been stolen. It doesn't make sense."

"It makes perfect sense to whoever's doin' it," Michael said.

Rebecca crossed her arms. "Warren, do you have the mausoleum key?"

"No, ma'am, I sure don't." His moustache wilted, hurt.

But Michael's jaundiced gaze sustained her into another question. "Did you know we found the will you signed for James on August twenty-fourth?"

"Yes, Mr. Adler said it'd turned up."

"Do you know why James never got anyone else to sign it?"

"No. When I left him that afternoon, he was putting away the chess pieces, chuckling over how he was going to surprise Mr. Adler . . ."

"What?" interrupted Michael, standing up straight. "James didn't want Adler to know about that will?" Rebecca shot a keen glance at him. Interesting point, but do you have to raise it with such relish?

"James hadn't told him about it when I left," Warren replied. "But he knows about it now, so James must've told him later."

"Weren't you curious," Michael persisted, "why the will you signed, the one that didn't provide for relatives, wasn't the one in effect?"

Warren glanced from Michael to Rebecca and back, obviously wondering why a higher education had left them so obtuse. "James's wills were his business. I signed where he asked me to sign. If he changed his mind again, that was no concern of mine."

Michael caught Rebecca's warning eye and subsided against the sarcophagus. "Thank you. Much obliged for your help."

Mollified, Warren glanced at his watch. "If you want that lock changed again, just say so. Someone must've copied one of the keys to the other one."

"The dead bolt you brought ought to do it," replied Rebecca. "And thank you for the smoke detectors. I'll make sure Eric reimburses you."

Lansdale settled his hat firmly on his head. "No rush. I feel bad enough about this—you come to do your jobs and all this happens to you." He backed into the rain. "I'll let you know if the lab finds anything."

The squad car swished down the driveway. Michael exchanged a careful glance with Rebecca. "Is he hidin' something, or is he just unimaginative?"

"I wish I knew." She dived out the door and padded across the wet lawn to the toolshed.

The small clapboard building smelled of soured grass clippings, fertilizer, and gasoline. In the light of a single bare bulb Phil and Steve crouched amid rakes, flowerpots, boards, and cobwebs, absorbed like Roman soothsayers in the entrails of a lawn mower. "Excuse me," Rebecca began. "Would you mind putting up some smoke alarms and installing a dead bolt on the door before you quit today? They're on the kitchen table."

"I'll do it right now," Phil said, unfolding himself from his crouch. To Steve he said, "Make sure you get those bolts on tight."

Just inside the door two milk jugs encrusted with brown goo stood next to a fresh red gas can. No wonder the place stank of gasoline, Rebecca thought. Surely Eric didn't know they'd been keeping it in plastic jugs.

Maybe the lab would find traces of gasoline in the trash can. She looked narrowly at Steve, but his lock of hair was as effective as a highwayman's mask in concealing his expression. Innocent until proven guilty, she reminded herself, and started back for the house.

The clouds were so low they touched the top of the castle, the weather vane looking like it was packed in cotton batting. It wasn't much warmer in the entry, and the breath of the house was damp and musty in Rebecca's nostrils, but the lights shone with comforting halos. She was telling Phil where the smoke alarms needed to go, on second-, fourth-, and sixth-floor landings, when she heard Dorothy's indignant voice.

The housekeeper had already given them chapter and verse for calling her on her day off. Rebecca had had to invoke Eric's name, coupled with the words "overtime pay," to do the trick. "You told me to clean it and I'm cleaning it!" Dorothy was saying.

"But you're muckin' it aboot!" protested Michael.

Rebecca found Dorothy and Michael confronting each other

just inside the Hall. Oh, my God—the woman had taken a scrub brush to the original gilt frame of a two-hundred-year-old Romney portrait.

Rebecca intervened, muttering whatever soothing phrases came to her mind—lack of communication, no harm done. Michael carried the painting away like a fireman rescuing a child from a burning building. Dorothy, frowning ferociously and muttering about people who couldn't speak English right, turned to the soot scum on the window. Rebecca fled.

Michael was in the kitchen, tenderly wiping the frame and murmuring assurances to the portrait. He was oblivious to Rebecca standing in the doorway. They must've been suffering from smoke inhalation last night, she thought with an affectionately exasperated smile, falling on each other like that. Nice hug, though. Absolutely first-rate.

She headed upstairs, replaced the glass bottles left in the fourth-floor hall, and went into James's bedroom.

She sealed the boxes of baby clothes. The poor little girl hadn't even lived long enough to have a name. If James haunted the house because of unfinished business, then, perhaps, so did Elspeth, looking for the baby she'd never accepted was gone.

Elspeth's clothes were fusty and limp, rather nasty, like plants growing in a stagnant pond. Cautiously Rebecca bundled them into black trash bags for the Historical Society, waiting to be gripped by some paroxysm of anger or grief. But whatever spirit of Elspeth lingered in the house had long since deserted its mortal clothing. Not the briefest whiff of lavender stirred the close, still air in the room. At last Rebecca got up, brushed off her sweater and jeans, and opened the window.

A shrill angry voice smacked her like Michael's wet towel. There, on the drab winter-brown lawn behind the castle, Steve stood hunched truculently while Heather's entire body gesticulated rage at him. Her words were lost in the rush and rustle of the rain.

Steve shrugged and turned away. Typical male. Heather stood there with her guts strung out beside her and he decided to sweep the shed or something. Heather grasped his arm and turned him back. He threw her away from him so forcefully she went sprawling. Rebecca gasped, clenching her fists on the windowsill. But Steve was already helping Heather up with every appearance of remorse.

Arm in arm, Heather sulking, Steve cajoling, they walked

around the corner of the building. A few minutes later a car revved, loudly and unnecessarily, in the parking area. Heather's stepmother's Datsun, no doubt; the girl drove it with the heedless swoop of the newly licensed.

Well! Rebecca thought. Heather was turning out as surprisingly as Elspeth had. There must be something in the atmosphere at Dun Iain that made mice into lions. And what had that argument been about, anyway?

Phil appeared in the door. "Alarms are up. Dead bolt's fixed."

"Thank you," she replied. His steps disappeared downstairs. Dorothy's voice echoed upstairs. The front door slammed twice.

A preternatural silence fell over the castle, the usual creaks and pops of the house swallowed in the white noise of the rain. Rebecca started down the stairs and walked right into Darnley's steady gaze as he crouched in the corridor, playing Greyfriars Bobby yet again. She stopped, a chill running its cold fingers down her spine.

He'd seen James lying there dead. Had he seen him fall? Or had he seen the old man pushed? The cat roused itself, looked up, meowed. Rebecca picked him up and laid her cheek against his soft fur, his little body thrumming comfortingly against her face.

Maybe some food would soothe the vague unease like a poison-ivy rash in her stomach. She found Michael in the kitchen heating up the leftover soup. "Great minds think alike," she said. "I'll make some bran muffins." They cooked and ate, jostling for the last crumbs, and when at last the food was gone Rebecca said, "You go on, I'll clear up."

Michael departed waving the bottle of Laphroaig and two glasses. "Usquebaugh was invented for a dreich night like this one. The museum, at least, expect their scholars to be drinkers."

"I won't tell the state if you won't," Rebecca replied.

That was what she needed, she thought as she finished the dishes, threw the dead bolt, and started upstairs. A good hot meal to dull the nerves. As dismal day clotted into dark night outside, the inside of the castle became cozy, even the ghosts dozing in the gentle swish of the rain. The stone shed its gray chill, the dark paneling glowed warmly in the lamplight, and the steps spiraled like the petals of a sunflower. Like Michael, the house was very appealing when well behaved.

His voice wafted down the stairs. As Rebecca took down and

brushed out her hair she listened to the song, then laughed. No wonder she couldn't understand the words; he was singing Runrig's "Chi Min Geamhradh." She went on to the fourth floor and stepped into the bedroom as his voice leaped upward with emotion. He saw her and stopped. The next phrase fell silently, like a silk scarf, through her mind. "What do the words mean?"

"I dinna ken. I dinna have the Gaelic; I learned the song by rote." He smiled reminiscently. "I knew a lass from Skye when I was at university. In moments o' emotion she'd start talkin' Gaelic. All those soft gutturals like puffs o' thistledoon in my ear." He reached for the bottle perched atop the bureau and poured a generous dollop into the empty glass. "Here you go."

"Thank you." What dynamic of rain and Scotch had brought forth that confidence? Rebecca smiled, admiring the sinuous dance of the light in the amber liquid in her glass. "Here's to the little man in the velvet weskit."

"Which means?" asked Michael teasingly, raising his own glass.

"The mole who dug the hole into which King William III's horse stumbled, killing him. William, not the horse. I assume the mole was sitting there smoothing its little plaid and snickering."

"Very good." Michael bowed graciously and sipped, swished the whiskey around his mouth, and with a blissful smile swallowed.

The whiskey detonated inside Rebecca's mouth and nose, filling her head with peat smoke and heather. She settled down on the floor next to the apothecary's chest. The space heater sighed. The rain, muted by the stone walls, crooned a siren song about burns and braes. The smell of leather books and furniture polish mingled with the tang of whiskey inside her sinuses.

More old maps were in the first drawer. The next one held postcards and candy wrappers. The third . . . "Uh-oh," Rebecca said, "a contraband copy of Carnegie's *The Gospel of Wealth*. The title's been scratched off the spine. James, hiding it from his father? Or John, checking up on the competition?"

"Look at these novels," said Michael. "All wi' Elspeth's name written on the flyleaf. Mrs. Holmes, Mrs. Southworth— sentimental moralists, I'd expect. But Ouida and *Lady Audley's Secret*. Racy stuff."

"I'm getting to like Elspeth," admitted Rebecca. She opened

another drawer and was rewarded by a mint copy of Boswell's *Tour of the Hebrides*.

"How old are you?" Michael asked suddenly.

"How old am I? Twenty-seven. Why?"

He laughed. "You're so girlish at times. And yet you have such matronly gravitas. Gey contradictory."

She sat with the book in her lap and stared at him. He found *her* contradictory? She countered, "How old are you?"

"Altogether too close to thirty, hen."

Again he'd called her a pet name. Her cheeks burned—from the whiskey, no doubt. Rebecca opened the next drawer. In it was a wool-cloth, green Forbes tartan. She took it to the bed and spread it out. It had a distinct odor of mothballs, but only two tiny holes. "Are you going to want this?"

Michael glanced around. "Bundle it up wi' Elspeth's clothes." He turned back, singing under his breath, *"I'll roll you in my green plaid while we lie upon the grass."*

Rebecca quelled a giggle and reached for the far end of the cloth. "Did you ever want to play the pipes for one of the folk-rock groups? You're as good as any I've heard."

"Why, thank you. You heard me playin', then?"

"The great Highland pipes are a little hard to miss." She overbalanced and climbed onto the bed. "Although I almost wish I hadn't; they made me hideously homesick for a place I've barely been."

He was looking at her again; she felt that exacting blue gaze on her back. "No so surprisin'. You've been livin' there in your mind for years."

"Oh. You're right. Very perceptive." She glanced around appreciatively. He shrugged, smiling back. She sat down and pulled the ends of the cloth toward her.

"Mind you," Michael said, "I would've liked to play wi' a group. But I wisna keen on livin' on the dole between engagements. So I contented mysel' playin' for the Glendhu band at the occasional festival."

"Have you ever tried Rizzio's guitar?"

"And Baron Ruthven wi' his wee dirk comin' after me like he did poor Davy Rizzio? I'm never touchin' that again."

"Another booby-trapped artifact? In the ashes of time you do find the odd live ember." Rebecca laid the cloth on the foot of the bed. Compared with some of the other rooms in the house, this one was not at all haunted. Not one object they'd found here had that strange resonance, as compelling as music. "I played the accordion," she said. "We couldn't carry a piano around with us. But after endless repetitions of 'Beer Barrel Polka' and 'Fascination' I gave up. It was only later I realized I could've been playing the old Scottish and Irish songs, like the ones you grew up on."

"I grew up on the Beatles, Led Zeppelin, and Willie Nelson." Michael stood, rescued her glass of Scotch, and brought it to her.

"Thanks." Tilting her head to drink, she saw that the underside of the canopy was stitched with intricate floral figures. She set her glass on the bedside table, flipped off her shoes, and lay back. "Well, look at that!"

Michael peered under the overhang. "Aye?"

"Beautiful embroidery." And, as he moved, "Take off your shoes."

He sent her a look of amusement and exasperation mingled. His Reeboks thudded on the floor and his head thumped the pillow. He balanced his glass on the cross on his chest; X marks the spot. "Victorian. Elspeth's?"

"Seaming her sanity with embroidery floss? I bet this is where she met Rudolph. No wonder this room isn't haunted. She was happy here."

"Depends on how you mean happy." Michael raised his head to drink.

"Wasn't Elspeth engaged to a man in Dundee before John carried her away? It's like you said—he always wanted things that belonged to someone else. At least he couldn't keep her."

"Ah, she had him knackered right and proper. Takin' trophies in the battle of the sexes, she was."

"And it can be a battle," Rebecca said. She reached for her Scotch, sipped, put it back. The room had a warm golden aura, as if she were looking at it through her glass. "Why did you ever take up with Sheila to being with?"

He tensed. "It was almost two years ago. I was workin' on the Jacobite exhibit at the British Museum. The same Jacobites the English used to shoot like rabbits—noo they're fair romantic. Sheila was publicity director. I was lonely and randy and she was lookin' for entertainment. It was like a nettle rash. It's no good to scratch it but you do, anyway."

"Quite lethal," Rebecca agreed.

"And why did you take up wi' Ray?"

"I was the classic ugly duckling. Braces on my teeth, glasses, nose in a book, no idea how to make friends, scared to death of boys. When I finally grew up, lonely and randy, there was Ray. He wanted me."

Michael turned his head to look at her. "All it took was him wantin' you? I was right—your standards are awful low."

"I got what I wanted at the time. A family, more or less. At least he was never cruel to me, like Sheila was to you."

That deflected Michael's scrutiny. "I widna play her game of kiss my hand and thank you for civilizin' me."

Yes, he defended his territory. Even if he was a closet romantic. Rebecca's mind frothed with satiny whiskey-scented bubbles. Aren't we a couple of goofs, lying here with our bodies separated by a foot and a half, when the Atlantic isn't wide enough to separate our minds?

Michael leaned across her to set his glass on the bedside table. He rapped the top approvingly. "Sheraton."

"Oh?" she said, more for his posture than his comment.

He stayed propped on his elbows, his body angled across the bed, half beside her, half over her. His forefinger appeared in her peripheral vision and traced a line down her temple to her jaw. "Do you ken," he murmured, his breath warm with peat smoke, his eyes sparkling with clean-washed Caledonian sunlight, "that I'm a Scottish pervert?"

"You are?"

"Aye. I like women better than whiskey."

"I see." She raised her hand and twined her fingers in the long, soft hair at the nape of his neck. "I thought, though, you didn't like me."

He grinned. "I've been likin' you as much as you've been likin' me."

"That bad?" She grinned back.

"Just aboot." The fingertip moved to her mouth and stroked her lower lip. "But then, I do like a woman wi' a tart tongue in her head."

"Show me," said Rebecca. Her hand pulled his head down to hers. He parted his lips and showed her. Just as the whiskey had detonated in her mouth and nose, the kiss detonated in her entire body. Some shred of rationality said, What do you think you're doing? The rest of her sighed and said, It's about time.

"Ah, lass." Michael laughed against her lips. "That's right magic."

She would've laughed, too, at the delightful absurdity of it, except laughing spoiled the shape of her mouth for kissing.

It must have been the lifetime of burred r's and rounded vowels that gave his lips and tongue such flexibility. He covered her face, her ears, her throat with little licks and nibbles, a bit haphazardly, but not, thank God, sloppily. He tasted different from American men, but that was probably the benign influence of the whiskey. If he smelled of anything beyond his own subtle scent, it was soap. Her hand found the gap between the hem of his sweatshirt and the top of his jeans, hungry for that cool yet warm skin.

His hands were delicate, strong, inquisitive. Sleight of hands, touching her as he touched the chanter of the pipes until she, too, sang in a high, clear melody played over the drone of his breath.

Rebecca didn't wonder what elemental fires burned beneath his surface. She saw them, touched them, tasted them, in the intricate pattern of flame and ash that was his face close to her face, that was his body beside hers. He was hiding nothing; whatever he was, was there in her arms, beneath her hands, sheening her lips with the flavor of grain and peat and something indefinable that was Michael.

Hail spattered into the humming in her head.

Michael's body went stiff. His head lifted and turned toward the door. Footsteps. James's heavy steps, bloody great tackety boots, thudded down the staircase and up the hall toward the door. Rebecca's mind stuttered. This time they were going to see him.

The steps stopped in the doorway as if repelled by something inside. But nothing was there. Not the least hint of a shape moved in the bright light of the hall. A gust of cold air, like an exhalation of hurt and disillusionment, chilled Rebecca's forehead. Then the presence was gone.

The rain spit and drizzled. The lights glared as crudely as those in an operating room. This room is haunted, after all, Rebecca thought. This bed is haunted, we've been overcome by an echo of lust. And yet touching Michael wasn't lustful clawing at an itch. It was the slow friction of music in the mind, soothing and exciting at once.

Michael caught his breath in a wheeze and looked down at Rebecca. His affectionate expression melted and ran, exposing his mask of crisp appraisal. Then that, too, evaporated, revealing doubt and pain. His eyes frosted, barriers rising. Whatever insight she'd had into the light and shadow inside him was cut off with the finality of a door slamming shut.

He slid down her body, lifted her sweater, and laid his face on her bare skin in the hollow where her ribs curved and parted. The moment stretched, a note of music held to an excruciating length. Her mind played two melodies in counterpoint, please stop, don't stop, please stop, don't stop.

Then in one shuddering movement Michael pulled himself away, stood up, and walked out of the room.

Rebecca looked at the canopy without seeing it, her thoughts tumbling like pebbles in a mountain stream, their edges smoothed by bewilderment. She had seen pain in his face. She had seen conscience.

Her stomach was cold. She yanked her sweater down and rolled off the bed. The floor seemed to hiccup beneath her feet. "Michael?" His shoes lay beside the bed, pigeon-toed with perplexity.

He was leaning against the frame of his door, presenting her with the crumpled back of his sweatshirt. "Michael, it's all right, talk to me."

"Sod off," he said.

She'd expected any remark but that. "What?"

"You're needin' a translation? Sod off—go away, let me be." For once his back was eloquent, quivering with rage and bitterness.

Each word hit her like a brickbat. Her stomach cramped. "Michael!" She took a step toward him, whether to embrace him or hit him she didn't know.

He slammed his door in her face. The crash reverberated through the house and was echoed by a sharp blow inside the room.

"Michael!" Fool, Rebecca told herself, to stand here childishly calling his name. I got carried away by one side of a two-faced inconsiderate slug. I am setting my standards pretty damn low. His name backed up in her throat and swelled painfully in her chest.

She blundered back into the large bedroom. The bottle of Scotch still sat on the bureau. She grasped it and raised it toward the stone windowsill—this is what happens when alcohol takes control of your senses . . . Swearing viciously, she lowered the bottle and set it down. Wasteful, to break half a bottle of Laphroaig. It would make a terrible mess. Eric gave it to me. Remember Eric? I know where I stand with him.

Rebecca turned off the lights and the space heater and smoothed the bedcovers like she'd pat dirt around a land mine. She stalked down to her room to discover Darnley sleeping on her bed. He looked up with a smugly masculine expression. She considered throwing him, too, but it wasn't his fault she was a certified idiot.

The house was no longer cozy but suffocating. The breath of air in the staircase was laughing derisively. The taste of Scotch was rancid in her mouth, and her stomach gulped bubbles of nausea. She scowled at Elspeth's portrait. "It's all your fault, leaving your cheap lusts lying around like bear traps."

But she and Michael had sensed no memory but that of shared experience. Those few moments hadn't been cheap. Not cheap at all.

Rebecca's body went as limp as if she'd been gutted and flayed. With a moan of pain she took out her contacts. She crawled onto the bed and stared toward the ceiling. But she heard no sound from the room upstairs.

Chapter Twenty

REBECCA WOKE UP knowing something wasn't right. She was fully dressed, with a vile taste in her mouth that made her look suspiciously at Darnley as he slept at the foot of her bed, his tail curled over his nose.

Then her thoughts congealed. Remembering was like picking at a scab. With a groan she rose, dressed, and combed out the tangles in her hair. Outside her window, thin clouds were shredded by a cold wind, revealing pennons of blue sky. Waves of sunshine raced across the lawn and hurdled the trees

Michael's eyes were blue. Michael's eyes were closed, locked, and guarded by armed sentries.

Rebecca braced herself before going into the kitchen. Sure enough, there he was, brooding over a mug of tea, a rack of toast untouched on the table before him. "Good morning," she said.

"Good mornin'," Michael replied, equally flat. He didn't look up.

Rebecca nestled a filter into the coffeepot, measured the coffee, added water. Steam rose and she inhaled the delectable odor. Caffeine was much more dependable than a man.

Michael was wearing a red sweatshirt emblazoned with the sentiment "Renegade Time Lord." His mouth was such a thin, tight line she couldn't believe it had been so flexible the night before. His right hand, cupped around his mug, was red and swollen. That's what that crash had been after he slammed his door in her face. He'd driven his fist into the stone wall. Rebecca's face crumpled into a grimace somewhere between a smile and wail. "Would you like me to fix some ice for your hand?"

"No," he replied. And, a moment later, "Thank you."

She poured coffee and drank. It wasn't as good as she'd anticipated.

"I'm sorry," Michael said to the toast. "I had no call tonguelashin' you like that."

She wanted to retort, What makes you think I care? But last night she had cared only too obviously. "No, you didn't," she said.

The silence stretched like a rubber band. Then Michael slammed back his chair and strode out of the room muttering something about work to do. He hadn't once looked at her.

Rebecca watched her coffee slop back and forth in its cup. Typical. You might as well skin a man alive as expect him to verbalize his feelings. The circumstances were pathetically banal, after all; they'd been forced together in trying times, they were only human, they'd gone overboard. No harm done. Thanks more to a ghost than to her own good sense.

But God, how good it had been to hold him! Not just felt good, was good, body, mind, and soul, right down to those purring kittens of her wits.

She slammed her mug into the sink so hard it cracked. She stared, appalled. Damaging estate property. Things were going downhill fast.

Rebecca picked up the fifth-floor inventory from the Hall. Michael could finish the fourth floor by himself, she wasn't going anywhere near that demon-possessed bed. James's steps had stopped in the doorway. Maybe as a child he'd seen his mother and Rudolph in that bed. The sight might have been enough to shock him into celibacy for the rest of his life. There was a good case to be made for celibacy.

Rebecca started in one of the smaller rooms on the fifth floor. She cataloged the collection of Victorian paper theaters, the cutout dolls dressed as shepherds, kings, and clowns carefully bundled into envelopes. She checked off the scrapbooks filled with old stamps—have to get them appraised. She opened the jeweler's boxes containing seventeenth-century *objets de vertu*, a cup carved from carnelian, a turquoise pomander, a tiny jeweled casket that smelled faintly of roses.

But more objects were listed on the inventory than were here. Either they were in another room or had been de-accessioned. She tapped her pencil on the notebook, sympathetic to James's reluctance to part with his possessions but wishing he'd realized what a headache it would mean to the innocent historian. In the gaps in the inventories was space for plenty of mischief.

Maybe Michael was pleased she hadn't made it with Eric because he wanted her himself. And yet, men didn't seem to have much of an impulse toward exclusivity. Masculine games of power being what they were, he might have taken what he could get just to score off Eric. But he hadn't. He buried his face in her stomach and clung to her as if he were being dragged away by some outside force.

It was all just fun and games. She played with Eric, Michael played with her. He'd said he wouldn't play Sheila's games. Hypocrite. She laid down her pencil and rubbed her throbbing temples. Just shrug it all off, that's what the rules say, that's what he's done.

Rebecca looked up to meet the painted eyes of young Queen Victoria gazing steadily from a Winterhalter portrait. "I'm not particularly amused, either," she said.

Footsteps. Rebecca turned sharply, only to see Dorothy and her basket of cleaners and scrubbers stepping into the hallway. The housekeeper held a cigarette clenched in her lips, her face screwed around it like a prune around its pit. "Mrs. Garst," Rebecca called, "would you mind not smoking indoors, please? Some of Mr. Forbes's things might be damaged by smoke."

Dorothy dumped her supplies and trudged back down like *Winnie-the-Pooh*'s Eeyore told he couldn't play. The woman grew more bloated every day. Overeating, perhaps. Or too much medication. If stuck with a pin, Dorothy would deflate into a puddle of flesh and double-knit.

But for the grace of education and opportunity, Rebecca thought, that could be me in thirty years. A menial scorned by smart-alec college girls as something less than human, embittered by the sour dregs of custom and ignorance. For a few months in her youth Dorothy had been young and free. Now she had nothing except her son and his family to look on with pride or hope.

Rebecca laid down the inventory. Dammit, she was making no progress at all with the vertical hold of her mind tuned to rapid scan.

She looked into the large bedroom; at least the ghosts there were not her own. There was the portrait of Mary Stuart. There was Elspeth's furrow in the bedclothes. There was the portrait of John Forbes and his self-righteously male scowl. Five cutglass bottles stood on the dresser. Rebecca frowned. Five, not seven. Maybe they'd gone up this time, instead of down.

She went up. The ballroom was washed in air and light, blocks of quicksilver sunlight making a tartan pattern with the planks of the floor. No bottles. But Phil's battery-operated screwdriver and a box of screws lay on a tabouret by a Queen Anne wing chair.

Rebecca picked up the tools, walked down all the flights to the entry, picked the key to the shed off the hook by the door, and stepped out into the sunshine. It was cold, but a nice day for a walk. She should ask Michael—no, better go alone. It would be so much easier if she hated him.

The shed still reeked of gasoline. Rebecca put the tools on a bench next to a broken lamp and glanced at the grimy milk jugs. They were empty. She checked the gas can. It was full, the lid on securely. Oh, well, give the place time to air out.

She returned to the house to find Dorothy leaving yet another foil-wrapped bundle in the kitchen. "Heavenly hash," she announced.

"Thank you," Rebecca said. She left the front door open for Phil and went back upstairs. Michael was sitting at the bureau in the fourth-floor room, leaning on his elbow, just as he'd been when she'd gone down.

As she went up the next flight of stairs she heard footsteps ringing on the treads above her head. Hello, James, she thought, and quickened her pace to the room where she'd been working. She stopped dead in the doorway.

The pile of old paperbacks that had been on top of a wardrobe now lay stacked neatly on the floor. If they'd fallen, they'd have spewed paper shrapnel all over the room. They'd been lifted down. Michael? He apparently hadn't moved while she'd been gone. James, maybe. Why?

Rebecca sifted through the books. Among the yellowed pages was a sheet of rag paper covered with James's handwriting, one end torn roughly off. The back of her neck shriveled. She'd seen that paper before.

She trotted down the stairs, pausing on the fourth floor to ask Michael perfunctorily if he'd been upstairs. "No," he replied without looking around.

Rebecca brushed past Dorothy on the landing and hurried into the Hall. The boxes holding James's diaries and scrapbooks were lined up beside the table. Not in this one, not in that one . . . There! Rebecca opened the one with the photograph and the torn scrap of paper. The scrap fit the bottom of the letter as perfectly as one puzzle piece dovetailing into another.

Rebecca smiled with satisfaction, feeling like Miss Marple. She read, "June 3, 1952. My dear Mrs. Brown. Yes, your parents were valued servants to my father, and it is for their sake and that of your childhood here at Dun Iain that I am troubling myself to answer your last letter. You must realize, Mrs. Brown, that your demands are growing more unreasonable all the time. What makes you think that any newspaper today would be at all interested in a scandal that happened in 1901?"

Rebecca glanced at the photo of Katherine Gemmell. She must be Mrs. Brown. Most people got married, despite the testimony against it.

The letter went on, "However, for the sake of your parents I will offer D., their grandchild, work at Dun Iain. Mrs. O'Donnell will be with me for a few years yet, but I will try to work something out. I repeat, though, that sympathetic as I am to your financial and marital difficulties, whatever problem you are having you have brought upon yourself. I cannot help you any more than I already have. Your threats are an embarrassment to the memory not only of your parents but mine."

Well! thought Rebecca. Katherine Gemmell Brown must've been desperate to resort to blackmail. And James was right: who'd care about Elspeth's death now? Katie's dark eyes gazed out at her from their paper, frustratingly silent. A failing marriage, and financial difficulties, and children. 1952. She would've been fifty-one. Her kids would have been grown, or almost so. James offered "D.," Athena and Rudolph's grandchild, work at Dun Iain.

James might've torn the letter pulling it out of the desk in the prophet's chamber, written another to Katie, and used the torn original as a bookmark. Now he came back from the grave to make sure it was found.

A shadow fell across letter and photo. Rebecca looked up. Dorothy stood just behind her, staring at the picture. Something slid from one side of Rebecca's mind to the other, clicking as solidly as a key in a lock.

D for Dorothy. Dorothy was Katie Gemmell's daughter. She'd replaced Louise as housekeeper here because of her mother's pleas. Maybe Katie had looked dubiously at the wild teenager Dorothy had been and so had planned for her future. Nineteen fifty-two—it had been several more years before Dorothy had actually come to work here. And despite Katherine's bullying, Dorothy had gotten along with James well enough. James had trusted her.

But even in Dorothy's fits of possessiveness she'd never pointed out her long relationship with the house. "Do you know who this is?" Rebecca asked, indicating the photo.

The housekeeper's sallow eyes snapped and then dulled. "I'm going to clean your room," she said. "At least you bother to make your bed and keep your clothes tidy." She turned on her heel and walked stiffly out of the Hall and up the stairs.

My goodness, Rebecca thought. Either Dorothy was embarrassed at the way she'd gotten her job, or else she was afraid that Rebecca or Michael or Eric would realize what a strong motive she had for embezzling the collections. She could well believe that her grandparents, the Gemmells, deserved more than they'd received in helping to prevent a scandal over Elspeth.

I'll ask Louise about it, Rebecca promised herself. It's only a string of circumstantial evidence. Although I suppose Eric would tell me that people have been convicted on less.

The phone was ringing downstairs. Bundling the photo and the letter into the diary and the diary into its box, Rebecca hurried down to the kitchen.

It was Warren. "Here's the lab report on your fire. Just greasy rags and scrap paper. No gasoline or other flammables. And no fingerprints."

"Someone was either very clever," Rebecca told him, "or very lucky."

"Judging by those singed curtains, it's you and Dr. Campbell who are the lucky ones. I doubt if the perpetrator meant more than to frighten you, but a fire can easily get out of control."

"Tell me about it."

"Call me immediately if you think something else is going on," Warren concluded, and Rebecca assured him she would. Not that it would necessarily do any good, she added to herself as she hung up.

Rebecca plopped down at the table and absently crunched a piece of Michael's dried toast. Her headache, if not dissipating, was at least less insistent than her rumbling train of thought.

No fingerprints. Damn. Warren must have Steve's and Heather's prints on file. Did he have Dorothy's? Hard to believe she would deliberately damage the house. Easier to believe Steve would be reckless—Heather had been angry with him about something. And yet Dorothy could have the stronger motivation. And there was Phil, too hangdog honest to be genuine.

On cue, Phil Pruitt's voice sounded from the entry counterpointed by Steve's whine. They were haggling over whether transplanting a rosebush or repairing a tread in the back stairs was first on the agenda. Both sets of footsteps went upstairs.

Darnley sauntered in the door and made for the pantry, turning his skeptical gaze on Rebecca. "All right, then," she said. She stood up, brushed the crumbs off her hands, and picked up the phone. It took her a moment to cajole Brian into fetching his mother, but soon Jan said brightly, "Sorensons' fun house— nervous breakdowns our specialty."

"Then I've come to the right place," Rebecca told her.

"Hey, are you all right? Margie Garst said you had a fire out there."

"Someone decided to get funny with the kitchen trash can, that's all. No big deal." Sure, Rebecca said to herself.

Jan wasn't convinced, either. "Why don't you come and stay with me? Michael, too, if he'd like."

"Run away? A fine thrawn lass like myself?"

"Say what?"

Rebecca grimaced at the flotsam her memory would spit out. "Never mind. I called to ask if you know what Dorothy's maiden name is?"

"I assume there's some reason you don't just ask her. I mean, I'm a trusting soul. I trust you're going to explain all this to me someday."

"If I ever find any explanation, I'd be glad to. Now, what was Dorothy's maiden name?"

"Gosh," said Jan. "Something like, like—Barton?"

Rebecca twisted the phone cord. "How about Brown?"

"I don't know. She was born in Columbus, I remember Margie telling me that. I think they're all gone; Chuck said something about never having grandparents on that side."

"Good as far as it goes. Do you know anything else about her?"

"Well, Margie was griping about how absentminded Dorothy's getting—she promised one of the kids a toy and then didn't bring it when she came, and the poor little tyke was beside himself. Early senility?"

"Maybe she's been under a lot of pressure lately." Darnley jumped onto a chair and Rebecca stroked him. He looked up, amber eyes inscrutable.

"Maybe you'd like this one," said Jan, with the air of a salesperson offering different pairs of shoes. "Margie and I were talking about the Tuchman girl—married on Monday, divorced on Wednesday, hadn't even written her thank-you notes—and Margie says Dorothy went through a quickie marriage to a boy in Columbus back in her flaming-youth days, before Chuck Garst.''

"Not too much of a scandal even then, I guess. But right now I'm more interested in her parents. Can you ask Margie what her maiden name is?''

"Sure. It may not be Barton, it may be . . .''

Darnley leaped down and fled into the pantry. Rebecca spun around and saw the figure standing in the kitchen door. Her mind fell into her stomach with a crash that rattled her teeth. She gasped, "Jesus H. Christ!''

"No,'' mused Jan, "that's not it . . .'' Her brain caught up with her mouth. "Rebecca, what is it?''

"Ray just walked in the door.''

Ray stood smiling at her, glasses gleaming in anticipation. The blond wave across his forehead was still marked by the teeth of a comb. He wore a checked shirt, the pocket stained by ink, and his favorite corduroy jacket with the patches on the elbows. He was trying valiantly to hold in his stomach.

"Good grief,'' said Jan. "You want me to call the exterminators?''

"I'll call you back.'' Rebecca hung up the phone and forced a breath into lungs that seemed to have petrified.

"Kitten!'' Ray exclaimed. He set down his suitcase and came toward her, arms outstretched, face bifurcated by a grin. "I've missed you!''

He had her trapped where the cabinet met the wall. Paralyzed, she let herself be swept into his embrace. He smelled of pipe tobacco and Old Spice. She'd forgotten that; her mind had been filed through like the bars on a jail cell. He kissed one corner of her mouth and patted the back pocket of her jeans. "Getting a little hefty in the starboard beam, huh?''

"I'm not a coed anymore,'' Rebecca returned. She pointedly glanced up and down Ray's slightly beefy body, broad shoulders that kept on going right down to his knees. "You haven't lost any weight yourself.''

"I've had to live on fast food and TV dinners. Your cooking is so much better than mine.''

She realized she was clinging to his lapels, more to push him away than to draw him near. She released them and struggled out of the corner into which he'd backed her. "Ray, where on earth did you come from?''

"I started driving yesterday and spent the night in Indianapolis. It's a long way out here, you know."

They'd had too many conversations just like this, not quite in the same language. "I mean, why are you here?"

"You asked me to come, Kitten," he explained patiently. "The message you left with Nancy in the departmental office— send me a pretty nightie and we'll spend Thanksgiving together giving thanks." He had the decency to try and suppress his smirk. "That got around the department pretty fast, let me tell you. Everyone was teasing me."

Rebecca gaped at him. She'd thought that headache was getting better. It had merely turned a corner, gathered steam, and come back to hit her again.

"I had to get Gene to take my classes, and you know how he always expects a bottle or two of wine in return. But I figured a reunion with you was worth it."

The negligee. A reunion. Oh God let me wake up this is a bad dream!

Ray remained substantial. Rebecca forced another breath and said, "I didn't leave a message for you. I would've called you at home with something that personal. It was the same person who sent you those postcards. It had to have been. They called the department because they knew you'd recognize my voice." A woman, she thought. It was a woman.

"Well, I didn't know. I never can figure you out. I thought you wanted to make up, maybe you'd been reading *The Total Woman* or something." He pulled her close to his chest. Once she'd lived to cuddle against the breadth of his chest. It had been so safe, so comforting. Now it was like hugging a couch-sized marshmallow. "I've been worried about you, Kitten, so far from home and among all these strange people."

Now she was going to have to hurt him again. Damn and double damn whoever was harassing her, making innocent Ray his—her—victim, too. But no and no again, she wasn't going to let some nut drive her away.

He bent toward her. She dodged, steaming his glasses. "Ray, listen to me. I didn't call Nancy and ask you to come. I don't know a thing about it. It was the prankster. I'm sorry—it's not fair, none of it."

His glasses cleared. Behind them his gray eyes flickered, understanding, not wanting to understand. She looked around for some alley down which she could duck, but no, hiding wouldn't help.

A tattoo of footsteps and Michael bounded into the doorway, held out an ancient leather-bound book, and said, "Rebecca, look at this!"

She shook off Ray's grasp. Ah, hell—Michael had been ready to resume normal diplomatic relations. But now his eyes were slightly crossed, his brows arched, as if someone had just hit his forehead with a hammer. His mouth was tucked in at the corner, with surprise, with humor—she couldn't tell.

Ray looked Michael up and down. He was broader, but Michael was taller. Rebecca croaked, "Dr. Kocurek, Dr. Campbell."

"How do you do," said Michael, his lips loosening into a fair approximation of a smile. He stepped forward, hand outstretched.

"Hello," Ray said. Warily he shook Michael's hand. "You've been living here with Rebecca?"

"Aye," said Michael. His smile took on death's-head proportions, his eyes went glassy.

Ray glanced from Michael to Rebecca as though he were considering dusting her for fingerprints. Realization swept his face. No, no, no, Rebecca wanted to wail, that's not it at all. The silence in the room was like quicksand.

"So you like Dr. Who?" Ray said gamely, gesturing toward Michael's shirt.

"Aye."

"Rebecca likes that, too. It's pretty amusing. Pitiful production values, though. Might as well be filmed in the BBC coffee shop. The special effects in *Star Wars* are much better done . . ." His voice trailed away. He looked down at the toes of his shoes.

Michael looked dubiously at Rebecca. He makes eye contact for the first time today, she thought, and it's because of Ray. "Nice to meet you," he muttered, and vanished out the door, clutching the book like a shield.

Rebecca's jaw hurt. Oh, she was grinding her teeth.

"So," Ray said, trying but not attaining a jovial tone. "That's the Englishman. Seems nice enough. I'd always heard they didn't talk much."

"I wouldn't let him hear you call him English." She inhaled, keeping her anger from leaking into her voice. It wasn't his fault. "Ray, I'm sorry you came all this way for nothing. It was a dirty trick."

"Don't worry about it," he returned. "I had to come out this way, anyway. I mean—well, I was saving the news for a surprise.''

"Oh?'' For one dizzy moment she thought he was going to admit vandalizing the castle. But no, he hadn't done that.

"I've been offered a position as the head of the philosophy department at Ohio Wesleyan. They liked my magazine articles. But a department head needs a wife—parties and stuff, you know. I'm a bachelor, I might not get the job . . .'' Even Ray realized that wasn't coming out right. He sighed and shook his head. "I'm sorry.''

"So am I,'' she managed to say calmly. "But it's not just that I don't want to marry you, I don't want to marry anyone. I have work to do, research, teaching. I don't think I'll ever marry.'' She sounded like Peter Pan asserting he'd never grow up.

"I see.'' Ray picked up his suitcase.

"The negligee's very pretty,'' Rebecca said. "Would you like it back?''

"Keep it, Kitten.''

"Thank you.'' She kissed his cheek. "You'll get the job, you'll see.''

"Goodbye.'' He gazed at her a long moment, as if imprinting her image on his retina. Then with an anemic smile he turned and walked out the door, back straight, gut tight, cloaked in dignity.

Rebecca followed, glancing around. No Michael. No Dorothy, no Phil, no Steve. They were probably ranged in the windows of the castle like Romans in the Colosseum, eating popcorn while innocents were savaged below.

Ray put the suitcase into his Escort. He climbed in, shut the door, and slapped the steering wheel with as much hurt and anger as Rebecca had ever seen in him. He drove away with the spatter of gravel and not one backward look.

He hadn't deserved this. Rebecca swore and kicked at the door.

Car horns shrilled from the end of the driveway. She waited, but the sound was not followed by rending metal and crashing glass. Rebecca sagged against the cold stone coping of the door. *I will never commit myself to a man again. It hurts too much. It hurts.*

The sky arched blue, clear, and indifferent overhead. The house was silent. The draft through the door and into the entry was chill on the back of Rebecca's neck.

Chapter Twenty-One

REBECCA LEANED AGAINST the stone coping of the door, her arms crossed tightly. She must be hallucinating. Up the driveway came Eric's gray Volvo, gleaming like a silver dollar in the sunshine. It stopped. Eric got out. "Who was that idiot in the Escort?" he called. "He came blasting out of the driveway right in front of me, didn't even stop."

She straightened, rotated her shoulders, rubbed her temples, and said mockingly, "Oh, hi, Rebecca, I got back early, how are you?"

Eric grinned. "Sorry." He came across the gravel toward her. "I called in this morning and my secretary said you'd progressed beyond vandalism and theft to arson. I was pretty much finished, anyway, so I caught an early flight back and came right out from the airport."

He reached for her but she dodged. "That idiot in the car," she told him, "was Ray."

"Ray? Oh, Ray. Has he come to steal you back?"

"Not funny, Eric. Someone called his office and said that I wanted him to come for Thanksgiving."

"That's a low blow, not only hounding you here at Dun Iain but interfering with your love life."

"I don't have a love life," Rebecca said, with such vehemence Eric took a cautious step back. "Sorry," she told him in turn.

He opened his mouth, shut it, and presumably decided discretion was the better part of bewilderment. "Come on inside. Show me the damage." The first thing he noticed was the dead bolt on the door. "That's new."

"Warren brought it out, and some smoke alarms, too."

"Should've thought of a dead bolt myself. Of course that as sumes that the intruder is coming from the outside." Rebecca darted him an aggravated glance. "Okay," he added hastily, "whatever Campbell's scam is, he wouldn't set himself on fire."

Rebecca shook her head, smiling ruefully at her waspishness. Come on, get hold of yourself. None of this emotional inquisition is Eric's fault.

She led him up the main staircase. "Someone lit some trash in the garbage can and left it here The front door was standing open—someone else has a key, right?—and the smoke went all through the house."

He examined the singed edges of the curtain and threw the material against the wall. "Idiot," he said under his breath. The muscle jumped in his jaw. "Not a clue, I suppose, as to who did it?"

"Warren called with the lab report. Nothing. Nada. Zilch."

Eric stepped into the Hall and inspected the ceiling. "We may have to do some repainting in order to sell the place, but it looks all right. Not as bad as I feared."

"Sell it?" Rebecca asked. "What about Ohio and its youth hostel?"

"I haven't had a chance to tell you I tracked the Dennisons, Rachel's descendants, to California. Only a matter of time until we have some heirs."

"Oh. I see." She was surprised that she was disappointed. But that was what James had wanted, she reminded herself. "California, huh? Everyone kept moving on west until they came to the ocean, then they bunched up behind the beach and built freeways."

Eric looked at her doubtfully. "What?"

"I'm not too coherent this afternoon, sorry. I mean, you're from California, too. Small world."

"Oh. Well, yeah, California's a big place. You don't happen to have any coffee, do you?"

"Sure." Rebecca led the way back downstairs. It certainly was quiet. Phil and Steve weren't hammering. Dorothy wasn't vacuuming, Michael wasn't—well, the only thing that he did that was noisy was to play the pipes.

She threw out the old coffee, started a fresh pot, got out bread, lunch meat, and mayonnaise. There they'd been in the Hall, and she hadn't shown Eric the letter she'd pieced together. Not that

she should. Just because she'd got it in her head that Dorothy
had something to do with the repeated threats didn't mean Eric
would follow her reasoning. He might even laugh at her. Dorothy was about as innocuous as they came.

Eric's chair scraped and he gasped. She spun around. Darnley
sat in the pantry door staring at him, front feet primly together,
tail twitching from side to side like a cobra fascinated by its
master's flute. Eric stared back, hands clenched, face pale.

Rebecca swooped down on the hapless cat, carried him
through the entry, and dumped him outside. Darnley flounced
away, nose and tail in the air. "Why," said Rebecca to Eric,
"are you so afraid of cats?"

He swallowed, blinking rapidly. "My grandmother hated
them. Had hysterics when she saw me playing with a kitten
once. But it never seemed like something it was worth paying a
shrink to fix." He smiled sheepishly. The tan returned to his
face. "Embarrassing, though. Half the little old ladies wanting
wills made out have cats."

It was some measure of the regard he had for her that he didn't
pull out and dust off that line about allergies. "I'm not too partial to big dogs myself," Rebecca said, and laid a sandwich in
front of him. "Eat. Good for you. Soothe the nerves."

"Yes, dear," he said indulgently, and ate.

There, at last, was a sign of life from elsewhere in the castle:
footsteps came down the front staircase and went out the door.
It couldn't be Michael—he'd have come into the kitchen looking
for food. Unless he'd heard Eric's voice. Rebecca plunked Michael's sandwich into a Baggie and put it in the fridge. She
joined Eric. "Tell me about Nebraska."

He told her, making her laugh with an account of a waitress
in a steak house in Lincoln who'd solemnly advised him against
ordering his meat rare—not cooked properly that way, she'd said.
Footsteps went back up the stairs, then another set—or the same
one—advanced and retreated again.

"Thank you," Eric said. "About time you cooked something
for me."

"Definitely." She picked up the dishes.

"I'm going to poke around outside," he said, "especially around
the mausoleum, since the key hasn't turned up. Just to make sure
the local punks haven't decided to use it as a clubhouse."

"There weren't any new scratches on the lock last Thursday,"

Rebecca told him, piling the dishes in the sink. "But I haven't looked recently."

Eric's voice was stretched just a bit taut. "Thank you for the deposition. I'll be back in a little while."

She turned to look at him, but he was already out the door. If he makes one more joke about my being curious, she thought wearily, or noticing something, I'll lose my temper with him. Not that the care and feeding of Eric's ego was all that difficult; she simply had to act less intelligent. And she'd had years of practice doing that. At least he didn't demand decorative idiocy, no matter what Dorothy had said.

Unfortunately her tension headache had abated only a little. Ignoring it, Rebecca started up the stairs. This was turning into yet another day when nothing got done. Nothing constructive, anyway. The faint creakings and hammerings from the back staircase must be Phil and Steve. The vacuum cleaner roared into life on one of the upper stories. She wondered what book Michael had been wanting to show her, the one he'd thought more important than keeping his emotional drawbridge pulled up.

As she walked past the door of his room something flashed multicolored light. She stopped. There were the two crystal perfume bottles, sitting on the desk beneath the window. She went to get them.

The desk wasn't as messy as it usually was. Papers, envelopes, and books were stacked in orderly shoals around the bottles. Odd—why did Michael arrange the papers like that instead of simply putting the bottles away?

Leaning against the bottles were the two snapshots he'd received in the mail the other day. He'd already showed them to her, it was all right for her to look at them again. She considered Michael in a kilt—nice, in spite of everything—and Colin and him on the icy mountainside. On the back of that photo was scrawled "Buachaille Etive Mor, February." No one climbed that mountain without some expertise, especially in the winter.

Rebecca wondered suddenly if Michael was afraid of her. Or, not of her specifically, of becoming involved. He'd just been burned, damn Sheila-bluidy-Fitzgerald, anyway. Rebecca emitted a sound partway between a laugh and a snort. Maybe she should be thanking Sheila. The last thing she needed was to get involved with Michael.

Beside the snapshots was Michael's passport, open to the page with his photograph. Unlike the others, that one wasn't flattering; he looked like a cat burglar caught in the sudden beam of a searchlight, surprised and resentful. Rebecca turned the page. He'd been through New York Customs only once, on October 11. He'd arrived in this country just when he'd said he had.

The light refracted by the bottles made prisms across half a dozen newspaper clippings lined up across the desk. Rebecca had seen that one, about a firebombing in the Western Highlands, sticking out of an envelope on Michael's bedside table last month. The dates on two of the others were just a couple of weeks ago; one of his correspondents was keeping him supplied . . .

The word "arson" jumped out at her. She read that clipping, then the next and the next, faster and faster as though the letters were evaporating before her eyes. The noise of hammering and the roar of the vacuum faded behind the rush of blood in her ears.

A house in Aberfeldy had burned down. It was owned by an Englishman and used for only a month or so in the summer. Arson was suspected. A burning Saint Andrew's cross had been planted on the lawn of a shooting lodge near Meggernie owned by an English company. Like one in Onich, a house near Largs had been bombed; the police found bits of a Molotov cocktail. There had recently developed in Wales a pattern of firebombings of properties owned by "incomers." Police suspected that a similar group of Scottish nationalists were committing terrorist acts.

Come on now, Rebecca said to herself. No way.

The letters that had just come lay unfolded in a tidy row behind the bottles. Rebecca hesitated, looked around guiltily, then picked up the first. Michael's sister—domestic commentary. His mother—ditto. Colin. Something about the Buachaille Etive Mor. Something about Ben Nevis. Something about Bruce Springsteen. And the sentence, "When you bring home the lolly, I know an agent in London who deals with some of the Arab groups."

Lolly, Rebecca translated. Money. An agent who deals with—no, Colin hadn't said "who sells arms to terrorists" in so many words. She closed her eyes a moment, keeping herself from hyperventilating. Her hands shook so hard the thin paper of the letters rustled. No, it couldn't be.

Like a battle-ax through her mind she heard Michael's words to Mrs. West: "It makes you want to pluck up sword and gun and fight it all ower again! All we're askin' is justice!"

Isn't poor tattered justice, she shouted silently, usually dragged in to rationalize bloody-mindedness?

The bottles blazed like cold bonfires in her eyes. In a chill sick sweat Rebecca saw, to one side of the desk, a photostat of a letter in John Forbes's copperplate hand.

Her knees folded and dumped her onto the desk chair. The words scattered, ran, and coalesced before her eyes. "1924. Dun Iain Estate. Director of the Museum of Antiquities. Having been fortunate enough to acquire one of the greatest treasures of Scottish history—yes, I am asking a high price, but I have provided a reliquary made of jewels that were once my unfortunate wife's—please let me know if you accept my offer." At the bottom of the page was a sentence in someone else's handwriting, "Reluctantly refused, funding limited."

There it was, the Forbes treasure. But Forbes hadn't had the decency to say what it was. The Stone of Scone? Malcolm Canmore's crown?

Rebecca laid the page down on the desk blotter and stacked the letters, the clippings, the passport, and the photos neatly on top of it. All this time, and Michael had known positively there was a treasure. Only one explanation fit all the evidence. He was after it for his cause—whatever that cause was.

Her mind leaped from its track and spun briskly away like a hoop bouncing downhill. She'd been snooping—she'd asked for a shock. But she needed to know . . . There must be some other interpretation. Michael was her friend. He'd come too damn close to being more.

He'd lied to her. She'd defended him and he'd stabbed her in the back. He could've taken some of the items missing from the inventories. He'd been here alone for a week. He'd been here alone while she'd been out indulging herself. No telling what he'd found, what he'd hidden. What better cover, to conscientiously finish his job here, conceal the stolen items in the shipment, and unpack them himself back in Edinburgh?

He could've set the fire, after all. He could've caused the trouble with Ray. He could've done any damn thing . . . But she had no proof he'd done anything other than lie to her.

Rebecca touched the icy side of one of the crystal bottles. Hell of a crook he was, to arrange the clippings so tidily, to leave the letters unfolded, to put Forbes's missive right out in the open. It was as if he'd wanted her to find them.

Or, she thought suddenly, as if Elspeth had wanted her to find them, just as James had wanted her to find the rest of his letter to Katie. Both of them, working to protect Dun Iain. Not that she'd expect Elspeth to have much of a proprietary interest in the place.

Her shoulder blades contracted. She stood up, the chair falling with a crash, and spun around. Michael was standing in the door, his face askew with puzzlement. "I came in here to get the bottles," Rebecca said. "The papers were already spread out like this."

"Aye?" His eye moved to the desk. Puzzlement clotted into horror.

"I just found the letter from John Forbes to—whom? Some retired director of the museum? Did you dig that letter out of the files, was that what made you volunteer to accept this job?" She bent, picked up the chair and replaced it. Still her hands were shaking.

Michael's face went blank, like a chalkboard wiped clean.

"I'm sorry, but I had to read Colin's letter. And look at the clippings. I bet you think you're a modern Robert the Bruce, don't you?" The hammering and the vacuum stopped. Her voice echoed loudly in the silence.

He actually seemed to be turning that over in his mind. Come on, she urged him silently, her hands knotted on the back of the chair, come on, answer me, produce some logical explanation for it all!

His eyes fell. "Aye, that's what it looks like, right enough."

She jerked as if he'd hit her. "Talk about self-delusion and gilded weeds!" she spat, and started for the door.

That statement was hitting below the belt, but he deserved it. Michael didn't move aside. His eyes snapped back up and fixed her face, his brows tightened. She turned toward the other exit, the bathroom door. "Rebecca," he said. Just one word, her name, cracking like a whip.

She glanced back. "Yes? I'm listening. Please, explain."

His face twitched and then went blank again. The hand he had raised toward her, the one that was red and swollen, fell back to his side. He not only hoisted his Do Not Disturb sign, he dug ditches, threw up a rampart, and lined it with cannon like the half-moon battery at Edinburgh Castle.

She wanted to scream at him, I would've believed anything, you fool. Why start telling the truth now? And she answered herself, because Michael Campbell gives no quarter, and expects none.

She stumbled through the bathroom and into the large bedroom. The green plaid still lay at the foot of the bed. There was something decent in him, there had to be—she'd glimpsed it last night. But where?

Eric was calling from downstairs, "Rebecca?"

No, she thought, looking at the plaid. No, I won't tell Eric. Eric would love to have Michael arrested, deported, returned to Scotland in disgrace. For the sake of that half hour when we held each other, when nothing else mattered and everything else mattered, I'll give him a chance to straighten up and fly right. But I'll watch him, I'll search the boxes, he won't leave a whisker in the sink but that I'll know it, and if he makes one more shady move, then he'll have forced me to turn him in.

"Rebecca?" Eric's footsteps came up the stairs.

"Coming!" She hurried past the bedroom door. Michael stood by the desk, his back to her as she passed in the hall, cold and still. The bottles glistened in his hands. Elspeth had certainly made her point.

Rebecca forced down the lump in her throat, making her jaw ache like an abscessed tooth. She met Eric on the landing outside her room. "Find anything?" she asked in brittle tones.

He quailed at her ghastly expression and replied cautiously, "No, the lock hasn't been touched."

"Excuse me," Rebecca returned, and fled into her bathroom. She allowed herself one long cry of agonized frustration, muffled in her bath towel. Then she splashed her face with cold water, massaged the back of her neck, and tried again, without success, to smile.

When she went back into the corridor, it was empty. The open door to her bedroom was on her right, the closed door to the piper's gallery on her left . . . The door was swinging slowly open. Her voice started to say "Eric?" but nothing came out of her throat. The door was opening all by itself.

No, not all by itself. A sudden patter like rain on a tin roof was James's boots. The door crashed open against the wall; the steps pounded through the opening and down the stairs. She'd never heard James in such a rush before. The ghosts were active today. No wonder, with the impending discovery of heirs. Rebecca waited until her heart started beating regularly again, and then walked into her room.

Eric was contemplating the portrait of Elspeth. Elspeth's jew-

els decorated the treasure . . . Stop it. Don't think about it.
"Did you hear that?" she asked.

"What? You mean Campbell or someone charging down the
stairs like a water buffalo? Doesn't he know to be careful on a
spiral staircase?"

She walked around him and looked out the window. It was helpful, in a way, that he kept denying the supernatural. What a shame
that old James hadn't been able to be careful on the staircase.

Steve, she saw from her vantage point, was ambling across
the lawn toward the shed. The westering sun was right in her
eyes and she had to squint; through the lace of her lashes it
seemed as if the many brown hues of grass, trees, and gravel
fragmented into a mosaic beneath the blue of the sky.

Steve stood on the stone step of the shed rolling a cigarette.
Tobacco? Rebecca wondered. He pulled a package of matches
from his pocket, struck one, lit the cigarette, and nudged open
the door of the shed all at once.

Rebecca jolted upright. James had run down the stairs. The
shed reeked of gasoline, gasoline stored in cracked old milk
jugs. Steve's hand shook the match. She shouted, "No, Steve,
don't!"

Steve, startled, glanced up instead of stepping inside. His hand
completed the motion and the match fell. A sudden *whump!* and
flame erupted from the doorway of the shed, engulfing him.

Eric bolted. Other footsteps pounded down the staircase. Rebecca realized her own feet were skimming the stone treads, the
walls spinning by her. The landing and the Hall, the main staircase, the entry. Eric was racing across the lawn. Michael was
three steps ahead of him, carrying his bedspread.

Steve was running, arms outstretched, his voice hung in a
shrill scream, yellow flame licking greedily at his hair, his shirt,
his pants. Michael brought him down with a clumsy but effective
flying tackle and smothered him in the spread. Eric was on them
both, rolling them across the grass. The grass was singeing,
tendrils of smoke curling upward around the struggling mass of
arms and legs. The shed emitted gouts of black smoke that blotted the sunlight and coagulated on the lawn.

"Sweet Jesus!" said Dorothy behind Rebecca.

Rebecca didn't stop. "Call an ambulance! Call the fire department!" There'd been a freeze, they'd reeled in the hoses . . . No,
Michael had reattached one to wash his wellies.

Phil stood beside Dorothy, his face empurpled. "Steve," he gasped. "Steve!"

Eric and Michael wrapped Steve in the heavy bedspread and beat on him. He fought back, screaming and coughing, like a giant caterpillar struggling in its chrysalis. Only his black boots showed, their heels hacking divots from the lawn.

The hose was still connected. Rebecca fumbled at the faucet and wrenched it open. Water spurted. Trembling, the water drops dancing madly, she sprayed the pile of bodies. The black hair matted on Eric's brow and Michael's red sweatshirt darkened into the crimson of blood.

Steve was no longer on fire, but flames were leaping from the doorway of the shed and crawling over the eaves toward the slates of the roof. Michael jumped up, snatched the hose from Rebecca's hand, and trained it on the still untouched area of the wall. His hair was singed, she saw, his face pink, and both hands were blistered.

Eric pulled the spread away from Steve's head. Rebecca was actually grateful to hear the boy crying. He was alive. She didn't look at his face. Phil came stumbling forward, arms outstretched, and fell wheezing to his knees beside Steve's pathetically twitching form. Eric groped in the man's pocket, produced an inhaler, helped him use it. Dorothy hurried from the doorway and began swathing Steve in wet towels.

The wind was ice cold. No, Rebecca realized, she was wet. She was standing in a puddle on the spiky grass. Her eyes burned and tears ran grittily down her cheeks. Michael advanced on the shed, containing the fire, his face set in deep lines around the whiteness of his clenched teeth. She reached toward him. He was hurt. He didn't see her.

She gasped and started coughing. Her lungs turned themselves inside out and yet still she was smothering in smoke. Her hands and feet tingled. The battlements of Dun Iain reeled above her.

Steve was crying, the pitiful, high-pitched mewl of a hurt child. Eric growled, a long way away, "I knew the kid was a walking disaster area. Where in God's name was he keeping that gasoline?"

With a long shuddering inhalation Rebecca answered mutely, In a gas can . . . Her thought detonated, spewing images into her mind. The milk jugs had been empty. The gas can had been full, the lid on tight. The fire had not been an accident.

Steve's crying was absorbed into the distant sound of sirens.

December

Chapter Twenty-Two

REBECCA TOOK A deep breath. She was frequently taking deep breaths, as though she wore corsets like Elspeth and her lungs weren't able to expand. Garden-variety stress, she thought. Maybe even hothouse-orchid stress. A few more weeks and she could go home.

Wherever home was. "Maybe I should move to Columbia," she said. "Even though I'd miss teaching, it'd be easier to work on my dissertation there on the Missouri campus."

"And make a clean break from Ray and Dover?" Jan replied. "Assuming he stays there." She maneuvered the station wagon from its parking place, threaded her way out of the shopping center, and turned onto the street.

Rebecca sighed. "I'm surprised that finally making a complete break with him hurts so little. It's simply a relief, one less thing to worry about."

"Poor Ray. I remember when you thought he was Mr. Right."

"There's no such animal as Mr. Right."

"Uh-huh," Jan said sagely.

Rebecca made a face at her and turned to the window. Gray houses lined the gray street under a gray sky. Except for the red and white candy canes and gold tinsel affixed to the lampposts, Putnam was as colorless as an artist's preliminary sketch. "At least with Ray gone we've eliminated one suspect. Not that he was a particularly viable suspect, I'll admit. I was really embarrassed just calling Nancy in the departmental office at Dover to check on that phone message."

"So someone did leave a message telling him to come here, that you wanted to get back together?"

"Nancy said it was a bad connection, but she doesn't know my voice that well, anyway. Obviously it was our malefactor trying yet another way to get me out of Dun Iain. It's frustrating that everyone around here appears so ordinary. If only someone would start playing with ball bearings or wearing a black hat, something to give us a hint."

"Perfectly ordinary people can conceal all sorts of devious little quirks. Like my neighbor who was sweeping her driveway on Thanksgiving. She's so afraid of germs she dips the phone receivers in Lysol, and then fusses at the telephone company because they won't work."

"You make these things up," Rebecca accused her.

"Cross my Girl Scout cookies," returned Jan.

The station wagon passed under the interstate and turned toward Dun Iain. Rebecca nodded toward the bags of groceries in the back. "Thanks for sacrificing your Mother's Day Out to come shopping with me. I had to get away for a little while."

"Keep looking over your shoulder?"

"You'd better believe it. But nothing's happened since Steve's so-called accident three weeks ago. It's like waiting for a centipede to throw down a whole battery of shoes."

"At least you're letting poor Michael alone for a while."

"Hey, he's the only suspect who's done anything suspicious!" Rebecca protested. "Whose side are you on, anyway?"

"Yours," said Jan. "And don't you forget it."

"No, ma'am." Good-natured, nonjudgmental Jan. Rebecca would've gone crazy without someone she could trust. And Peter, too; it was hard to believe she'd ever suspected him, even for a moment. Talk about paranoia.

"I've told myself over and over again," Rebecca said, "that just because Michael has those clippings and that letter from John Forbes, he's not necessarily a thief or a terrorist. Maybe he had second thoughts and wrote to Colin to start the revolution without him. Maybe he's up to something else entirely." She sighed and pulled her coat more tightly around her. "No matter what else he is, he really is a historian for the National Museum. His superiors must've thought I was nuts, calling all the way across the Atlantic to ask about him."

"And you still haven't told Eric about the clippings and the letter?"

"No. It doesn't seem fair to cause a confrontation on so little evidence. Not that Eric confronts. He slides."

Jan's brows rose, but all she said was, "Eric should understand better than anyone else the principle of innocent until proven guilty."

"Proof," said Rebecca. "That's just it. Proof."

The road was a strip of licorice between the gray fields on one side and the gray stone wall on the other. There was the graffiti-painted gap in the wall; Rebecca peered at it as they drove past. Tire marks. Well, the roadside was always crisscrossed with tire marks. If anyone had parked there and sneaked in to splash gasoline over the shed three weeks ago, those marks had long since been obliterated by rain, snow, and more cars.

"And what," Jan asked, "does Michael think of your breathing down his neck waiting for him to prove something?"

"Not much. He stood there, every cannon loaded and run out, while I ransacked the place looking for something, anything he'd hidden. And then he let go with that blasted little smirk when I didn't find a thing. Professionally I can't fault him; cool competence all the way. It's as if what he's out to prove is that my suspicions are wrong. But if they're wrong, why doesn't he just say so?"

"Have you asked him?" Jan turned the car into the driveway.

"Not since the day I found the papers. Why bother? It's no better than an armed truce around there as it is. Something has to give soon, or . . ."

"Or what?" inquired Jan.

"I'd like to make something give." In the last three weeks she and Michael had not only ignored the delicate subject of the papers, they'd never once acknowledged that delightful, disturbing moment of intimacy. If only she would wake up tomorrow and find it January 3, Michael on his way back to Scotland and out of her life forever, she and Eric winging their way to the Caribbean for that casual, virtually meaningless fling . . . Rebecca squirmed. Eric was fun to be with, no doubt about it. And yet she hoped he hadn't put down any deposits on that cruise.

There was the castle, shouldering aside the grasping limbs of the trees. Its face was getting to be that of an old friend, the windows winking with puckish humor, the battlements edged with truculence.

Heather's Datsun sat in the parking area. Dorothy had called in sick three times now—flu, she said—and of all the unlikely substitutes it was Heather who'd come after school to sweep and dust. In fact, there was the girl now, leaning against her broom like a soldier against his pike, eyeing the burned patch of grass and the blackened and boarded-up shed where Steve had been injured She started at the sound of the engine and headed purposefully for her car.

Jan stopped her station wagon, got out, opened the rear gate. "Hello, Heather," Rebecca said.

"Hi," the girl returned, putting her cleaning implements away.

"How's Steve?"

"A lot better. His dad's going to bring him home from the burn unit in Columbus tomorrow. He says he doesn't want to see me. Not because he's going to need some work on his face, he's embarrassed he lost his hair."

"Better his hair than his life! Hang in there, Heather. He'll need you, you'll see."

Heather slammed the trunk lid and looked up, her shoulders curled shyly, her gaze between her black-rimmed lashes earnest and direct. "Miss Reid, Mr. Pruitt says you saved Steve's life, yelling at him and keeping him from stepping into the shed."

"Not necessarily." Rebecca's neck crawled. James had tried to warn her of the impending fire, she was sure of that much. What bewildered her was the flash of clairvoyance that had led her to correctly interpret his message. Maybe living among the odd resonances of the house had driven her slightly mad. As it had James himself.

She seized a bag of groceries. Heather claimed another. Michael appeared at the far side of the lawn, attired in coat and wellies, and tramped forward to pick up the third. Rebecca went inside without waiting for him. Three weeks, and not once had they gone walking companionably together.

She was laying out the cat food when he came in, shed his coat, and revealed the T-shirt of the day. It was black, emblazoned with the legend "I'm not stupid, I'm not expendable, and I'm not going." A shame he hadn't expressed that sentiment when he was offered this job.

"How's the haircut holding up?" Jan asked him.

"Quite well." Michael brushed self-consciously at his forehead. But, unlike Steve, he'd lost barely a quarter inch of his hair. "Thank you kindly for trimmin' it."

"I wasn't going to let all those burnt, frizzled ends fall into the cranberry sauce," Jan told him.

Rebecca placed the teakettle on the burner and mopped at her own brow. The Thanksgiving haircut had started her and Michael talking to each other again after forty-eight hours of stiff silence. His pleas of "No so short" in response to Peter's teasing threats had made them all laugh and had led Rebecca into the daredevil plunge of asking Jan to cut her hair as well. Symbolically cutting off Ray and her old life, probably. Now it was so much easier to care for, waving around her face instead of down her back.

Heather declined Rebecca's offer of tea, murmuring something about a homework assignment, and Michael escorted her out. "Glad to see his hands are healed," Jan said. "I felt so sorry for him, eating his turkey with those horrible blisters."

A shame to see such fine instruments as Michael's hands damaged, Rebecca had to admit. "The first time he picked up the pipes after the bandages came off, his fingers were so stiff he botched every tune. He stood there swearing and trying to do better until he was white from the pain. I was afraid he was going to faint. 'A fine thrawn lad like yourself,' I told him, and took the pipes away. Then he got huffy with me."

"Of course he did. You threatened his manhood."

Rebecca shot a sharp glance at her friend but Jan was discreetly folding a grocery sack. By the time the kettle whistled Michael had reappeared to make the tea. "How'd things go this afternoon?" Rebecca inquired.

"Found a mouse that had snuffed it beneath the dresser. Elspeth's lavender was no bad after that." He meticulously opened the new box of shortbread. "Thank you for the biscuits."

Michael's and Rebecca's eyes met like swords raised in salute before a duel. One of his brows quirked upward and his mouth crimped into a speculative grimace. She tilted her head questioningly, and he looked away. "You're welcome," she said, picked up the teapot, and poured.

"You two have more nerve than I do," said Jan, "working with ghosts."

"The ghosts are no dangerous," Michael asserted as he doctored his tea and turned to go. "The work has to be done."

"It's people who've caused all the trouble around here," said Rebecca, but he was already out the door. "Case in point," she added under her breath.

Jan opened her mouth, apparently decided not to comment, and ate a cookie instead. "Did Warren believe you when you said you'd seen that gas can full and capped a couple of hours before the fire?''

"It'd be a lot easier on him if the fire had been an accident. Awkward, isn't it, that I happen to know it wasn't?''

"So who do you think poured the gas out of the can? I assume it wasn't Dorothy choosing a drastic way to prune Steve's hair.''

"Dorothy smokes,'' replied Rebecca. "She could've been the victim just as well, except she would've been less likely to go in the shed. You think I'm twitchy, she's halfway round the bend. She knows more than she's letting on.''

"I don't doubt it.''

"Dorothy could've poured the gas,'' Rebecca continued. "Or Michael. Or Phil himself, not planning to trap his own son. Or it could be Eric. Although I can't see him sloshing gasoline around in those Italian shoes.''

Jan contemplated and ate another cookie. "Or the fire might have been set by one of Steve's friends. Maybe Steve didn't pay him for his last joint or something.''

"So person A covers up for person B, and person C helps person D, and here is person X that we don't know anything about.'' Rebecca glanced uneasily at the door. It was empty.

"Maybe the dog and cat are masterminding the whole scam,'' said Jan. "Whatever the scam is.''

Rebecca laughed, but there was an edge in her laughter. "You know what it is. Money—the artifacts and the treasure. Someone's willing to go to drastic lengths to keep the state and the museum from getting them.'' She replenished her cup and stared into it without drinking. The castle was even quieter than usual, the gloomy afternoon pressed like foam packing against the walls and muffling the clink of the dishes.

Rebecca jerked herself to her feet. "Come on upstairs and I'll show you that letter James wrote to Katherine Gemmell.''

"Ah, yes. Dorothy as scam mistress.''

From the upper stories emanated a faint strain of music; Michael, after asking very politely, had this morning borrowed Rebecca's tape player and was now playing a Silly Wizard album. "Pretty song,'' said Jan as they crossed the landing into the Hall. "I like the line about 'kiss the tears away.' ''

"Very romantic,'' Rebecca told her, "even though it's a cheerful ditty about a young couple drowning in a shipwreck.''

With the chandelier and a ceramic lamp both shining, the Hall wasn't too dim. The brass implements on the fireplace were a bit tarnished. Not that it mattered, they'd belong to someone else soon.

Jan pulled a chair up to the row of boxes while Rebecca knelt on the floor and opened the closest one. "I looked at the letter again several days ago, wondering whether the issue was worth pursuing. I did try to get Dorothy talking about her family, but all she wanted to tell me was how her grandkids played chipmunks in a church pageant."

"I asked Margie about Dorothy's maiden name," said Jan.

Rebecca looked up. "Not Brown, or you would've called me."

"Sorry. It was Norton."

"Rats." Rebecca moved to another box and continued to dig through the diaries. "So much for that bright idea."

"But if Dorothy isn't Katie Gemmell's daughter," asked Jan, "why did she shy away like that when you showed her the picture?"

"Galvanic reaction?" Rebecca sat up, peeling bits of black paper from her palms. "Darn it, I know I put it in here somewhere."

"Maybe Mr. Brown was Katherine's second husband," Jan suggested. "Dorothy's father was her first husband, somebody Norton. I know I'm constantly getting hung up over some of Peter's cousins who have yours, mine, and ours families."

"There's a thought. Do you suppose Louise would know?"

"No harm in asking her. Or we could go down to the Bureau of Records in Columbus and look up Dorothy's birth certificate."

"Yes!" Rebecca brightened, then dimmed again. "But it might be a wild-goose chase, and I have so much work left to do."

"I can't decide that for you." Jan glanced at her watch. "You'll have to show me the letter some other time. I have to get back to being a mother before they throw the munchkins into the dumpster behind the church."

"But it's right here," insisted Rebecca, peering at the label on the box. The tea gurgled in her throat and she sat back on her haunches. "Jan, it's gone. Someone's taken it, and the photograph, too."

"Maybe someone just put it back in the wrong place. Here, let me help." Jan went down on her knees and opened another box.

"No one knew they were here but Dorothy and me, and I'm

not even sure she saw the letter. I never told Eric or Michael or Warren or anyone about that letter—I didn't know whether it was important, or who I could trust.''

Jan's mouth tightened. "Rebecca, calm down.''

Rebecca forced a deep breath into her chest and started methodically working her way through the boxes. Fifteen minutes later she said, "Okay. That's it. The letter and the photo are gone."

"They sure are. I'd say that answers your question."

"It's important enough for someone to steal. So I guess we have a date with Louise, right?"

"How about tomorrow afternoon? My shift at Golden Age starts at one."

Rebecca pulled herself up, helped Jan to her feet, and scooted the chair back under the table. "I can't go off and leave Michael alone again. It's not fair to him, and it's not fair to the state to give him free rein."

"Bring him along. We'll sic Mrs. West on him again. Or you could even tell him about it and put those tartan brain cells to work."

"But he's a . . ." Rebecca began, and then shook herself, trying to seize some kind of logical thought. "Of all the suspects he has the least reason to have taken that letter. Everyone else has been in this area for years. Even the sheriff. Unless Michael's got such a heck of an elaborate scam going . . .'' Logic, she reminded herself.

"Yes?" Jan prodded.

"All right! Part of my job is to protect the house and the artifacts. This is the only lead I've got. I'll see you tomorrow, with or without the shady customer upstairs.''

"Okay, then." Jan grinned encouragement. "See you tomorrow."

Rebecca saw Jan to the door and then went through the boxes one more time. The letter and the photograph hadn't magically reappeared. Hell, she said to herself. This is ridiculous. I'm just an innocent little drudge of an academic, all I wanted out of this was some self-respect.

She started piling the diaries back into the boxes. In the silence the taped melody playing on the fifth floor was faint but clear, coiling down the staircases like translucent smoke. She recognized this one, too—"Fhear a Bhata," "The Boatman." Michael's voice, singing along with the tape, lifted and then died away, leaving one phrase hanging in the air: "You call me faker, you call me false one."

He's doing that on purpose, Rebecca thought with an aggravated snort. She, too, began to sing, first under her breath and then more loudly, almost defiantly, blanking out his voice.

Which, she realized suddenly, had stopped. She spun around and saw Michael standing in the doorway, a taut smile about to break his face. He held one of two inventories toward her. "You worked on this one, did you?"

From her crouch halfway across the expanse of the floor Rebecca squinted at the label. "Dressing room, fifth floor. Yes, I did."

"Were all the little jeweled things there?"

"No. There're some missing. Eric said some things were sold that James refused to mark off." She put the last book in its box, closed the lid, and stood up.

Michael's jaw jutted belligerently. "He's been sayin' that all along. Wi' no receipts, no notes about where things were sold, naething at all. Can you no own that's a bit dicey?"

Rebecca set her hands on her hips and raised her own chin. "Sure it's questionable. I never said I liked it."

"And this one." He held out the other book, the thick inventory of the main bedroom. "Elspeth's necklace, the one in the portrait, is listed as present and accounted for. But it's no there."

"Eric told me ages ago that was long gone." One corner of Rebecca's mouth twitched and tensed. Go ahead, she ordered herself. Say it. "Besides, if anyone knows about that you do. The letter John wrote to the museum, about making a reliquary out of his wife's jewels for the treasure. Remember that?"

"Half a minute." Michael's expression, already crisp, petrified. "John said it'd been used to make a reliquary, but Eric said it'd been sold?"

Darn, Michael slipped aside from that jab as adroitly as Eric himself. "The choker wasn't here when Eric came on the scene," Rebecca rationalized. "And John never said those were the jewels he was talking about."

"Aye, he was a canny one, old Johnnie was." They looked at each other, frustrated glare glancing off frustrated glare. "James must've known there was a treasure," Michael said at last. "Do yon diaries tell where it is?"

"I don't have time to read all the diaries. Neither do you."

"If it's a Scottish treasure, then I'm entitled to it."

"You're entitled to it? Or Scotland is?"

"As far as you're concerned," he snapped, "we're one and the same."

Rebecca strode to within a foot of Michael, her head and shoulders tilted back to erase the six inches of difference in height. "The same? Not sodding likely."

He smiled again, crescent lines cut in his cheeks as though the smile were in parentheses. "Sorry to have interrupted your work. If you happen to step on a wee jeweled casket for rose petals, do tell me."

"A jeweled casket for rose petals? That was there three weeks ago. I marked it off."

"Aye. So I see. But it's no there the noo."

Sparks swirled across her vision. "*You're* checking up on *me*!"

"It's only fair." The sparks were reflected in his eyes.

She doubled her fists. She and Michael were acting like bloody-minded fools. If they were anything, they weren't fools. "It's too late," she hissed, "for you to be playing the offended innocent."

"It is, rather. And it's no good your playin' judge and jury."

"True enough." Rebecca released her fist and shook out her hand. The marks of her nails made a neat row of gouges across her palm. "But you lied to me. You've been lying all this time."

"No a' the time, lass." His voice dropped abruptly into such a low register she hardly heard it.

She stared at him. His teeth were clenched so tightly his cheeks were corded. His brows crumpled over eyes glinting with pride, pain, and resentment, more at himself, she thought, than at her. For once he wasn't trying to hide.

Rebecca's rage sizzled like a drop of water on a hot iron and evaporated into a thin, dry weariness. "Have you been trying to scare me away? Have you taken any artifacts, or a letter from those boxes of diaries?"

"No."

"Are you some kind of terrorist?"

"No."

"What're you up to, then?"

"Naething that concerns you." He didn't flinch. His eyes didn't leave hers. He didn't insult her by saying winsomely, "Trust me."

No quarter, she reminded herself. "Why won't you come clean with me?"

"I already had a bath the day, thank you just the same."

Laughter swelled in Rebecca's chest and she couldn't hold it in. "Damn you, Michael!" she exclaimed, and she punched halfheartedly at him. "This is ludicrous!"

Michael dodged the punch. His expression cracked and softened and he, too, started laughing. "It's a proper cock-up, and no mistake."

"I want to believe you."

"Then feel free to have a go at it."

His wry humor was infectious. "So don't trust anyone," she told him with an expansive gesture. "You're safer that way. Come on. I'll help you search for that box." Michael rolled his eyes toward the ceiling in an unmistakable expression of relief.

A casket for rose petals, Rebecca thought as she led the way up the stairs. A showy little thing that would sell quickly. Anyone could have taken that. But not Michael. If he had, he wouldn't have pointed out its disappearance. Maybe Dun Iain was generating multiple interlocking conspiracies, but she simply couldn't see how Michael Campbell, the last suspect on the scene, was their prime mover.

She glanced back. He looked at his feet on the stone steps, his face hidden by the fringe of his hair, and his body language that could be so compelling was once again mute. He hadn't asked her to trust him. But she did.

Chapter Twenty-Three

THE SIXTH-FLOOR BALLROOM was so still the silence hummed in Rebecca's ears, so chilly her flesh contracted, trying to snuggle closer to the bone. Last night's dusting of snow reflected the watery sunshine. The pale, blurred light bleached the walls and floor not of color but of definition, so that the room was filled by a subtle mist.

Rebecca drained her coffee, opened an inventory, and went to work. Nineteenth-century landscape prints, check. A tiny casein painting, check. An exquisite Clouet miniature of Mary, Queen of Scots, check. The book Michael had tried to show her the day Ray had come, an elegant mint copy of Johannis de Fordun's *Scotichronicon Genuinem*, was listed on this floor even though it had turned up on the fourth. The claymore from the study had already been checked off.

Last night she and Michael had ransacked the house like eastern and western bloc armies on formal maneuvers. The little casket was gone. Even after Michael had given up and gone off muttering braid Scots curses, Rebecca had continued doggedly on. She'd come out of the lumber room, skin, clothing, and mood equally grimy, to hear Michael playing the pipes. Playing every difficult piece in his repertory, no doubt to prove that his manhood was no longer damaged, thank you. As she'd stood on the staircase, listening, her puzzled itch seemed to emanate from a phantom limb, impossible even to reach, let alone scratch.

The steps coming up the stairs to the ballroom were those of Michael's Reeboks. "What was the final song you played last night?" she asked.

He studied her for a moment as though wondering if she'd turn his answer against him. "Mo Nighean Donn, Gradh Mo Chridhe," he answered.

"Okay," she said. "Thanks."

He nodded toward the storerooms in the back. "So they're comin' the day to collect the books for the library?"

"I took out the ones that were in really bad shape, as well as the ones that're worth something. A first-edition Hemingway, for example."

Michael shrugged, unimpressed by Hemingway. Rebecca opened a cabinet. With a slide and a thud the top sash of Elspeth's window flew open. As one they jumped, and then shared a shamefaced smile. Michael tiptoed across the room and shut the window. "Would you like me to work in here wi' you?"

"I can make it until noon, thank you," Rebecca replied stoutly.

"Noon? What happens then?"

Rebecca considered his face. His cannon had been rolled into the armory for maintenance and his porcupine prickles were reduced to the texture of a hedgehog's. Smudges of fatigue under his eyes looked like bruises on his fair skin. The lines at the corners of his mouth and between his brows were more deeply defined than they had been two months ago. His face wasn't that different from the one staring back from her mirror. Shaking her head at herself and him both, she told him about the letter, how it and Katie Gemmell's photo were gone, how she suspected Dorothy. "Would you like to come?"

"Oh, aye, I'd like to hear what Louise has to say."

"Michael," Rebecca began, and then heard a faint hammering from downstairs. All right—she hadn't really had anything to say to him.

Taking four flights of spiral stairs without pausing left her dizzy. She threw open the front door and stood blinking at a dark figure in a a pallid halo of daylight. "Miss Reid?" it said, solidifying into a uniformed workman. "We've come to pick up your shipment."

"Certainly. Come in."

The hood of a silver-gray car peeked from behind a truck whose panel read "Ace Moving and Storage—you tag it, we bag it." Of the two men talking by the truck's cab, Rebecca recognized one. "Eric! What're you doing here?"

Eric followed the workmen into the building, greeting Rebecca with a peck on the cheek. "I was at Golden Age, so I'd thought I'd run by and supervise. Hard to believe the day has come to start clearing the place out."

"Just some nondescript books," she replied.

"And those boxes for the Historical Society."

Rebecca stopped dead outside the Hall. "What? Already?"

"The donation has to be made this year," Eric explained, "if the estate is going to get the tax deduction. I thought you'd said they could go."

"I did, it's just . . ." She looked through the door. The men were stacking the cardboard boxes of diaries and scrapbooks and the sacks of old clothes. "We were hoping there might be something in James's diaries about the gaps in the inventories."

"But you told me you didn't have time to read them all."

"No," she admitted. "I don't."

"They'll be safe and sound at society headquarters anytime you want them." Eric pulled her aside as the workmen struggled to get their loaded dolly down the stairs.

"Oh, all right," said Rebecca, "take them away, get it over with."

Eric gauged the crumples in her brow and mouth. "Tired? We'll go to a movie this Friday. Get your mind onto something else."

As if that were possible. She inspected Eric's smooth, handsome face, his tailored clothes, his slightly quizzical, slightly amused look. What a frivolous relationship, she thought, discreet and superficial. Just what she'd been looking for. She offered him an anemic smile. "Thanks, I'd like that."

The workmen came back up. Phil Pruitt was just behind them, his quilted vest scented with motor oil and fish. "How is Steve?" asked Eric.

"Doing just fine," Phil replied. "Mr. Adler, I'm sorry to bother you, but what you said once about the hospital bills. Steve's going to need some of that plastic surgery, they tell me."

The workers manhandled the dolly down the stairs. "Of course," said Eric. "I talked to Dun Iain's insurance company, and since Steve was working here when the—ah—accident occurred, his medical bills should be covered."

"I sure do appreciate it," said Phil.

The workmen asked about the books. "I'll show you," said Rebecca.

Eric guided Phil to the study. Rebecca led the men upstairs.

Michael looked curiously up from the cabinet she'd left, inventory open on his lap. Elspeth's window had opened itself again, the usual three inches from the top.

The boxes holding the books were imprinted with the brand names of catsup and toilet paper. When the men hoisted the first two, the flimsy cardboard gave way and books crashed to the floor. The men shot aggrieved glances at Rebecca. She decided her presence was inhibiting their commentary and headed back down, passing Phil, his mission accomplished, on the way.

On the stairs to the second floor Rebecca heard Eric's voice. Now it was in velvet mode, soothing, almost caressing, too soft for her to make out the words. Dorothy's barbed voice ripped his. "—deserve it!"

Rebecca stopped, her hand on the rope banister. Deserve what?

Eric's voice rolled over Dorothy's like a buffing wheel, polishing its sharp edges. Rebecca caught the words "job" and "pension." Oh—if the estate could do for Phil, surely it could do for Dorothy. Apparently the woman was going to make darn sure it did, legally or otherwise.

Eric walked Dorothy out onto the landing, his dark styled cut bent over her steel perm, and held her arm as she worked her way painfully down the stairs. The woman seemed shriveled, her once bloated flesh a couple of sizes too big for her, as if someone really had stuck a pin into her and deflated her. Having the flu was a drastic way to diet.

Rebecca peeked around the corner after them, then dodged into the study door ahead of the workmen as they wrestled boxes around the bend in the staircase. There was Dorothy's purse sitting on a corner of the secretary. She picked it up and went on downstairs.

The vinyl bag was heavy, clinking as she walked. Unzipped, it gaped open to reveal several pill bottles sporting the labels of more than one pharmacy—and more than one doctor's name. Valium, Rebecca read. Ativan. Elavil. Inderal. The last was for high blood pressure; her father took it. The others were tranquilizers; her mother had gone through several different kinds over the years. But all at once? No wonder Dorothy looked so ghastly. She needed detox more than Steve had.

Rebecca guiltily closed the purse and walked out the door holding it at arm's length, like a vial of nitroglycerin.

Dorothy wasn't there. Eric was leaning against her car talking to Heather. Rebecca squelched a grin. He was nondiscriminatory, he was going to vamp every female on the place. Heather was gazing at him through her lashes, slightly cross-eyed, as though she already had a bit of a crush on him. Girls that age don't know superficial from bananas, Rebecca told herself. It's girls my age who deliberately choose surface gloss over substance. She said, "Dorothy left her purse upstairs. Where is she?"

Heather jumped and blushed, making her heavily made-up face look like a jack-o'-lantern. Eric's polite smile broadened into an outright laugh. "In the kitchen. Here, I'll take it to her."

Rebecca handed over the purse. The workmen tramped by. And, just to complete the circus atmosphere, Warren Lansdale's squad car came up the driveway. He had to stop by the mausoleum since the parking area was full. Rebecca, shivering, went to meet him.

The sheriff's moustache was fluffy with glee. "Look what I found!"

"Not the mazer?" returned Rebecca.

His moustache wilted. "That was a low blow," she apologized. "What do you have?"

He mimed a magician producing a rabbit out of a hat and held up a massive key. "The mausoleum key!" The metal was cold in her hand, sticking to her palm like a Popsicle to her tongue. "Where on earth did you find it?"

"I went out to the Pruitts' house yesterday evening, after Steve got home. He looks terrible, but the accident did wonders for his disposition."

"He handed over the key."

"That's right. He took it off your kitchen table three weeks ago with some idea of letting his friends into the mausoleum. Kids and their macabre ideas these days. It's those horror movies, if you ask me."

Rebecca nodded agreement. "But no one's opened the lock. I go out and check it every few days. Yesterday, as a matter of fact."

"He had second thoughts. He never really said why. Maybe he realized if those punk pals of his vandalized the place he'd not only do himself and his dad out of their jobs, this time he'd end up in jail."

Rebecca thrust the key into her pocket. Its weight made her feel lopsided. "But how did he get it? I'd swear that the only times the front door was open, someone was in the kitchen . . ." She frowned, unable to separate those particular details from the welter of details crusted on her mind.

Eric came toward them carrying Rebecca's coat. A slender shape stood in the sixth-floor window—Michael, Rebecca realized with a start, holding a bundle of butterscotch and white fur. Both man and cat were no doubt agog with curiosity over what Warren and Rebecca were talking about. Clutching her coat around her shoulders, Rebecca smiled a thank-you to Eric and turned back to Warren. "And what's Steve's version of the fire?"

The sheriff tilted his hat back on his head. "Well, Phil says he told Steve to transfer the gasoline from the milk jugs to the can. Steve says he did it. Now I know you think, Miss Reid, you saw the jugs empty and the can full. But the shed is pretty dark . . ."

"And I could've been mistaken," Rebecca finished for him. They'd already beaten that horse to death.

"Even Phil will admit," Warren went on, "that when they were handing out the carelessness, Steve was at the head of the line. Maybe the pain and shock made him forget whether he did it or not. Maybe he's too embarrassed to admit it. Maybe the jugs were cracked and leaked over the floor."

"I don't suppose we'll ever know," said Eric, "if the fire was set deliberately. If so, it was just part of the pattern of harassment."

Warren went on, "We talked to some of Steve's buddies in town and even to Dr. Kocurek in Missouri. Nothing. I'll stick by my theory that it was an accident. Poetic justice, I guess, that Steve was the only one hurt."

Poor Steve. Rebecca looked long and hard at Warren's guileless teddy bear face. Arguing with him was like sculpting Silly Putty. "As long as you're here," she said, "would you like to hear about another missing item?"

"What?" Eric and Warren exclaimed simultaneously.

She told them about the jeweled casket. Warren got out his clipboard and laboriously wrote down the details. A box for keeping rose petals—she suspected he'd much rather be out tracking down a stolen car. Eric looked tight-lipped at the house, his profile more like an eagle's than ever.

Rebecca glanced at the dovecote, each stone edged with a lace of snow. "At least the key is back. That's one tiny comfort."

"What?" Eric shouted this time.

"Oh!" said Warren. "You didn't hear. Steve had the mausoleum key. He gave it back to me last night. Sorry he took it, he says."

"Steve gave it back to you?" Eric's voice grated harshly. His eyes flickered and stilled, like embers stirred. "He had it all along?"

"No harm done. I gave him a very stern warning, believe me."

Rebecca's brows rose at Eric's white, pinched look. Even his superhuman patience must be wearing thin.

"Sorry," he said, his face relaxing, his eyes cooling. "You ambushed me with that one."

The sheriff muttered something conciliatory, climbed into his car, and with a quick salute drove away. Rebecca looked after him, mouth tight. The doors of the truck slammed with a crash. One of the men proferred a couple of forms to Eric. He signed, and waved as the truck lumbered off.

Enveloped by the cloud of exhaust, Rebecca and Eric retreated toward the house. She glanced at her watch; it was almost time to go pump Louise for a hint that would explain something, anything at all. Eric had already been at Golden Age today, no reason to ask him to go back. Especially not with Michael in tow. "See you Friday," she told him. "Thanks for your help."

"My pleasure." He pecked her again, the other cheek this time, and with another affable wave drove away.

Michael came trotting out of the house wearing his coat and carrying Rebecca's purse. He handed it over, saying, "Dorothy and Heather are tryin' to decide whether I have a body hidden in my bedcovers. Phil's bangin' on the fourth-floor loo. Are we leavin' them alone in the house?"

"If anything disappears in the next couple of hours," she told him, "we'll definitely know who took it, won't we?"

"Aye, hen, that we will," Michael said, and then caught himself. His face collapsed into the wry, apologetic smile of a boy caught with his hand in the cookie jar. Averting his gaze, he headed for the car.

No, Rebecca thought, unable to work up a good head of exasperation at him, you didn't say "hen" and I didn't hear it. She locked the door, joined Michael in the car, and started toward town.

Chapter Twenty-Four

MICHAEL SLUMPED BESIDE her, his legs folded against the dashboard. All she could see of his face was its reflection in the window. Trees and fences glided through the transparent image without making any impact on its pensive expression. When she told him about Steve and the mausoleum key, he nodded. "I'm no surprised he had it, and less he gave it back. A wee taste of the inferno to make him see the error of his ways."

Rebecca darted his back with a sharp glance. You're one to talk about errors. But there was no point to goading him. Whatever he was dealing with he'd chosen to deal with alone. Instead she asked, "Do you think the fire was an accident? The shed's always smelled of gas."

"A smell would no have exploded. The petrol was poured out, maybe splashed over the door. I wonder, though, why no one stank of it."

"Whoever it was could've changed clothes. Or someone came in from outside, so we never had a chance to smell gas on them."

Michael muttered something about how nice it was in Edinburgh this time of year, and fell silent.

In today's tentative sunlight the preliminary sketch of Putnam was touched with color. The snow-dusted evergreens in front of Golden Age Village looked as if they were trying out for a greeting card. A couple of workmen nailed strings of lights to the eaves of the building. Through the windows of the sitting room Rebecca saw several old-timers, assisted by staff members, decorating a Christmas tree.

Jan came to meet them, trailing tinsel through the bustle and chatter. "There you are! I told Louise a little bit about what's been going on, and she wants to talk to you."

The building was toasty warm, redolent of pine branches and Lysol. Rebecca shed her coat, hoping her fingers and toes would take the opportunity to thaw out. Michael looked as if he'd like to shed his sweatshirt as well as his coat. "Too warm for you?" Rebecca asked.

"What're they tryin' to do, cook the old folks for Christmas dinner?"

She grinned at him. "Just lie back and think of Scotland."

With a part groan, part guffaw, Michael turned to say hello to Mrs. West, whose wheelchair homed in on him like a tartan-seeking missile.

Jan led the way to a small room down the hall. Louise was propped up in bed, wearing a frilly pink bed jacket, a small Bible open on her lap. At her throat, almost concealed in ruffles, she wore the clay beads Phil had found in the sixth-floor fireplace at Dun Iain.

"Good afternoon, Mrs. O'Donnell," said Rebecca. "Thank you for talking to us. This is Michael Campbell."

Michael took Louise's frail fingers in his most delicate grasp. "Oh my," she said. "Another handsome one. How do you do it, my dear?"

I don't, Rebecca replied silently. Michael, at his most non-committal, pulled up a chair for Rebecca and inspected a print of Dun Iain on the wall above the dresser. "Lithograph. Very nice."

"Little Jamie—Mr. James Forbes, I should say, left that to me." Louise closed her Bible. "Everyone's gone now. It hardly seems worthwhile . . ." Her voice faltered and died. Her oddly magnified eyes went dull with memory. The two bright spots of rouge on her cheeks made the rest of her face seem very pale. "Well!" she said. "What did you want to ask?"

Jan leaned against the wall. Michael settled on the floor beside Rebecca. She wanted to pat his head as if he were a giant puppy, charming but not quite paper-trained. "About Katherine Gemmell. Do you know who she married and if she had children?"

"She had a son and a daughter, but I don't remember their names."

"One name started with a 'D,' " offered Rebecca.

Louise shook her head. "Her husband was from Pittsburgh. Bill Brown."

"Was he her first husband?" asked Michael.

"As far as I know."

"When did Katherine and her family leave Putnam?" Rebecca asked. "Where did they go?"

"Sometime in the forties. They went to Columbus; Bill got a job there, since she was always after him to make more money."

"She liked her consumer goods, I take it?" queried Jan.

"Oh, yes. She never had enough nice things. Always made sure to get exactly what she wanted, too. She kept saying it was her due."

"She deserved it," said Rebecca quietly.

Louise nodded. "Exactly. She sure took after Athena; strong-minded."

"They left in the forties?" Rebecca repeated, hoping that in Louise's mind one decade had run into another.

"During World War II. Bill went to work in an airplane plant."

Michael glanced up. Rebecca glanced down. I hate to lead the witness, she told herself, but there seems to be no help for it. "Mrs. O'Donnell, we're also wondering about Dorothy Garst."

"Dorothy. I haven't talked to her in years, since I turned Dun Iain over to her. Always rather avoided her, to be honest; she's a lot like her parents, constantly telling you what's best for you. It served them right she was so wild when she was young."

"Margie thinks she may have been estranged from her folks," said Jan.

"Sam and Ruth Norton," Louise said, blithely unaware she was dropping a bomb on her audience. "They moved to Columbus, too, but later than the Browns. In the early fifties, I think."

Michael sighed. "There's another theory gone west."

Rebecca slid down in her chair. Damn. For a moment everything had been so tidy. The mausoleum key, still in her pocket, stabbed her waist. "We thought maybe Dorothy was Katherine's daughter," she said.

"Dorothy, Katie's girl?" exclaimed Louise. "Oh, no, no. Katie's children moved to Texas or some outlandish place like that, years and years ago. James helped them out."

In the distance someone played "Joy to the World" on a tinny piano. "James helped them out?" Rebecca repeated. "Katherine wasn't able to, then?"

"The last time I saw Katherine," said Louise, "she came out to Dun Iain with Dorothy. This was right after the Nortons moved. Katie said Dorothy had just joined her church in Columbus and needed help, too."

"Oh?" Rebecca sat up. Michael leaned forward, his shoulder pressing against her knee. She barely noticed.

Louise's eyes blurred, seeing a scene from another place and time. "Katie and James had a terrible row. He was very put out with her, believe me, to come and ask him for money when she'd made such a hash of things."

"What kind of hash?"

"I'm not really sure. When I came in with tea, he was saying something about her leaving Bill Brown for another man—Ed? Fred? Ted?—who he didn't feel was a good influence on the children."

"That's why he helped them to push off," Michael commented.

"Just so, dear." Louise smiled benevolently on his upturned face.

"And then?" prompted Rebecca.

"Jamie and Katie just sat there staring at each other, white-faced and tight-lipped, while I served the tea. And Dorothy—well, she was standing by the sideboard looking at the mazer. That's a big fancy drinking cup."

"We know what it is." Michael said hastily.

Louise went on. "Dorothy was a sprightly little thing when she was a girl. Jamie told me later that he might hire her to take my place when I retired, rather than give her a handout. It was three or four years later that Dorothy came back to Putnam and married Chuck Garst. Jamie did hire her then."

Dorothy, sprightly? Hard to believe they were talking about the same person. Time did peculiar things. "That was the last time you saw Katie?" Rebecca asked. "It wasn't 1952, by any chance?"

"Yes, I believe it was."

Rebecca indulged in a brief, silent aha! Michael realized he was leaning against her and sat up with a start.

"Is Katherine still alive?" asked Jan.

Louise shrugged. "I have no idea. Her children left that same year; maybe she went with them. Maybe she went away with that Ed person. Maybe she's still in Columbus, and simply gave up badgering Jamie."

Rebecca shook her head. "I don't know. It's just too damned elusive. Excuse me," she added to Louise.

Louise didn't notice. She fingered the necklace at her throat and closed her eyes. "Poor little Katie. We didn't think at first she'd survive."

"I beg your pardon?" said Rebecca. The sudden veer of Louise's thought gave her a crick in the neck. Michael turned back to the bed, his head tilted. Jan leaned on the back of Rebecca's chair.

"She was born there at Dun Iain. And she was terribly little and weak. It was a miracle from God that she blossomed out, got so big and strong."

"I thought it was Elspeth's baby that was little and weak," Jan said. "Athena's baby was sickly?"

"Oh, yes. And there was Mrs. Forbes's little girl, bouncing and blooming. No wonder people wondered if she was Rudolph's baby."

"And Johnnie took a scunner to the one they called his daughter, did he?" asked Michael.

"He didn't like her very much, if that's what you mean. But Mrs. Forbes raged at him, and at Athena, and even at little Katie. Oh, things were very stiff and sharp there for a time. Then the baby died."

Rebecca sat forward, her spine prickling. "Which baby died?"

Louise's eyes roved confusedly for something that was no longer in front of them. "Elspeth blamed that letter. She went through the house looking for it, saying she'd destroy it if she found it. But she couldn't."

"Do you know what she means?" Jan asked Rebecca.

Like an explosion run in reverse, Rebecca's mind detonated not outward but in, shrapnel fitting together instead of flying apart. "The Erskine letter! It has to do with switching a living baby for a dead one!"

"Thank you," said Louise. Her voice broke. Her eyes closed in sudden weariness. "That's what I've always wondered. Thank you."

"Switching babies? Oh, my God." Jan came around the chair, sat on Louise's bed, and took her free hand. "It's all right, Mrs. O'Donnell. It all happened a long time ago."

Michael clambered to his feet and braced himself against the dresser, looking slightly dazed. Louise settled even further into her pillows, a porcelain figure nested in white tissue paper. "It was so long ago. There's no one left, it's hardly worthwhile to go on."

"To go on hiding the truth?" asked Jan gently. "To pretend that Athena's baby miraculously turned into a healthy one?" The old lady tried to speak and couldn't. Jan motioned to Michael for the glass of water on the dresser and helped Louise to drink. "You don't have to tell us anything."

"Yes, I do," Louise replied faintly, looking from Jan to Rebecca and Michael. "You shouldn't go to your grave carrying other people's sins."

"Why not?" muttered Michael. "Happens all the time."

Jan made soothing noises. Rebecca winced. "If you'd like to tell us, we'd like to hear."

Louise took a deep breath. "Athena went in to get Katie in the morning and found her dead. Only I suppose it wasn't Katie, was it?"

"Cot death?" Michael asked. "Naething apparently wrong with her?"

"Athena swore up and down she'd been smothered by one of the cats. You know the old story, how cats will curl up on an infant and smother it. But Rudolph thought he knew what had really happened. He went to John and claimed Elspeth had smothered the baby in a fit of jealousy."

"Ouch," exclaimed Jan.

Rebecca said, "John believed him, didn't he?"

"He'd been living with Elspeth's temper for years. He believed him."

"And the Gemmells," said Michael, "wanted Elspeth's bairn."

"Do you think they blackmailed the Forbeses?" asked Rebecca. She scooted forward to the edge of the bed, folding her arms on the coverlet.

"There was plenty of talk. Charges and countercharges. I wouldn't be surprised if it came down to blackmail."

"What a scandal there would've been if the Gemmells had accused Elspeth of murder," said Jan. "Not to mention that an investigation would've brought out the affair with Rudolph and the doubt about who the baby's father was."

"I think John could've bought Rudolph off," Louise said. "I think he tried. But Athena wanted the child."

"And she got it," Michael concluded. "Losin' her own baby finally pushed Elspeth round the twist. Not that she had far to go."

"Did John push her out of the window?" Rebecca asked.

"I don't know," replied Louise. "All I heard was Mrs. Forbes screaming, 'I want my baby back, give her back to me.' And then she fell."

"Unpremeditated murder in a moment's rage," Rebecca

mused. "Or quite intentional if misguided 'justice' for her infidelity and for killing Athena's baby. Although I daresay even John didn't know whether she really had."

Jan frowned. "With all due respect, Mrs. O'Donnell, do you really remember which baby was born strong and which weak? Could it be that Elspeth herself switched babies because she wanted the healthy one? What if it was Elspeth's baby who died in Katie's bed of perfectly natural causes?"

"It's hard," the old lady admitted. "I could have the details confused. But somewhere, somehow, the babies were switched. And I know for sure that Mr. Forbes was not only in the house but in the ballroom when his wife fell." Her trembling hand fingered the beads. "He promised me a piece of her jewelry if I never told."

"Guilty conscience?" asked Michael. "Blood money?" He inspected the lithograph of the castle as if expecting its cool Scottish baronial facade to suddenly crack, slough away, and reveal love and hate snarled like brambles.

"Switching babies and—well—letting Elspeth die solved John's problems," Rebecca pointed out. Her shoulders were cramping from her intense crouch over the edge of the bed. She sat up.

"Elspeth had led him a merry life," Louise said. "She threw over the young man in Scotland to marry him, because she wanted his money. She used his money, too. And then there was Rudolph and the baby, and her madness. That was just too much, I think. The last straw."

Rebecca visualized Elspeth's portrait with its dark, self-absorbed eyes. She saw the height of Dun Iain and the open window. She saw the woman falling, skirts fluttering, face set in exaltation and terror mingled. She saw the young servant girl watching in horror, knowing the truth but unable to blow the whistle on the laird of the castle. Louise had been holding baby Katie when Elspeth fell. Except it wasn't the same Katie, it was a new, improved Katie.

A slightly off-key "Silent Night" jangled down the hall. Lusty bellows from the staff accompanied various cracked voices. The bedroom was so quiet Rebecca could hear the tick of Louise's clock, so hot, close, and still she detected a faint sour odor beneath that of bath powder. She looked up, her cheeks burning. Sweat sheened Michael's forehead, sticking down the strands of his hair. Jan bent solicitously over Louise as the old lady lay back, the clay beads dull against the ruffles of her jacket

"Did you ever get any jewelry?" Rebecca asked. "Or did he only give you those beads and a photograph of what you were promised?"

"No, he never gave me any jewelry. Why should he? I didn't know anything. I only suspected. Katie got a family, much better than having a bitter old man for a father and no mother at all."

"And Katherine knew all of this, did she?" Michael asked.

"She didn't hear it from me. I promised I wouldn't tell and I didn't. It was Athena, filling Katie's head with nonsense about wealth and power."

"That was Katherine's claim on James," Rebecca said with a tight smile. "Not the manner of Elspeth's death, but that she might have been his sister."

"Half sister," corrected Michael. "Possibly. No matter whether her mother was Elspeth or Athena, her father was Rudolph."

"Was it?" Rebecca stood up. "What if she believed she was John's daughter? Then she'd have some claim on the estate, wouldn't she? Did she ever ask you for a deposition, Mrs. O'Donnell?"

"Why should she?" scoffed Louise. "Couldn't prove a thing. Couldn't get a penny."

"So," said Rebecca, "lacking proof, Katherine resorted to threats and to subterfuge to get what she thought she had coming to her. And yet she dropped out of the picture thirty years ago."

"If she was still around," Jan said, "would James have been so vague about leaving Dun Iain to relatives? Who did Eric find, some lady out in California descended from John's sister?"

"Yes." Rebecca jiggled the mausoleum key in her pocket.

"Do you want to go to Columbus tomorrow?" asked Jan. She glanced down at Louise. The old lady had fallen asleep. "We could look for Katie's death certificate. And Dorothy's birth certificate, for that matter."

Rebecca exhaled. "Yes, I think we ought to check the records."

"Occam's razor?" asked Michael brightly.

"The simplest explanation is most likely to be the right one," Rebecca explained to Jan. "All this about babies and blackmail. It has to have something to do with what's going on today."

"There is some connection between Dorothy and Katie," Jan pointed out. "Do you suppose Katie's lurking out there somewhere directing operations through Dorothy?"

"Ah, the spider in the middle o' the web. Waitin' for us to

find the treasure, no doubt." Michael's smile was as pure as the driven slush.

"If they wanted us to find it for them, they'd hardly be trying to drive us out, would they?" rejoined Rebecca. She wasn't sure whether to scowl at him or smile with him.

Louise twitched and awoke, blinking owlishly. "What do you know about John Forbes's treasure, Mrs. O'Donnell?" Michael asked.

"He used to say that no matter what happened, he had his treasure. Although he did talk about selling it when the market crashed in 1929."

"We know," murmured Rebecca.

"Mr. James would say the same thing," Louise went on, "except I don't think he knew where it was. Or even what it was. And the Lord knows I haven't the foggiest idea. Never did."

"That figures." Shaking the sweaty ends of her hair out of her face, Rebecca leaned over and kissed Louise. "Thank you, Mrs. O'Donnell. We do appreciate your taking the time and the energy to help us."

"You've helped me," Louise replied. And, to Michael, "You may kiss me, too, dear." Obediently he did, eliciting a delighted girlish giggle.

"See you tomorrow," Jan said to Rebecca. "I'll pick you up at nine. Would you like to come with us, Michael?"

"I'll hold the fort. Someone has to keep workin'—in the house," he added quickly.

Jan stayed to fluff Louise's pillows and bring her more water. Michael and Rebecca plunged out the front door like swimmers into an icy pool. The cold clean air took Rebecca's breath away. Even Michael zipped up his coat.

Rebecca unlocked the car, turned on the engine, let it idle until it warmed. "And then," she thought aloud, "did someone kill James? Brian heard his ghost say 'Don't push me.' "

"On that evidence I'd believe he tripped over the ghost of Athena's killer cat." Michael assumed his slump against the window.

Rebecca shot a jaundiced look at his ear, peeking at her from beneath a wing of hair, and put the car in gear. "If he was killed, it was because he was about to blow the whistle on the embezzlement scheme."

"Obviously. The man was ninety-six; it would've been easier to let him go in his own time. But can you see Dorothy chuckin' him down the stairs?"

"People can do just about anything if they think they're justified."

"Aye." Ignoring the personal implications of her remark, Michael said nothing more until they were back at the castle. The parking area was empty. Darnley was prowling around the dovecote.

Once in the kitchen Michael put on the kettle and prepared the teapot. Rebecca leaned wearily against the cabinet. She'd thought she had brain overload before. Now her mind seemed to bulge against her skull, like yeast bread rising in too small a container. If she'd had a home, she'd have gone there, buried her head under the pillows, and screamed.

Elspeth, a pillow, a baby. The Erskine letter. Rebecca started up so abruptly she almost crashed into the mug Michael was holding out. "Cuppa?" he asked, brows arched warily. "Good for what ails you."

"Will it cure my habit of trotting merrily up primrose paths and finding them only weeds?" She took the mug and set it on the counter.

"Primrose paths?" Darnley meowed peremptorily from the pantry and Michael reached for a can of Fancy Feast. "They're no so many weeds, lass. Gilt-edged or otherwise."

"Thank you, lad," she returned, smiling in spite of herself. She took a paring knife, headed upstairs, and tucked the mausoleum key back into the secretary. Where it should've been all along, she scolded herself.

In her room she lifted down the portrait of Elspeth. The crackling brown paper that covered the back was signed and dated: "John Singer Sargent, New York, 1900. Mrs. John Forbes."

Elspeth's face was only paint on canvas, a mask made of brush strokes. Rebecca visualized her posing for the artist, flirting and smiling, and Sargent searching for the quiet desperation below the surface. Or perhaps Elspeth had deliberately chosen that sweet, sad face, as an alternative to her reality.

Carefully Rebecca slit the backing, took the flashlight from her bedside drawer, and inspected the narrow gap between canvas and paper. Nothing. Well, no one had ever accused John of having a sense of humor, black or otherwise. He hadn't hidden the Erskine letter in his wife's portrait.

Rebecca took the painting and set it in the piper's gallery, face to the wall. She closed the door on it and went to report to Michael.

Chapter Twenty-Five

REBECCA SAT ABRUPTLY up in bed, the blankets clutched to her breast. What was that noise? Oh, the dishes in the pantry. This time they had gone at five forty-five. Elspeth kept early hours.

Rebecca fell back into the covers. The vertical scan of her mind clicked on—birth certificates, convoluted plots, Jamie, Katie, Dorothy. So much for sleep. Thanks, Elspeth. She crawled from the bed and hit the light switch. Nothing happened.

The electricity wasn't out; her night-light glowed brightly enough to illuminate the pallid square on the wall where Elspeth's portrait had hung. "Don't like to hear the truth, do you?" Rebecca whispered. She opened her door and looked out into the gloomy corridor. A palpable aura of lavender hung on the draft from the stairwell.

Rebecca grabbed an armful of clothing and scurried into her bathroom. That light didn't work, either. The sound of running water was like thunder in the silence. Quickly she pulled on the silk long johns she'd found on sale in the mall, corduroy pants, blouse, sweater, and socks. The fabrics were chilly against her shrinking skin, but not as cold as the air.

Gagging on the miasma of lavender, Rebecca took her flashlight and crept down the stairs. The chair in the study scraped as if someone were standing impatiently up to see what was going on. At the sound the odor vanished. Rebecca scurried by. She was beginning to think that James and Elspeth were not working together but at cross-purposes. And yet they both seemed determined to protect the house.

Queen Mary's alabaster features leaped suddenly out of the darkness, caught in the beam of light. Rebecca sprinted into the kitchen and tried that switch. The bank of lights blazed. Through the open door of the pantry the shelves, the boxes and cans, the dishes stared innocently out.

A light thump was Darnley bounding down the staircase, his whiskers at full food alert. Smiling, pleased with herself, Rebecca turned off her flashlight, fed the cat, put on a pot of coffee, and started making toast.

A few minutes later Michael appeared in the door. His face looked like his jeans and sweatshirt, crumpled but clean. He smoothed the antennalike ends of his hair and asked, "Here noo, what's a' this, then?"

"The dishes crashed again. So I got up."

"Hell o' an alarm clock." He groped toward the stove, seized the kettle, opened the cabinet where the tea canister was. His eyes flew fully open. "I'll be damned."

Rebecca turned to see him pluck the tiny jeweled casket from the shelf. "I thought that had gone missing!"

"It had done." He opened it, turned it over, and shut it as if waiting for it to disappear in a puff of smoke. "If I went back upstairs and started ower again, do you think it would help?"

"No." Rebecca took a linen napkin from a drawer and wrapped the box in it. "Someone took it and brought it back. If we're lucky it'll have fingerprints on it. Besides yours and mine."

Michael groaned and peered dubiously into the tea canister.

A gallon of caffeine later they advanced on the top floor, inventories in hand. "All right," Rebecca said. "Jan's coming to pick me up at nine. You can call Warren about the box then. I'll try to be back by one or so. Probably without any more information than we already have."

With a glance of long-suffering patience Michael settled himself in front of a cabinet. Rebecca turned her chair away from the black oblong of Elspeth's window. The pernicious draft nibbled her ankles and slithered up her legs to gather in the small of her back. The glow of the coffee in her stomach flickered like a candle in a breeze.

The cabinet contained more letters. She flipped through them hopefully, the papers crinkling. John Knox, Hume, Mills. Alexander III, that was a good one. Robert the Bruce.

"He was Anglo-Norman, you know," said Michael.

"Another cherished myth crushed," Rebecca replied. "And

clan tartans didn't originate until the nineteenth century, and the pipes are indigenous to Portugal or some such place.''

"Surprise, surprise." Michael pulled a thick piece of parchment from the rest. "Here, look at this.''

She took it. The last vestige of warmth in her stomach winked out as though she'd been plunged into a snowbank. The hair on her brow stirred in an icy wind, that on the back of her neck tightened in fear.

The letter had been written by John Dalrymple, Master of Stair, in 1691. "I believe you will be satisfied it were of great advantage to the nation that thieving tribe were rooted out.''

"It's one of the orders for the Glen Coe massacre," she croaked. Michael's face swam before her eyes, blurred by swirling snowflakes. "Robert Campbell of Glen Lyon quartered his men on the MacDonalds and then turned on them, violating every rule of hospitality. They killed everyone, even the women and children, who didn't escape through the snow into the mountains.''

She stopped with a gulp and threw down the paper. Her teeth were chattering. It wasn't that cold in the ballroom, but it had been at Glen Coe.

"The Glen Coe MacDonalds were bandits and bullies," said Michael, thrusting the letter back into the cabinet. His face was white, his lips thin. "Campbell o' Glen Lyon was just the executioner, he didna gie the order. That was Dalrymple, and King William.''

"You're saying he was just following orders? I thought that excuse went out of style after Nuremberg." Rebecca paced up and down, trying to force some blood back into her skin.

"It's always easier tae swallow the simplistic version.''

"You know what Charles II said—there's never trouble in Scotland that hasn't been stirred up by a Dalrymple or a Campbell.''

"Dammit, woman, I didna go shoppin' for a family name!''

"That's not what I meant." He knew what she meant, and he chose not to answer. She stood holding herself defensively against Michael's annoyed glare. The dark apertures of the windows lightened just a bit. Barely dawn, and already they were fighting. Dawn lay gently on the bloody snow . . . "Sorry. That letter ambushed me. Talk about the artifacts wanting to go home!''

"Aye," said Michael, his glare dissipating. "Some o' them should be in cages wi' warnin' signs, right enough.''

Rebecca moved to a cupboard across the room. Her fingers were still cold, her toes numb, the back of her neck twitchy. But she managed to get through a couple of hours of sorting. Her head had just fallen forward in a doze when the phone rang downstairs. "I'll get it," she said to the blank expanse of Michael's back, and he sat up with a start.

Her watch said eight-thirty. The windows admitted a fine platinum sunlight, lifting the shadows lurking in staircase and corridor. "Hello," she said into the receiver outside Michael's door.

"Rebecca!" said Eric. "Sorry to bother you so early in the morning."

"You're not bothering me," she replied, pleased to hear evidence of a world beyond Dun Iain.

"Just wanted to let you know contact has been made—I've found Charlotte Dennison Morris."

"Who? Oh! Rachel Forbes Dennison's granddaughter?"

"The very same. In a nursing home in San Francisco. Eighty-five years old and in very poor health. But she has children and grandchildren of her own, someone to pass the proceeds of the estate on to. The unexpected inheritance for them, just like you said that time."

She'd said that? When? "So Mrs. Morris wants you to sell it?"

"The cost of keeping it up would be ridiculous. And we do have that offer from Bright."

"What will Bright do with the place?" She paced down the hall, the friendly threadbare carpet muffling her footsteps.

"Make it into a corporate retreat, I imagine. New furniture, exercise equipment, hot tubs. That jazz ensemble on the piper's gallery."

Rebecca looked down the stairs, at the golden stone and the quixotic rope banisters. The state of Ohio would use the place as a youth hostel. They couldn't afford to replace stone and wool with plastic and polyester.

"Rebecca?"

"Sorry. Hard to imagine the place being refitted like that. The historical preservationists . . ."

"Have enough to do already. Bright won't tear the place down, Rebecca. They'll just scare away the ghosts."

That wasn't particularly funny, even though she knew he meant it to be. "Eric," she said, and then stopped. No, she wouldn't tell him she was going to be in Columbus today. Jan's kids didn't need to lower the tone of whatever exclusive restaurant he frequented for lunch. And Rebecca didn't want to listen to his smooth, ever-so-slightly condescending comments about her curiosity and initiative. "See you tomorrow night. Thanks for calling."

"See you then."

Rebecca went on down to her room, put on some makeup, gathered her coat and purse. The Sorensons' station wagon came clattering along the drive and she shouted up the staircase, "I'm leaving now."

"Happy huntin'!" Michael shouted back.

The dark, clean limbs of the trees shone in the morning sun. The dusting of snow was gone, leaving only a fragile rim of ice on the dovecote. Darnley was basking on his stone wall. Rebecca climbed into the car, buckled up, and said "Good morning!" more brightly than she really felt.

The radio was predicting a winter storm on Saturday. "Can we build a snowman?" asked Mandy from the back, where the children were immobilized like papooses in snowsuits and car seats.

"Of course." Jan turned the car onto the road. "And how are you?" she asked Rebecca.

Rebecca told her.

"You found it in the kitchen cabinet?" Jan exclaimed. "Hadn't you already looked there?"

"I'd looked everywhere. Someone brought it back, that's all. Maybe they're all in it together, Warren, Katie, Dorothy, the Pruitts, the cat. There're traffic jams of malefactors at night."

"I must admit," Jan said, "that at first I thought you were being a bit paranoid. But you're not being paranoid when someone's really out to get you."

The countryside sparkled as if it had been varnished, brown fields transformed into bronze, gray houses into silver. The sky was a deep cobalt blue, implying unplumbed depths of light. The last time I came this way, Rebecca thought, Eric was playing "Music from the Hearts of Space."

The brightness of the day made even the city look attractive. They passed the Ohio Historical Society on the outskirts of town and Rebecca waved at the diaries. Jan actually found a parking place not too far from the Bureau of Records. Soon they were in a long room beneath fluorescent lights which glanced off nondescript linoleum, desks, and microfiche readers.

Margie had said Dorothy was born in 1933. Rebecca got the appropriate transparencies from the gum-chewing girl behind the counter while Jan hauled an orange plastic chair into a corner. She plunked the children down behind it and opened a sack of toys. "Okay," she said. "Imagine the chair is concertina wire. Do not pass." Brian and Mandy began to fight over a G.I. Joe figure.

Rebecca settled herself at a reader and started plugging in plastic sheets. Names and numbers crawled like neon insects across the screen. "Well," she said when Jan appeared in her peripheral vision, "that didn't take long. Dorothy Anne, born to Samuel Norton and Ruth Kordelewski."

"Okay," said Jan. "On to Plan B."

"Katherine Gemmell Brown's death certificate? Yeah, well— she was born in 1901. She's probably long gone." Rebecca flicked the switch on the viewer and the screen went out. A tiny bulb in the back of her mind went on. She swung around in the chair. "What was it Margie said about Dorothy that time? That she'd had a quickie marriage and divorce back in her flaming-youth days?"

Jan's brows shot up her forehead. "You think she might have . . ."

"Married Katie's son!" Rubbing her hands in anticipation, Rebecca turned in her transparencies and claimed some new ones. "Nineteen fifty-two. It had to have been. They got married, couldn't live on love, Katie tried to hit up James for a handout for them!"

Jan scooted in Rebecca's chair. "And Louise never knew about it!"

"Why should she? She didn't overhear the entire conversation between Katherine and James. And the marriage was just a flash in the pan, here in Columbus beyond the range of the Putnam gossip radar. It didn't work, he left, Dorothy married Chuck Garst and settled down."

"It's worth a try," Jan said. "I'll check some of the death records while you go through the marriage licenses."

The lurid green letters unreeled before her. Nothing. Rebecca blinked, her eyes hurting, and turned around with a frustrated sigh. Jan was feeding her children animal crackers and paper cartons of juice. "Any luck?"

Jan mopped at a small mouth. "If she died, she did it some-where else. How about you?"

"If Dorothy got married, she did it somewhere else."

"It was just a rumor," Jan returned. "You know how rumors are."

"Yes, I do . . ." Another mental bulb flared. Rebecca leaped up, did a modest approximation of a grand jeté, and distracted the attendant from her bubble gum by asking for the birth certificates for 1952. "Rumors," she explained to Jan. "How better to handle rumors of pregnancy than to claim a marriage? If Katie was at Dun Iain with Dorothy in 1952, and Dorothy was pregnant, the baby might've come in early 1953."

"All right!" Jan's wicked grin was tempered with caution. "But that doesn't explain why Katie butted in. Maybe her son was the father, yes, but then, why didn't she get him to marry Dorothy?"

"Let's make a leap of faith and assume Katherine was actually telling the truth. She met Dorothy in church. An unwanted pregnancy would sure drive me to prayer. Maybe Katie had had some kind of born-again experience and was trying to make up for her past greediness by helping poor little Dorothy. They were both from Putnam, after all. Maybe that letter from James, about shaming the memory of her parents, brought her to her senses. That's why he never heard from her again after helping her kids and Dorothy, too."

"Sounds good to me," said Jan, and Rebecca turned back to the reader.

She realized she was whistling "The Trooper and the Maid" under her breath as the blotches of print unfurled. "Bonnie lassie, I'll lie near you now; bonnie lassie, I'll lie near you—something, something, in the morning I'll no leave you." Yeah, that's what they always say.

"There it is!" Rebecca exclaimed, and bit her lip, hoping she hadn't disturbed anyone else in the room. Then her thought exploded, emotional shrapnel searing bloody tracks in her mind. "Jan! Oh, my God, oh, Jan!"

"What is it? I thought you found it."

"I found it, all right." Rebecca's trembling finger indicated the words on the screen. "Look."

Dorothy Norton, Ronald Adler. Male child. Eric. March 27, 1953.

"Adler?" said Jan. "Hey, there's got to be lots of people in the world named Adler."

"Eric Adler? My—our—Eric Adler is thirty-five years old. It's him." Rebecca's voice thinned and twanged like a rubber band.

"Lord," Jan croaked. "Of all the things I thought we might find, this sure as heck wasn't one of them."

The lines of print on the screen blurred and ran. Rebecca

closed her eyes and opened them again, but the accusing name was still there. The letters were fuzzy, especially the "R" of Ronald and the "th" of Dorothy; "Norton" looked rather like "Horton." It was only a copy of an old birth certificate, after all. The original had been typed on some clerk's long-suffering typewriter, and the transfer to microfiche hadn't helped. Only "Eric" was crisp, hand-printed in ink after someone—Dorothy? his adoptive parents?—had given him that name.

Jan looked at the screen, brow furrowed. "Eric's named Adler, though. Maybe Dorothy *was* married to Ronald, and Eric was taken into a foster home rather than adopted. Maybe his father's family took him in. Did he ever tell you what happened to the people he called his parents?"

"Some kind of accident, I gather. It's not the type of thing you ask." Rebecca's lips were so numb it was hard to speak.

"Looking for your roots has become fashionable," Jan went breathlessly on. "Maybe he grew up under the name of his adoptive parents and then took 'Adler' after he found out who his father really was."

Rebecca flicked off the screen, but the name still danced in front of her eyes, little smeary letters wriggling like bacteria. "He knows Dorothy is his mother."

"Him *not* knowing would be stretching coincidence to absurdity. But I can see why he never told you, or anyone else, for that matter."

"Pearls before swine? No, someone who's worked as hard as Eric to smooth his rough edges would never claim a relationship with a small-town slob like Dorothy. But he knows. So does she. No wonder she's so partial to him."

For a moment the women were silent. The fiche machines hummed only slightly less shrilly than the fluorescent lights. Car horns honked outside. Mandy's and Brian's voices ricocheted off the hard floor. More than one patron of the room sent dirty looks first at them and then at Jan.

"What about Katherine?" Jan said, sidling hurriedly toward her offspring. "Or do you even think she's important anymore?"

"How the hell do I know?" Rebecca stood up, her knees and back locking themselves upright. "Sorry. Let's get out of here."

Either the day's bright sunshine had become as smudged as the old records, she thought, or the smoke of her burning assumptions clouded her vision. On the outskirts of Columbus Jan turned into a Shoney's. They found a booth in the corner, ordered kid meals for the children and coffee and club sandwiches for themselves. Brian painted his plate with catsup, using a french fry as a brush. Mandy peeled the pickles from her hamburger.

Rebecca took a bite of her sandwich, chewed until it was the size of a baseball, then tried to wash it down with a gulp of coffee. Choking, she shoved the plate away. "And Michael said, way back when, that Eric was up to something. Did I listen to him? No."

Jan raked her friend with an acute gaze, and for a moment Rebecca was afraid she was going to say something about Michael. But she said, "Is Dorothy blackmailing Eric into fencing the missing items for her?"

"The envelope from Sotheby's? I'd wondered how someone with Dorothy's limited background could sell something like the mazer."

"Or is Eric masterminding the whole scheme?" Jan went on.

Rebecca rubbed her temples, rearranging rather than soothing the pain. "But it's not a lucrative enough scheme to be worth the penalties. So petty, an item here, an item there. You don't buy Volvos with that. You don't risk disbarment. Only Dorothy would think such small amounts were worthwhile."

"Maybe he's just covering up for her, trying to get matters straightened out before anyone finds out. He must've been appalled to look up his long-lost mother only to find she's up to her perm in embezzlement. How'd that go over with Benjamin Birkenhead?"

Rebecca snorted. "Real well."

"You see? Come on, eat, it'll make you feel better." Jan followed her own advice by wrestling a piece of bacon from the edge of her sandwich.

Rebecca picked up her sandwich again. She nibbled at a piece of turkey, got that down, tried a bigger bite.

After a time Jan said, slowly and carefully into the depths of her cup, "Eric had access to the house without romancing you, you know."

"I know."

"But the shine's already gone off that relationship, hasn't it?"

"That obvious, huh?" Without waiting for Jan to reply, Rebecca went on, "I know there's something beneath that glossy surface. But I'm beginning to wonder if he's spent so many years hiding it he's lost it himself. Such slickness is a kind of dishonesty, I think."

"I think so, too. But that was what you wanted, once. What do you want now?"

"The truth." Rebecca smiled wanly at her friend, motioned to the waitress. and grabbed the check.

On the way back to Putnam she listened only halfheartedly to the prattle of the children and to Jan's remarks on the landscape and the weather. Her thoughts crawled as painfully as wounded soldiers across the no-man's-land of her mind. *And I thought this was going to be such an easy job. Instead of the Erskine letter, I find assorted ghosts, a punk, and an alcoholic housekeeper, a slick lawyer, a teddy bear of a sheriff, and a porcupine of a historian with a tartan chip on his shoulder and sensibilities deeper than any heart of space.*

Jan dropped Rebecca off in a parking area deserted except for the Toyota and the Nova. The two cars were facing different directions, giving each other the cold fender. "You going to be all right?" she called. "I'm just at the end of the phone line."

"I'm okay. Thank you for putting up with all of this." Rebecca walked into Dun Iain, where the ashes of the past drifted like snow, piling up in the corners, making ridges and banks in the corridors, muffling all footsteps but those of the dead.

Michael galloped onto the landing. "It's you."

"Who else? Dorothy and Phil aren't due again until tomorrow."

He glanced over his shoulder. "James has been trampin' up and doon the bluidy stairs all bluidy mornin'."

"Even the ghosts are getting nervous." Rebecca said, frowning.

"Warren says he's right pleased to have the box back again, we must've overlooked it, thank you very much. If we really insist, we can take it into the lab in Putnam, but why bother?"

"Great."

Michael started to go, caught himself, and came back. "Did you find anything in the records place?"

"We found that Dorothy isn't related to Katherine Gemmell," Rebecca answered, not looking at him.

"Ah. I see. Well, then." He went back upstairs.

Rebecca found Darnley asleep in a patch of sunlight on her bed. She sat down and stroked his soft fur. "No," she said, "I can't tell anyone else about Eric until I've talked to him. It just wouldn't be fair. If Michael has some things to work out alone, then so do I."

Darnley regarded her with skeptical yellow eyes, as though asking just what truth she really wanted.

Chapter Twenty-Six

THE SKY HAD an ominous tint. It was still blue, but it was no longer deep; it arched above Dun Iain like a lid. The icy wind left a metallic tang in the back of Rebecca's throat.

She hurried past Dorothy's and Phil's cars into the house. Her first stop was her bathroom, where she scrubbed black ink from her fingertips. The Putnam police had looked at her with thinly veiled amusement when she marched in, handed over the jeweled casket, and asked them to dust it for fingerprints; Warren had never told them she was coming. After they'd taken her prints they pointed out with the patient reasonableness reserved for children and the mentally impaired that they'd need prints from everyone else at Dun Iain as well. Maybe they'd get back to her on Monday. Maybe later in the week. She'd barely made it outside before she blushed with rage and embarrassment.

There, her fingertips were pink again. Rebecca got her notebook from her room and glanced up the stairs. Michael must be on the sixth floor, doing more than his share of work. From the sound of water running and the odor of furniture polish she deduced Dorothy was on the fifth floor. Phil was banging the plumbing on the fourth floor, the pipes reverberating like gongs.

Her mouth tight, her shoulders stiff, Rebecca went into the kitchen, poured herself a cup of tea from the still warm pot, and placed the telephone and the phone book on the table. She sharpened her pencil, opened a fresh page in her notebook, and made the easiest call first. "Hi, Jan!"

"How're you doing?" Jan responded.

"I haven't committed hari-kari with my nail scissors yet. The mood I'm in I'm much more likely to commit the Dun Iain nail scissor massacre."

"Spare the cat, at least. What can I do for you?"

"Tell me if you know whether Eric is doing any legal work for Louise."

"No, she's got somebody else. Why?"

"Just wondering if he had some influence over what she told us the other day. Grasping at straws, I'm afraid."

"If I see any answers on sale at the Big Bear, I'll get some, okay?"

Rebecca laughed. "Thanks, Jan. Check with you later."

The next number was that of the Ohio Historical Society. She wended her way through three different extensions until she ascertained that the diaries and scrapbooks had indeed arrived safely. She wrote, "OHS okay."

Michael strolled into the kitchen, warmed up the teapot with hot water from the kettle, refilled his mug, and strolled out again. From the corner of her eye Rebecca registered his inquisitive glance. He was just like a cat, auburn whiskers always at the alert.

Rebecca dialed Information, wrote down a number, and dialed again. A voice answered, "Sotheby's New York."

Again Rebecca persisted through several extensions until she found someone who either knew what he was talking about or cared what she was asking. "Nineteenth-century Edinburgh silver work," repeated the male voice. "Is that the piece that was recently stolen from some place in Ohio?"

"That's where I'm calling from," said Rebecca. "I'd like to know if anyone's offered the mazer for sale through you."

"Oh! You must be from the insurance company." Rebecca didn't enlighten him. The voice went on, "Since we've been notified that the piece was stolen, we would, of course, let you know if it came in. There're collectors who could've been contacted privately, but I'm not at liberty to divulge their names."

"Of course not," said Rebecca through her teeth. "Thank you, anyway." Her pencil jerking with disappointment she wrote, "Sotheby's? Collectors???"

She poured herself more tea and checked her watch. Barely past noon. Eric was coming at five. Her chest bubbled like ginger ale—let's get it over with, the accusations, the explanations, the cold hard looks. Her heart was a lead weight suspended amid the bubbles—no, let it go, don't confront him.

Don't confront him? No way. Her own whiskers were twitching like mad. She dialed again. "Benjamin Birkenhead, please. Rebecca Reid at Dun Iain."

The receiver emitted insipid music and she held it away from her head. Then Ben's voice boomed, "Miss Reid?" so loudly she hardly needed to move it closer. "What can I do for you, honey?"

Reminding herself to keep her voice sweetly breathless, Rebecca asked him her rehearsed question: Her nephew Joey was just out of law school, and Eric always said how much he enjoyed working for such a prestigious firm. How did he get his position with you?

Just as she'd guessed. Punch the right buttons and Ben would respond like a candy machine depositing a Snickers bar. "Why, honey, Eric called us to see if there was an opening. He had such glowing references from the firm in Los Angeles where he'd interned we told him to come for an interview."

"At his own expense?"

"Sure thing. Nice to see a young buck with such enthusiasm. He even agreed to a clerk's salary to begin with, just to work for us. Of course we've raised his salary since then. He does good work, and makes such a fine appearance for the firm."

You give him every job associated with a woman, right? Rebecca asked silently. She wondered just how far Eric was in debt, raise or no raise.

"If your nephew would like an interview," continued Ben, "I'll have my secretary set one up. You come with him. There's a little place near here that serves a real businessman's lunch, two martinis and a bloody T-Bone."

Rebecca gagged. "Why, thank you. How kind. I'll write and tell him. I know he'll be very grateful." Even if thoroughly bewildered; her nephew Joey was only ten years old.

Birkenhead hung up. With the receiver still at her ear Rebecca gulped tea, washing away the sour taste of her own lies. There was a fine distinction between lying and simply not telling the truth, but she wasn't up to fine distinctions. She was infected with Dun Iain's virus of dishonesty.

A distinct click broke the silence in the receiver. Someone had just hung up the fourth-floor extension.

Rebecca threw down the phone, catapulted out of her chair, and raced up the stairs. She almost collided with Dorothy between the third and fourth floors. The housekeeper's pale, dull eyes barely registered Rebecca's suspicious glance.

Phil was disassembling the sink in the fourth-floor bathroom. Michael was scrutinizing a Raeburn portrait in the stairwell between the fourth and fifth floors, one of Elspeth's crystal bottles in his hand. Rebecca returned his curious look with a glazed grin, spun, and thundered back down to the kitchen. Could've been any of them. Great.

She wrote "BB&D!!!" on her paper and surrounded it with lightning bolts. Then she dialed the sheriff's office but hung up before the dispatcher answered. Warren might not be guilty of anything more than a too-casual attitude, but she wasn't convinced.

Swearing under her breath, Rebecca turned to a fresh page and wrote down everything she'd discovered. Little enough, she thought, tapping her pencil against her teeth. But she needed all the ammunition she could get. If Eric griped about all the long-distance calls on the phone bill, tough. It was his own fault. And once she'd trusted him.

The odor of cigarette smoke wafted from the entry. The water pipes gonged. Darnley prissed in, sniffed around, left. Someone walked down the stairs and out the front door whistling the derisive "Hey, Johnny Cope, are ye waulkin' yet?" Ah, yes, it was time for the mail. Michael was helpful, to a certain extent. To whatever extent she could trust him.

Don't start that again, Rebecca ordered herself. She stamped up to her room slapping her notebook against her thigh. Her mind felt like an eggbeater, thoughts, images, fear, and frustration whirring frantically but never meshing.

Phil passed her as she went on up the stairs, touching his cap like a medieval serf. "I'll be leaving now, Miss Reid. See you Monday."

"See you Monday, Mr. Pruitt. Thank you."

Dorothy was standing on the fifth floor looking at John Forbes's portrait, the painted features showing more animation than the living ones. She said to Rebecca, "I forgot to bring your dinner tonight, sorry."

Rebecca said politely, "It's very good of you to think of us, Mrs. Garst. We'll manage until next week."

"Have a nice weekend," said Dorothy like an automaton. She shuffled off down the stairs.

Michael had disemboweled some of the smaller rooms on the

sixth floor, leaving boxes strewn across the floor. The metallic sunshine blanched the room so that it resembled an overexposed photograph. The claymore, propped by the fireplace, shone with a cold steely gleam. The wind wailed around the turrets, and on the roof something loose banged an uneven rhythm. The place suited her mood. Rebecca sat down, picked up the inventory, and chose a box.

Slow footsteps clomped far below, on either the front or the back stairs. "Hello, James," she said. "I'm beginning to understand why you never married, with Elspeth and Athena, Katie and Dorothy setting such fine examples of womanhood." She glanced warily at the slitted window. Silence. The ghosts had been silent recently. Saving up for something, no doubt. Maybe Rebecca herself would explode, just to amuse them.

That set of steps bounding toward her was Michael's. "So many cars were comin' oot the drive I doot you'd turfed them all oot good and proper."

"How's your girlfriend today?" Rebecca asked.

"The postie? She's on holiday. This one's a man. Didna ken a word I was sayin'." Shaking his head incredulously, he threw down a collection of form letters and ads and went back into the smaller rooms.

Rebecca turned the pages in the inventory. Box 576—all right! She lifted a finely tooled wooden box from the large cardboard one and opened it. Yes, just as the inventory said. It was Mary Stuart's gold rosary. The filigree beads tingled between her fingers, and the crucifix was oddly warm.

Rebecca crouched beside the box, barely able to breathe. In a piece of cloth was a prayer book. When she opened the brass latches and turned the pages, the four-hundred-year-old illuminations leaped out at her, fresh and vital. The cloth was Mary's veil, its history embroidered around the edges in Latin: *"A nobiliss matrona . . ."* "My God," Rebecca breathed. Mary had held these things at her execution.

Rebecca sniffed. Crybaby. She was just so tired. Her back curved, weighted down with despair, with a life of struggle so futile that death was welcome. Mary, too, had lost her child; he'd been taken away from her and raised to hate her. For twenty years she'd been imprisoned in alien England, ill and reviled, and still had knelt before the executioner like a queen.

The floor was hard beneath Rebecca's knees. The cloth, the rosary, the book tingled in her hands. The Hall at Fotheringhay

was cold. Mocking faces looked at her, voices buzzed and were
then stilled by awe and respect. No, not despair. Desperate hope,
the light in a long tunnel. Not an end but a beginning. Faint and
faraway a woman's voice said, *"In manus tuas, Domine, confide
spiritum"*—"Into your hands, O Lord, I commend my spirit."
The lips of Mary's severed head had continued to pray for a
quarter hour after her death.

Something touched her shoulders and Rebecca started up with
a gasp that was almost a scream.

Michael was on one knee, looking into her face, his brows
puckered with sympathy and alarm. Cautiously he took crucifix,
book, and veil from her hands, checked them against the inventory, and sat down on the floor, eyes bulging.

Rebecca watched, half crying, half laughing at how despair,
terror, and elation swept his features just as they had hers. At
last he laid the items reverently back in their box and cleared
his throat. They looked at each other, dazed. "Is that the Forbes
treasure?" Rebecca croaked.

"Canna be. James had it on the list. And John said he'd made
a reliquary for the treasure from Elspeth's jewels."

"It should be the treasure. Romantic Mary and all." Again
tears spilled from Rebecca's eyes and down her cheeks. No—
this was a torture of embarrassment. But the tears were the fluid
drained from a sore, relieving pain and fear. She cried, sputter-
ing apologies. Michael's hands touched her again. His supple
fingers worked the quivering fibers of her back and neck until
they relaxed and nestled into his grasp. "Ah, well," he said,
"there's naething wrong wi' a bit o' romance. And a good greet
if it'll ease your mind."

Rebecca leaned back into the sanctuary and the danger of
Michael's arms. This was what she'd wanted, her mind hiccuped, the reassurance and support of which sex was so often
only a counterfeit. But she and Michael were both too good at,
if not lies, then certainly half-truths.

She rested, her shoulders against his chest, his arms locked
around her waist, her hands on his slender wrists. No, she
wouldn't turn toward him, even as his cheek pressed against the
side of her head and his lips touched her ear. "Rebecca, whatever happens, I want you to know . . ."

She waited, each deep breath following quietly on the next.
He rocked her in his arms and murmured, "Never mind, lass.
Never you mind."

With a shuddering gulp and a choked "thank you" she put his arms aside and sat up. He let her go without protest. She pulled out a tissue, mopped at her face, and retrieved her wandering contact lenses. She must be a mess, her eyes red, her nose running.

"Go have a bit of a lie-down before you leave tonight," Michael said. "You've been workin' yourself too hard."

"No, I haven't. You've done most of it."

"I don't mean wi' the artifacts." Michael stood, heaved her to her feet, and pointed her toward the door. "Go take a snooze."

Rebecca walked out of the room without looking at him. She didn't want to see his expression, be it affection, conjecture, or some peculiar combination of the two. He had spoken perfectly calmly and coolly, as if nothing cither good or bad had ever happened between them.

What did he mean, whatever happens? Rebecca lay down on her bed and stared at the canopy. Yes, the house drove everyone who lived here mad.

She dozed, dreaming quick images that twisted and twirled just beyond her grasp, and woke to find the house drowsing in the brassy afternoon sunlight. Maybe it, too, had needed a good cry. After tidying up she found Michael in the kitchen reading *MacKay* over a sandwich. His glance was uncharacteristically shy. "Did you put a warning on that box?" she asked. Rats, her voice had come out pitched too high, artificial.

"Aye," he said with a rueful grin that looked like her voice sounded. "Right dangerous with those emotional land mines scattered about the place."

Where we keep stepping on them. For a moment Rebecca wondered what would have happened if she'd met Michael somewhere else. Then a knock on the front door snapped her away from the blue eyes and the appealing lopsided grin that called to her across a bottomless chasm. "See you later," she said. He gave her a stoic British palm-outward salute.

Rebecca walked through the entry pulling on her coat, symbolically girding her loins. This was it, then. Eric.

Eric stood hunched into his overcoat. "Cold," he said succinctly, and swept her into the warm, leathery interior of the Volvo.

The sunlight made the tiered windows of Dun Iain into sheets of flame. Dark clouds massed on the northern horizon. The wind tasted of snow. Eric guided the car past the dovecote and down the driveway, saying, "They're predicting several inches by Sunday. The first big snow of the year."

Rebecca responded with something appropriate. She made appropriate if monosyllabic responses all the way into town. By the time they passed beneath the interstate Eric was glancing at her curiously. "Something wrong?"

"Could we skip the movie tonight and just go someplace quiet where we can talk?"

"Oh, now that's ominous, when a woman says she wants to talk." His voice wasn't quite as light as he'd obviously intended; it roughened, rubbed against the grain. "Let's go back to Gaetano's. I'll ask Mohammed for the table in the corner."

"Thank you." She bit her lip and realized she was getting lipstick on her teeth.

Long shadows stretched across the streets of Putnam. The candy canes on the lampposts looked sickly in the yellow sunlight, but Gaetano's door sported a Della Robbia wreath whose brilliant lacquers only shone the brighter.

Eric seated Rebecca in the banquette, paused while the waiter lit the candle on the table, and ordered appetizers and wine. In the dim light his sculpted features looked like the funeral mask of a pharaoh, precious metal molded and polished. Oh, he was pretty. But only outside.

No. That wasn't fair. Give the man a chance to tell his story. Rebecca accepted a glass of Asti Spumante and sipped, the bubbles tickling her nose. She asked, "Eric, why is your last name Adler?"

He swung toward her, his thick gold ring glinting beneath the curve of the wineglass he held, brow furrowed with perplexity. "What?"

"Usually adopted children take the name of their new parents."

Perplexity faded into complete mystification. "Rebecca, what are you talking about?"

"I'm a historian. I'm trained to follow a paper trail. Birth certificates are very useful items." She picked an olive from the antipasto tray and nibbled at it, remembered she hated olives, and laid it down again.

The mask of his face thinned and she glimpsed the heat behind. His voice was very soft. "My birth certificate?"

"I wasn't looking for you. I was looking for Dorothy. She's your mother."

Eric's eyes flashed and dulled. His mouth fell open and snapped shut. He turned away, staring at a print across the room, his hand clenched on the stem of the wineglass, his mouth so tight it was only a crease in his face.

So. Rebecca thought, she'd finally managed to turn Eric's flank and take him by surprise. Not that that was anything to be proud of. It wasn't Dorothy, then, who's been listening on the extension: she'd have warned him that Rebecca was being so irritatingly curious again.

She presented her suspicions as methodically and emotionlessly as he would have done himself, omitting only that Jan had been with her at the Bureau of Records. He would just be hurt worse if he knew someone else knew.

Eric inhaled, set his glass on the table, and took Rebecca's hands. The gleaming intensity of his black eyes mesmerized her. Maybe it was just as well she'd chosen a public place for the confrontation. But no. Eric was not one to shout or make a scene, even in private. That night at his condo had proved that. "I've lied to you," he said, his voice slightly fuzzy.

"Yes, you have."

"I haven't been using your affections, I promise you that."

"Oh?"

"My adoptive parents were named Schnerk. Can you see a judge ever taking me seriously with a name like that? And my grandmother's name was Matwiejow—I spent years spelling that out. So when I foolishly decided to look up my biological parents, I was delighted my father's name was a simple, straightforward Adler. The change is quite legal. I did it myself, ten years ago in California, long before I came here."

His hands tightened. He was hurting her. She flexed her fingers and with a quick shake of his head he released her. Still his eyes, dark crystals each containing a solitary flame, held her trapped.

"That was three years ago. I found out very quickly that my father was dead. As for my mother—well, I don't know what I envisioned, but it wasn't that pitiful, addicted, bitter woman old before her time. Can you imagine walking innocently into a spider's web, being caught in it, knowing there's no way out?"

"You didn't have to help her," Rebecca said. Brutal, but true. She felt as if her skin, too, was matted with sticky, grimy web.

"She's my mother. If it ever came out how she'd been skimming the till all these years . . . Well, I felt the least I could do was obtain a position with the firm that represents Dun Iain and help to, if not make good the losses, at least make sure no more occurred."

"What about the mazer?"

"I got to her too late. She destroyed it and sold it for scrap. I did get her to return the little box."

"That beautiful artifact, ruined!" Rebecca knotted her hands, trying to keep her voice quiet "At the risk of stating the obvious, you never should've told that first lie. If you'd gone to Birkenhead to begin with . . ."

"I know! I should've gotten help for her right at the beginning. But I didn't want to—to admit she was my mother. Selfish and callous, I know. But there it is." At last his eyes fell.

Without the pressure of those eyes Rebecca felt almost deflated. "Was she paying Steve and Heather to make trouble around the place—my room, the chair, the small fire?"

"I think so, yes. But the fire in the shed must really have been an accident. Steve was trying to hide that he'd been using the gasoline."

"And what about Michael?"

Eric darted a swift, sharp glance at her. "What about him?"

She asked, "Did you really suspect him of working his own embezzlement scheme? Or were you just trying to deflect suspicion from Dorothy? And from yourself."

"Oh." He looked back down and poked at a piece of cheese. "No, I've never had any evidence that he was dishonest "

Rebecca wanted to laugh, to shout, I could've given you plenty of evidence! But she could never have given him the truth. She looked back at Eric's immaculate profile, ran her tongue over her lips, and asked, "Did James suspect?"

"Yes, he did, there at the end. Dorothy was pushing too hard, wanting too much. He was my friend, and I lied to him, too. Believe me, Rebecca, if I could go back and change things, I would." Eric's eyes caught her again, as if she touched a high-voltage wire. "It's been an impossible situation right from the start. I tried to help, and I only made it worse. I just hope that Mrs. Morris gets her fair share of the proceeds and that it'll all be over soon."

The waiter was hovering, offering menus. Eric waved him away.

Yes, Rebecca thought, she was sympathetic. But Eric was so quick with those facile lines, so adept at telling her what she wanted to know. She took a healthy swallow of her wine and followed it with a bite of prosciutto and cheese. It tasted like sawdust.

"What're you going to do?" he asked grimly. "Have me disbarred?"

"Will that set things right? Dammit, Eric, you didn't go shopping for a mother. We're all stuck with what we get." He gazed into his glass, ego wilted and yet still distinguished. She was impressed in spite of herself. "Monday, you go to Warren and Chief Velasco in Putnam, too, and explain it all. Surely if you come clean before you get caught, that'll help matters. Maybe you can get Dorothy off on an insanity defense. I don't know, that's your department."

A reluctant wry humor tickled the corner of his mouth. "You're right. Confession is good for the soul."

If Warren isn't on the Dun Iain take, Rebecca thought. If I shouldn't go to the police myself. She squirmed. With what? Until Eric made a formal, witnessed confession, what she had was still circumstantial. Including her conclusion that James Forbes was murdered, reached because a three-year-old talked to his ghost. She was sick and tired of being condescended to by male officialdom. No, she had to give Eric a chance, the equivalent of the quaint old British custom of leaving the accused alone in a room with a loaded gun to take the gentleman's way out.

Eric lifted her chin and turned her face toward him. His eyes narrowed slightly, glinting between their lashes. Concern, calculation, pain—she couldn't tell. "And what about us, Rebecca?"

She pulled gently away from his grasp. "I'll be leaving in a couple of weeks. It's just as well. Even though that cruise would've been . . ." She groped for a word and finally produced a lame ". . . nice."

"We would've had a good time, wouldn't we?"

"We already had some good ones. I'm sorry."

"Oh, no, I'm the one who should be apologizing." He picked up his glass, drained it, looked at the tray of food, and shoved it away. "Would you like dinner, or would you like me to drive you home?"

"Neither, thank you. I'll ask Peter to take me back out there.

Or Michael can come and get me.'' Although, she added to herself, that was one perceptive eye she still didn't want to face.

Eric's features were taut and pale, but his armor never cracked. He summoned the waiter and paid the bill. He helped Rebecca up, poured her into her coat, stood dutifully by while she called the Sorensons and Peter said he was on his way.

In the dark deserted hallway at the front of the restaurant they kissed one more time. Then, without another word, he walked out the door. Rebecca's lips burned from the ferocious regret of that kiss. That much of his performance, at least, had been sincere. She decided she was getting much too good at breaking up relationships.

A blast of cold air and the glare of neon burst the darkness around her. ''Rebecca?'' said Peter. ''I barely got out of the house without Jan fixing me a little keg of brandy to wear under my chin. What's going on?''

''I'm not sure I know myself.'' Gratefully Rebecca took his gloved hand and walked outside. Tiny snowflakes swirled through an iron-gray dusk, stinging her cheeks. Her thoughts melted and ran down her mind like snow down the car windows. No, it wasn't over yet.

Peter, driving in discreet silence, took her home.

Chapter Twenty-Seven

REBECCA TWITCHED AND moaned. A man stood in the door of her room. Michael? She saw then it was an old man, so shriveled that decay seemed to have set in before death. "No," he rasped, "don't push me, help."

Except for that quick glimpse when she'd first arrived, she'd never actually seen James before. She started up and found herself alone except for Darnley, who sat on her bed eyeing the doorway with feline equanimity. "I'm trying to help," she whispered, but there was no answer.

Rebecca looked out the window into the diffused light of the morning. Snow had smoothed lawn and drive into one white expanse. The trees stood like dark candles in a cake, and the mound of the dovecote and tomb was softly lapped by white. The clouds were a low and gauzy gray, of that matte texture betraying cargos of yet more snow. The wind moaned and the castle hushed its own creaks and settlings to listen.

Shivering, Rebecca clambered into half the garments she owned and went downstairs. The teapot was warm and dirty dishes lay in the sink. She fixed herself eggs and toast and ate two leftover pieces of bacon.

She and Michael had spent last evening impassively sorting artifacts. Only his expression had reacted to her early arrival home, not so much with a query as with a kind of satisfied relief. She hadn't been able to bring herself to ask him about his early suspicions of Eric; that would've required altogether too many explanations from them both.

Rebecca cradled her cup between her hands, but it had already

cooled. Eric would either go to the police and brazen it out or
he would run for it. He was more likely to brazen it out. His
story sounded good. His stories always sounded good. He would
wiggle out of the charges of theft, harassment, and embezzlement even if he had to throw his own mother to the wolves. And
what could the wolves do to her? She'd end up in a hospital, not
in a jail.

Probably the first thing he'd done after leaving the restaurant
was to tell Dorothy that Rebecca was threatening to blow the
whistle on them. James had died because he'd threatened the
same thing.

Rebecca leaped up and tidied the kitchen, her abrupt move-
ments making the cutlery clatter and the dishes jangle. It was
too late now to take back those accusing words. She would have
to hedge her bets.

She went upstairs, got her typewriter and her notebook, put
together sandwiches of plain and carbon papers, and typed three
letters outlining her suspicions. When she'd addressed the envelopes she put the letters in her purse. They wouldn't be mailed
to Sheriff Lansdale, Chief Velasco, and Benjamin Birkenhead
until Monday. She'd give Eric and Dorothy a chance. If they
didn't take it . . . Well, she'd told each recipient of her letter the
other two had a copy; each man would have to act to save face.
They couldn't all be involved.

Rebecca went upstairs feeling slightly sick to her stomach.
Michael was layering paper. kindling, and pieces of wood from
a crate in the sixth-floor fireplace. "Does the chimney work?"
she asked.

"I've laid muckle fires in mountain bothys wi' poor excuses
for lums. Look." He took a match from the box on the mantelpiece, lit a spill of newspaper, and held it in the maw of the
fireplace. A chill draft whisked the smoke cleanly away. The
wind whimpered in the chimney. Michael looked up at her with
a slim, distracted smile.

"Okay," she said, returning the smile in kind.

Rebecca selected an inventory and sat down. She checked off
a stack of Minton tiles, each carefully nestled in tissue paper. A
bell-shaped pot, a Bronze Age funeral beaker. Brass Victorian
kitchenware from Neidpath Castle. A coin of King James V.
When a faint swish-crunch of wheels penetrated the moan of the
wind, she rose and hurriedly clutched the back of the chair. Her
limbs were petrified with cold, her feet numb. She hobbled to

the window and saw a Datsun creeping through flakes of snow the size of saucers. What was Heather doing out here on a Saturday morning? Afternoon, she corrected, noting with surprise the angle of the hands on her watch.

Michael was sitting by the wooden box containing the haunted artifacts of Mary Stuart. But he was staring beyond the box at Elspeth's window, abstractedly, not as if he saw something there.

Rebecca went off flapping her arms and stamping her feet, trying to get her blood circulating again. By the time she arrived in the entry it was reverberating with dull thunks. She pulled back the bolt and opened the door. A small bundled figure was kicking at it, arms filled with a knapsack and a wicker picnic basket. Rebecca had to look twice at the circle of face peeking out between stocking cap and muffler to make sure it was Heather. My goodness, the girl had quite attractive hazel eyes. Rebecca had never seen them before, impacted as they'd always been in black liner, mascara, and shadow.

She took the basket. Heather laid down the knapsack and emerged from her polyester chrysalis. "Hi!" she said, with the brittle, and probably equally false, cheer of a department store Santa.

"Hello," returned Rebecca quizzically.

Heather threw her garments over the recumbent form of Queen Mary. Rebecca blinked; the marble face seemed to wince at such lèse-majesté. "I was over at the Pruitts," Heather said, "and Mrs. Garst came by with some food for them, and she said she was going to bring you some, and since I was coming out here, anyway, I said I'd bring it for her."

So Dorothy's cuisine tracked them through the storm. "Thank you. Would you like some cocoa?"

"Yes, please."

Rebecca put on a pan of milk and peered into the basket. A congealed salad peered back at her, queasy orange Jell-O clotted with carrot strips and crushed pineapple. Another dish held gray hunks of hamburger meat laced with green peas and instant rice like bits of Styrofoam.

Exhaling through pursed lips, Rebecca closed the basket, fixed Heather's cocoa, and made a fresh pot of tea. The girl's hair, she decided, must be dyed that dismal black; it contrasted shockingly with a rosy complexion that owed its beauty to youth, not to artifice. But her expression was middle-aged, abused by gravity into a tragic mask.

Heather realized she was under surveillance. "I'm sorry, I rushed out of the house without my makeup."

"You look just fine," replied Rebecca, understating the issue.

"I've run away from home."

Rebecca stood, teapot aloft, as if the squashed remnants of the girl's spiky hairdo had been the snaky coiffure of Medusa. "What?"

"I've run away from home."

Yes, that was what she'd thought she said. Rebecca laid down the pot, pulled out a chair, and sat. "Your parents must be terribly worried," she said, although what she wanted to say was, Why descend on me?

"My dad's away on business. He's always away on business. My real mother lives in Indonesia. Sandra went to her garden club. They're making wreaths for the mall or something. I decided I just wasn't going to take it anymore." With a quick smug smile Heather drank some of her cocoa.

"Take what?" Rebecca asked.

The child uttered a word she had no business knowing. "Sandra lost her cool because I came in late last night. She just doesn't understand."

"You know mothers," said Rebecca with a wan smile, "their ears just fold up on you."

"Stepmothers at least. I couldn't have told her, anyway. I thought maybe you could help."

Rebecca frowned; she'd missed a conversational connector somewhere. "Help with what?"

"I mean, when I was in your room that time—sorry about that and everything, but we've been over that . . ." The girl waved her hand airily, dismissing past mischief. "I saw your birth-control pills, so I figured you were, well, experienced."

Rebecca wasn't sure what to reply to that. She doubted the girl wanted a lecture on the sharp pecks of the birds and the harsh stings of the bees.

Heather said, "I think I'm pregnant."

"Good God!" Rebecca took a gulp of tea and it stuck like a thistle in her throat. She sputtered, "And you're afraid to tell your parents?"

"You know what they'd say?"

"I can make a pretty good guess." Someone moved in the entry. Michael and his British sixth sense had scented a cuppa and arrived in the doorway just in time for the shocking news. Heather turned, saw his stunned expression, and ducked into a defensive huddle.

Rebecca fixed a mug of tea, took it to the door, and pressed it into Michael's hands. "Christ," he hissed under his breath, "don't you people have all-night chemists' shops? All the lad had to do was buy . . ."

"And I suppose you've always been a paragon of self-restraint," interrupted Rebecca, turning him around and applying a firm push to his shoulders. "Go away. The last thing she needs now is a man!"

"Well, excuse me!" he said, and went back up the stairs.

Heather emerged from her crouch. "Is he gone?"

"Have you told Steve?" Rebecca asked.

Heather's face wavered into the most peculiar expression, part exasperation, part amusement. "No, I haven't. What could he do?"

"I'm not sure marriage is an option." Foolish little Heather—she had her life ahead of her—look at Dorothy, her past sins returned to haunt her. Rebecca sat wearily down at the table. Her job description hadn't included being Putnam's Dear Abby. "How much overdue are you?"

"A couple of weeks. More or less. I'm never that regular."

"Then it might be a false alarm. But for heaven's sake, Heather, if it is . . ." She wanted to say, Don't do it anymore, but the girl's trusting gaze made every one of her own past indiscretions float wraithlike before her. "Get some information on birth control, okay?"

"Okay. But if it's not a false alarm?"

"Tell your parents. And Steve. You can't run away from it."

"Oh." Heather considered that, her face set with the artless adolescent self-absorption that drives adults mad. "Can I stay here tonight?"

Rebecca caved in. "If you call Sandra and ask. Tell her the snow's too heavy for you to drive safely. That usually works."

Heather jabbed truculently at the phone. Rebecca sipped her tea and listened to the girl's half of the conversation. Although she could also hear most of Sandra's; the woman was shrieking so loudly Heather held the receiver a foot from her ear. Finally Rebecca, suppressing a groan, interceded. "Mrs. Hines, this is Rebecca Reid. Yes, Heather is here with me. You know she helps with the cleaning. Yes, the roads are pretty bad, she should stay. Yes, I'll make sure she earns her keep." What Sandra said about ungrateful stuck-up stupid Heather made Rebecca wince.

She hung up and turned to the girl. "You're all right for tonight. I suggest you use the time to do some serious thinking. About Steve, for one. I'm sure he's a nice kid, but . . ."

"Love is worth everything," Heather said.

"No, it isn't," retorted Rebecca. "But that particular romantic fancy is one you simply have to outgrow." The girl shrugged, unconvinced. Rebecca sighed—people who live in emotional glass houses shouldn't throw advice. "Are you hungry? Get some food and then come on up to the top floor."

"Thank you!" Heather dived on the picnic hamper. "I'll wash the dishes, too, okay?"

"Okay," Rebecca said, smiling at the girl in spite of herself. Had she ever been that young? These days she felt as if she'd been born forty.

She found Michael in the ballroom, holding his cup and staring out a window. She walked up beside him and looked down on the tire tracks in the driveway, on the trees and dovecote half concealed in swirling white confetti. The wind sang, its words just beyond hearing, only the eerie melody audible. "There's some food downstairs if you want it. Dorothy's, I'm afraid. The Jell-O doesn't look too bad."

He turned to her, but his eyes were focused about two feet beyond her back. The angle of his brows indicated deep thought. "Right. Thank you kindly." He wandered off across the room, still holding the cup she'd seen was empty, and sat down by a pile of boxes.

So she'd insulted his masculinity. Tough. Rebecca sat down, shifted, cataloged a few items, shifted again. She forced herself to concentrate. More ephemera, letters and documents. A Chinese vase from Fyvie Castle. A collection of 1950s advertisements for refrigerators, including one for the model downstairs. It was some time later that she stood and stretched, pleased at the boxes standing properly labeled. Almost five o'clock.

Michael was gone. When had he left? Shaking her head, Rebecca started downstairs. The stairwell was dim, evening seeping in already. No one was on the fifth floor, or the fourth. Michael's room was its usual defiant mess. Her own room was inhabited; Heather lay on the bed. She stirred as Rebecca looked in and she muttered, "Thought I'd take a nap."

"Go right ahead. Be my guest." Rebecca tucked the girl under the blankets and flicked on the heater. Usually cold gloom made her sleepy, too, but not today. Today her nerves wriggled like insects stuck on pins.

The second floor was deserted. Drifts of shadow filled the corners of the Hall. On the gallery Elspeth's portrait was turned so that her face peeked through the railings. In the empty kitchen the teapot was cold. No Michael.

Rebecca looked into the storeroom. The dark mass of the boxes seemed to shift and grumble, inching forward in the corner of her eye. She shut the door on them. Of course. Michael was in one of the little rooms on the sixth floor. She started back upstairs not sure just why she was looking for him. On a stretch of staircase that five minutes before had been empty lay all seven crystal bottles in a neat row like a roadblock.

Rebecca stood staring. The chill lavender-scented draft in the stairwell raised the hair on the back of her neck. And then the hush was broken by the grotesque crash and clatter of the dishes in the pantry.

She spun around. The crash of the dishes was a natural phenomenon, nothing alarming . . . She went back down, anyway, leaving the bottles, turning on lights as she went. The pantry was closed. She opened it.

China shards lay strewn across the stone floor amid the crumpled shapes of the covering cloths, their bright colors like blood on a wound. One entire shelf of dishes had been swept clean, only shapes in the dust marking where they'd been stacked. Rebecca's jaw dropped, her brain stammered.

No lavender. Not one whiff did she smell in the pantry. Michael? Why would he throw down the dishes? She looked into the sitting room. Darnley was curled up on the couch grooming his tail. He looked at her. She looked at him. No, he was too surefooted to have knocked the dishes down.

Rebecca turned. A dark faceless figure stood just behind her. She leaped back. Her heart exploded in her chest, pushing a gasp from her throat.

"Miss Reid, it's me." The nasal voice was trimmed of its adolescent whine. Furtive lashless eyes peered through the holes of a ski mask. Black coat, jeans, gloves, and an eye-searing Cincinnati Reds scarf—it was Steve Pruitt.

Rebecca collapsed against the sitting room door as oxygen percolated painfully into her brain. "Where did you come from?"

"I—er—I had a key," Steve said. "I came to get Heather. She said she was coming out here. I don't want her out here."

A little late to be assuming responsibility, Rebecca thought. "She's here. Come on." Rebecca hauled herself up the staircase, Steve's boots clomping behind her. On the one hand she was grateful for the noise, on the other she wanted to tell him to be quiet, he was disturbing the tense silence of the house. "Did you walk in from the road?"

"Yeah. Snowplow's been there already."

In the bedroom Steve called Heather's name and shook her. No response. Rebecca, frowning, got a wet cloth and slapped her face. Heather moaned and fell inert again. "What's the matter with her?" Steve lifted one of her hands and dropped it. It fell limply, with a small thud.

Rebecca tried to remember what her sister-in-law the vocational nurse had once told her. She gently pried open one of Heather's eyes. Her pupil was a grain of black in a dull iris.

"She's on something?" Steve asked.

Rebecca shot a sharp glance at him. No, Heather hadn't been despondent. It must be . . . Oh, come on now. She led Steve back downstairs and swept Darnley from his perch on the couch. In the kitchen she offered him a piece of meat from Dorothy's casserole. He sniffed at it, hissed, contorted his body, and with a snag of claws in Rebecca's sweater leaped and ran.

Rebecca threw the casserole, dish and all, into the trash and washed her hands. With all those pill bottles clanking in her purse Dorothy hadn't had to go far for inspiration. But she'd intended the drugged food for Rebecca and Michael, not Heather. Rebecca didn't have to guess why. She'd forced Dorothy's hand by telling Eric the game was up.

She threw down the dish towel and turned to Steve, hovering like a giant mosquito behind her. "Tranquilizers, I imagine."

"Is she going to be all right?"

"If it's Valium or something like that, she can just sleep it off. Hardly any of the casserole is gone." But Heather was small. What if she was pregnant? "It wouldn't hurt to call the paramedics," Rebecca concluded.

First an ambulance, then—no, not Warren, the Putnam police. Even if she couldn't convince them Dun Iain was in danger, maybe the activity would scare Dorothy and her minions away. Rebecca picked up the telephone receiver. Silence. She jiggled the buttons. Nothing. She clunked it down and sagged against the cabinet, her face in her hands. Calm down, she ordered herself. Heather wasn't having trouble breathing. "A branch must've fallen across the line. Come on. Let's do what we can, then you'll have to go back into town and get help."

"Yeah." Surrounded by the dark blue ski mask, Steve's pale eyes made his head look like a skull in negative image. Rebecca didn't need to see his disfigured face to sense his fear. Having your employer try to burn you to death didn't generate loyalty. He glanced over his shoulder more than once during their trip up the stairs, but no more often than Rebecca.

The next half hour was the most unpleasant Rebecca had ever spent. But by the time they walked Heather out of the bathroom and up and down the corridor her eyes had cleared and she was muttering curses at them. Steve, with surprising tenderness, tucked her back into bed. "I'll bring help, I promise," he said. His eyes glinted with terror, but his voice was firm.

"Thank you," Rebecca replied. "I couldn't have taken care of her alone." And she thought, Michael sure had found something interesting in one of the small storerooms. The turkey, they could've used his help.

When Rebecca opened the front door a blast of wind buffeted her and she clung to the handle. *"Bon voyage,"* she said as Steve plunged past her. For a moment he was a silhouette amid swirling white confetti. Then he was gone.

Rebecca stood squinting into the darkness. Steve's steps were deep holes in the drifted snow, deeper than the set he'd made coming in. Heather's steps were almost filled. Three sets of tracks. Rebecca's teeth were chattering. She slammed the door, shot the bolt, trudged wearily into the kitchen, and started clearing up the broken dishes.

She stopped suddenly in midstoop, dustpan dangling. When she'd opened the door for Steve to leave, the dead bolt had been open. But she'd shut it when she'd admitted Heather. If the dead bolt had been closed when Steve came, no key could possibly have let him into the house.

Rebecca dropped the broom and dustpan and raced upstairs, vaulting the barrier of crystal bottles. "Michael! Michael, where are you?" He wasn't on the sixth floor. His coat and his wellies weren't in his room. Neither was his flashlight. He was gone. Not in his car—it was still in the parking area under its shroud of snow.

Rebecca's knees dumped her onto a stone step. Her mind shattered like the dishes, shards of thought tumbled in indiscriminate piles like a thousand-piece puzzle. She scrabbled among them; some had to fit together.

Three sets of footprints. Heather coming. Steve coming and going. Michael going . . . That wasn't right. Somebody had levitated.

A movement. Rebecca spasmed to her feet. Darnley sat at the foot of the stairs, bristling, staring upward, not at her, but through her. James's steps plodded down the stairs behind her. She shrank against the wall. A shape brushed by her, too solid for air, too insubstantial for flesh. Her eyes burned, but she could see nothing.

The steps stopped. Darnley looked up, meowed, and arched his back as if petted by an invisible hand. Then the cat glanced at Rebecca as if to say, Yes, something wrong with you?

Silence. Rebecca started to breathe again. With a tangible click her thoughts dropped into place. James had fallen down these stairs and been buried in the mausoleum. Steve had taken the mausoleum key without apparently coming in the house. Darnley went in and out of the dovecote. Michael had looked through her when he turned away from the window, lost in thought. Elspeth's jewels made a reliquary.

"Why that sneaky underhanded two-timing rat!" Rebecca exclaimed. "What a muckie great idiot I am, and with all the evidence he had!" Her voice echoed mockingly up the stairs. She left it behind as she galloped to the study. The mausoleum key was gone. Not one puzzle piece, then, but two, fitting back-to-back like the dovecote and the mausoleum.

She grabbed her coat and hat, gloves and boots—not that she was cold, she was burning with rage. She ran to Michael's bedroom, pulled two blankets from his bed, and spread them over Heather. The girl's forehead was cool, but not cold. Her breathing was nice and even.

Rebecca finished sweeping up the dishes, the shards rattling into the trash pail. There—that was the shelf that had Darnley's hole beneath it. No coincidence that the one next to it was the one the dishes had fallen from. Steve, a klutz at the best of times, probably couldn't see much through that ski mask.

She poked, prodded, and with a fierce oath kicked. The shelves moved. Subtlety, she told herself, not force. She pulled, and with the hiss of oiled hinges the entire section of shelves and the wall behind them swung open. Rebecca aimed her flashlight into darkness. John's paranoia? An idle moment for the architects? A joke of James's?

It didn't matter. A short muddy stairway led to a tunnel that was so low she had to stoop. Stone walls traced with root tendrils leaned toward her. She was beneath the huge, heavy walls of the castle. Contracting her body into as little space as possible, she shone the light ahead. The path was perfectly clear, the stone flags of the floor marked with foot- and pawprints. Grand Central Station.

A small hole was Darnley's detour to the moggie gate behind the rosebushes. The main track led on. The odor of mildew and dirt choked her. The skin between her shoulder blades prickled but she didn't turn around. Ahead of her was a rounded three-foot-high opening like the door of a hobbit hole, outlined by the faint silvery glow of the night.

She emerged inside the dovecote, the wind whining through the frost-rimed interstices in the stone. Hinges gleamed murkily on the inside of a stone that was, on close inspection, only plastered wood. A handy-dandy little entrance indeed.

Rebecca opened the door and stepped out. The snow around the side of the mausoleum and on the steps down to the entrance was pocked with footprints. The lock, glinting with bright bronze streaks, hung open. A dim yellow luminescence leaked between the door and its frame.

Here in the lee of the structure the wind was stilled. The laden tree branches creaked sadly. If Rebecca turned around she might see spectral faces among them. If she went inside the tomb she might see worse. She stood palpitating, listening, sensing. Malice, yes. A sad tired malice, gnawed almost to nothingness. A terrible patience worn so thin and fine it had at last snapped. Perhaps as the things in the house were sorted through, John lost his last hold on existence. He'd defined himself through his possessions.

"Do you want it found, John?" Rebecca whispered. "Are you as tired as I am of this charade?"

Fortunately there was no answer. Taking a deep breath of ice and mold, Rebecca threw her shoulder against the massive door. It gave. Her momentum carried her inside, and her feet stumbled down a short flight of steps.

She had a quick impression of shelves built into the stone walls, for the most part filled with nothing but dust, cobwebs, and darkness. A flat stone bench like a druid altar stood in the center of the building's semicircle. Michael sat there, his elbows resting on his knees, his head hanging, his flashlight lying beside him. He twitched but didn't look up at Rebecca's sudden entrance. His light seemed as bright as a strobe flash, illuminating one arc of the curving wall. Above it shadows clung like bats to the ceiling.

Rebecca tightened her teeth, filtering a stench of mildew and decay so thick she expected it to deflect the beam of her own flashlight. She ignored the slow crawl of her skin and swept her light around the tomb. To her left was a shelf holding a dusty coffin, its brass nameplate tarnished. But she knew what it said: "John Forbes, 1847-1931." Just below it was another coffin, its wood still bravely gleaming beneath a thin patina of dust. That nameplate was quite legible: "James Ramsey Forbes, 1892-1988."

Michael faced a third coffin, even grayer and more dismal than John's. It had no nameplate, but Rebecca knew whose lovely mortal shell lay there broken but not quite abandoned. "Elspeth," she whispered. Her breath was shockingly loud. Michael stirred but still didn't look up.

Below that shelf was a miniature coffin as sad and derelict as Elspeth's. The baby might not have been hers. It probably wasn't even a Forbes. But whether mother and daughter or murderer and victim, the woman and child were spending eternity side by side.

In the glare of light, trailing cobwebs back into the shelf beside the baby's coffin, was a box. Its tilted lid was smeared with handprints revealing the rich sheen of mahogany. A screwdriver lay on the floor beside it.

Michael was sitting a good three feet away. As Rebecca stepped closer she saw tears like drops of ice glistening on his cheeks. Her rage died with the sudden flare of a magician's flame paper. "The Forbes treasure? You've found it?"

He wiped his face with a gloved hand. "Oh, aye, I've found it."

Rebecca walked forward. The cold air seeping through the door made odd little whorls with the clammy air inside the tomb, stirring dead leaves across the stone floor and licking at her ankles. Malice, patience, pain . . . She ignored the bulk of Elspeth's coffin just above her and focused her light into the shadow-filled box.

A face looked up at her. Her breath escaped in a short cry. She jerked away and spun toward Michael aghast.

"Got me, too," he said. "Payin' me back for a' those jokes aboot her. But it's no her head. Look again."

With an audible swallow Rebecca looked again. The beam of her flashlight wobbled and steadied. The face was plaster; each eyelash of the closed eyes was defined, the cheeks were slightly sunken, the nose sharp. The mouth curved in a delicate, chillingly tranquil smile. It was the face of the effigy, of the Curle portrait—the face of Mary Stuart, Queen of Scots. Rebecca went down on her knees in the dust and litter. "My God. It's beautiful. It's horrible."

"You said yoursel'," replied Michael, "the face o' her effigy was modeled on her death mask, but the mask at Lennoxlove's no like it. And that one's too small. This is the real one."

"Provenance?" Rebecca's voice thinned to a wisp.

Michael knelt beside her and opened a small drawer in the base of the box. It was filled with yellowed papers. "Provenance a' the way back tae the Great Hall of Fotheringhay. Queen Elizabeth ordered the mask made. She'd never actually seen Mary, mind you, and this was her last chance. That face is hers. It's really hers . . ." He stopped to regain control of his voice. After a moment he said, "The Erskine letter's no here, either."

A draft snaked along the floor and beneath the hem of Rebecca's coat. Stone grated on stone. She glanced up and swung her light around the tomb. Nothing was there, just shade and sorrow and stench.

Michael indicated the cloth in which the mask was nestled. "John cut up an Aubusson tapestry for her. Cheap at the price. I dinna ken aboot this, though." He flipped aside a fold of fabric next to the plaster chin.

Cold flame danced around the face. Elspeth's garnet, jet, and diamond choker wrapped the severed neck of the dead queen. "John loved Mary," Rebecca said. "She'd never lied to him . . ." She leaped to her feet, away from Elspeth's coffin. But nothing happened. Elspeth's spirit was in the house.

Michael heaved himself up beside her. "James never kent where the necklace was. He lied, Adler lied, it's a' been lies, a' but that face."

"Lies?" said Rebecca. The unwholesome air clogged her chest and made her slightly dizzy. "Lies?"

Michael flinched.

"Why did you come out here alone?" she went on, not in a shout but in a mild perplexed weariness. "Is that how you were able to look me in the eye and tell me you hadn't stolen anything, because you hadn't yet found what you were planning to steal?"

"No!" he protested, and then, on a long, agonized sigh, "I dinna ken what the hell I was plannin'."

"You might not be able to sell the mask," said Rebecca remorselessly, sparing neither of them. "But the necklace would sure bring a tidy sum. No one need even know it was here."

"You would," he said under his breath.

"Don't mind me. I'm the one who thought that line about 'the greed of the Campbells' was just propaganda. Well, you and Colin can get what you want now, guns or fancy cars or whatever you've been after all this time."

"Nae guns. We never wanted guns."

"No. I don't think you did." Her voice trembled but she was too tired to steady it. Maybe Michael's shoulders were shaking. It was too dark to tell. Rebecca herself shook, the clamminess of the tomb permeating coat and sweater and oozing into her bones. The mask looked upward. She wasn't so sure its lips weren't moving in prayer.

Quickly she covered the cold, pale, compelling face with a piece of tapestry, set the cover back on the box, and replaced the screws. "We might as well leave it here. Cold and damp— a museum couldn't preserve it any better."

With a heave and a startlingly loud scrape and crash Rebecca put the box back on the shelf. She stood, dusted herself off, and turned away from Elspeth and Mary and the link, a dead child, that bound them together throughout time. Holding the screwdriver toward Michael, she said, "Here. If you decide you want the necklace, you'll need this."

He didn't take it. She could hear his ragged breath in the silence, edged with the distant wail of the wind. With a snort of exasperation that was close to a sob she thrust the screwdriver into his pocket. "Here, dammit!"

His flashlight rolled slightly on the bench and the shadows swirled and steadied. His ravaged face turned away from her toward the darkness.

Rebecca spurted into the cold but fresh air. Around the corner of the tomb the gale-driven snow slapped her face and ran like tears down her cheeks. The lights of the castle hung in the seething darkness before her as if they were strung in midair. She stood, snow drifting over the tops of her boots, and looked at them. Dun Iain's impassive face made no response.

For once I had my priorities straight, she thought. Michael and I were friends before ever approaching love, physical or otherwise. For us there wouldn't have been a boundary but a ford, a gate, a bridge. She spun and shouted toward the misshapen hump of the mausoleum, "But there's no such thing as truth, is there?"

Her words were shredded by a gust of wind so strong she staggered against the icy side of the dovecote. From the woods came a rumbling thud and a wet hiss. Every light in Dun Iain went out. Rebecca stood blinking. Another branch, this time breaking the power line. She wasn't surprised.

Beyond the snow-filled beam of her flashlight loomed the merest suggestion of blackness, of solidity in an insubstantial world. Rebecca opened the door in the doocot, trudged inside, and shut it behind her.

Chapter Twenty-Eight

THE KITCHEN WAS as dark as the tunnel. At least the walls and the ceiling didn't seem like a throat threatening to swallow her. The clock gyrated in the beam of Rebecca's flashlight as her hand shook to the pounding of her heart. It was seven-thirty. She could've sworn it was midnight.

She shut the secret door and the door to the pantry itself. She stood breathing deeply and rhythmically of the still, warm air of the kitchen with its undercurrents of dust and toast, forcing her heart to steady.

"Whatever happens," Michael had said, "I want you to know . . ." What? Had he still been planning to steal the treasure as late as yesterday?

And yet, no matter what his intentions had been, she couldn't believe he'd ever actually stolen so much as a paper clip. He'd lied, yes. But his expression in the mausoleum had been that of a man who'd struggled through the hell of his own worse nature and emerged bloodied but unbowed.

Rebecca pulled her gloves off with her teeth and threw them in the direction of the counter. As if she didn't have some rather more important things to worry about. Dorothy had intended for them to be deep in pharmaceutical dreamland when she and her minions came to take what they could and run. Circle the wagons, batten down the hatches, raise the drawbridge . . . None of which would make any difference to people who no doubt had a key to the house and burglars' tools to open the dead bolt.

She'd done enough already, naively assuming they'd choose the honorable way out. With a snort of disgust Rebecca pushed the table against the pantry door, blocking it. She took another flashlight from the drawer, put it in the pocket of her jeans, and walked into the entry.

Heather's outer garments still lay across the sarcophagus. Rebecca scooped them up and focused her light on the cold white face of the effigy. Yes, even in half-scale it was the same as the mask, the fullness of the face emphasized by middle age, the slightly aquiline nose emphasized by death. Rebecca shuddered in awe and horror mingled.

Forcing herself away from that face, she opened the bolt on the door. In spite of everything Michael was still the only friend she had tonight.

She plodded to her room. No electricity, no space heater. She couldn't carry Heather upstairs to the fireplace. She pulled her hat onto the girl's lolling head and arranged the collection of coats across her body. Running away was no option, especially when it would mean leaving Heather, a discarded pawn, behind.

Rebecca turned off her flashlight and leaned against the window embrasure, arms crossed tightly. The wind sobbed, blowing the snow horizontally across the glass. Maybe she could play possum, pretending to be asleep while the predators helped themselves; she could always testify against them later. But if Steve had been sent to scout, not to get Heather, they'd know she hadn't eaten the tainted food.

Maybe they wouldn't come tonight, discouraged by the weather . . . Not bloody likely. Not after all the time and effort they'd already expended.

Rebecca moaned between her teeth. She was hideously vulnerable in the dark, in the cold, in the labyrinth of the old house. So were the artifacts, their haunting memories destined to be sold like boxes of cornflakes. Her mind tested the razor's edge of hysteria and recoiled. Stop it! She doubled over, grinding her fists into her ribs. How dare they scare me like this! How dare they make me feel so helpless!

There was a flashlight, a shivering firefly almost obscured by snow. She tracked its path toward the house. A moment after it disappeared below her the door slammed and the dead bolt snicked. That was Michael, wasn't it?

Scowling with rage rather than whimpering with fear, Rebecca crept to the stairs and felt her way down far enough to see Michael's lanky form following the gleam of his flashlight into the Hall. In the backspill of light his mouth was pinched shut, his jaw outthrust. Before long he'd remember the fire he'd laid upstairs. Maybe by then she could face him.

Gingerly Rebecca climbed upward, turning on her flashlight only when she was past the third floor. Coffins lurched through the darkness in the corners of her eyes. Mary's serene white face floated behind her, the open eyes fixed in mild surprise on the back of her neck. Every black doorway like a gaping mouth made her skin crawl as though it wanted to escape her body and hide. The profound silence of the house blanked out even the wail of the wind. No matter how carefully she climbed, her footsteps tolled on the stone.

The bottles were no longer on the steps. Rebecca peeked into Elspeth's bedroom. Crystal flashed from the dresser. The furrow in the bedclothes moved, as if the sleeper woke and turned to rise. She shut the door and scampered up the next flight of stairs. Yes, the fatal window was open a crack, snow sifted onto the sill. No point in closing it, too.

Rebecca lit the fire, her hands so cold they fumbled three matches before one caught. She poked the burning kindling and leaned the poker against the brick. When the fire was throwing out bright yellow light, she turned off her flashlight. She had the extra one, but it would be a long night.

The light of the flames danced on the walls, making the shadows writhe. The wood snapped and sighed. Rebecca set a cushion behind a couch to one side of the hearth, where her back was against warm, solid brick. The claymore leaned in its corner beside her, gleaming with fiery reflections. She saw herself standing at the top of the stairway like Joan of Arc . . . Yeah, remember what had happened to her.

Something brushed by her, a palpable fall of fabric. Rebecca leaped to her feet. Beneath the odor of woodsmoke that of lavender swirled in the air. Rebecca heard a giggle, quickly muffled. "What do you know I don't?" she asked under her breath, but there was no answer. She swept both flashlights around the room. The light glinted on the brittle blackness of the windows. Nothing and no one was there, just lavender, shadow, and chill.

Rebecca turned off the lights, pocketed them, sat back down behind the couch, and pressed against the brick. Shutting her eyes against the weird patterns of the light, she counted out several slow breaths. Too many plots, she thought. Too many malefactors, living and dead. She could try a little creative problem-solving, that was better than mindlessly waiting for . . . Well, whatever.

She focused. Here Phil had found Louise's necklace, a bribe to forget Katie Gemmell's mysterious birth. It was Athena who'd remembered. She'd convinced Katie she deserved part of the estate. But Katie had been conspicuous by her absence for thirty-six years now.

James's last will, the unsigned one, hadn't mentioned relatives. But that one wasn't the legal one. The estate was going to be an unexpected inheritance for the Morrises . . . Aha! That was when she'd made that comment about an unexpected inheritance—the first time she and Eric had gone to Gaetano's. That night she'd still been innocent, not yet savaged by plot and time. The food and conversation had sparkled like Eric's gold ring A diamond, and his engraved initials, "EFA." His middle name was Frederick.

Her eyes opened, seeing nothing but the gleaming image of that ring. Frederick. Where else had she heard that name? Frederick. Fred.

Louise had said that Katherine Gemmell Brown left her husband for someone named Ed, Ted, or Fred. Who was a bad influence on her son.

Rebecca banged her forehead against her fists, trying to knock perception into her mind. What if Katie's paramour had been named Fred—Fred Adler? Then Ronald would have been . . . But no. James's letter had said something about their grandchild "D." Unless "D." was the daughter.

Again something moved. Rebecca started up. A man stood watching her. She squinted, and saw nothing but a chair and a bookcase illuminated fitfully by the ebb and flow of the firelight. She had to look more carefully, she told herself. She had to clear her mind of preconceived assumptions.

Grandchild "D." Deborah, Diane, Doris. Darnley. David, Dennis, Daniel, Donald. Donald? Rebecca saw the smeared letters on the screen in the records office. She hadn't interpreted the one word as "Horton" because she'd already known Dorothy's name was "Norton." But the man, Eric's father—his name she hadn't known in advance. Maybe it wasn't Ronald but Donald. Maybe Donald was Katie's son, who'd taken the name of his stepfather, Fred Adler.

Fireworks exploded in her head. That was it! The link between Katherine and Dorothy and Eric! Rebecca leaped to her feet, did a quick jitterbug on the hearth, and plumped back down onto her pillow.

Where was Donald Adler? Where was Fred, for that matter? Why had Dorothy returned to Putnam but Katherine hadn't? Because Katherine had taken the child to California and filled his head with her mother's stories of cats smothering babies and property hoarded by the undeserving! Katherine might still be sitting out in California, an old spider weaving her web over Dun Iain and everyone who belonged to it.

Every link sounded true, right down to Eric's cat phobia. Motive, opportunity, ambition. Rebecca visualized the portrait of John Forbes. His eyes were onyx marbles. Eric's eyes were dark, too. But then, so were Rudolph's. And Elspeth's. Donald Adler might have had Rudolph's and Eric's devastating good looks. No wonder Dorothy had been swept off her feet.

A shame, Rebecca thought, she had at last come up with a viable theory too late to do her or the house any good . . . She stiffened, her muscles keening with tension. Footsteps were coming upstairs. James? Michael? If it was Michael, he'd be calling to her.

The floorboards squeaked. A light flickered. Darnley's little head appeared above her, looking at her quizzically over the back of the couch, his tail waving like a semaphore. Rebecca made shooing gestures. Darnley said in conversational tones, "Meow."

Two quick steps and hands seized her, one around her chest, the other pressed over her mouth. Her scream was only a choked gurgle. Eric's hands were sturdy, Warren's were large, Phil had picked her up bodily from the broken chair . . . The strong arm across her chest was deceptively slender. The fingers that crushed her right breast were long and flexible. "Hush," said Michael's rounded vowels in her ear. "You'd think I was Jack the Ripper."

"Then stop acting like him!" she mumbled, and bit him.

"Ow!" Both hands vanished. She swung around. He was shaking the hand she'd bitten and inspecting the other, just realizing what it was he'd been holding. "Sorry. But I didna want you tae go screamin' on me. I heard something movin' aboot that wisna the cat nor one o' the bogles. Someone's in the hoose."

"Already?" Rebecca sat hard on the wooden floor but didn't feel a thing. "How'd they get in? If it'd been when you were outside, there'd have been four sets of footprints. And I closed off the tunnel.''

''Tunnel?'' Michael peered over the back of the couch like a soldier looking from his trench into no-man's-land. Darnley sniffed at him, made a face, trotted away. Michael settled back down beside Rebecca, so close she could smell his breath. So he'd had a swig of whiskey while he was in the Hall. He could've brought her some.

''Of course there's a tunnel.'' Even as Rebecca explained about Heather and the drugged casserole, about Steve and his ambiguous promise to bring help, she remembered that scrape of stone, that quick draft in the tomb. That was when the predators had come inside. They'd been inside all this time.

Michael laid his hand on her arm. The fingers pressing her skin through blouse and sweater were wonderfully firm. In the glow of the fire his features were stark, ravaged by self-knowledge, tired and yet stubbornly denying the tiredness. He could tell her it was a balmy summer day outside, she thought ruefully, and she'd believe him. ''You look terrible,'' she said.

''Seein' that face in the tomb was damn close tae a religious experience,'' he replied. And added, ''You're no sae lovely yoursel'. Half-Hangit Maggie looked fitter when they pulled her oot o' the coffin.''

''Thanks.''

''You're welcome.'' And he said, low and urgent, his accent so thickened by his agitation she could hardly understand him, ''Aye, I'd been thinkin' o' theivin' something. I'm sick tae death o' cheese-parin'. But what made me think I could steal when I never had the gumption tae park illegally I dinna ken. I came here tae work, no tae steal. That was lunacy.''

Odd how she'd once thought Eric's eyes were compelling. They were blank slate compared to Michael's hot, demanding blue gaze. ''You don't owe me any explanations.''

''Oh, aye?'' he replied. ''If I dinna owe *you*, lass, I dinna owe a soul.''

Rebecca looked up at the plaster ceiling and down at the planks of the floor, trying to evade those immeasurably deep eyes. But they followed her. She said, ''You told me several days ago your scheme didn't concern me.''

''I didna ken what was goin' on here, did I? The only thing I was sure I wanted was for you tae get away free and clear. No right you're bein' mucked aboot because I was gey daft.''

"It was too late for that even then! Besides, how do you know I haven't been in on the plot all along?"

"Just for one, you'd no have written a' that incriminatin' evidence doon in your wee book, would you?"

"You read my notebook?" Rebecca demanded indignantly, and clapped her hand over her mouth. Nothing moved in the ballroom but light, shadow, and that insidious tang of lavender.

"You had the wind up when you came back from the records office. And you were talkin' tae Birkenhead—aye, I listened in. You twigged it and never said naething to me. I'm no the only liar."

"I didn't lie for personal gain, like you did—at the beginning, at least," she amended.

"Nae, you were coverin' your arse for actin' a gowk ower Adler!"

"I never told him about your letters!" Rebecca shook off his hand, bounced to her feet, and started around the couch.

Michael came around the other side and they met nose-to-forehead. "Never grassed on me, did you? That's fair obligin' o' you."

"No, it wasn't, I just wanted to be impartial . . ." Her thoughts raced in circles, panting. "I don't know what it was."

Michael pulled her, none too gently, against his chest. "Aye, you ken what it was right enough. The same thing that had me wantin' tae protect you."

"Yes," she said. Her hands got away from her, running around his sides to embrace him. She watched bemusedly as her mind stilled and puddled in his grasp. His warm smoke-scented breath stirred her hair. The fire popped and shrank to orange incandescence. The wind cried.

Then the dorsal fins of thought sliced the still pool of Rebecca's mind. No. Not now. Not yet. She straightened abruptly and Michael dodged, guarding his chin. "The mausoleum key was gone for three weeks. Who knows about the mask?"

He emitted a wry laugh and released her. "No one's touched it in years. You could hardly see it for the dust and cobwebs. But then, I was lookin' for it."

If she'd gotten control of her feelings, then he'd managed to bring his accent to heel. "Obvious once you know the answer?"

"Aye . . ." Suddenly Michael looked around and held up a warning hand. Slow footsteps reverberated in the air. The sifting

of snow on the windowsill exploded softly into the air and settled, sparkling, onto the floor.

"How many of them?" Rebecca asked.

"Only the one. Which staircase?"

"I can't tell. Do you want to face him—her—down? Or do
you want to play hide-and-seek through the house until Steve
brings the cavalry?"

"I'm no puttin' my trust in Steve, thank you just the same.
Maybe we can throw something at him and distract him."

Rebecca didn't argue with Michael's choice of pronoun. If
only one person had come, instead of a pack, she knew who it
had to be. "This way," she said, tugging at Michael's sleeve,
and started toward the storerooms.

Too late. A burst of light caught them poised in the center of
the room just as Heather had been nailed by the headlights of
the Volvo. He was only a dim shape behind the glare as he
stepped from the storerooms into the ballroom. Of course he
would have one of those big Black and Decker spotlights.
"Well," said Eric's smooth, perfectly moderated voice, "there
you are. Punch up the fire, would you, please?"

"Damn," said Rebecca, and walked across to the fireplace.

"Careful with that poker," Eric said, as her hand touched
warm iron.

"Do as he says, hen," said Michael. "These American yobbos, they have to have their guns."

Rebecca glanced around. The gleaming black shape in Eric's
right hand was nothing less than obscene. With another curse
she flailed away at the fire. Sparks flew and flames clawed high
up the chimney. She sidled back to Michael's left hand and said,
"Eric Frederick Adler. You shouldn't have told me your middle
name. I've figured it all out."

"Really?" In the combined reflections of fire and spot Eric's
face wasn't a stiff, cold mask. One side of his mouth twitched
and his teeth glinted between his lips in a vulpine smile. "Well,
you're wrong. The 'F' stands for Forbes."

"Grabbed your step-grandfather's name out of the air, did
you?" If she didn't keep talking she might start screaming, and
there was no way she'd let him know how frightened she was.
"All right, Forbes is close enough. Named by your grandmother, Katherine Gemmell, in a fit of wishful thinking."

Michael gasped. "So that's it!"

"Not wishful thinking," Eric said. "As a promise, that I'd

one day regain what had been kept from us by John and by James.''

"Sure," snorted Michael. "Katie could never prove a thing. You could never prove a thing. No one kens whose bairn was whose.''

"So you understand why I had to take a slightly more subtle approach.'' Eric strolled closer to the fireplace, his smile cramping.

"All that blether about Dorothy,'' said Rebecca. "It was your scheme all along, not hers. You were using her. And you weren't after a few artifacts. You wanted the entire estate.''

"I'll have the entire estate. Haven't you figured out that Charlotte Dennison Morris and Katherine Gemmell Brown Adler are one and the same woman? And I'm Katie's heir, perfectly legal.''

"I would've gotten there eventually,'' Rebecca replied. "Is Katie waiting for you to sell the place, pocket both the proceeds and your commission, and come home to California?''

"No. She died five years ago. But she trusted me to carry on without her. It's the principle of the thing, you see. Justice.''

"Justice,'' Michael repeated, his breath hissing between his teeth.

Katherine must've been a Tennessee Williams character, consuming her offspring. Rebecca shivered. The estate. The only way he could get it now was to eliminate the people who'd figured out his scheme. He hadn't come tonight to get a few paltry artifacts, he'd come to kill them.

Her mind leaped and twirled in denial, tripped, and fell sprawling. Don't think about that, think about how to get away. He didn't know about the letters she'd written, he didn't know that Jan knew his ancestry. He wouldn't get away with it, no, but threatening him with that would only put Jan in danger and make sure the letters were destroyed. None of which would help her and Michael now. Keep him talking and pray for a distraction.

"The only one who had any money to begin with and you wanted more,'' scoffed Michael. "You're a right bastard, you are.'' He took Rebecca's hand. Their sides pressed together. Lavender wafted through the firelight. Rebecca could almost hear Elspeth laughing with glee. Eric, her great-grandson, come for vengeance, come for justice.

Eric's hands holding flashlight and gun were perfectly still, his face thoughtful, even regretful. "Yes,'' he said, his voice slipping into a lower register. "Cozy up together—that's the idea. He appreciates your type, Rebecca, more than I can. A love triangle, except the foreigner won't take no for an answer, one thing leads to another, and there's a gun to hand."

"Clever," said Michael. "Murder/suicide."

Oh, God, wailed something in Rebecca's stomach. He can't, he can't! Eric was wearing gloves. No fingerprints would be on the gun except hers or Michael's, which didn't matter. "Where would we get a gun?" she asked.

"I reported it missing from my car yesterday," Eric replied. "I'm sorry, I wish there were some other way, but there isn't."

"Yes, there is," said Rebecca. "What about Dorothy? What about Steve and Heather? They've all been working for you. They can all turn you in, and probably will."

"Poor pitiful Dorothy, with all her pills and booze. She's suicidal, can't you tell? Has been for a long time. Steve was supposed to have eliminated himself. It was certainly handy, that day, to still have my suitcase in my car so I could change my shoes. But you had to interfere. No matter. He never knew where his orders were coming from."

Michael said, "So I have you to thank for burnin' my hands?"

"You had to be a hero, didn't you?"

Michael didn't reply. Rebecca's mind sparked and sputtered and successive waves of heat and cold ran down her spine. Heather had been furious at Steve after the fire in the trash can. She'd said, "Love is worth anything." "Steve wasn't taking his orders from Dorothy but from Heather," Rebecca said. "What'd you bribe her with? Clothes? Makeup? Drugs?"

Eric stared at her. "You're too clever by half, aren't you? No, just for your information, I told her if she was going to be seen with me she had to take off the makeup. She's much prettier without it."

Pathetic kid, he'd once called her. "She might be pregnant, Eric. Is the baby Steve's? Or is it yours?"

Michael muttered an outraged four-letter word. Eric took a step backward. It was hard to tell in the ocher firelight, but Rebecca thought sure he'd paled. "She what?"

No wonder Heather had been out so late last night. He'd gone to her when Rebecca had thrown him over. She felt queasy. "For God's sake, Eric, you should know the laws about statutory rape."

"Oh, it wasn't rape, I assure you. She's a sweet little thing.

I'd never hurt her. It's just as well she's down there asleep. She won't know a thing about—about this."

"And what about the child?" Rebecca demanded.

His brows rose with indignation. "It'll have everything I never had. What do you think I am, anyway?"

"I take it," said Michael, "you dinna want an answer to that."

The fire popped. Eric's dark slacks and jacket didn't reflect the light. His eyes did, black gemstones faceted with flame on the surface, not in the depths. The depths were as cold as the draft from Elspeth's window. "You," he said to Michael. "I could've worked a deal with you, bought you off, couldn't I?"

"No," growled Michael, but Rebecca felt him shudder.

She groped for topics of conversation—oh, for half of Scheherazade's tales. "Is the mazer really destroyed?"

"No. A collector has it. It's quite safe."

Even now that was a relief. From the corner of her eye Rebecca saw the box where Mary's rosary and prayer book lay. He wouldn't feel anything for them, either. "Why, Eric? Why?"

"It's all Dorothy's fault. She had to take things, just a few little things, enough to raise James's suspicions. And that idiot Steve, taking the mausoleum key, setting that fire. And you." His eyes blazed and Rebecca had to stop herself from shrinking back. "I tried to scare you away, I tried to get your moronic boyfriend to take you away. The plan was faultless, not a hole in it, until you came along and started asking questions."

"You didn't have to hurt Ray like that . . ." He's right, Rebecca told herself. I forced him into this corner. His little financial caper, his life's justification, hadn't included murder. Or had it? "I wasn't here when you pushed James down the stairs. No wonder Darnley scares you so much. He saw you, didn't he? Every time you see the cat your guilty conscience twinges."

"James was going to change his will," Eric explained, his rationality more chilling than any draft. "He had no business doing that to me. Dorothy made him suspicious of me, the fool woman."

"You weren't surprised when Peter found that new will," Rebecca went doggedly on, "because Dorothy heard us talking about it and warned you."

Eric shook his head as though bothered by a stinging insect. "You're too damn smart, Rebecca."

Michael said scornfully, "Ah, a woman wi' no intelligence is like a sandwich wi' no fillin', there's no point to the eatin'."

"Thank you," said Rebecca toward Michael's frosty profile. Half his mouth smiled at her, the other half stayed crimped shut. Eric's brows tightened. He swung the light around the room, objects quailing in its brilliance, as if he'd heard something. But nothing was there.

Keep him talking, Rebecca told herself. "So you were just using me."

"Not really. There's no harm in some mutual pleasure, and you were available." She winced at that. Eric went on, "I had to keep on good terms with you to get reports of what was happening here. But it wasn't work. We had some good times, if not quite as many as I'd intended. You could've had your cruise, you know. You didn't have to give that up."

"That would've been the cap to your scheme, wouldn't it? Taking me on a cruise paid for by the goods stolen out from under my nose!"

He grinned, his uneven teeth flashing. "You wouldn't have known that. And you would've benefited. Nothing stimulates the libido like success."

Rebecca grimaced, wanting to hate him. All she felt was pity for that charming, handsome, sick face. Beside her Michael's infuriated expression moderated to curiosity and his head went up as if he, too, heard something. The cat, maybe, prowling downstairs. Eric was afraid of cats. Darnley, Rebecca thought, trying to protect telepathically, here, kitty, kitty.

The scent of lavender hung heavy in the air. Eric glanced at his watch, the light of the spot dipping and swaying and sending the shadows fleeing. "Tell me. What were you two doing in the mausoleum tonight?"

As one, Michael and Rebecca stiffened. Their hands clenched together. Neither said a word.

"Something was hidden in there?" Again Eric grinned, slowly, a wolf scenting its prey. "Now, that's a thought. Did old John hide his treasure in the mausoleum? I'll have to look. Later. It's a shame you two aren't asleep like you were supposed to be. It would have made things much easier."

Michael stared ahead, scowling. She could, Rebecca thought, try pleading with Eric, but that wouldn't make any difference. Did it matter if she died with the last shreds of her self-respect intact? Yes, it did.

Her mind stuttered. She wasn't going to die. Impossible. No way . . . Now she heard something. Not the light thump of the cat, but the clump of boots on stone. Steve? No, anyone he'd bring would come in shouting. James? James! she screamed silently. Don't let him get away with another murder! Help us, James!

Three more steps, far down in the house, then three more. Bloody great tackety boots. Michael glanced at her, brows arched. His eyes went abstract. He, too, was calling for help.

"Let's go on downstairs," said Eric, with a tight, pained grimace, "and get this over with. Come on." He gestured with light and gun.

Michael stood firm. Rebecca didn't move. James! she shouted, projecting the shout from her mind into whatever passed for another dimension in Dun Iain. James! Come up the stairs! Please!

James started up the stairs. Each step was sharp and clear, cutting through the moan of the wind. Eric darted a quick glance over his shoulder. "Great! You two, get back in there." Michael and Rebecca, pushed at the point of the gun, retreated toward the storerooms. "In there." Eric shooed them up the narrow stairway beneath the platform.

Footsteps pealed through the house. Michael dragged Rebecca up the steps to the little room. She stumbled and he caught her just as the door slammed behind them. They hung on to each other, knit as snugly as they could get, clothed and standing up. "And I thought you were a terrorist," Rebecca croaked into his shoulder. "Some terrorist you are, intimidated by a gun."

"Dinna be daft," he replied. "What I am is terrified."

"That makes two of us."

The room smelled of decay, which, at the moment, suited Rebecca considerably better than lavender. The windows rattled in the force of the wind. A draft fanned her hot cheeks, sucking the warmth from them. She clutched Michael, wondering incoherently if she was going to crack his ribs, asking herself if it really mattered, anyway.

The wind cried as though it wanted inside. Rebecca heard no other sound except the quick, steady beat of Michael's heart against her ear. For a long moment that was enough.

Chapter Twenty-Nine

MICHAEL AND REBECCA untangled themselves. She pulled one of the flashlights from her pocket, pattered down the steps, and checked the door. "It's locked, but the key's still in it."

"We're on the wrong side," Michael returned. He produced his own flashlight and swept its feeble beam around the room. Nothing was there but the plank floor, the lath ceiling, and the trapdoor, and four walls, each with its window as blank as an aristocrat's monocle.

"Maybe Steve's bringing back help . . ." Rebecca began as she climbed back up the stairs, and cut herself off. Steve no longer counted. "How long will it take Eric to search the house and realize no one's there?"

Michael threw up the sash of a window and leaned out. The beam of his light was consumed by snow-spangled darkness. A gust of wind blew his hair back from his face and curled Rebecca's toes. "We're proper experts at searchin' the house. For him, fifteen minutes. Twenty at the most. We have to be oot o' here by then."

"Sure," Rebecca said stoutly, even as she thought, And if we're not? She inhaled the cold draft that stirred the clammy, slightly rotten air of the room. Eric wasn't going to kill them. They wouldn't let him. "You can say 'I told you so' if you like."

Michael extricated himself from the window and slammed it shut. "Because I've been tellin' you all along he was up to something? No, gloatin' over you widna help; I wish I'd been dead wrong." He tilted his head and his flashlight and considered the trapdoor. "I'll have to go ower the roof and try to open a window."

"The slate's glazed with ice," Rebecca protested. "You'll fall!"

He lowered his eyes to hers. His face was as uncompromising as the basalt upon which Edinburgh Castle had stood for a millennium. "If I'm goin' to die, it'll be on my own terms."

Rebecca forced down the lump in her throat. "If you fall I'm coming after you. You won't get away from me that easily."

"I hope not." Michael's cold hand cupped her cheek, soothing the ache in her jaw. For just a moment the ice blue of his eyes melted. Then he said, "Let's get to it." Tucking his flashlight into the sleeve of his sweatshirt, he climbed the ladder to the ceiling and heaved on the trapdoor. It flew open with a creak and a crash lost in the keening of the wind.

Rebecca frowned, visualizing the plan of the house. "Michael, wait. Elspeth's window in the ballroom—it's next to one of the turrets, right?"

"Right." He clung to the ladder, looking down at her, the light of the flashlight in his sleeve pooling on the ceiling.

She waved her hand at the window across from the one he'd opened. "It's below that window. It's a tall one, above my head. You wouldn't have to go onto the slates at all."

"Her window's open, is it? I could hang on to the sill o' this one and get my foot into the gap at the top o' the other." Michael slammed the door and jumped from the ladder. He opened the sash and shone his light downward.

It's also a sheer drop all the way to the parking area, Rebecca thought. "Three. four feet of wall between the sill of this window and the top of the other? I could do it, but your extra inches would make a difference."

A gulf of blackness opened beyond the window, the ground so far down that its covering of snow reflected only implications of their lights. Rebecca fought down a wave of vertigo. Michael stood up, squared his shoulders, and stuffed his flashlight into his pocket. His voice was thin but firm. "Colin took me up the Buachaille Etive Mor in February. I'm no bad at scramblin' ower ice the noo, although one o' his nylon belayin' ropes widna come amiss."

Nylon, Rebecca thought. A nylon rope . . . She laid her flashlight on the floor and started pulling off her shoes, her shadow dancing grotesquely on the far wall. "A rope. I'm wearing silk long johns. Light but strong."

Michael stared. "What?"

"Tights. If you stretch them out toe-to-toe, they'd make a kind of a rope. Better than nothing." Her socks followed her shoes to the floor. She unbuckled her belt and ripped open the zipper of her jeans.

Michael's teeth flashed in a delighted grin, as much at her impromptu striptease, no doubt, as at her suggestion. He did a precise about-face and considered her shadow instead of her person. "Only you'd be wearin' tights and socks together. Have you been that cold, then?"

"Yow," exclaimed Rebecca, dumping her jeans and peeling herself out of the silk. She broke out in gooseflesh. "I'm that cold now."

His back shook with a laugh. She threw the now limply snaky garment at him and scrambled back into her jeans. "There. Tie yourself a mountaineer's knot that would make Colin proud."

"I hope I'll have a chance to tell him aboot it."

"With suitable embellishments," added Rebecca dryly, tying her shoes.

"No, lass, no time for embellishments." He made a loop in one leg of the material and draped it beneath his arms. "Sorry, Phil." He drove his foot through the bottom pane of the glass in the window. It fell tinkling into oblivion. Michael tied the ankle of the other silk leg through the empty panel, around the thick wooden frame of the window. "There. That'll help, psychologically at the least. If I can get that window open far enough, I'll slip oot o' the bowline—the loop—and into the room. Got it?"

"Got it," said Rebecca. She didn't add, if Elspeth doesn't slam her window on you. But she was much more frightened of Elspeth's great-grandson and his nasty little gun. Michael sat on the windowsill, one leg outside, one inside. Rebecca knelt, clasped the makeshift rope near its knot on the window sash, and held her flashlight poised. He looked down and winced.

Her mind burped and words spilled from her tongue. "Michael, what were you and Colin going to do with the money you brought back?"

His eyes glazed. "Noo?"

"Now."

"We wanted to buy property. I thought if I saved my salary—

and if something valuable fell into my lap . . ." He grimaced
and plunged on, "Colin didna ken that. He'd be right ashamed
o' me if he did."

"That's why you were saving the clippings about firebombed
houses?"

"We hoped the estate agent in London could get damaged
property on the cheap. But neither o' us had a mind to set those
fires, or to thank the yobbos who've been doin' it. They're livin'
in the wrong century. Economic power, that's what it's on aboot
the day."

"So the bit about Arabs . . ."

"The last time I was in Harrod's the prices were in Saudi rials
as well as pounds." Michael clasped the back of her neck, pulling her face to his. "Property. Land. A bit o' the Auld Sod. A'
right?"

"All right." She laughed. "Sorry."

His cold lips landed a kiss on the corner of her mouth. Then
he was gone. His hands flexed on the windowsill. The strip of
silk tightened. Rebecca braced herself inside, one hand clenched
on the straining knot, the other holding the flashlight pointed
out and down. The wind whipped her hair, bits of ice stung her
face. Her lungs burned; she realized she was holding her breath.
The top of Michael's head was a dark splotch, his elongated
body splayed against the pale wall. The bubble of light around
him appeared deceptively substantial against the encroaching
dark. He stretched. Rebecca felt her lips move, "*In manus tuas
Domine . . .*"

Michael's hands disappeared. The strip of cloth jerked and the
window creaked. From below, as if from the bottom of a well,
came a sliding crash and a thud. Rebecca leaned further over
the sill. He wasn't there. The nylon loop swung wildly in the
wind. The ballroom window stood open.

The wood beneath her knees bucked. With a silly grin Re-
becca fell back into the room—he was all right, he was inside.
She untied the ridiculous pseudo rope and closed the window.
The door opened. "Rebecca!"

She catapulted down the stairs and into Michael's arms. His
shirt was cold, his face felt like marble, but his eyes blazed with
triumph. He shut the door and locked it. "We've got him the
noo. Come on."

They crept into the ballroom. The fire had subsided into glowing embers; the central portion of the room shimmered with

diluted orange light while the shadows in the corners shifted like deep water. Michael handed her the poker, whispering, "You're no too squeamish to use this on him, are you?"

"Don't be daft. If I can get the drop on him, he'll see stars."

Michael nodded approvingly. "Good. Find yourself something to throw, something that'll make muckle noise but that's no valuable."

"Got it," Rebecca replied. Michael turned off the flashlight. She tiptoed toward the end of the room to the right of the main stairway; he faded into the shadows on the left. As he passed the corner of the fireplace there was a scrape of metal against brick. Good God, had he taken the claymore? It wasn't even sharp. It was heavy, though.

Footsteps. Again Rebecca couldn't tell which staircase. If Eric came up the back stairs, as he had before, he'd unlock the door and discover them gone. But she'd used up every profane expression she knew. She thrust her hand into the first box she came to and found a Toby jug. It was fairly valuable, but not so much so as her life.

A movement pricked the corner of her eye, the sway of a long skirt, shadow sketched on twilight, trailing lavender. Light steps glided across the floor. Elspeth, no, don't warn him!

Eric stood at the top of the main staircase, the dazzling light in his hand glancing off a picture frame here and a vase there. He'd heard something, or maybe felt something, and he knew he wasn't alone. But the brightness of his light obliterated firelight and shadow equally, streaking the room with undiscerning black and white. The steps stopped, the suggestion of a skirt vanished, but the lavender lingered, clogging Rebecca's nostrils.

Eric started across the room, his steps cautious, his light circling like a spotlight at a Hollywood premiere. Rebecca huddled behind a love seat, her knuckles white on the poker, the ceramic jug trembling in her other hand. The light struck the wall above her hiding place, making the shadow in which she crouched even thicker.

Ghostly fabric brushed her back and she bit her lip. No, I won't let you scare me into jumping up. No.

A thump. Once again a tiny head peered down at her, its butterscotch and white fur clearly defined. Eric's steps stopped. The cat turned, its eyes gold in the light, and a low rumbling hiss emanated from his throat.

Another thump as Darnley leaped to the floor. Rebecca flattened herself against the floorboards and peered beneath the love seat. Just beyond its legs, festooned with swags of dust, she could see four paws braced in front of a pair of loafers. The loafers took a step backward.

Dust swirled into her face, spurting away from a print made by an invisible foot. Rebecca laid down the poker and suffocated her mouth and nose to keep herself from sneezing. Her mind was emitting puffs of smoke so tangible she was afraid Eric would see them wafting wraithlike through the firelight. He's handicapped by holding the gun and the flashlight both, she thought. If I throw the jug—no, if he's looking at the cat he'll see me, he'll probably start shooting, wait until he turns.

To her hyperextended senses the quick scrape from the opposite wall sounded like a three-car pileup. The light swung around, the loafers turned. Now! Rebecca grabbed the poker and vaulted up, striking her kneecap against the leg of the love seat. She hurled the jug as hard as she could.

From somewhere in the black well of the staircase came the horrendous crash of antique Staffordshire. The light zoomed through the darkness, flaring in each succeeding window, as Eric whirled and took several running steps toward the stairs.

In her mind's eye, like the afterimage of a lightning flash, Rebecca saw standing beside the love seat an old man holding the arm of a long-skirted woman. Yes, they'd both been protecting the house, but for different reasons. Mother and son stared at each other, opposing forces locked in time.

Rebecca leaped to her feet, poker at the ready. Her knee shrieked in pain and buckled. She fell on one arm of the love seat. Darnley bounded up beside her, tail like a bottle brush, whiskers quivering.

At the top of the stairs Eric spun around. His light struck Rebecca full in the face, blinding her. Still she clutched the poker, her other arm across her face. Dive! Every muscle in her body contracted. She plunged from light into oblivion. Fire rent the night and an explosion ricocheted through her head. Somewhere, six or seven miles away, glass shattered.

She bounced and jackknifed violently toward the back of the couch. Light struck her—this time he wouldn't miss . . .

The light winked out, whisking away from her. A shout rang through the room, echoed, re-formed. "Cruachan!" Rebecca scrambled up the arm of the love seat. Michael leaped from the side of the room. He brandished the claymore before him, its blade a brilliant streak of reflected light.

Eric swore viciously, realizing his momentum wasn't great enough. Gun and spot were still aimed to Michael's left when the sword connected. The sound of the blow was muffled by Eric's gasp of pain. Light gyrated madly across the room and with a shattering crash the spot went out.

Rebecca blinked, straining through the abrupt orange gloom. Darnley clawed frantically up her thigh. Eric's face was twisted in rage and indignation. One arm dangled limply at his side, the other was raising his gun. Michael was bringing the claymore up in an arc from the floor, struggling to set it swinging again. His expression, terrified rage, would've sent the closest redcoat racing for the English border.

Eric aimed his gun, teeth set, eyes narrowed. Rebecca dropped the poker, swept up the cat, shouted, "I'm sorry," and threw him.

With an earsplitting squall Darnley sailed through the air. Eric's shot went wild. He raised his arm protectively, his angry face gaping into panic. The cat struck and clung, teeth and claws tearing like scythes. Eric screamed, staggering backward, and scraped the cat off his chest onto the floor. But his feet had already carried him to the top of the staircase. They skidded, groping for more floor. He fell. His scream was cut suddenly short, but the sickening thuds and crashes of his plummeting body continued on and on.

Rebecca was draped bonelessly over the corner of the love seat. Her mind gasped for air, for coherence, for anything other than the numb, dumb sludge that clogged it. Get up, run—no, no need . . .

Michael, still clasping the claymore, crept to the staircase. Darnley crouched on the top step, a bristling blob of fur seething like a teakettle. No sound came from the lower floor. Michael started down, using the sword as a cane. Rebecca forced herself to stand, working through each step of the process like a child learning to walk. Right leg. Left. Twinge from the knee—ignore it. Flex ankle. Step.

She found her flashlight, turned it on, shone it down the throat of the stairwell. Eric lay facedown, head twisted at an impossible angle to his shoulders, beneath the portrait of John Forbes. The painted black eyes and desiccated face focused beyond him, beyond satisfaction or sorrow, beyond even caring. Elspeth's rages, John's anger, Rudolph's opportunism, and Athena's resentment; none of it mattered, not anymore.

The gun lay against the far wall. The claymore lay on the carpet, gleaming in the light of Michael's flashlight. Michael knelt by Eric's head, staring appalled at the red smearing his fingertips.

"Michael?" Rebecca took each step one at time, the stone treads and their dusting of ceramic shards skewing beneath her feet. "Michael!"

Lavender surged through the corridor. Something glinted in the black open door of the large bedroom and shot into the hallway. Glass shattered against the wall just beside Rebecca's head, raining splinters on her hair and shoulders. She jumped the last two steps. Michael leaped up to catch her. They went sprawling on the floor together, limbs enlaced, heads covered. Another whiz, crash, and sprinkle of glass. Another.

Rebecca counted seven. Seven crystal bottles hurled by the frustrated hand of a woman dead eighty-seven years. As the last sliver fell tinkling onto the staircase the air was ripped by a shriek, a banshee's wail shrilling until the very stones of the castle cringed, then dying slowly into nothingness. Like a bubble popping, the scent of lavender disappeared.

Warily Rebecca looked up. Michael was staring over her shoulder. She turned. A shape moved in the darkness at the top of the stairs.

The tall, thin shape of the man was just a form in the darkness, a hint of humanity. For a long, breathless moment it stood as though watching. Then it faded into the shadows. Solemn footsteps rang down the flight of steps, and the next, and the next, until they died away in the depths of the house, and their vibration was absorbed into cold silence.

It was over. It was all over.

Rebecca forced herself to look at Eric's body. She could see only the dark hair tousled on the back of his head, not, thank goodness, his face. One of his hands was outstretched, reaching futilely for the unattainable, perfectly still. If it weren't for his glove, she'd see the gold and diamond ring, its initials gleaming in icy mockery.

Michael looked at the blood on his hand, his face contorted with horror. "His forehead, against the floor—it's smashed right in—his neck's broken . . ." His voice leaped into another register. "He's dead."

Eric was dead. Dead, like Elspeth, like James. Eric was dead. We killed him. Rebecca turned away from the crumpled body, from the handsome intelligent face destroyed forever by love, by hate, by justice.

No. It hadn't happened. It wasn't true. She curled double over her knees. Tears oozed from her eyes and down her cheeks, draining her fear, draining her anger into a soft, dark nothingness. She was the shell of Dun Iain gutted by fire, ravaged and hollow, snow sifting down to smooth the harsh edges—ashes drifting in the empty corners, gathering on the hard rim of reality—ashes, ashes, all fall down.

Michael wasn't there. In the distance water ran and stopped. The beam of his light came through the darkness. His hands, cool, damp, smelling of soap, drew Rebecca to her feet and down the staircase. They found Heather still asleep, her features smooth and innocent.

They lay on the bed in the large fourth-floor bedroom, wrapped in the green wool plaid, Darnley hunched and quivering beside them. The freezing cold of the night permeated Rebecca's body and even in Michael's arms she shivered. Only her tears were hot, burning creases in her face. Michael's mouth touched her cheeks and eyes, not so much kissing the tears away as mingling his own with hers.

Somewhere between five minutes and an eternity later red lights pulsed in the windows and tires crunched in the driveway. Help had come. Too late. Much too late. Michael and Rebecca propped each other up and went to open the door to the outside world.

Chapter Thirty

THE HAPPY SHOUTS of the children rang through the Hall. Rebecca stood in the window, slitting her eyes against the glitter of the snow. Brian and Mandy, so bundled in snowsuits they could hardly walk, were urging Peter on as he maneuvered the head onto their snowman. The maple trees were black stitches basting together white lawn and brilliant blue sky. The mausoleum was an unobtrusive white mound by the churned ruts of the driveway.

Rebecca smiled. The movement cracked her face and sloughed several layers of anguished frown. She turned, limping, back into the room.

Michael sat at the table, his mug of tea in front of him, looking at his hands as if he were about to launch into Lady Macbeth's "Out, damned spot." Rebecca rubbed his shoulders and laid her cheek on the top of his head. "Don't," she whispered. "Remember how brave you were. Did you realize what it was you shouted? 'Cruachan!'—the old Campbell war cry."

"Racial memory." He looked up at her with eyes drained into gray by weariness. "I wisna brave, I was scared spitless."

"So was I." Her mind was still buffeted by the sound of Eric falling down the stairs. It might have been poetic justice, but that didn't make it any the less horrible. He had told her, "No one knows the end is near—a mercy, that." But he wouldn't have been merciful to them.

Darnley lay asleep on the carpet in a patch of afternoon sun, paws splayed, looking like a lady's fur wrap tossed carelessly down. "The vet says he isn't hurt," said Rebecca. "Nice of the man to make a house call."

"I doot he was as curious as everyone else." The telephone rang for the fiftieth time. Jan's voice answered and calmly interceded.

It had been a dark, cold midnight when police, paramedics, Warren Lansdale, and both Pruitts descended upon Dun Iain. It had been an even darker four-thirty when they'd retreated, taking an already twitching Heather and Eric—what had been Eric—with them. Despite infusions of coffee from Phil's thermos, Michael and Rebecca had been numbed beyond speech long before they were left to lapse into blessed oblivion.

Rebecca had regained consciousness at ten to find the morning bright with promises, not the least of which was Michael's bleary, unshaven face on the pillow beside her. Next time, she thought with a wry smile, she'd notice she was sleeping with him. Complicating relationships were the only ones worth the effort of having.

There was another knock on the front door. She kissed Michael's forehead and went to see who Jan was dealing with this time.

Alerted by the Putnam grapevine, Jan had arrived with breakfast just as Rebecca finished a cold water spit bath, flinching from her face in the mirror—it'd looked as squashed and slept in as her blouse.

The lights had flashed on within the hour. The telephone had taken a little longer. Not only were the lines down in the woods, they'd been neatly cut just where they entered the house. Rebecca had promised herself she wouldn't think about that.

Phil had appeared next. He'd plodded upstairs in delightful silence to fix the broken windows, the one Michael had kicked out and the one shattered by Eric's first shot. Elspeth's window, the one Michael had climbed in. Rebecca wasn't going to think about his precarious climb, either.

A reporter from the *Putnam Enquirer* had come about noon. Rebecca and Michael had agreed to talk to her; the dramatic events at Dun Iain were, after all, going to bump the breakdown of the traffic light at Elm and Main off the front page whether the actual participants had anything to say about it or not. When the reporters from Dayton and Columbus had arrived soon after, Jan sent them off to the *Enquirer* office to copy the prepared statement.

Now the voice echoing up the stairwell was Warren Lansdale's. He stood holding his hat next to Queen Mary's supine marble body, talking earnestly while Jan nodded understanding. ". . . I never realized—God rot me for a complete idiot—excuse me, ma'am . . ." He saw Rebecca at the top of the flight of stairs and stopped. His moustache was looking distinctly motheaten.

Rebecca summoned a smile for him. "Come on up, Sheriff." Poor complacent Warren had been severely shaken last night. He'd been just as much a victim of the plot as she had.

He shook hands and settled at the table, clasping the cup of coffee Jan brought him and staring up at the piper's gallery. Rebecca turned to see what he was looking at. Elspeth's portrait still peered out between the railings. But her face was just paint on canvas, her body a husk in the mausoleum; her awareness was gone. "You can't blame it all on her," Rebecca said quietly. "Everyone made wrong choices, including me."

"And me," said Michael as Jan wafted discreetly away.

"Well," Warren said, "let me begin by apologizing. I knew Eric had a gun, he'd reported it missing. I never dreamed . . ."

"You did enough apologizing last night," Rebecca told him.

"Oh, well . . . I should've suspected something was going on right before James died, when he was so upset about the taxes. I bet Eric was telling him the taxes were a lot higher than they really were, not only so he could skim off the top but so James would agree to willing the estate to those imaginary relatives."

"What if," Rebecca asked, "there really are some relatives of Rachel Forbes's out there? Do they get the estate, after all?"

"I got hold of Benjamin Birkenhead this morning. Once I convinced him that Eric really was—gone—and that he'd been manipulating all of us out here . . ." Warren cleared his throat. "Birkenhead says the state can sue to have that will thrown out and the one James made several years ago reinstated. That wouldn't affect you. You'd still get the artifacts."

Michael nodded. "So Eric began simply wi' a campaign of harassment, tryin' to scare us out, or, failin' that, to keep us from takin' all the dearest things."

"And then he had to cover up what he'd already done," said Rebecca, "by making me suspect Dorothy or Phil or you, Sheriff, or even Michael." Beside her Michael stared down into his cup. So he'd had a half-baked scheme of his own—that hadn't helped. But that, too, was finished. "Dorothy'd been part of Eric's plan all along, hadn't she?"

"Chuck found Dorothy overdosed on tranquilizers and vodka last night. Suicide attempt. She'd left a note saying she never meant things to get away from her. Apparently she'd drugged your food as Eric told her, and then realized he meant to kill you. She'd already come around by the time I got to the hospital this morning, and she wanted to talk. Did she ever want to talk!"

Warren drank, fortifying himself. "The only prints on the jeweled box, besides yours, were hers. She'd been taking things all along, in spite of Eric warning her to wait for the payoff. We even found that picture of Katherine Gemmell and James's letter in her pantry, behind a flour canister."

"Eric was going to share the inheritance with Dorothy?" asked Rebecca.

"He'd promised to pay off Chuck and Margie's house and set up a college fund for their kids. She still believes that she was using Eric, not the other way around. But then, how can you tell who was using who?"

"You canna," muttered Michael.

"She never suspected Eric killed James, not until the last few weeks," Warren continued. "What could she have done if she had? She was in it too deep herself."

"What happened to Eric's father?" Rebecca asked.

"Dorothy says she was never married to Donald Adler. By the time she knew she was pregnant he was in jail on a burglary charge. Taking after Fred, his stepfather, who was a petty thief and hoodlum. I checked with Columbus, his record's as long as your arm. But Donald was killed by another inmate before Eric was born. Katie and Fred took the baby to California, and then Fred walked out. Or so Eric told Dorothy."

"Funny, it was Eric's middle initial that tipped me off, and I was wrong about that. She'd named him 'Forbes.'" Rebecca shifted on the hard chair. Her head ached, her shoulders ached, her knee throbbed. Even her mind was tired, sprawled as limply as the cat in the confines of her skull. "Maybe Katie intended to start over. We'll never know if she deliberately drove Eric into going after the inheritance, or whether he simply picked up so much of her resentment he decided it was something he should do. Eric said she always pushed him to make something of himself. Strange what love will make you do. And hate, and how thin the boundary is between them." Beneath the table Michael took Rebecca's hand and squeezed it against his thigh.

Warren puffed his moustache uneasily. "Dorothy didn't know where Eric was until he appeared on her doorstep three years ago and started playing on her guilt about giving him up as an infant."

"Would he have told her who he was if she wisna so cozily bidin' here at Dun Iain?" Michael asked.

No one answered. The happy voices of the children rang through air sparkling like cold club soda. Darnley twitched, stretched, and yawned.

"As for little Heather," continued Warren, "Dorothy didn't know a thing about her and Eric. Heather was running Steve, and Eric was running Heather, just to hedge his bets. That's one reason things got so complicated. Every now and then the different teams would start working at cross-purposes."

"Like Heather eatin' the drugged food," said Michael.

"His plan wasn't nearly as tight as he imagined," Rebecca said. "Is Heather all right?"

"She was sitting up and demanding to know what happened when I left the hospital a couple of hours ago. I imagine Sandra will tell her all about it."

"I hope Sandra decides to make friends with her. If the kid had more self-esteem, she wouldn't have . . ." Neither would I, Rebecca thought. "Was Eric giving her drugs to pass on to Steve?"

"Yes, I'm afraid so, although the boy'd been hooked for years. That fire was the best thing that could've happened to him, considering. Once he was off the dope he realized it was time to start controlling his own life. George Velasco said he was hysterical when he came in last night, shouting that they had to get out to Dun Iain right away before something terrible happened. But they had to put the snow chains on the ambulance first." He stared out the window. "I can't believe Eric's dead. And like that."

Michael clutched Rebecca's hand. "Eric would've gone to prison, right enough, but no forever. We'd have been lookin' ower our shoulders the rest o' our lives, waitin' for him to catch up wi' us."

Amen, thought Rebecca. She returned the pressure of Michael's hand. Eric was at peace, boldness burned away, intelligence wasted, charm soured. He'd cheated himself the most.

Warren said, "Eric must've set the fire in the shed to catch Steve because the fire Steve set in the trash can made us put a dead bolt on the door. Eric had to be careful, then, how he used the tunnel, or you'd have realized there was another entrance. Dorothy didn't know about the tunnel, by the way—Eric must've wormed it out of James when James still trusted him."

"But I didn't tumble until it was too late to hurt him," said Rebecca. "And Phil, I guess, is completely innocent."

"Just not too bright," Warren returned. "He let Steve go without supervision much too often. Never asked questions like he should have. Kind of like me, I guess."

Rebecca made soothing noises. Michael smiled with dry sympathy. The front door slammed. Up the stairs echoed the voices of the children demanding food and Peter bellowing for coffee.

"It turns out," said Warren, "that Heather's the one who took the mazer, not Dorothy, and she handed it right over to Eric. I'll get onto Sotheby's tomorrow morning, see if I can get the names of those collectors."

"Thank you," Rebecca said.

"Steve suspected there was more to Heather's wanting to harass you than she was letting on, but he couldn't admit to himself she was—er—with Eric. A lot of the things Steve did were without her instructions, trying to get back in her favor. Like setting the fire in the trash can and stealing the mausoleum key right out from under us. He also locked you in the storeroom, Michael, and tore up your tape. He says he'll get you another one."

"I'll get me one when I get home," replied Michael. "It's hardly important the noo."

"Scared the heck out of him, though, when all the lights in the house came on by themselves," Warren added with a short laugh. "Served him right."

Phil trudged down the staircase carrying his tools. He stopped in the doorway. "Is there anything else, Miss Reid? I need to get home."

"Thank you," called Rebecca. "And don't worry about Steve. Mr. Birkenhead knows that the estate is to cover his medical bills."

Phil shuffled his feet, tugged on the bill of his cap, and fled. What must it be like, Rebecca wondered, to have a mind that moved like a snail crawling laboriously up a single leaf, thinking that leaf the entire world? For a moment the prospect was almost tempting. Then she caught the acerbic gleam in Michael's eye. No, she didn't want to be a snail.

"Well," said Warren, picking up his hat and standing, "I need to go fill out some more reports. This is going to generate more paperwork than the tornado of 1972."

"Sorry," said Rebecca. Reluctantly she laid down Michael's hand.

"It's not you who should be apologizing." Warren smoothed his hair and fingered his moustache. "The inquest into Eric's death won't be for a few days. I know you're leaving the country in a couple of weeks, Michael, but it won't take long."

A couple of weeks, Rebecca repeated silently. Michael frowned.

"The inquest will bring in a verdict of self-defense," the sheriff assured them. "No one doubts it happened just as you said. I'll keep you posted."

Warren's descending footsteps were crossed by approaching ones. Jan ushered in a pale, willowy figure. "Heather!" Rebecca exclaimed. "You're supposed to be in the hospital!"

"I checked myself out. I'm okay. I had to talk to you. Sandra drove me out here. She's really been halfway decent about all this, especially since I'm not . . ." She rolled her eyes at Michael. He looked back, brows arched. ". . . pregnant," she concluded defiantly. "I was just upset because everything seemed to be falling apart, Steve hurt and Dorothy acting weird, and Eric—well, he was getting to where he kind of scared me."

"Sit down," Rebecca told her. Heather sat, her hands folded on the table in front of her. Michael muttered something and went upstairs, Jan mumbled something and went downstairs, where Sandra's brassy voice was trying to coerce Peter into helping light the living Christmas tree at the mall.

Heather's complexion was pristine. Even her stark black hair lay softly around her face instead of standing up in spikes. Her features clung desperately to an expression of stubborn pride.

"Why?" Rebecca asked.

"I loved him," Heather returned. "He said he loved me. He made me feel good."

"Three pretty good reasons, depending on your point of view. What about the drugs?"

"Those were for Steve. They made him feel better. I mean, I smoked a joint or two with Eric, just to—to make things different, you know? He really didn't like it. Said it slowed him down."

Rebecca laid her chin on her fist. Her fist was trembling. "I've heard my students say it has that effect."

"It started last summer, before you ever got here." Heather's expression cracked slightly, revealing bewilderment. "He was good, so much better than Steve. Men are just supposed to know what to do, aren't they?"

"No. Why should they?" Rebecca's whole arm was shaking. She stood and started pacing, her hands clenched behind her back, her knee twingeing.

"He didn't want anything kinky, nothing like that."

Just that he was thirty-five years old, and you're sixteen. There was some kind of psycho-anthropological wrinkle to that, the wealthy mature male and the nubile female, but Rebecca wasn't about to explore it now. She turned at the window and paced back.

Heather's bewilderment shattered into sorrow. A tear ran down her cheek and hung on her jaw. She didn't seem to have the energy to brush it away. "Sometimes he'd only want to hold me. He was awfully lonely. And then you came. He told me to mess something up in the house, he didn't say what. I picked on your room because I was jealous. I mean, you're so much more sophisticated than I am, I thought he liked you better."

"But that's just what he didn't like about me."

Heather shrugged. "He asked me to call that place in Missouri, pretending to be you. That was really clever of him."

"He was using me," said Rebecca. "Much more so than he ever used you. He cared for you, Heather."

"It would never have worked," the girl replied. More tears rolled down her face and she laid her head on her arms. "He told me he had to take you away for a cruise, but then he'd come back, and you wouldn't be here anymore, he'd be all mine. He said for me to finish school, not drop out like Steve. He wanted me to go to college, he said I could be a paralegal. But he didn't really need me, he didn't need anybody. I think I knew that all along."

The lonely little girl, and the lonely man. Rebecca stopped behind Heather's chair and laid her hands on her shoulders. She felt as if she could crush the girl's fragile bones. "If you want to believe it would've worked, go ahead. You may have been the only person he ever did need."

Heather shook her head against her arms. "I never meant to hurt you."

"I never meant to hurt you," Rebecca replied. "Get some counseling, Heather. Talking about it'll help. And stick with Steve. If anyone needs you, he does." Gently she heaved the child to her feet and dried her tears with a tissue from her pocket.

Jan appeared, murmuring about cups of cocoa, and led Heather away. The girl paused in the doorway, glanced up the stairs, then called conspiratorially to Rebecca, "He really is cute, you know, even if he talks funny. Good luck."

Rebecca blew her nose. Surely she had milked her tear ducts dry the last few days. For the rest of her life she'd never cry again. Or be angry again, or be frightened again . . . She collapsed in the closest chair, giggling insanely. Of all the epithets she'd applied to Michael, "cute" wasn't one of them. And she didn't think he talked funny at all.

The castle dozed in the crisp sunlight. The voices in the kitchen were only a subliminal murmur. Steps padded across the floor and hands touched her shoulders. Long, strong, flexible fingers rubbed the back of her neck.

Rebecca leaned her head against his sweatshirt. "Michael, this would be a great time for you to trot out the Erskine letter."

His sigh ruffled her hair. "That would come a treat, right enough. But I'm afraid it's gone. Elspeth or John must've destroyed it."

"Maybe it doesn't matter so much anymore. There's plenty of other work yet to do."

"Aye. We're no in the clear yet, are we?"

Rebecca closed her eyes and nestled against his chest. His fingers caressed her face, stroking smooth the lines of worry and sorrow and fear.

Chapter Thirty-One

THE SNOW LOOKED like Rebecca felt. Road and sidewalks were edged with piles of slush, kept from slumping into nothingness only by splotched crusts of ice. Even the snow covering the fields around the cemetery was fragile gray. But the sky was a blue as deep and clear as Michael's eyes.

Rebecca edged a bit closer to him. He glanced down at her with the thinning of his lips he no doubt meant as a smile. Their clasped hands tightened between the folds of their coats.

A mist of exhaled breath hung in the crisp air over the open grave. The minister, a young and nervous assistant pastor of Dorothy's church, droned doggedly through the burial service. Rebecca wondered if anyone were listening any more closely than she was. The words were supposed to be comforting. Maybe in different circumstances they would have been.

Peter stood, reassuringly stolid, on her other side. Jan clasped his arm, eyes not quite focused. Beyond the Sorensons stood Chuck Garst, looking as if a cattle prod had been applied to his spine. As well he might, burying a brother he'd never known he had. His mother was propped between him and Warren Lansdale, the sheriff respectfully bareheaded despite the cold. Dorothy's head was swathed in a drab brown scarf, her face was that of a battered mannequin. She'd wanted Eric buried in the Forbes mausoleum, but in that, too, she'd been disappointed.

A pallid Heather stood stiffly with Steve, whose glazed eyes peered like a cornered rabbit's through his ski mask. Sandra Hines stood next to the young couple, her lipstick turned down in a scowl. Phil Pruitt, his cap in his gnarled hands, watched with his mouth hanging open, as if he were offended by something but wasn't sure just what. Benjamin Birkenhead huddled in his wool overcoat on the opposite side of the grave from the reporters clustered in the cemetery gate. When he wasn't glancing at his watch, he was staring in baffled resentment at Rebecca, as though it was all her fault.

The minister closed his book and threw a clod of earth onto the coffin. The meager crowd silently dispersed. Chuck and Warren steered Dorothy past the cameras and microphones into the back of the sheriff's squad car; her next stop was the state psychiatric hospital.

Michael and Rebecca thanked the minister. He uttered a few conventional words and sidled away. Cemetery workers scuffed forward to fill the grave. In an hour nothing would be left but a pile of dirt and an index card in a metal holder: "Adler, Eric Forbes; 1953–1988." From her pocket Rebecca pulled a spray of lavender wrapped with Louise's clay beads. "Mrs. O'Donnell wanted you to have these," she murmured, laid the flowers and the beads down, and turned away.

Peter pushed a path through the reporters. Already their numbers had diminished; the few days from Sunday to Wednesday had produced more immediate stories. Jan opened the door of Michael's Nova and shoved Rebecca inside. "See you Sunday for Christmas tree and turkey," she said. "And anytime before, if you want to come."

Michael maneuvered the car from the muddy parking area onto the road. Rebecca leaned back against the seat and closed her eyes, her thoughts emitting the little pops and sighs of subsiding embers.

The mazer, swathed in plastic bubble wrap, had returned via Federal Express on Tuesday. The Connecticut collector testified he'd bought it from a dark-haired, dark-eyed man with crowded teeth who'd said he represented Dun Iain Estate. When he'd told me he was searching courthouses in Nebraska, Rebecca thought. Not only had Eric's debts forced him to sell the mazer prematurely, it even turned out he'd been the one who'd contacted Bright, touting the estate's virtues as a corporate retreat. He'd once said, "God, I'll be glad when this is all over." And now it was.

Rebecca opened her eyes to see Dun Iain waiting beyond its alley of maples, rising disdainfully above the dreary lumps of ice at its feet, its windows winking in the sun. The stone and harl of its face seemed lighter, shedding its burden of worry like a phoenix rising from the ashes.

Michael opened the door for her and together they walked inside. By the time they'd taken their cups of tea into the store-room they were able to smile at Darnley sniffing, stalking, and pouncing on their bedraggled shoelaces. "I'm glad Jan's going to adopt him," said Rebecca.

"You need a cat," Michael replied, "just to keep you in your place."

Rebecca opened the inventory and peered into a crate. "An old bell. The tag is labeled 'Iona.' " It was surprisingly heavy, cold and rusty in her hands, but the clapper was still attached. When she gave it a push with her forefinger, the bell rang with a muted resonance. Green lawns, gray stones, and the murmur of the sea. Rebecca smiled again.

"It sounds like an abbey bell," said Michael, "callin' you to vespers, quiet, and peace."

Rebecca laid it carefully down. "What've you got?"

"Carved oak roundels from Stirling Castle," he announced, lifting a circular piece of wood cut with the bas-relief of a woman in a Renaissance headdress. "They'll fill the gaps in the collection quite nicely."

Rebecca added them to the list. "How many more crates to go?"

"No too many. We'll be rushed gettin' it all packed, though. You've booked the removal lorry for next week?"

"Yes." She sipped at her tea. Next week. Michael would be leaving for Scotland in less than two weeks, taking the artifacts back home to the museum, to assorted collectors, to his own satisfaction. Although his satisfaction, she thought, needed more than artifacts.

They'd spent the past three evenings close together in the sit-ting room, listening to music ranging from Mozart to Silly Wiz-ard. Sharing an occasional noninvasive kiss had seemed like reckless bravado to sensibilities as raw as tenderized meat. They were tired, Rebecca told herself. They were frightened. Two out of the last three nights she'd waked up screaming, racked by nightmares of fire and darkness and bodies falling into snow. Two out of the last three nights Michael had come to her and held her, lying circumspectly outside the covers, until she'd gone back to sleep. His own dreams, he'd admitted, were just as bad.

For someone who'd once been a thunderstorm on her horizon, being with Michael now was like sitting before a glowing hearth, the kettle bubbling on the stove, the kittens of her wits purring in his lap, and the rain falling softly, gently, harmlessly outside.

"Right," said Michael from the depths of another crate. "Here's a grand paintin'. Landseer, 'Queen Victoria on Horseback.' And her ghillie Brown holdin' the reins. I've seen photos o' this one—thought it'd been lost. And look here. 'The Entry of George the Fourth at Holyroodhouse.' Dinna he look a treat, kilt and all."

Rebecca peered over his shoulder as he pulled the painting half out of its box. "You're going to have a choice collection to take back."

"Aye," he said, but with a frown rather than a smile. Darnley's padded paws on the stone were suddenly loud.

"Why," Rebecca asked, "did you tell me that night to sod off? Trying to protect me from implication in your scheme?"

"Like I'd warn you away from toxic waste, lass. Serves me right, takin' a notion to you." Michael's expression implied he'd turned around in a dark alley and found her behind him, knife upraised. "And meddlin' aboot in other folks' bluidy plots," he added.

"It's over now, Michael. Can't you come down off the guilt trip?"

"When the trip ends, I'll be comin' doon." He cupped her face, his thumb teasing her cheek. "I also left you that night because—well, wi' you, hen, it'll no be cheap, or casual, or anything but honest."

Rebecca felt herself blush against his hand. But he wasn't making any assumptions she hadn't. "So I've gone from being a kitten, fuzzy and helpless, to being a squawking, scratching hen. That's an improvement."

He grinned that heart-stoppingly candid grin. "Aye, that it is."

She kissed his hand. "There're more boxes to open, love."

"Then let's be gettin' on wi' it."

In amiable companionship, they got on with it. That evening and all day Thursday they worked and talked. Thursday evening Rebecca reluctantly poured the last drops of the Laphroaig down the kitchen drain and threw the bottle away. That night she climbed to the top of the house and sat on the shadowed steps where Eric had died. She remembered it happening, and yet it was like a play she'd seen years ago, images but no sensations. The portrait of John Forbes stared into oblivion, personality erased by time and passion. Nothing of him lingered. Nothing of Elspeth or James. Nothing of Eric.

The sound of the pipes coiled sensuously up the stairwell and with a sigh of acceptance Rebecca went down to listen.

Neither Wednesday nor Thursday nights did she have nightmares. Neither night did Michael come to her bed. And she didn't approach his, even as the kisses in the sitting room grew less cautious.

By Friday afternoon they'd worked their way to the last items in the inventories, the regimental flags in the entry. Michael unfurled a tattered cloth, saying, "My middle name's Ian —quite appropriate."

"Mine's even better," replied Rebecca. "Marie." She took the end of the flag. "Oh, nice. Cameronian Rifles, World War I."

"Last night there were four Maries," sang Michael, his tenor vibrating in the small room. *"Tonight there'll be but three. There was Mary Beaton, and Mary Seaton, and Mary Carmichael, and me."* He shook out another flag. "Black Watch. I'll be takin' these."

Rebecca closed her notebook and regarded the serene marble face of the Queen of Scots. "And the death mask."

"Dr. Graham, my boss, he'd no let me back in the country if I left that behind."

Rebecca yawned. "Then there's the sarcophagus. I guess the state'll just have to leave it here. A solid chunk of marble must weigh tons . . ."

They turned and looked at each other, eyes lit by wild surmise. "Why should it be solid?" Michael demanded.

"How fast can you get that crowbar?" Rebecca dropped the notebook with a thud and fell to her knees beside the carved marble of the tomb. A dark line ran beneath the lid where it overhung the sides by two inches. Shadow? She cursed the dim ceiling light, scrambled up, ran into the kitchen, grabbed the flashlight, and ran back.

No, by Mary's garters, that wasn't a shadow, that was a hairline crack. Michael galloped through the storeroom door, crowbar held like a knight errant's lance. "Stand aside," he ordered.

With a tooth-grating squeal the effigy shuddered and the lid slid aside. Rebecca shone the light into the dark interior of the sarcophagus. But there wasn't much to see, only a thin leather portfolio gray and dismal at the bottom of the hole. Michael reached, strained, and hauled it out. Dust eddied and he sneezed.

"Bless you." Rebecca snatched the portfolio from his hands. Art Deco tooling. Nineteen twenties. The papers inside were from the same era, receipts, a list of the items in the storeroom—thanks a lot, they'd had to make their own—and a letter from an art dealer in San Francisco. Amid the papers was a thick piece of parchment, yellowed with age. The ink on it was faded, the writing absurdly spiky. She squinted, turning it this way and that, Michael's breath hot on the back of her neck.

It was written in sixteenth-century Scots. ". . . being departit from the place quhair I left my hart . . . remember zow of the purpois of the Lady Reres . . . remember how gif it wer not to obey zow, I had rether be deid or I did it; my hart bleidis at it . . ." At the bottom was a scrawling signature, "Zour gude sister, Arabella."

Rebecca whooped, "This is it! This is it! The Erskine letter!"

"I'll be damned!" exclaimed Michael. "The first place and the last in the whole blasted house!" He swept her up and danced her across the entry and into the kitchen, where he plucked the parchment from her hand and spread it out on the table. "You'll have a' the copies you want, I promise you that. And I'll translate it for you before I go."

"I can handle a translation," Rebecca said, recovering her breath.

She bent over the table, her head colliding with Michael's, mouthing the words. Ten minutes later she sighed. "Well, so much for that."

"It's no good, is it? James was Mary's right and proper?"

"Arabella here did have a baby, but it died. That's why she's talking about her heart bleeding. Lady Reres—Margaret Forbes—hired someone else to be James's wet nurse but took the credit herself."

"Too little scandal there," Michael commented, "to wake a good gray historian from his afternoon snooze in the library."

"I didn't have any stake in the answer one way or the other." Rebecca shook her head. "No scandal. That figures. I can't decide if that makes it an anticlimax or a relief."

"It's all in the writin' up. If anyone can make it into a—what do you call it, a dog and pony show—you can."

"Thanks." She tickled him affectionately, and went to find a cardboard box for the precious parchment.

That night she sat up late translating the letter, Michael dutifully keeping her pencils sharp. It was only when she was making coffee the next morning she realized it was Christmas Eve. In honor of the occasion Michael laid a fire in the Hall, and went into town to get wine, fruit, cheese, and crackers for a picnic on the hearth. While he was gone Rebecca wrapped up the present she and Jan had found in the mall, a sweatshirt version of a soup can label reading "Campbell's Cream of the Crop." Then she set her typewriter on the Hall table and began typing packing lists. The end was altogether too near. But Mary Stuart herself had said, "In my end is my beginning."

When Michael returned with the food, he also had the mail. A box from L.L. Bean he whisked away before Rebecca could see it, leaving her to deduce it was her present—a tartan flannel nightgown, probably. A box from Rebecca's mother turned out to be a CARE package of cookies and fruitcake, the enclosed card admonishing Rebecca to share the goodies with "that English guy."

It was the nicest Christmas Eve she could remember. In some celestial alchemy the hazy day alloyed itself into clear night, moon and stars hanging in the almost invisible branches of the maples like ornaments on a Christmas tree. In the glow of the fire the Hall was pleasantly cool, not cold, and the light of the chandelier was soft and subtle. The wine was smooth and fruity, the crackers crisp, and the cookies melted on the tongue.

Later, Michael played the pipes while Rebecca filled boxes with books, her mind doing an effortless backstroke through the music—"The Sound of Sleat," "Finley McRae," "The Cowal Gathering," "Bonnie Dundee," "The Sweet Maid of Mull." And, again, he played "Mo Nighean Donn, Gradh Mo Chridhe," slowly, lyrically, like the touch of a kiss upon a lover's skin.

She'd just packed a book of Gaelic songs. She pulled it out again and checked the index. There it was, translated as "My brown-haired maiden, love of my heart." Suppressing a grin, she put the book back in the box.

Michael started playing his own transcription of Runrig's "Going Home." He was getting to go home. He had a home to go to. When the melody ended, the hum of the drones lingered on, stroking her senses. Michael laid down the pipes and pulled Rebecca to her feet, his hands squeezing her arms, his face set with resolution. Say it, she thought. I'm ready to hear it.

"Rebecca, come home wi' me."

Home. A place to settle down. Someone to settle down with.

The hearth, the kettle, and the kittens, enough to withstand any thunderstorm . . . Something in her chest punctured and deflated. "I can't."

"I had a bed-sitter in William Street," he went on, as if she hadn't spoken, "but I could get something larger for us. What I'd like is a flat off the Royal Mile. The old wynds are bein' tarted up by the MacYuppies. But I canna afford one o' those. Yet."

She echoed his manic grin, spread her hands across his shirt, and felt the rhythm of his breath. His strong and gentle arms slipped around her waist. "I couldn't get a job there. An American professor of British history looking for a position in Edinburgh? Talk about coals to Newcastle!"

"We'd find something for you, love."

"I have to write my dissertation," she insisted, as much for herself as for him. "If I don't get that Ph.D., Michael, I don't want to be able to blame it on you."

"Ah," he said, as though she'd just hit him in the stomach. His brows were clouds over the clarity of his eyes. "But I have tae go back, I have tae tend tae the artifacts."

Rebecca pressed herself against his chest. Medieval executioners had ripped the living hearts out of their victims. When he left, she'd find out just how that felt. "I'll come next summer. Even though we'd be as poor as Burns's church mouse."

"Poor, but hardly timid." He released her and picked up the wine. The cork was attached to a metal cap—one flick of his thumbs and it popped out of the bottle. The broken seal left a metal ring around the bottle neck. He pulled that off, lifted Rebecca's left hand, settled the thin strip of metal around her fourth finger. "There. We're engaged. To have substantive talks as soon as possible, at the least."

He gave no quarter, and expected none. "You lunatic," Rebecca said. "I love you." She pulled his head down and kissed him, savoring wine and the elusive tang of peat smoke on his tongue.

"It's high time," he said against her mouth, "we were makin' love."

Yes, it was, time ripened to inevitability. "My place or yours? Mine's closer."

An expression of gratified relief swept his face. Rebecca laughed. He took her firmly by the shoulders and steered her toward the door. She couldn't resist saying after two steps, "Of course you have to rush out to the chemist's shop now, don't you?''

He retorted, ''I've already done my shoppin' the day.''

''Confident, weren't you? But I'm teasing you. Matters are— well, taken care of.''

''Aye, I saw the packet of pills in your room.''

''Who didn't?'' Rebecca moaned, and started up the stairs.

With perfect timing, the phone rang. They shared exasperated grins. ''Go answer it,'' Michael said with a kiss and a tickle. ''I'll tidy the Hall.''

It was Jan. ''Hi!'' she said to Rebecca's slightly jaundiced hello. ''Just called to wish you a happy Christmas Eve. If you don't have any plans, we were mulling some wine . . .''

''Thank you, Jan, but we have plans.''

''Don't forget your plans for New Year's Eve are our party. For which I'm asking a favor. Can Michael play the pipes for us? Does he know 'Auld Lang Syne'?''

Michael came into the kitchen to throw the wrappings of their picnic into the trash. Rebecca said, ''Jan's asking if you know 'Auld Lang Syne'?''

''Does she ken 'Yankee Doodle'?''

''I've been bragging to her how well you play, and she wants you to play for her New Year's Eve party.''

''Oh?'' He nodded, ego purring like Darnley stroked under his furry chin. ''The state'll no be sendin' someone to snatch the pipes from my hands at midnight. I'd be pleased to play.''

''Oh, aye,'' said Rebecca to Jan, ''he'll be playin', right enough.''

Jan giggled. One of Michael's eyebrows tilted in playful af- front. He cornered Rebecca in the angle where the cabinet met the wall, licked his lips, and starting nibbling her neck.

''We'll expect you about eleven o'clock tomorrow,'' Jan said. ''The kids'll be having their stockings first thing, of course. It'd be cruel and unusual punishment to make them wait past six. But we'll have the presents beneath the tree when you get here. I've got the turkey in the sink thawing, and I'm going to fix that cranberry relish of your mother's.''

''Who?'' Delicious frissons ran down Rebecca's spine. Chas- ing them, Michael lifted the back of her sweater and excavated her blouse from the waistband of her jeans.

''Maureen Reid, your mother.''

"Oh?" Her mother's name, not to mention her face, was absolutely the furthest thing from Rebecca's mind.

"It's the funniest thing about that recipe," Jan went on. "Sue next door has a similar one. We were comparing notes, and she said something about cooking the cranberries."

Michael's hands slipped up under Rebecca's blouse and unhooked her bra. He began exploring the joys of bilateral symmetry. His extraordinarily sensitive fingertips, she thought, must be the result of years of playing that chanter. She let her eyes cross in delight.

"But," said Jan's distant voice, "I've always made the relish with raw cranberries. It tastes all right to me. What do you do?"

Michael whispered in Rebecca's unoccupied ear. "My jeans are gettin' awful tight. You need tae come peel them off me afore anything's damaged."

"Rebecca?" Jan asked. "Are you listening to me?"

"No," Rebecca replied. Making one last grab at coherence, she explained, "Jan, we have plans tonight. There's something I need to tend to. I'll have to let—you—go . ."

The line rang hollowly. Then Jan exclaimed, "Oh! Oh, my gosh! How inconsiderate can you get. I'm so sorry—bless you, my children."

Rebecca laid the receiver somewhere in the vicinity of its cradle. She turned, inserted her right hand into the back pocket of Michael's jeans, and pulled him close. They stood clasped together, one of her legs hooked around his steady stance, his hands splayed on her bare back. Her senses, her wits, her cautious nature all cheered, Go for it!

In some kind of amatory instinct they managed to get up the stairs without disentangling themselves. They found Darnley curled on the foot of Rebecca's bed. He looked up, stretched, and sat with his head cocked in a benign smirk while she took out her contacts and laid the metal ring reverently in her jewelry case.

Michael picked up the cat, solemnly informed him, "We'll be takin' it from here wi'oot your help, thank you just the same," and set him down in the corridor. Rebecca turned down the bed, drew Michael back inside the room, and shut the door. They looked inquisitively at each other, smiling with something between glee and amazement, in perfect accord.

All the windows of Dun Iain went dark. The castle closed its observant eyes and drowsed, finally at peace with love and time.

Printed in the United States
103155LV00001B/4/A